W9-BIJ-028

F   Werfel, Franz.
WER   The song of Bernadette.
#9022

CHRIST UNITED METHODIST CHURCH
4488 POPLAR AVENUE
MEMPHIS, TENNESSEE 38117

The Song of Bernadette

TO THE CHILD

MANON

IN REMEMBRANCE

F
Wer

FRANZ WERFEL

The Song of Bernadette

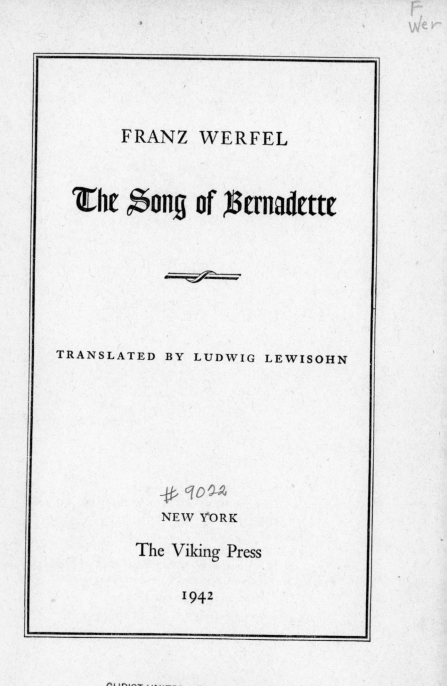

TRANSLATED BY LUDWIG LEWISOHN

9022

NEW YORK

The Viking Press

1942

CHRIST UNITED METHODIST CHURCH
4488 POPLAR AVENUE
MEMPHIS, TENNESSEE 38117

DAS LIED VON BERNADETTE

COPYRIGHT 1941 BY BERMANN-FISCHER VERLAG, STOCKHOLM

THE SONG OF BERNADETTE

COPYRIGHT 1942 BY THE VIKING PRESS, INC.

PRINTED IN U. S. A.

PUBLISHED ON THE SAME DAY IN THE DOMINION OF CANADA
BY THE MACMILLAN COMPANY OF CANADA LIMITED

PUBLISHED IN APRIL 1942

THE HADDON CRAFTSMEN, INC., CAMDEN, N. J.

A Personal Preface

=====================================

In the last days of June 1940, in flight from our mortal enemies after the collapse of France, we reached the city of
Lourdes. The two of us, my wife and I, had hoped to be able
to elude them in time to cross the Spanish frontier to Portugal.
But since the consuls unanimously refused the requisite visas,
we had no alternative but to flee back with great difficulty
to the interior of France on the very night on which the National Socialist troops occupied the border town of Hendaye.
The Pyrenean *départements* had turned into a phantasmagoria
—a very camp of chaos. The millions of this strange migration
of peoples wandered about on the roads and obstructed the
towns and villages: Frenchmen, Belgians, Dutchmen, Poles,
Czechs, Austrians, exiled Germans, and, mingled with these,
soldiers of the defeated armies. There was barely food enough
to still the extreme pangs of hunger. There was no shelter to
be had at all. Anyone who had obtained possession of an upholstered chair for his night's rest was an object of envy. In
endless lines stood the cars of the fugitives, piled mountain-high
with household gear, with mattresses and beds; there was no
gasoline to be had. In Pau a family settled there told us that
Lourdes was the one place where, if luck were kind, one might
still find a roof. Since the famous city was but thirty kilometres
distant, we were advised to make the attempt and knock at its
gates. We followed this advice and were sheltered at last.

It was in this manner that Providence brought me to Lourdes,
of the miraculous history of which I had hitherto had but the

most superficial knowledge. We hid for several weeks in the Pyrenean city. It was a time of great dread. The British radio announced that I had been murdered by the National Socialists. Nor did I doubt that such would be my fate were I to fall into the hands of the enemy. An article of the Armistice provided that France turn over certain civilians to the National Socialists. Who could these civilians be but those who had fought the modern pestilence in the days of its modest beginnings? In my friends' eyes I read the same conviction, although their words sought to calm me. A few of the initiated pretended to know the number of those who were to be turned over and the very order of their documented names. At such moments the boundary between rumour and fact is obliterated. The most stubborn reports predicted again and again the conqueror's occupation of the Pyrenees on the following day. Each morning when I woke up it was in ignorance as to whether I was still a free man or a prisoner condemned to death.

It was, I repeat, a time of great dread. But it was also a time of great significance for me, for I became acquainted with the wondrous history of the girl Bernadette Soubirous and also with the wondrous facts concerning the healings of Lourdes. One day in my great distress I made a vow. I vowed that if I escaped from this desperate situation and reached the saving shores of America, I would put off all other tasks and sing, as best I could, the song of Bernadette.

This book is the fulfilment of my vow. In our epoch an epic poem can take no form but that of a novel. *The Song of Bernadette* is a novel but not a fictive work. In face of the events here delineated, the sceptical reader will ask with better right than in the case of most historical epic narratives: "What is true? What is invented?" My answer is: All the memorable happenings which constitute the substance of this book took place in the world of reality. Since their beginning dates back no longer than eighty years, there beats upon them the bright light of modern history and their truth has been confirmed by friend and foe and by cool observers through faithful testimonies. My story makes no changes in this body of truth.

I exercised my right of creative freedom only where the work, as a work of art, demanded certain chronological condensations or where there was need of striking the spark of life from the hardened substance.

I have dared to sing the song of Bernadette, although I am not a Catholic but a Jew; and I drew courage for this undertaking from a far older and far more unconscious vow of mine. Even in the days when I wrote my first verses I vowed that I would evermore and everywhere in all I wrote magnify the divine mystery and the holiness of man—careless of a period which has turned away with scorn and rage and indifference from these ultimate values of our mortal lot.

FRANZ WERFEL

Los Angeles, May 1941

Characters

The Kinsfolk of Bernadette

François Soubirous ⎱ her parents
Louise Soubirous ⎰
Marie, her sister
Jean Marie ⎱ her brothers
Justin ⎰
Aunt Bernarde Casterot, her godmother
Aunt Lucille Casterot

Bernadette's Schoolmates

Jeanne Abadie
Cathérine Mengot
Annette Courrèges
Madeleine Hillot
Antoinette Gazalas

Neighbours of the Soubirous

André Sajou, mason
Madame Sajou
Jean Bouhouhorts
Croisine Bouhouhorts
The Bouhouhorts child
Piguno
Madame Ourous
Madame Germaine Raval
Madame Gozos
Louis Bouriette, stone-breaker
The cobbler Barringue

Papa Babou

Madame Millet, a wealthy widow

Madame Baup ⎱ members of Lourdes's "good society"
Elfriede Lacrampe ⎰

Antoinette Peyret, dressmaker
Antoine Nicolau, miller
Mother Nicolau

Personalities of Lourdes

Marie Dominique Peyramale, dean
Abbé Pomian ⎱ chaplains
Abbé Penès ⎰
Père Sempet

Adolphe Lacadé, mayor

Courrèges ⎱ his secretaries
Capdeville ⎰
The imperial prosecutor Vital Dutour
The chief of police Jacomet
Rives, examining magistrate
Duprat, justice of the peace

CHARACTERS

PERSONALITIES OF LOURDES (*Continued*)

d'Angla, commander of the gendarmerie

Belhache } gendarmes
Pays

Callet, municipal police officer

Dr. Dozous, municipal physician

Dr. Lacrampe

J. B. Estrade, revenue officer

Clarens, school principal

Duran, proprietor of café

Cazenave, postmaster

Doutreloux, driver

Maisongrosse, baker

THE STATE

Emperor Napoléon III

Empress Eugénie

Madame Bruat

Roulland, Minister of Worship

Fould, Minister of Finance

Delangle, Minister of Justice

Baron Massy, Prefect of the Hautes-Pyrénées

Duboë, Sub-prefect

Falconnet, Attorney General

THE CHURCH

Pope Pius XI

Bertrand Sévère Laurence, Bishop of Tarbes

Monseigneur Forcade, Bishop of Nevers

Monseigneur Thibaut, Bishop of Montpellier

THE CONVENT OF THE LADIES OF NEVERS

Mère Joséphine Imbert, mother superior

Mère Marie Thérèse Vauzous, mistress of the novices

Sœur Sophie

Sœur Nathalie

*   *   *

Hyacinthe de Lafite, a poet and man of letters

Contents

Evocation of February 11, 1858, at Lourdes

CHAPTER ONE

In the Cachot

FRANÇOIS SOUBIROUS gets up in the dark. It is just six. Long ago he lost possession of the silver watch which was a wedding present from his clever sister-in-law Bernarde Casterot. The ticket for it as well as the tickets for other poor little treasures issued by the municipal pawn brokerage had lapsed the autumn before. Soubirous knows that it is six even though the chimes of the parish church of Saint Pierre had not yet rung for early Mass. The poor have the time in their bones. Without dial or bell they know what hour has struck, for the poor are always afraid of being late.

The man gropes for his wooden shoes. But he holds them in his hand so as to make no noise. Barefoot he stands on the icy stone floor and listens to the various breathings of the sleeping members of his family. It is a strange music which weighs upon his heart. Six human beings share the room. He and Louise have managed to keep their good wedding bed, witness of a once hopeful start in life. But the two adolescent girls, Bernadette and Marie, must sleep on a hard enough couch. The youngest two, finally, Jean Marie and Justin, are bedded by their mother on a sack of straw, which she rolls up by day.

François Soubirous, who still does not stir from his place, casts a glance at the open hearth. It is really not a proper hearth, but a crude fireplace improvised by the stonemason André Sajou, owner of this magnificent dwelling, for his tenants. Under the ashes glimmer and crackle remains of fresh branches too wet to burn up. Now and then a pale gleam quivers. But the man lacks the energy to stir the remnants of the fire. He turns his glance to the windows and watches the night turn grey beyond. Therewith his deep discomfort turns into angry bitterness. A curse trembles on his lips. Soubirous is a strange fellow. What annoys him more than this wretched room is the two barred windows, one larger, one smaller, these two abject squinting eyes turned on the filthy yard of the Cachot where the dunghill of the whole neighbourhood stinks to heaven. For he is, after all, no vagabond or ragpicker but an honest-to-God miller and even mill-owner and so in his way as good a man as Monsieur de Lafite with his big saw-mill.

The Boly mill below Château Fort could stand comparison with any mill for miles and miles around. Even the Escobé mill at Arcizac-les-Angles was not bad at all. The old Bandeau mill was nothing to be proud of, yet it was a mill. Was it perhaps the fault of the good miller Soubirous that the Lapaca brook which used to turn the wheels had been dry for years or that the price of grain had risen or that there were more and more people out of work? God was responsible, if you liked, or the Emperor or the prefect or the devil knows who—not a decent man like François Soubirous, even though he likes an occasional glass and an occasional game of cards at the inn. Guilty or not, what is the difference? There he is with his family in the Cachot. And the Cachot in the Rue des Petites Fossées is really not a dwelling at all but the former town jail. The walls sweat with moisture. Fungi crouch in the cracks. The boards are warped. Bread mildews in an hour. In summer one roasts, in winter one freezes. It is for this reason that, several years ago, Monsieur Lacadé, mayor of Lourdes, ordered the Cachot to be abandoned and the vagabonds and evil-doers to be housed in the building of the city gate of Baous by reason of the emphatically better hygienic conditions there. But the conditions in the Cachot are good enough for the Soubirous family. We have the proof, the former miller reflects. He had heard Bernadette's lungs hissing and whistling again half the night. This thought makes him feel so lamentably sorry for himself that he is absolutely determined to creep back into bed and go on sleeping.

But this cowardly retreat from reality is barred to him, since in the meantime Mother Soubirous has arisen too. She is a woman of thirty-five or -six but looks fifty. She busies herself with the fire at once, blows the sparks out of the ashes, heaps on them smoking straw, shavings, and a few dry branches, and finally hangs the copper kettle over the new flames. Soubirous regards his wife's silent activity with a lofty and sombre air. He does not speak, either. Another day is beginning with its burdens and its disappointments—a day such as yesterday was and such as tomorrow will be. Now the tinny bells of the parish church are heard. The day is inescapable.

François Soubirous has but one yearning at this moment—to feel the good burning of brandy in his desolate stomach. But Mother Soubirous keeps the bottle with the vinous demon well locked up. And he cannot bear to put his passionate desire into words, for the demon in question is a source of conflict between the couple. He hesitates another minute or two, then slips into his wooden shoes. "I'll be going now, Louise," he growls softly.

"Have you anything definite in view, Soubirous?" she asks.

"One thing or another has been offered me," he opines mysteriously. The same dialogue takes place daily. For Soubirous's sense of dignity prevents him from admitting to himself or to his wife the entire wretched truth.

The woman moves hopefully back from the hearth. "Was it at Lafite's maybe? At the saw-mill?"

"At Lafite's!" he jeers. "Who's thinking of Lafite? But I'm going to talk to Maisongrosse today and also to Cazenave, the postmaster, you know. . . ."

"Maisongrosse, Cazenave . . ." In a disappointed voice she repeats the names and goes on working. He puts on his Basque beret. His gestures are slow and faltering. Suddenly his wife turns and faces him. "I've been thinking hard, Soubirous. We should send Bernadette away from this place," she whispers.

"What do you mean, send her away?" Soubirous has just lifted the heavy latch on the door. It is a prison door. Whenever he opens the door he recalls the worst time of his life—those four weeks the year before, when, utterly innocent, he had been remanded for investigation. His lifted hand falls. He hears his wife's whispering: "I mean to her aunt Bernarde. The country would be even better—down in the village of Bartrès. The Laguèses would surely take her in again, and down there the air is good and she gets goat's milk and honey on white bread. She loves it, too, and the little work she does can't harm her. . . ."

François Soubirous feels the bitterness of life rising in him again. Although he sees Louise's excellent reasons, rage chokes him. He has a weakness for big words and dramatic gestures. Some ancestors of the Soubirous probably came from Spain. "So it has come to this! I am in very truth a beggar whose children starve and must be given to strangers. . . ." He gnashes his teeth.

"Be reasonable, Soubirous," his wife interrupts him, to prevent his being noisy. She observes him as he stands there with bowed head, desperate, dignified, weak of will. She takes the bottle out of the cupboard and pours him a little glassful.

"Not a bad idea—that," he says awkwardly and gulps down the burning liquor. His soul cries out for a second glassful. But he restrains himself and goes out. In the bed shared by the two sisters the older, Bernadette, lies very still with her dark eyes wide open.

CHAPTER TWO

Of an Infamous Place Called Massabielle

THE RUE DES PETITES FOSSÉES is one of the narrow alleys which surround the castellated rock of Lourdes. It straggles trickily uphill before it ends at the municipal square, the Place Marcadale. Morning has now come, but Soubirous sees only a few paces ahead, for the grey sky hangs low and a veil of rain and thick snowflakes flaps against his face. The world is empty and without edge. Nothing breaks in upon the desolateness but the leaping morning signals of the bugles blown by the squadron of dragoons up in the citadel and in the barracks of Nemours. Although down here in the valley of the Gave the snow melts at once, yet strange puffs of icy cold pierce to the bone. It is the breath of the Pyrenees in ambush there behind the clouds, the sharp-edged message of those thronging crystalline peaks, from the Pic du Midi to the terrifying and demoniac Vignemale yonder between France and Spain.

Soubirous's hands are red and clammy, his stubbly cheeks wet, his eyes on fire. Yet he stands a long time in indecision in front of Maisongrosse's bakery before he enters. He knows it to be in vain. During last year's Carnival Maisongrosse had hired him as porter now and then, for during that festival the brotherhoods and guilds have their celebrations. The tailors and seamstresses, for instance, give a ball in honour of their patron saint, Lucia. The ball always takes place in the Post Hotel, and Maisongrosse furnishes the bakery goods, from simple breadstuffs to elaborate cream-tarts and apple-fritters. On this occasion Soubirous had earned the considerable sum of a hundred sous and had, moreover, brought home to his children a bag of bakery goods.

He plucks up his courage and enters the shop. The maternal fragrance of the warm bread swathes and nearly stuns him. It makes him feel almost tearful. In the middle of the room stands the fat baker, his white apron over his mighty belly, and orders about his two assistants, who sweatily draw out of the oven black tin pans full of fresh small loaves.

"Couldn't I be of some use to you today, Monsieur Maison-grosse?" Soubirous asks carelessly. He lets his hand slip into one of the open sacks and the wheaten flour glides voluptuously through his sensitive miller's fingers. The fat man does not deign to look at him. He speaks in a goitrous voice. "What day is today, *mon vieux?*" he grunts.

"Thursday, if it please you—*jeudi gras.*"

"That makes how many days to Ash-Wednesday?" Maison-grosse continues his questioning like a sly schoolmaster.

"All of six days, Monsieur," the miller answers hesitatingly.

"There you are!" The fat man acts as though he had won a bet. "Six more days will see the end of this whole rotten Carnival. Furthermore, the societies don't give me their orders any more. They buy at Rouy's. The good old times have gone to the devil. People go to the pastrycook's, not to the baker's. And if this is the state of business during Carnival, you can imagine what it will be in Lent. This very day I'm going to kick out one of these two good-for-nothings."

Soubirous reflects whether to ask the baker straight out for a loaf. The word chokes him. But he has not the courage to utter it. I'm not even a good beggar, he reflects. Like a dissatisfied customer he twiddles his cap and leaves the shop.

To reach the post-office he has to cross the square. Cazenave stands very authoritatively in the big yard surrounded by his teams and coaches. A former sergeant of the regiment of the line stationed at Pau, the man is an early riser. He had seen service many years ago, in the days of the fat citizen-king. He likes the thought of subsequent imaginary advancement and is flattered if he is addressed as an officer. He wears high, shining boots at all hours and carries a riding-crop with which he strikes his boot-tops with a military air. His face is purple and swollen and he wears the turned-up moustachios, dyed a careful black, made fashionable by the Emperor. Accordingly Cazenave is a convinced Bonapartist, adherent of a political programme that consists, as far as he is concerned, in a strict riming consonance between the expressions *la France* and *gloire* and *progrès*. Since the building of the railroad from Toulouse by way of Tarbes and Pau to Biarritz—a favourite resort of the Emperor and especially of the Empress Eugénie—the business of this postmaster flourishes more than ever. Every tourist and every valetudinarian bound for the health resorts of the Pyrenees must stop at Cazenave's. For Cazenave is sole purveyor of all "conveniences" which, dear or cheap, comfortable or the reverse, take those in need of cure to Argelès, Cauterets, Gavarnie, and Luchon. Just now the "season" is, to be sure, far off. With what lures to prolong it and thus increase the frequentation of tourists, such is the inexhaustible subject of discussion between Cazenave and the ambitious mayor of Lourdes, Monsieur Adolphe Lacadé.

Soubirous himself had served with the armed forces in his youth for just two weeks. He wasn't wanted for longer. So he assumes as best he can a soldierly bearing and faces Cazenave. "Good morning, Postmaster! Do you happen to have some small job for me?"

Cazenave fills his cheeks with air and expels it again disapprovingly. "You back again, Soubirous? Aren't you ever going to make ends meet? A man must make his place in the world. None of us get presented with what we have. . . ."

"God isn't pleased with me, Monsieur. I've had no luck for years."

"Good luck comes from God; it's possible. Ill luck is our own doing, my friend. . . ." The riding-crop whistles through the air in confirmation of this maxim.

Soubirous lowers his eyes. "My children surely are innocent of their misfortune."

The postmaster shouts a command to the groom Doutreloux. Soubirous holds himself straight once more. "Maybe there's something after all, *mon capitaine?* . . ."

Cazenave becomes almost benevolent. "I always like to help an old soldier. But today I really haven't a thing."

The miller's body visibly droops with heaviness. Slowly he turns to go. At that moment Cazenave calls him back: "Hold on, old man. Maybe you can earn twenty sous after all. Not very clean work, to be sure. The Mother Superior of the hospital asks that a lot of refuse be called for and burned somewhere outside the city. Bandages, operative remains, linen of contagious cases, and the like. Hitch the roan over there to the small open cart, if you like. . . . Twenty sous!"

"Couldn't you make it thirty, *mon capitaine?*"

Cazenave does not think it worth while to answer.

Soubirous does as he has been bidden. He hitches the rickety roan, the poorest horse on the place, to the open cart. The team clatters on to the hospital, which is conducted by the sisters of Saint Gildarde of Nevers, the same sisters who teach in the school. The hospital janitor has the three boxes of refuse ready for carting away. They are not heavy, but stink like the pest itself of all the miseries of the flesh. The two men lift the boxes onto the cart.

The janitor, knowing in medical matters, issues a warning:

"Be careful, Soubirous! The very devil of infection is in that
stuff. Take it far out to Massabielle; burn it there and throw
the ashes into the Gave!"

Rain and the flying of snow have ceased. The wagon rattles
over the uneven stones. The Hospital of the Sisters of Nevers
lies at the northern gate of the city where the national high-
ways from Pau and Tarbes cross. Soubirous has to use his
brake to get his cart down the steep Rue Basse in order to leave
Lourdes by the western gate of Baous. Not till he has crossed
the Pont Vieux, the old Roman bridge, does his frozen hand
relax. He lets the nag trot indifferently along the cart-road
that follows the bank of the river. Here the Gave makes a
sharp bend. As with a thousand voices angrily roar the immemorial mountain waters; the almost rectangular bend seems
to strain and irritate them. Everywhere huge blocks of granite
impede the river's raging course. Soubirous does not listen
to the waters. He didn't say "No" outright, the postmaster;
surely he'll pay me the thirty sous. I'll buy four loaves of
bread—eight sous—but not, faith, at Maisongrosse's; oh, no, not
at Maisongrosse's. I'll buy half a pound of sheep's cheese—
nourishing—that, added to the loaves, makes fourteen sous.
Add two litres of wine and we have twenty-four sous. Last,
a few lumps of sugar, so that the children have something
sweet and strong with their wine. . . . Nonsense. Better to hand
the thirty sous over to Louise at once and let her do the spending. Then I don't have to do the reckoning. And I won't keep
a button's worth for myself, so help me God. . . .

Despite the prospect of the thirty sous—a very gift from
Heaven—Soubirous's heart grows heavier and more desolate.
His hunger feels like nausea, abominably sharpened by the
stench of his lamentable load. He has to drive past the estate
of Monsieur de Lafite, the man of legendary wealth from
Lourdes, who like Soubirous himself had started out in life

as a simple miller before a demonic fate raised him to his dizzy height. The vast estate lies on the so-called Chalet Isle, which is formed by the bent bow of the Gave River and the taut bow-string, as it were, of the brook called Savy which empties itself into the river a few feet beyond the rock of Massabielle. The estate consists of the manor house built in the style of Henri IV with many little towers and bay-windows, of the park, of broad meadows, and of the impressive saw-mill. Reverently the folk of Lourdes call the mill "the factory." It is an extensive building, and a magnificent dam concentrates the waters of the meagre brook so that they achieve wonders. There is another mill, old and small, beside this brook. Soubirous can see it now from his box. It belongs to Antoine Nicolau and his mother. He envies Nicolau a hundred times more than he does Monsieur de Lafite for all the latter's manor and factory and carriages. Excess inspires no envy. But there is a common denominator between Nicolau and himself. In what way is he worse than Nicolau? Probably better, in fact —older and more experienced assuredly. Inscrutable the decrees of Heaven which cause the worthier to sicken in want the while the less worthy calmly watch, from the threshold of the Savy mill, the mill-wheels turn and turn. Soubirous brings his whip down over the nag's bony crupper, so that it gives a leap and begins to trot. The road is lost in the rust-hued heather, and far behind lie the silvery poplars of Monsieur de Lafite. The Chalet Isle grows desolate. Nothing grows here but wild boxwood and a few hazelnut-bushes. The two ranks of alder-bushes which line the Gave at the right and the brook Savy at the left seem to race toward one another.

At the left of the two streams rises the rocky height of the Montagne des Espélugues. It is but a low, insignificant ridge, this mount of holes or caverns. More elegantly it could be called the Mountain of Grottoes, for nature has blasted a couple of caverns into the solid rock. The largest of these, the grotto of Massabielle, is now directly under Soubirous's gaze. It is a hole in the chalky cliff, twenty paces in breadth, twelve in depth, not unlike a baker's oven. Bare, damp, filled with the rubble of the Gave which floods it with its moderately high water, the cavern is no gay sight. Sparse ferns and colts-foot sprout from amid the rubble. Half-way up the side of the grotto a single meagre thorn-bush clings to the rock; and there is a wild rose-vine which clambers about an oval or, rather, arched and pointed aperture, a small doorway, as it were, that opens upon a stony side-chamber of the grotto. One has almost the impression that this gate or Gothic window had been hewn into the rock aforetime by the hands of primitive men. The cavern of Massabielle is no favourite place among either the people of Lourdes or the peasants of the near-by villages in the valley of Batsuguère. Old wives will tell you many a tale of dread and ghostly happenings on this scene. When storms drive fishermen or shepherds or old women gathering faggots in the little Saillet wood to seek shelter in Massabielle, they do not fail to cross themselves.

Now, Soubirous is no old woman. He is a man fortified by experience, and tales of ghosts have no power over him. He brings his cart to a halt on the tongue of land between the river and the brook. He climbs down from his box and considers where and how he may most quickly execute his commission. It might be best to cross the shallow brook in the cart and to burn the hospital refuse in the cavern itself, where fire will burn more easily than out in the air. Soubirous hesitates. The rotten wooden cart might be damaged by the jagged stones in the brook.

François is no man of quick decisions. He scratches his head and becomes aware of a dull grunting mixed with hoarse cries. That must be Leyrisse, the swineherd, who comes running to

CHRIST UNITED METHODIST CHURCH
4488 POPLAR AVENUE
MEMPHIS, TENNESSEE 38117

the river-bank the while his black sows wallow in the morass between Massabielle and the municipal forest. There is another man whom God has stricken. Soubirous despises him not a little, for in the first place he is little better than an idiot; secondly, he has a cleft palate and hence barks and howls when he speaks; and, thirdly, he herds all the swine of the valley, which seems to the expert miller Soubirous the lowest of human occupations. Leyrisse is a short, stocky fellow with an enormous red-haired head on his goitrous neck. His body is wrapped from top to toe in raw skins, which has caused the school principal Clarens to declare that the aboriginal Pyrenean man must have looked like Leyrisse. The latter gestures excitedly to Soubirous. The swineherd is always highly excited, like all those unhappy creatures who, because of an impediment of speech, find communication difficult. The miller beckons him to approach. With great strides Leyrisse wades through the brook as though it were dry. His shaggy dog, no less excited than he, follows upon his heels.

"Hey there, Leyrisse," Soubirous calls out to the swineherd, "do you want to help me?"

Leyrisse is a good-natured creature whose highest ambition it is to prove his usefulness and his human efficiency. His powerful arms lift the boxes from the wagon and he carries them, as Soubirous has bidden him, to the extreme tip of the tongue of land, where he empties their contents on the ground. There arises an evil-smelling pyramid of blood-soaked cotton, pus-stained bandages, and filthy linen rags. The miller, accustomed to the cleanest of occupations and hence easily sickened, lights a pipe to get a pleasanter aroma into his nose. He imagines he has caught sight of unspeakable things amid the refuse, such as, for instance, an amputated human finger. Quickly he tosses his box of matches to Leyrisse to set the heap on fire. The cold has become intense, but no wind stirs.

The horrid combustible pyramid flares up on the instant. The swineherd and his dog dance merrily about this strange sacrificial pyre, whose smoke, graciously accepted by Heaven, rises in a straight line.

Soubirous, sitting on a stone, smokes and looks on. After a while the good swineherd sits down beside him. Out of his provender bag he takes dark bread and a hunk of bacon. He cuts equal portions of both. Barking amiably, he offers Soubirous a share of each. The latter is tempted to eat ravenously. The food is tasty and he has had no nourishment today. But he restrains his greed and chews slowly and thoughtfully, as befits an honourable miller whose station is so far above that of the swineherd and village idiot. His eyes upon the fire which is swiftly consuming its strange fuel, he murmurs: "If only there were a shovel here. . . ."

No sooner has the obliging Leyrisse heard the word shovel than he leaps up, runs across the brook again as though it were dry, and produces two shovels from the depth of the grotto. Workmen who were building a dam against the Gave in flood must have left them behind. Meanwhile the fire has reduced to ashes those awful remains of the suffering flesh. It costs the two men little trouble to shovel the ash-heap and sundry remnant of tinder into the Gave River, which accepts this gift in its own choleric manner and will carry it by way of the River Adour out into the ocean.

It is still far from eleven o'clock when François Soubirous, no longer with empty stomach and hopeless soul, faces Cazenave once more.

"Your order has been executed, *mon capitaine!*" After lengthy chaffering and several ever more tensely uttered *"mon capitaine's,"* Soubirous finally holds twenty-five sous in his hands. At the corner of the Rue des Petites Fossées Soubirous is still determined to hand over the full amount to Louise.

But by the time he reaches the bar of Papa Babou, the tempter assails him, and after the exertions of this forenoon his resistance is feeble. The original pay offered for his work was twenty sous, one single round silver piece. The five big copper coins represent surplus. Where is it commanded that a good family man who plagues himself as few do in the cold of winter to provide for wife and child is not to use these wretched coppers and sinful extras for himself? The price that Papa Babou asks for his home-distilled corn demon is no more than two sous for an eighth of a litre. Soubirous thinks that extremely reasonable. But he lingers at Babou's no longer than is necessary to consume a single measure.

In the Cachot a pleasant fragrance meets him. No *milloc*, no corn-mush today, thank Heaven! Mother is cooking an onion soup. Fate can't get the better of a woman like that, he reflects. She always succeeds in providing something. Maybe it's the rosary always in her apron pocket that stands her in good stead. Soubirous busies himself indifferently for some time in the room before he hands his wife the silver coin with an air as though this were merely a small advance against the louis d'or which he expects tomorrow.

"You're an able fellow, Soubirous," she says, not without a blending of esteem and pity, and he, too, is convinced that life has not got the better of him today. She places a plate of onion soup on the table before him. He eats spoonful by spoonful with thoughtful severity, as is his wont. She watches him and sighs.

"Where are the children?" he asks, after he has finished his soup.

"The girls will be back from school any moment. Justin and Jean Marie are playing outside. . . ."

"Those babies shouldn't play in the streets," the former miller observes with a critical air appropriate to his station. But since

Louise refuses to be drawn into a dispute on this point of honour, Soubirous gets up, groans, and stretches himself wearily. "I'm frozen to the bone. Best to go to bed. I've earned my rest."

Louise opens the bed for him. He slips out of his wooden shoes, gets in, and draws the covers up to his nose. Even though a man be poor as Job's turkey and put upon by fate, there are moments when life is delicious, especially after duties well performed. Soubirous is aware of his satisfied stomach, of the rising warmth, and of a distinct satisfaction with himself which permits him to glide swiftly from wakefulness to sleep.

CHAPTER THREE

Of Bernadette's Ignorance of
the Holy Trinity

At her desk in the schoolroom sits Sister Marie Thérèse Vauzous, one of those nuns of Nevers who have been delegated to serve the hospital and the girls' school attached to it. Sister Marie Thérèse is young and might be considered beautiful if her mouth were not so very narrow and her eyes so deeply sunken in their hollows. The pallor of her delicately formed face assumes a morbid yellow tinge under the snow-white wings of her cap. Her long and arrowy hands bear witness to exquisite breeding. Regard them closely, however, and you find them red and frost-bitten. From the pitiless signs of ascetic self-torture you would judge the nun Vauzous to be the very picture of a medieval saint. The catechist of Lourdes, Abbé Pomian, who has a pretty ironic vein, has been heard to say: "Our good Sister Marie Thérèse is less a bride than an Amazon of Christ." And he knows her very well, since she has been assigned to be his assistant in giving religious instruction to girls. (His pastoral activities often keep Chaplain Pomian away from Lourdes for days at a time to work in the villages and market-centres, so that he is fond of calling himself a travelling salesman of God. His superior, Dean Peyramale, holds all such witticisms in horror.) Under Pomian's supervision Sister Marie Thérèse is preparing the children for their first communion, which is to take place in the spring.

A girl is standing in front of the teacher, a girl rather small for her age. The round face is quite child-like, while the slight body already betrays the early maturity of this Southern race. The girl is clad in a peasant smock. She wears wooden shoes. But everyone, not the children only, wears them here, except those very few who belong to the so-called better circles. The brown eyes of the girl are calm under the nun's gaze. Their expression is uninhibited and dreamy and almost apathetic. There is something in that expression which troubles Sister Marie Thérèse. "So you really know nothing of the Holy Trinity, dear child?"

The girl keeps her eyes on the teacher and answers unabashed in a high, clear voice: "No, Sister, I know nothing about it."

"And you've never even heard of it?"

The girl reflects at some length. "Maybe I've heard about it. . . ."

The nun closes her book with a little bang. Real pain shows on her features. "I'm puzzled, my child. Are you pert or indifferent or only stupid? . . ."

"I'm stupid, Sister. They used to say at Bartrès that I have a poor head for study. . . ."

"It is as I feared." The teacher sighs. "You are pert, Bernadette Soubirous."

The sister walks up and down in front of the forms. True to her duties as a religious, she must fight down a rising irritation. During her silence the eighty or ninety girls in the class begin to move about restlessly in their seats and to babble louder and louder.

"Silence!" she commands. "Am I lost among the heathen? But indeed you are worse and more ignorant than the heathen. . . ."

One of the girls lifts her hand and waves it.

"Aren't you another Soubirous?" the nun asks. She has been

in charge for a few weeks only and has not yet affixed the right name to each of these faces.

"Yes, Sister, I am. I'm Marie Soubirous. I just wanted to say that my sister Bernadette is always ailing. . . ."

"I don't remember asking you for information." Her tone is censorious. This sisterly support smacks of rebellion to her. Christian sweetness alone will not keep this horde of ninety proletarian girls in check. But Sister Vauzous knows very well how to make herself respected. "So your sister is ailing?" she asks. "What ails her?"

"They call it athma, or some such name. . . ."

"You're trying to say asthma. . . ."

"Yes, Sister, asthma! That's what Dr. Dozous calls it. She can't breathe. Sometimes . . ." Marie gives a vivid imitation of an attack of breathlessness. The class roars. The teacher lifts her hand and cuts short the immoderate laughter. "Asthma prevents no one from study or piety."

Sister Marie Thérèse frowns and looks over her class.

"Can anyone here answer my question?"

In the front form a girl jumps up. She has black, tousled hair, desirous eyes, and a pointed, puckered mouth.

"Well, Jeanne Abadie." The teacher nods. She has frequent occasion to call the name. Jeanne Abadie is quick to let her light shine before men.

"The Holy Trinity, why, that is the simply the Lord, our God. . . ."

The thought-worn face of the nun shows a smile. "Well, it isn't quite as simple as that, child. . . . But at least you have a glimmering. . . ."

At this moment the whole class rises to its feet as a mark of respect to Father Pomian, who has just entered the room. The young priest, one of the three chaplains of Dean Peyramale, lives up to his name of Pomian or Appleman, for he has apple-round red cheeks and waggishly smiling eyes.

"You're having a little trial here?" he asks, seeing the poor culprit who still stands in front of the teacher's desk.

"I'm sorry to have to complain of Bernadette Soubirous, Monsieur l'Abbé. She is not only ignorant but pert."

Bernadette motions with her head as though to interpose and rectify the accusation. Father Pomian's strong, hairy hand turns her face toward the light.

"How old are you, Bernadette?"

"I'm past fourteen," the girl answers in her high, clear voice.

"She's the oldest in the class and the least mature," Sister Vauzous whispers to the chaplain. He pays no attention but turns back to Bernadette.

"Can you tell me, little one, on what day of what year you were born?"

"Oh, yes, I can tell you that, Father. I was born on the seventh of January 1844. . . ."

"Well, look at that, Bernadette. You're not so stupid; you can answer intelligently enough. . . . Maybe you know too in what octave you were born or, to be simpler, what feast we celebrate on the day before your birthday? Do you recall? It's not so long ago. . . ."

Bernadette looks at the chaplain with the same strange blending of firmness and apathy with which she irritated her teacher. "No, I don't recall," she answers without lowering her eyes.

"Never mind." Pomian smiles. "I'll tell you and the others too. On the sixth of January we celebrate the feast of Epiphany. It is on that day that the three kings from the East bring their wondrous gifts to the Christ child in the stable at Bethlehem—gold and myrrh and frankincense. Didn't you see the manger in church and the figures of the kings from the East?"

Bernadette Soubirous comes, as it were, to life. Her face flushes delicately. "Oh, yes, I saw the manger!" she cries almost ecstatically. "All those lovely images just like real people, the Holy Family and the ox and the ass and the three kings with little crowns and golden staffs. Oh, yes, I saw all that. . . ." The girl's eyes seem themselves to become golden under the power of the images which she summons up.

"So we do know something about the three holy kings who came from the East. Remember them, Bernadette, and pull yourself together, for you're a grown girl." Father Pomian winks cunningly at the teacher. He has given her a little hint as to the proper pedagogical method to use. Next he turns to the whole class. "And the seventh of January is an important feast day in France, for on that day one was born who rescued our country from the deepest disgrace. That happened exactly four hundred and forty-six years ago. Think carefully, children, before you answer!"

A shrill triumphant voice comes from the class at once: "The Emperor Napoléon Bonaparte!"

Sister Marie Thérèse presses her hands to her middle as though a sharp colicky pain had gone through her. Some girls take this as an occasion to shriek with savage laughter. The priest preserves his bright seriousness. "No, dear children, the Emperor Napoléon was born much, much later." And he goes to the blackboard and writes in great angular primer letters, seeing that many of the girls are still struggling with the first principles of reading and writing: "Jeanne d'Arc, the Maid of Orléans, born on the seventh of January 1412 at Domrémy."

While the children begin in a dull and broken chorus to decipher this legend the school bell rings. It is eleven o'clock. Bernadette Soubirous still stands in the space between teacher and pupils. Sister Marie Thérèse Vauzous rises to her full height. In the pale February light her proud face seems to breathe suffering. "It is on your account, dear Bernadette, that we failed to progress in our study of the catechism." Her voice is very soft so that none but Bernadette can hear her. "Consider whether you are worth that!"

CHAPTER FOUR

The Café Progrès

On the municipal square called Marcadale, scene of most of
the public life of Lourdes, there is situated between the two
important eating-houses of the town the Café Français. It is not
far from the terminal of the post-coaches, that is to say, from
the most important point of connexion between the great world
and the smaller one of the Pyrenean town. The owner of the
café, Monsieur Duran, had gone to great expense the year
before to decorate and furnish his place of business: red plush,
marble-topped tables, mirrors, a huge tile-oven which resembles a battlemented Roman watch-tower. This very fortress of
an oven causes the Café Français to be the best-heated place in
Lourdes. But Duran has been thoughtful not only of warmth,
but of light as well. He has introduced a new system of illumination: powerful, green-shaded kerosene lamps hanging in
pairs from scale-like rods pour their white and cosy radiance
over the marble tables. The coffee-house owner is convinced
that even in Paris, the city mad for the instant use of every
modern innovation, few public gathering-places are yet blessed
with this type of illumination. Unlike most of his countrymen
Duran is not notably thrifty. At need he lets his light shine
even by day, as, for instance, on this day on which the winter
twilight lingers long. But his magnanimity extends even beyond this. It is his aim to let the light of the mind shine forth
as well. On the coat-racks, in solid holders, hang copies of the
great Parisian newspapers, and it is Duran who willingly pays
the price of the subscriptions. *Le Siècle* is to be found here,

L'Ère Impériale, Le Journal des Débats, La Revue des Deux Mondes, and *La Petite République*. Yes, indeed, even this *Petite République*, a highly revolutionary sheet, opposed to the Emperor and his regime, belligerent and run, as everyone knows, by Louis Blanc, the unspeakable Socialist himself. Hardly necessary to say that the local weekly paper of Lourdes, *Le Lavedan*, is to be found here. The management has made a mutually profitable arrangement with Monsieur Duran, according to which four fresh copies of the weekly are placed on the marble tables every Thursday. In view of all these efforts in the direction of the guests' intellectual nourishment it is easy to understand why not a few people call Duran's Café Français the Café Progrès.

Twice a day the café is crowded—at eleven in the forenoon, the hour of the *apéritif*, and at four in the afternoon, when the offices of the provincial courts close. The officials of these courts are among the most faithful customers of the Café Français. The French State seems to follow an almost eccentric policy in the location of its seats of authority. The prefecture of the *département* or province is situated in Tarbes. Accordingly the sub-prefecture should be at Lourdes, the second city in importance. Its seat, on the contrary, is in the tiny town of Argelès, where, together with the head office of the *gendarmerie*, it is cut off from the normal circulatory system of the provincial administration. The reason for this arrangement is not to be fathomed. Lourdes was, naturally, hurt and offended. Hence Lourdes had to be placated. This was done by making it the seat of the highest provincial court, which ought normally to have been at Tarbes. Thus it comes about that Monsieur Duran boasts as guests a genuine president of a provincial court, sundry judges, the imperial public prosecutor Dutour, a number of administrative civil servants, advocates, and court secretaries.

At this hour none of these gentlemen has yet put in appearance. All alone at a round table in one corner sits Monsieur Hyacinthe de Lafite. He is not at all *the* Monsieur de Lafite, but a propertyless cousin of the rich man. A tower room in the manor house has been put at his quite free disposal. The Lafite family is often absent on journeys. Hence Hyacinthe has more and more availed himself of this refuge recently. For a man with an empty purse this town of Lourdes is a place of recuperation, and as for Paris, to hell with that city which cannot tell the difference between the genuine and the pinchbeck! Who can work in Paris? Journalists, whores, salesmen of souls.

You have only to glance at Hyacinthe de Lafite to know that he is a far from ordinary person. His style smacks of a former age. The richly intertwined cravat of his stock, for instance, reminds one of Alfred de Musset. The hair combed back from the rectangular cut of the forehead brings up the image of Victor Hugo. Although he is still far below forty his hair is sprinkled with grey. Once upon a time he was almost Victor Hugo's friend, that is, the giant condescended to make a pleasant observation concerning Lafite, then a participant in the battles of the theatres in the cause of French Romanticism, one of that company of the elect, in fact, who wore the historic waistcoats of red. In addition to Victor Hugo, long since in exile, he is not unacquainted with Lamartine and with Théophile Gautier and many others. But he has had enough of this entire arrogant crowd. So Lourdes seemed the ideal place where, upon the bosom of a somewhat violent nature and far from the insulting disparagements of the Parisian salons and literary cafés, a man might dedicate himself to the composition of a mighty work. Bold to the point of madness is the plan that Hyacinthe de Lafite turns over in his head. It is nothing less than the reconciliation of the Romantic school, to which, according to his feeling, he himself belongs, with the classical

tradition. Limitless imagination embodied in stringent form—
such is his watchword. He is working at a tragedy, *The Founding of Tarbes*. His subject matter he owes to his old friend the
school principal Clarens, a zealous student of local lore and
legend and editor of a column in *Le Lavedan* called "The
Antiquities of Lourdes." The fable of the tragedy concerns an
Ethiopian queen named Tarbis who, smitten by an unreturned
passion for a biblical hero, flees westward to the lands of the
Pyrenees to forget her woe. Hither she comes, liberated from
the sombre deities of the East. The serene gods of the Occi-
dent magically heal her heart's torment. As their priestess she
builds a city called Tarbes.

No bad subject, as is obvious, and full of allegorical implications. The poet writes in pure, classical alexandrine verses,
in itself a rash challenge to the Shakespearian Victor Hugo. He
is unbendingly determined, as an inheritor of the tradition of
Racine, to observe the unities of time and place. It is a melancholy fact, moreover, that after two years of work all he has
to show is forty alexandrine couplets. Today's *Lavedan*, however, contains an article by him in which he gives an exposition of his stylistic principles. The editor had been more than
reluctant to print the article, arguing that it would make no
sense to his illiterate readers.

In front of Lafite lies today's *Lavedan*. It has appeared punctually, no common event. Usually this progressive weekly appears two or three days after the scheduled date. Father Pomian
is fond of saying: "An odd sort of progress that always comes
too late."

The friendly enemy of Victor Hugo is passionately eager to
have his article read. He is especially eager to have the philologist and humanist Clarens absorb it at the earliest moment. It
contains three sentences on Racine that should be permitted to
melt on the tongue. Clarens, however, who appears at this very

moment, is so passionately engrossed in a favourite preoccupation of his own that he pays no attention either to the paper or
to the author of the article. Such is always the tragic element
in these æsthetic or learned relations. Clarens is unwrapping a
heavy flattened stone from a cloth. Self-centred, he pushes the
stone under the poet's nose and forces upon him a magnifying
glass.

"Look at this find, my friend! Guess where I came upon it!
But you never will! On the mount of caverns in one of the
grottoes amid the rubble—there lay this stone and fairly cried
out to me. Look at it closely! Under the glass, please! You
recognize the coat of arms of Lourdes, eh? Fundamentally different from its contemporary form. I'd stake my life on its
being as old as the early sixteenth century. Over the towers of
the citadel floats the eagle with the fish in his beak. The towers,
however, differing from the present design, are in purest Moorish style. Mirambelle, as I need hardly tell you, was the medieval
name of our city. Miriam-Bell. Now, Miriam is the Moorish
form of Maria. The trout which the eagle holds in his beak is
none other than *ichthus*, the Christ symbol which is being
thrown down on the city, which has just been conquered for
Mary. As everywhere in this land you see the principle of the
worship of Mary. . . ."

Out of sheer annoyance Lafite interrupts and blankly contradicts him: "I can't in the least agree with you, my friend. It
is my considered opinion that all these heraldic animal symbols
are pre-Christian in origin."

"But you will not deny, my friend," the elderly Clarens pro-
tests, "that even the name of the River Gave contains an Ave."

The poet denies it categorically. Like all minds of his type he
lets the improvisation of the moment lead him along a path surprising even to himself, merely in order to arrive at the goal
which has preoccupied him from the start. "As a philologist,

my friend, you know better than I that in many languages the letter gamma is transmuted into iota, and vice versa. Why shouldn't Gave rather be identical with the biblical Yahve whose worship my Queen Tarbis, after her unhappy experience with her Hebrew, introduced here? If you will read my work, or, at least, the article in today's . . ."

He gets no further. The subtle conversation has to be interrupted. Eleven o'clock has struck. The hour of the *apéritif* is here. One by one they appear, all those who belong to the cultural or economic upper crust of the town. Conversations such as the one just recorded can scarcely be expected of these advocates, officers, civil servants, physicians. A pure and non-utilitarian humanism is hardly their line. First comes Dr. Dozous, physician to the municipality, a very busy soul. Always on the jump, always rushing from one case that needs him to another, he will not forgo his glass of port or Malvasier at this hour among the other big-wigs. Next there are Dr. Peyrus and Dr. Vergez and Dr. Lacrampe and Dr. Balencie, in spite of whom Dozous is convinced that the entire responsibility for medical science here rests upon his somewhat high shoulders. The passionate curiosity of the researcher has not yet been extinguished in his soul. Hence, despite his overcrowded days, he keeps up a lively medical correspondence to save himself from going scientifically to seed in this provincial town. The great Charcot, the famous Voisin, head of the Salpêtrière in Paris—how they must be astonished when their mail brings them those long letters and eager questionnaires from the municipal physician of Lourdes, which it takes hours to answer.

"I'll trouble you gentlemen just three minutes," says Dozous. It is his daily formula. He sits on the edge of a chair in his hat and coat, which, in view of Duran's mighty oven and the principles of hygiene, is a pretty bad mistake. He takes up *Le Lavedan*, pushes his spectacles to his forehead, and begins to nozzle his way through the paper. Hyacinthe de Lafite, though he is absorbed by the sight of the reading doctor, catches no sight of any expression that might betoken the finding of his article. Meanwhile Jean Baptiste Estrade, the chief revenue officer of Lourdes, has joined them. The poet considers this man with the dark, pointed beard and the melancholy glance to possess definite advantages. He says little and is a good listener. He seems not wholly deaf to intellectual cognitions and formulations. Indifferently the physician has passed the paper on to the revenue officer. Now Estrade turns the pages with careless fingers. But just as he comes to the page where Lafite's article appears in all its glory he is forced to put the paper down, for all the gentlemen are rising in their seats. It isn't every day that his honour the mayor drops in in person.

Benevolently, extending greetings to all sides, the weighty figure of Monsieur A. Lacadé makes its way among the tables. It is still clear why for the greater part of his life he was called the "handsome" Lacadé. In view of his belly, the pouches of his cheeks and under his eyes, there can no longer be any question of looks. Emphatically, however, one can speak of that well-oiled, even supple dignity characteristic of the politically gifted and corpulent. Although of humblest peasant origin in the district of Bigorre, he has magnificently identified himself with his role as a public figure. On his first election as mayor of Lourdes around the year 1848, malicious tongues stigmatized him as an out-and-out Jacobin. Today he is a trustworthy adherent of the imperial regime. But who does not change his views with the passing of time? Lacadé appears steadily in black, as though always prepared to let his ceremonial duties take him by surprise. His gestures are large, almost majestic. His tone is condescending. His conversation is always an allocution. He patronizes equally the two State functionaries who have entered with him. One of these is Vital Dutour, imperial prosecutor, rather young, bald, ambitious, and bored to death. The other is the police commissioner Jacomet, a man somewhat over forty with heavy hands and that ominous glance which even the most harmless creatures assume when they become criminalists.

The mayor shakes everybody's hand and gives his joviality full play. The coffee-house keeper Duran rushes up, takes the orders, and returns after a while to serve the drinks himself.

"Ah, Messieurs, I'm sorry to say that the papers from Paris haven't arrived this morning. What miserable postal service we have!"

"Bah! The Paris papers," someone jeers. "In February politics are as sombre as the weather. . . ."

Little Duran is reassuring. "But if the gentlemen want to see yesterday's *Mémorial des Pyrénées* or the *Intérêt Public* of Tarbes or today's *Lavedan,* which came out punctually, here they are. . . ." He bends down to Lacadé's ear. "And there's a little article in it, Monsieur le Maire, a beautifully wrought bit of work. . . ."

Lafite is all ears. Duran purses his lips in pleasurable appreciation. "It's a little article which the reverend clergy will scarcely find palatable. . . . Another Malvasier, Monsieur le Maire?"

Lacadé raises both a visionary glance and his rich, oily voice. "I can promise you and all of us, in fact, better postal service, my dear Duran. Great things will be done for our humble town. On the basis of my ceaseless protestations the highest quarters are contemplating connecting us with the railway system. . . . I trust that all you gentlemen share my local patriotism. Am I right, Monsieur le Procureur?"

Vital Dutour's answer is dryly courteous. "We members of the judiciary are like vagabonds. We're ordered from one place to another and our local patriotism hasn't much chance . . ."

"The railroad is coming, nevertheless," Lacadé prophesies.

Duran's face lights up. He remembers an exquisite formulation which he has read in one of the papers. Since he spends so much money for them, he feels it his duty to study them far into the night. It is a hard enough task, injurious to his unaccustomed eyes but very profitable to the cultivation of his speech. "Means of communication and the educational system are the two pillars of a truly developing humanity. . . ."

"Bravo, Duran!" Lacadé nods approval. "Especially the means of communication. Just see how this old waiter of ours furnishes me with a perfect formulation for my next ceremonial address. I mustn't forget it."

The mayor's praise lends wings to Duran. Stiffly he raises his right hand like an amateur actor. "When distances between men are shortened and their wealth of words increased, then will superstition, fanaticism, war, and tyranny disappear and it may be that the next generation or, at latest, the next century will witness the coming of the Golden Age. . . ."

"Where does that come from, my friend?" the mayor asks in suspicious astonishment.

"Just my own humble opinion, Your Honour. . . ."

"I don't place so high a value on either the means of communication or on the educational system as our friend Duran," Lafite says suddenly, unable to master his irritation any longer.

"Oho!" Dutour laughs. "Don't tell me that a Parisian poet is a reactionary."

"I am neither reactionary nor revolutionary. My mind is wholly independent, but for that very reason I don't see the meaning of human life in the higher development of the broad masses."

"Careful, careful, my friend," the humanist Clarens admonishes him.

"And what, then, is the meaning of life?" asks J. B. Estrade thoughtfully, as though to himself.

With unmotivated but evident bitterness Hyacinthe de Lafite takes the floor. "If humanity may be said to have a purpose it is this and this only: to give birth to the man of genius, to the extraordinary human being. That is my conviction. Let the masses live and suffer and die for this end, that from time to time there arise a Homer, a Raphael, a Voltaire, a Rossini, a Chateaubriand, and, if you like, a Victor Hugo. . . ."

"It's sad," says Estrade, "pretty sad for us poor insignificant worms to be nothing but the painful detour to these splendid ends. . . ."

"It's the philosophy of a poet," Lacadé declares indulgently and only half listening. "But since we have a poet in our city he should do something for Lourdes. Come, Monsieur de La-fite, write something for the Paris press, something about the beauty of our scenery, our great views—about Pibeste and the Pic de Ger and the overwhelming grandeur of our mountains. Then write about our municipal techniques and the cosy life which is led by our fiery little people, which demands, after all, so little. Why, you might write about this stunning Café Français! Whatever you like! But be sure to say unmistakably to Paris and therefore to the world: Why do you arrogant peo-ple neglect Lourdes in favour of the baths of Cauterets and Gavarnie? We are as well prepared to receive you and to pro-vide good lodgings and a first-rate cuisine. . . . For some time, Messieurs, I have been asking myself why second-rate holes like Cauterets and Gavarnie are preferred to us? Thermal baths? Mineral springs? Well, if there are medicinal waters a few miles from here in Gavarnie and Cauterets, why not near Lourdes? It's a simple problem in arithmetic. We've got to discover the springs. We must strike them from the rocks. And such is my firm intention. I have dispatched several memoranda on this subject to Baron Massy, the prefect. Better roads, improved postal service, higher appropriations. We will channel the stream of gold and civilization to Lourdes. . . ."

The mayor cannot deny even to himself that he has delivered a brilliant address over his *apéritif*. Filled with the warmth engendered by his eloquence, he is convinced anew that he is an incomparable magistrate. How orphaned will Lourdes be when some day he is no more! With satisfaction he empties the rest of his Malvasier. Almost at once all prepare to go. Their womenfolk have *déjeuner* waiting at home.

Wrapped in his cape, the solitary Hyacinthe de Lafite proceeds along the Rue Basse. No afterwarmth of eloquence is his, but biting cold of soul and weather. Suddenly he stops and stares at the dirty houses, which reply with their disconsolateness to his own disconsolate glance. What the devil am I doing here? I belong on the Boulevard des Italiens and the Rue du Faubourg Saint-Honoré. Why do I live in this filthy hole? As he walks on he answers his own questions: I live in this dirty hole because I'm a dirty dog, a poor relation to whom a bone is thrown and who must be grateful for it to this self-inflated provincial family and its charitableness. I've got a warm room and first-class grub and no chance to spend five sous a day. I associate with the mental dwarfs at the Café Français, to whom I am a closed book. I belong neither to God nor to man. The spirit is the perpetual outcast and poor relation in such a world as this.

CHAPTER FIVE

End of the Brush-Wood

Before Bernadette and Marie are home from school the
two little boys turn up in the Cachot for their midday meal.
The older brother, Jean Marie, wears an expression both reckless and sly, as though he has come victoriously out of an adventure. And so he has. At the end of the last morning Mass,
which Dean Peyramale usually celebrates himself, the parish
church is apt to be quite empty. At this moment the seven-
year-old Jean Marie slipped into the little side-niche where
stands the statue of the Virgin, for which the women of Lourdes
have a great devotion. There on an iron stand burn many candles dedicated to the Mother of God. Jean Marie has scratched
among the candle-drippings until he has several lumps of melted
wax. These he brings home in all good faith to his mother.

"Make candles of it, Mamma . . . or maybe you can use it
for cooking. I tasted it. . . ."

"*Praoubo de jou!*" exclaims Louise Soubirous. "I am to be
pitied!" The people of Lourdes rarely speak French. They
speak their own dialect, which is akin to Basque. "I am to be
pitied! I have a child who steals from the Most Blessed Virgin."

She snatches the wax from the child. On this very day she
will visit the chandler Gazalas and have him make a large candle for the Virgin. She is so outraged by the impiety of Jean
Marie that she pays no attention to the six-year-old Justin,
whose grimy hands are stretched out with a gift for her too. It
is a narrow strip of knitted wool.

"Look, Mamma, what I was given!"

47

"You little wretches, you've been begging. . . ."

"We haven't been begging at all!" The older boy is indignant at the accusation. "Justin got it from the young lady."

"What young lady, in Heaven's name?"

"Why, the one who always goes about with a basketful of things like this. And we didn't say a thing. We just stood there."

"Do you mean Mademoiselle Jacomet, the daughter of the police commissioner?"

"And she said," babbles Justin, " 'You're to have this knitted piece because you are the poorest child I know.' "

"You two had better be careful," Mamma says angrily, "that Monsieur Jacomet doesn't catch you just idling about! He's sure to put you in a dark hole. . . ."

"Am I really the poorest child she knows?" Justin asks, with the bright curiosity of one unconcerned.

"Oh, you stupids," Mother Soubirous hisses, and yanks the two urchins to the washtub, where she scrubs their hands with white sand, preaching at them the while. "The child of Madame Bouhouhorts is ever so much poorer than you. He's been paralysed from birth and can't move. But all day long you fool around in the street and can act and chatter as you like. And moreover, you're not poor children at all but sons of a former mill-owner and you're not to act like kinless vagabonds. Your mother's family is an excellent one. The Casterots were always held in high esteem. You've only to look at your aunt Bernarde; and an uncle of my father was parish priest in Trie and yet another uncle was stationed with the military in Toulouse. You're a disgrace to them all. Your father is looking for a new mill. Everything will be different then. It's a mighty good thing he's asleep and doesn't know that you steal from the Blessed Virgin and plague respectable folk. . . ."

After this sermon Louise Soubirous casts a lingering glance at her husband, who, flat on his back, sleeps the loud sleep of the just, though the just don't as a rule sleep during the fore-noon. But like all people who must share a room with many others Father Soubirous has long since learned not to let loud talk or any other noise break in upon his slumber. Neverthe-less, his wife lowers her voice.

"He wears himself out for you, your good father, and every day he brings home money. And children like you who have parents are not really poor at all. Tomorrow I do Madame Millet's washing and she's sure to give me a piece of cake for you. . . ."

"Will there be fruits in the cake?" Justin asks with the sus-piciousness of the expert. But his mother has no time to reply, for the two daughters, Bernadette and Marie, have come in and brought another girl with them, the prize pupil of the cate-chism class, Jeanne Abadie. This damsel of thirteen, with her quick black eyes and pursed mouth, is quite a lady in her demeanour. She begins with the neatest of curtsies.

"I'm not a bit hungry, Madame; I'll just watch the others. . . ."

Meanwhile Madame Soubirous has placed the pot of onion soup on the table. Bits of toasted bread swim on the soup. She sighs: "Help yourself, Jeanne. One more makes no difference. We have enough. . . ."

Marie hastens to explain the reason for the visit: "Jeanne came along because we're going to study together later. That Vauzous woman was terribly nasty to Bernadette and made her stand in front of the forms. . . ."

Bernadette looks at her mother with almost inattentive eyes. "It is true," she says, calmly just, "that I really didn't know a thing about the Holy Trinity."

"You know no more about anything else," the prize pupil observes cruelly. A human being who is objective enough to bare his own weakness becomes an easy prey. "You can't get along by just knowing your Hail Mary. . . ."

"Shall I recite the Hail Mary for you?" Justin asks zealously.

Marie comes to her sister's rescue. "Bernadette was in Bartrès for years and years. . . . You don't learn as much in the village as in the city!"

The mother has placed a glass of red wine in front of Bernadette. This special favour accorded to the delicate girl is accepted by everyone as a matter of course. Secretly, moreover, the mother has put three lumps of sugar into the wine. "Bernadette," she asks her now, "would you like to go back to Madame Laguès at Bartrès for a while? . . . I've already discussed it with your father. . . ."

Bernadette's eyes brighten as always when she sees a vivid image with the inner eye. "Oh, yes, I'd like it so much. . . ."

Marie shakes her head, quite angry. "I don't understand you, Bernadette. It's terribly dull in the village. All you do is watch the sheep crop the grass. . . ."

"I like it," Bernadette declares tersely.

"If she likes it . . ." the mother says in Bernadette's support.

"You're just lazy," Marie scolds. "You'd like best to sit in a corner all day and gawp. You're hard to get along with. . . ."

"Let her be," says Madame Soubirous. "She's not as strong as you are."

But Bernadette is hurt and will not have it so. "That's not true, Mamma. I'm just as strong as Marie. Ask Madame Laguès! If need be, I can even do farmwork. . . ."

At this point Jeanne Abadie, laying down her spoon, breaks in with premature strictness. "It's impossible, Madame! Bernadette is the oldest girl in our class. It's high time that she receive the body of our Lord. Otherwise she'll remain a heathen and a sinner and won't go to Heaven nor even to Purgatory. . . ."

"God have mercy on us!" the frightened mother cries and strikes her hands together.

At this moment Soubirous wakes up. Moaning, he sits on the

edge of the bed and blinks into the room. "Mass-meeting here, eh?" he murmurs and begins to saw the air with his arms. "It's damned cold in here. . . ."

Still drunk with sleep, he gropes his way to the fireplace and throws a few small logs on the meagre fire. There is left but a tiny heap of brush-wood and dry branches, and the head of the house must blame someone in sombre tones. "What's the meaning of this? Neither brush-wood nor logs! You just let the fire go out. After all my work, am I to go out to gather wood too? Am I to have no assistance at all?"

"We'll go out for wood, dry wood too!" the children cry merrily and with one accord. Especially Jean Marie and Justin are wildly enthusiastic.

Soubirous rebukes them harshly: "You two stay here. We've had enough of your excursions for one day. . . . Marie and Jeanne can go looking for wood. . . ."

"How about me?" Bernadette asks. She flushes and her tranquil countenance shows its first trace of sadness. Mamma tries to dissuade her.

"Be sensible! You're the oldest. Marie and Jeanne are well and hardened to work. But you'll come home with a cough and a cold. And then your asthma will get worse. You know how you suffer when that happens. . . ."

"But, Mamma, I'm really much tougher than Jeanne and Marie. Why, in Bartrès I had to be out of doors all day, whether it snowed or rained or thundered. And I was never so well as there. . . ." She turns to her father with a persuasive reason: "And three people can carry much more than two, can't they?"

"It's for your mother to decide whether you go or stay," says François Soubirous, who practises the advantageous and pleasant principle of interference or self-commitment in matters of the children's upbringing only in case of extreme need.

A knocking at the door is heard. Madame Bouhouhorts, the

neighbour, a very thin woman still young, slips in. She is exhausted and struggles for breath. "Oh, my dear Louise, oh, good neighbour," she laments.

Louise, about to begin washing the dishes, lets everything be. "God above, what's wrong, Croisine?"

"It's the baby, the poor lamb. . . . It's like the convulsion he had three weeks ago. . . . His eyes roll in his head and he clenches his little fists, and I don't know what to do. Do come and help me, for the good Lord's sake. . . ."

"It will pass, Croisine, as it has before. Do be calm. I'll be over in a moment. Look, I'm all confused with the troubles of my own brood. . . ."

The two boys ordered to stay home have raised a belligerent cry of protest. Louise has to go after them roughly to quiet them. And tears of compassion for Croisine Bouhouhorts are in her eyes.

"I'm coming now. Go on, girls, get started!"

"So you're permitting me to go!" Bernadette is radiant.

Louise Soubirous puts her hand on her forehead. "How is a poor woman like me to manage with all this foolishness?"

She goes to the cupboard and fetches a few things. "Here, put on these woollen stockings and this warm neckerchief and also the *capulet*—yes, that too—and don't contradict!"

The *capulet* is a little cloak with a hood which covers head and shoulders and comes down to the knees. It is worn by the simple women of Lourdes, but even more generally by the peasant girls of Bartrès, Omex, in the valley of Batsuguère and all the district of Bigorre. The *capulets* are scarlet or white. Bernadette's is white. Under the pointed hood her little face disappears in a bluish shadow.

CHAPTER SIX

Of a River's Rage and Woe

THE GIRLS have sundry encounters before they reach their goal.

Near the Pont Vieux, between the first bridge-pier and the fishing-hut, on the gentle slope of the river-bank, is the paved square of the washerwomen. In sunny weather the women of Lourdes are wont to stand in long rows to rinse their linen in the Gave, whose waters are reputed to be uncommonly cleansing and bleaching. At such times the eternally morose roaring of the waters blends with the many-voiced gossiping of the women and the impact of clothes on the washboards. Today there is but a single woman who is undeterred by the weather. She is called Piguno, but what that nickname means nobody knows. If it were meant to refer to the dove-like nature of this crone, it would be sheer euphemism, like that of the ancients when they called an especially treacherous body of water the "benevolent sea" in order not to anger it by a characterization of its real nature. Piguno is no dove; rather a crow hardened by wind and weather, a many-wrinkled crone, a demon of curiosity, and a dangerous know-it-all. Her real name is Maria Samaran and she is a distant kinswoman of the Soubirous. But the family regards her with a measure of haughtiness, for no one stands on so low a rung of the ladder of society but that, luckily, there is another on a still lower one.

"Hey there, you Soubirous girls," Piguno calls, "whither away?"

"We're being sent on an errand, Aunt Piguno," Marie shouts

through her cupped hands, for the roar of the waters makes speech difficult.

Piguno's red fists are against her hips. "Your parents must be crazy, by the Blessed Virgin! I wouldn't send a dog out into this frost!"

Bernadette reflects a moment and then cries: "Why shouldn't we go for wood, Aunt Piguno, when you do your washing in this weather?" This is one of those remarks of Bernadette which Sister Vauzous would have considered indisputably pert.

Piguno, who rarely fails to have the last word, approaches. "Easy to imagine the state of your wood-pile! Your father doesn't know how to cut his garment to suit his cloth, and as for your mother! . . . I'll speak no evil of her, for it's not your fault that you are her children. But you can tell them both that Piguno gave you a bit of good advice." She lowers her voice and whispers stealthily: "Monsieur de Lafite's manager has had several poplars cut down on the Chalet Isle, at the end of the park, close by the iron fence. There you'll find wood enough, by cripes, for seven families. . . ."

Jeanne Abadie curtsies. "We're very much obliged to you for your kindness, Madame."

The three girls do not take the same road which François Soubirous followed that morning with his pestilential load. They cut inland from the river on a path that leads to the Savy mill to the left of the brook. From there they can cross the little bridge later on to the Chalet Isle. Bernadette is reflecting slowly. The notion of having to cross the park fence to steal wood fills her with discomfort. But it also irks her to be called a "fraidy-cat" by her two robust companions if she confesses to her pang. Half their way lies behind them before Bernadette utters a protest. "Poplar wood is always green and mad. After all this rain it'll be wet and just smoke."

"Wood is wood," Jeanne says. "We can't pick and choose like customers in a shop."

Bernadette tries again. "And we haven't a knife, either, to cut off the branches."

Marie is triumphant. "I took along Papa's clasp-knife." She draws the clumsy tool from her apron pocket. The conversation is interrupted by Leyrisse and his grunting herd, which had started home at noon from Massabielle. The good swineherd grins sunnily and takes off his cap to Bernadette. She smiles back at him.

"Bernadette is a great favourite of Leyrisse," Marie jeers. To ingratiate herself with the superior Jeanne, Marie will now and then make fun of Bernadette. "The two are sort of colleagues, you know."

Bernadette is not at all hurt. She explains, that is all. "I never herded swine, only goats and sheep. . . . Ah, if you knew how sweet a little lamb is, a tiny new-born one. It lies in your lap so sweetly. . . ."

Marie is irritated at her sister again. She thinks of herself as a city girl and is contemptuous of all kinds of husbandry. "You big silly, with your sweet ball of wool. . . . She's crazy over anything that is tiny and kind of cute. . . ."

"I myself prefer pork to mutton," Jeanne Abadie asserts knowingly, although her family, too, is rarely as festive as that.

The sluice of the saw-mill is locked at this time in order that the sawdust-bin may be filled. Whenever this is done, the water in the brook is so low that the wheels of the Savy mill stop turning. Antoine Nicolau, the young miller, uses these occasions to mend those that are defective. Mother Nicolau stands outside her door, for though the cold has grown keener, the weather is a bit brighter. Not that the gusts of wind have torn the ceiling of cloud, but the wintry sun drenches that ceiling with a moist light which seems to spray the Chalet Isle with its faint beams.

"Those are the Soubirous girls," says Madame Nicolau. "I don't know the third one."

"I think her name is Abadie—a pert little baggage," says Antoine, laying aside his tools and drawing himself up to his full height. He is a tall, good-looking young chap with sincere eyes and an elaborate moustache of which he is not a little proud. The girls smile a greeting at Mother Nicolau.

"How are your parents?" Madame Nicolau calls out. "Don't forget to give them our regards!"

Although François Soubirous is no longer a miller in his own right but a day labourer out of work, Madame Nicolau consciously uses a condescending friendliness, seeing that the Soubirous were once her equals in rank.

"No one says good day to me," Antoine complains.

Bernadette goes up to him and gives him her hand. "I beg your pardon, Monsieur Nicolau!"

"Whither are you bound, ladies?"

"Oh, we're just strolling about a bit," Marie says prudently. "Maybe we'll pick up an armful of kindling along the way. . . ."

"May we use your little bridge?" Jeanne asks with her accustomed politeness.

Antoine makes a gallant gesture. "No toll charged ladies."

The bridge consists of three boards with cracks between as wide as the boards. Marie and Jeanne leap gracefully across. Bernadette lingers on the middle of the bridge in order to watch the leaping little waves of the brook. She adores gazing into water and no longer hears the voices of the miller and his mother.

"How quickly people go down in the world if they aren't careful," says Mother Nicolau. "Now the Soubirous send their children to steal wood in the park of the manor. . . ."

"Why not?" Antoine answers generously. "Maybe they're not thinking of robbing Lafite. Maybe they're just fetching brush-wood from the Saillet woods. We do that ourselves. . . ."

Madame Nicolau frowns. "I'm not talking about brush-wood. Our friend Soubirous has had trouble about freshly cut wood before."

Antoine takes up his hammer and proceeds to fasten a new board to the mossy wing of the mill-wheel. The girls hear the blows of his hammer on their entire way. Now they have reached the gate of the park that leads to the manor house, and a broad avenue of plantains gives them a view of the terrace. A solitary gentleman in a voluminous cape is slowly walking up and down the avenue. He seems in a bitter mood, for he does not return the greeting of the children; he talks to himself, with arms beating time. Now and then he stops to make memoranda in a little notebook.

"That's Monsieur de Lafite, the cousin from Paris," Jeanne Abadie whispers reverently. "No doubt he's counting all the trees in the forest to find out what they're worth. . . ."

That frightens Marie. "Dear God, maybe we'd better not follow Aunt Piguno's advice."

"You're right. That's quite impossible now!" Bernadette cries, and feels free and at peace.

"What cowards you Soubirous are!" the Abadie girl declares, but flees as swiftly as her friends to escape the eyes of the counter of trees. . . .

And this was the fourth encounter the girls had.

Now they tramp through the pathless, dank, thickly covered heath. Bernadette begins to break twigs from the bushes. The two insensitive ones laugh. "No one could so much as burn his fingertips on those twigs."

"Maybe we'd better go farther along here," says Bernadette,

though she scarcely knows this region. "We'll find more farther down. . . ."

Jeanne Abadie, proudly expert in geography, points grandly to the west. "If we run on here, we could easily get to Bétharram without finding anything."

She is wrong. They would meet a natural obstacle in the confluence of the brook and the river. They are standing on that tongue of land, covered by rubble and sand, on which this morning Father Soubirous for a wage of twenty-five sous conducted his *auto-da-fé* of the miseries of the flesh. They can see the spot blackened by the fire. At their left extends the low wooded ridge of the mount of caverns where the cave of Massabielle lies under the alternating light and shadow of the slothfully moving clouds.

"There!" Jeanne cries. "Do look at all those bones!" She points to a few whitish sheep- or cow-bones which the water has washed up to the foot of the rock. They gleam brightly amid the darker rubble.

"If you sell these bones to Gramont, the rag-and-bone man, you'd get at least two or three sous," Marie reckons, "and for that much Maisongrosse would sell you a big loaf of white bread and a large piece of rock-candy. . . ."

"I'm entitled to half!" Jeanne becomes passionate. "At least that. Actually the bones are mine. I saw them first."

Swinging them wildly she flings her wooden shoes across the brook, at this point no wider than seven paces, and wades with grim determination through the shallow water, which at its deepest point scarcely reaches her knee. Earlier on this day, when Leyrisse waded through as though there were no water, it reached to his hips.

Jeanne Abadie squeals. "It cuts like a knife! Oh, how cold!"

Marie is afraid she will lose her little trading venture. Hastily she takes her wooden shoes in her hands, gathers her

skirt high, and follows the other through the icy brook. She
utters little sharp cries of horror. Bernadette is seized by a
strange, wholly unknown revulsion. The sight of her sister's
naked gleaming thighs, though the girls share one bed, seems
to her a thing so hideous and fills her with such disgust that
she turns aside. The two who have now reached the farther
bank sit down and madly rub their legs while their teeth chatter. Tears run down their cheeks.

"And what's going to become of me?" Bernadette cries out.

"You'll have to condescend to do like us," Jeanne snaps.

"She mustn't," Marie objects, worried. "She'd get a bad
cold in the head, and then her athma would be so miserable
that she wouldn't be able to sleep all night."

"Yes, I'd get a cold and a cough, and Mamma would scold
like anything and even whip me."

In an access of magnanimity Marie jumps up. "Wait! I'll
come over and carry you across pick-a-back. . . ."

"Oh, no, you aren't big or strong enough, Marie. We'd
both tumble into the water. . . . Maybe you could find some
big stones for me to step over on. . . ."

"Big stones!" Jeanne jeers. "You'd have to hire a couple of
hod-carriers first. . . ."

"But you could carry me across, Jeanne. You're the strongest
and biggest."

Jeanne Abadie, the prize pupil, so up-and-coming as a rule,
gives way to vulgar rage. "Thank you so much for the charming invitation! Another dip into that icy mess? Not for pounds
of rock-candy. And if you're a born fraidy-cat and scared of
your mamma, stay where you are, you touchy little runt. To
hell with you!"

Bernadette has the child-like quality of visualizing the spoken
word. To her no phrases are empty. She fills the shabbiest
clichés with reality. Hell gapes invisibly behind her merely

because of Jeanne's imprecation. "That is an evil wish you have wished!" she calls across. "If that is your wish, you're not my friend and I don't ever want to have anything to do with you!" Indignantly she turns her back to the grotto and listens only to Marie's voice.

"Look, there's plenty of dry wood up there. . . . Wait for us, Bernadette. We don't need you."

Slowly Bernadette grows calm. She can see the other two bending down moving hither and thither between the rock and the woods, picking up the branches. Every time that she is left alone she experiences the same delicious release from tension and the homecoming to a form of existence so blessed, still, and equable as is not to be led among men. No breath of wind breaks in upon the calm of the world now, either. The light-drenched ceiling of cloud stands still. Bernadette looks about her. Yonder the feebly gleaming wavelets of the Savy melt into the raging spray-tipped whirls of the Gave. The cave of Massabielle is flooded with the steady, rosy light of a hiding sun. There is scarcely a shadow. The only dark spot is formed by the pointed niche which from the right wall of the inner grotto leads into the depths of the rock. Unstirring the wild rose-vine reaches forth from the thorn-bush. Bernadette listens. There is no sound save the disappearing voices of the girls and the old rough scolding of the Gave, which is as familiar to her as the roar in one's own ears when one awakens from an evil dream.

They do not need me. There is no bitterness in the thought now. Her sense of duty, however, awakens too. She is the oldest and should not shirk the work. That would be setting a bad example. And even though she does often have asthma, she is not a touchy little runt and she will not catch a cold just on account of a bit of cold water. Too bad that Mamma made her wear those stockings. . . . Bernadette sits down on

the same spot where some hours ago the swineherd shared his
bread and bacon with her father. She steps out of her wooden
shoes and begins to strip the white woollen stocking from
her right leg. But before she has reached her ankle she becomes
aware of a strange change. She peers in all directions with her
sharp child's eyes. Everything is as it was. No one has appeared. Only the clouds have become opaque again and the
light has a leaden cast. It is some time before Bernadette, who
is not quick, perceives that the change of which she is aware
concerns not seeing but hearing. The Gave River has changed
its tune.

It is as though the Gave were no longer a river but a public
road, specifically the highway from Tarbes on a market-day
in Lourdes during the busiest time of the year, during the
Easter season. A hundred open carts and wagons and omni-
buses and landaus and victoria-chaises and tilburies rattle down
the deeply rutted roads. And in addition a squad of the
dragoons of Lourdes. The painful, stubborn braying of donkeys is mingled with the echo of hoofs, the rolling of wheels,
the cracking of whips, the neighing of horses. All this tumult
is that of a wild flight full of dread and comes toward Bernadette in a cloud of dust and seems to be hurrying up the
stream. Another moment and it will sweep over her. Amid the
shrill confusion of voices, from which arise women's sharp
cries of woe, she seems to distinguish definite calls and brief
sentences: "Get yourself hence! Away with you! Flee while
you can! To hell with you!"

Yes, ever and again Jeanne's imprecation. The whole thing
roars toward her uninterruptedly and stands uninterruptedly
still. Bernadette clenches her teeth. I've had that same experience once before! But where? When? Thinking does not help
her. And of a sudden it is all past and gone and as though it
had never been, this howling of rage, this howling of woe.

And the Gave River blusters along with its usual tone and tune.

Bernadette shakes herself a little in order to forget. Now she holds the stocking of her right leg in her hand. She peers once more, this time shyly, in all directions. Her glance stops at the cavern. Storm-shaken, the wild rose-vine seems to writhe under the niche in the completely windless calm.

CHAPTER SEVEN

The Lady

BERNADETTE TURNS her eyes to the nearest poplar to discover whether at some height there be not, after all, some wind that got caught in the thorn-bush of Massabielle. But the usually quivering foliage of the poplar is still to breathlessness. She turns again to the cavern, which is no more than ten paces from where she is sitting. But now the wild rose, too, clings unmoving to the rock. It was an illusion of hers that it had stirred.

But there is no delusion possible now, for Bernadette rubs her eyes, closes them, opens them again, and repeats this process ten times. Nevertheless, what she sees remains. The daylight is as leaden as ever. Only in the pointed niche of the rock in the cavern there dwells a deep radiance as though the old gold of powerful sunbeams had been left behind. And in this remnant of billowing light stands someone who has come from the very depths of the world and issued here into the day after a long but painless and comfortable wayfaring. And this someone is not at all an unprecise and ghostly or a transparent and airy image, no changeful dream vision, but a very young lady, delicate and dainty, visibly of flesh and blood, short rather than tall, for she stands calmly and without touching side or arch in the narrow oval of the niche. The very young lady's garb is not at all common, but is in no wise old-fashioned. To be sure, she is not tightly corseted nor does she wear a Parisian hoop-skirt. Yet her easy, snow-white raiment is so cut as to indicate her delicate waist-line. Bernadette had had a chance recently to witness the church wedding of the youngest daughter of the Lafites, and the raiment of the lady was best comparable to that of a distinguished bride. For there is first the loose and precious cloak of veiling which reaches from the head to the ankles. Yet, charmingly enough, the small bridal lady seems not to wear the fashionable high coiffure, curled with irons and held by tortoise-shell combs, that would suit her rank. Wavy ringlets of her light-brown hair escape from under the veil. A quite broad blue girdle, lightly knotted under the breast, falls down over the knee. But what a blue! Lovely to the point of pain. Not even Mademoiselle Peyret, dressmaker of all the rich people in Lourdes, would be able to decide of what manner of fabric the white gown was made. Sometimes it gleams like satin or silk; sometimes it is duller, like some unknown, very delicate, ineffably snowy velvet; again it seems like a transparently thin batiste which transmits to its folds every stirring of the limbs.

Bernadette observes the most striking thing last of all: the young lady's feet are bare. And the tiny narrow feet give the effect of ivory, almost of alabaster. Their pallor shows no trace of rose or pink. These feet have never stepped or trodden. They form an extraordinary contrast to the normal corporeal aliveness of the dainty girl. The strangest thing, however, is this: two golden roses are placed above the beginnings of the slender toes of each foot. Impossible to tell by what means; nor can one tell of what substance the two roses are, whether of delicate jewelled craftsmanship or of painting in high relief.

First Bernadette feels a brief quivering pang of terror, next a steady fear. But this is no familiar fear, no fear that impels one to jump up and run away. It is as though someone softly clasped forehead and breast in an embrace and one desired this embrace to last and last. Later this fear melts into still

another feeling of which this child Bernadette has no idea and
can find no name. One might call it comforting or consolation. But until this instant Bernadette never knew that she was
in need of being comforted. For she is really not at all aware
of the hardness of her life: that she suffers hunger, that she
is housed with five other people in the dark hole of the
Cachot, that she passes long nights struggling for breath. This
has always been so and will probably always be so. This is
naked reality accepted as a matter of course. But moment by
moment now she is more deeply swathed in this consolation
which has no name, which is a hot flood of compassion. Is it a
compassion that Bernadette feels for herself? That, too. But
the self of this child is now so cleft asunder, so open to the
universe and so at one therewith, that the utter sweetness of
this compassion penetrates her shivering body to the very
points of her young breasts.

But while the waves of this love-thrilled consoledness roll
over Bernadette's heart, her independent eyes remain freely
fixed upon the countenance of the young lady. The latter, for
her part, is intent upon offering her countenance to the
girl as if it were a gift. Although it remains calmly yonder
in the niche, that countenance seems to come nearer as Bernadette's eyes are absorbedly upon it. She can count the lifting
and lowering of those eyelashes which, at long intervals,
shadow the noble whiteness and blueness of those eyes. Despite its perfection the hue of the skin is so vivid that it bears
the marks of the sharp wintry day upon the slight flush of the
cheeks. The lips are not solemnly closed. They are a little
open, unconsciously so, and reveal the gleam of the youthful
loveliness of the teeth. Bernadette, however, does not observe
these separate elements of beauty. The vision is a whole to her.

The idea does not strike her in the least that she is dealing
with a heavenly thing. Bernadette does not kneel as in the

dim nave of a church. She is seated on a fragment of rock near the confluence of the Savy brook and the River Gave, in this cool, clear world of February, and she holds her stocking in her limp hand. She is conscious of nothing but the undreamed-of beauty of this lady's image, with which she is intoxicated, insatiably so. The beauty of the lady is the first and last thing which has unlimited power upon this child and will not let her go.

In the paralysis of her rapture it suddenly occurs to Bernadette that her behaviour is improper. She is sitting the while the lady stands. It embarrasses her, too, that her right foot is bare while the other has a stocking on. What shall she do? Guiltily she rises. The lady smiles contentedly. This smile is but a deeper radiation of her graciousness. Bernadette thereupon uses the awkward gesture common to the schoolgirls of Lourdes when they meet a teaching sister or Father Pomian or His Reverence Peyramale on the street. The lady hastens to return the greeting, by far not so condescendingly as the persons in authority here named but with an air of free comradeliness. She nods repeatedly and her smile grows still brighter. This greeting creates a new situation. The web of the relationship between the two is being woven. Between these two, the blessed and the blessing one, arises and flows back and forth a stream of happiest sympathy, of immemorial unitedness, indeed the awareness of a very special solidarity that stirs the heart's core. Jesus and Mary, Bernadette thinks; she stands and I stand. In order to mark a reverential difference between her posture and that of the lady, she kneels on the rubble, her face turned fully toward the niche.

As though to prove that she has understood the girl's intention the lady's alabaster feet on which the golden roses glow take one small step forward from the portal toward the extreme edge of the rock. She either can or will not come farther.

Then she opens her hands a little, thus indicating a gesture of embracing or of raising another up. The hands resemble the feet in slenderness and pallor. There is no red or pink on the palms.

Now for a long time nothing happens. The young lady seems either obliged or, better still, willing to leave the entire initiative to Bernadette. But nothing occurs to the girl to do for a space and so she kneels and gazes, gazes and kneels. Thus there arises between the two a gentle embarrassment and the girl is a little oppressed thereby, for aware of a serviceable unworthiness within her she would do all in her power to ease the encounter.

At the same time there bloom and burst little awakenings in the rapt spirit of Bernadette; keen points pierce her consciousness to the extent of pondering: Whence has the lady come? Out of the inside of the earth? And can any good come thence? Does not the good and heavenly come from above? It uses clouds and sunbeams as the vehicles of its earthfaring, as the pictures in the churches illustrate. But whoever the young lady may be and whencesoever she may have come on her naked feet, whether by ways that are natural or not, one thing remains incomprehensible: why did she choose Massabielle, of all places, the filthy rock cavern, the place where the high water washes up the bones of beasts, the place of rubble, swine, and snakes, the spot detested by all the world?

Bernadette's suspiciousness seems not very serious even to itself. Her whole being is jubilant over the beauty of the lady. Now, there is no beauty that is wholly of the body. From every human countenance which we call beautiful there streams a radiance which, though bound to bodily forms, is of the spirit. But the beauty of this lady seems less of the body than any other beauty. It is that very spiritual radiance alone which we call beauty. Overwhelmed by this radiance and also a little to ascertain the true being of the lady, Bernadette is about to make the sign of the cross.

Crossing herself has been to Bernadette a well-proved remedy for the thousand terrors of the soul which have pursued her since early childhood. Not only for the monstrous dreams of the night; even in the bright light of day her eyes have ever had the gift of creating images within the frames of all visible things. The walls of the Cachot, for instance, are studded with great splotches of moisture. When one crouches in a corner or, sleepless in the early mornings, stares at the walls, these splotches assume a swift succession of incredible shapes. The shapes usually belong to the demoniac realm of things contorted or senselessly conjoined. Orphide, the big, bearded he-god of the Laguès farm in Bartrès, plays a frequently repeated role among these visions. Once the malicious brute with lowered horns had chased the little shepherdess across a meadow. Oh, why did she who so adores all that is sweet, charming, lovely, graceful, have to be so often the prey of abominable phantoms?

Her eyes upon the lady's bloodless feet, Bernadette is about to cross herself. She cannot. Her arm hangs down heavily and lame like an alien burden. She cannot stir a finger. This lameness is not unfamiliar. She has experienced it in nightmares when voice and muscles fail and one cannot summon the Saviour's aid against the powers of evil. But here and now her powerlessness to raise her arm seems to have a special reason. Perhaps the lady has read her pondering guesses and is punishing her therefor. Or perhaps Bernadette's attempt to cross herself has been an unforgivable breach of good manners and a shocking piece of awkwardness. For doubtless in any matter that concerns the cross, the lady there would have a precedent right.

And in fact the lady in the niche does now raise her right hand with its fragile fingers slowly, almost instructively, and

over her entire countenance makes a great, almost gleaming
sign of the cross, such as Bernadette had never seen a human
being make. And that sign seems to remain floating in air. At
the same time the lady's face grows very serious, and this seriousness is another wave sent out by that loveliness which leaves
the beholder breathless. Always hitherto Bernadette, like everybody else, merely tapped forehead and chest carelessly when
making the sign of the cross. Now she feels a mild power grasp-
ing her hand. As one takes the hand of a child and guides it
when one teaches a child how to write, even so that mild power
guides the girl's icy hand to make that great and inexpressibly
noble sign of the cross upon her forehead. And now the lady
nods and smiles again, as though a thing both important and
very precious had been accomplished.

Thereafter a pause ensues once more, fulfilled by rapturous
seeing and loving. Bernadette would like to speak, to burst out
in words or even in inarticulate sounds, stammering, reverential, tender. But dare she speak before the lady has spoken? She
takes her rosary out of her pocket. What better thing can she
do? . . .

All the women and girls of Lourdes constantly carry a rosary
upon their person. It is the authentic tool of their piety. The
hands of poor hard-working women have not the habit of stillness. A prayer with empty hands would be no proper observ-
ance for them. But the prayer of the rosary is to them a sort
of heavenly manual toil, an invisible needlework, a knitting or
embroidering busily wrought of the fifty Hail Mary's and the
nine other invocations of their string of beads. He who tells a
sufficient number of beads in the course of the years will have
woven a goodly web with which some day the divine compassion can cover a portion of his guilt. The lips, one may say,
murmur but automatically the words of the angel to the Virgin,
yet the soul traverses the pastures of holiness. Though the

thoughts often stray from the proper forms and lament the un-reasonable price of eggs, and though one even drowses now and then over an Ave, it is no great misfortune. The deep feeling of being at home and protected remains. Mother Soubirous uses her rosary as do all the other women of Lourdes. But Bernadette, who is still so young and anything rather than pietistic —she whom Sister Marie Thérèse Vauzous considers an ignorant heathen and who in fact has only the faintest inkling of the mysteries of the faith—Bernadette carries her rosary proudly as a sign that she has come to the estate of womanhood.

Now she raises her poor, simple little string of black beads encouragingly up toward the lady. The latter seems long to have expected that. Again she smiles and nods and seems deeply delighted by the girl's praiseworthy idea. In her slightly raised right hand a rosary becomes visible now too—not the meagre string of a day labourer's child, but a long chain of large gleaming pearls reaching almost to the ground, such as has not yet been seen even in a queen's possession. At the end of the string a golden crucifix is radiant in the sea of light.

Bernadette is happy to hear her own voice, though it sounds quite unfamiliar to her: "Hail Mary, full of grace . . ." she begins the first decade of Aves. She watches keenly whether the lady is praying with her. But those lips do not move. It seems not to be her business to utter the angel's greeting. But with a gentle devotion she seems to supervise, as it were, the child's murmuring. At the end of each Ave she lets a pearl glide between her index-finger and her thumb. But she always waits and lets Bernadette drop her little black bead first. Only when the decade is finished and followed by the invocation, "Glory be to the Father and to the Son and to the Holy Ghost," does a strong breathing pass through the lady's form and does her mouth silently repeat the words.

Never has Bernadette told her beads so slowly. But the rosary is doubtless a powerful means of keeping the lady with her. And that is all that matters to her. She is so afraid that that supremely lovely one, to the vision of whom her whole soul clings, will grow utterly weary and sick of staying in that inhospitable hole in the rock on the edge of a precipitous cliff (from which one could so easily plunge down) for the sake of a poor girl like herself. Probably, too, she does not at all relish being stared at uninterruptedly, and in such weather. Oh, soon she would go away and leave Bernadette alone. . . .

After the thirtieth Ave these accompanying thoughts of dread and shadows upon her soul vanish too. Though her eyes are not weary, Bernadette is but one act of seeing now. The life of all her other senses recedes. She does not feel the stones which her knees press. She does not feel the icy cold that is roundabout her. A warm and blessed drowsiness enfolds her.

How well it is with her, how well . . . how well. . . .

CHAPTER EIGHT

Of the Strangeness of the World

IT TAKES more than twenty minutes before Marie and Jeanne return to the brook. In the low-lying land between Massabielle and the municipal forest they had gathered a great mass of fallen branches. The girls can hardly carry their load. They pant and sweat and have no strength to glance at Bernadette. Marie is the first to be frightened. On the rubble by the brookside her sister kneels in a curiously rigid posture. Between the thumb and index-finger of her right hand she holds her rosary. A white stocking lies on the ground beside her. She is as pale as a corpse. Even her usually healthy lips are colourless. Her eyes stare in the direction of the grotto, but they are the eyes of one blind, in which the dull whites predominate. On the petrified little face, from which no breathing seems to come, lies a smile blissful and withdrawn, such as Marie had once seen on the face of a neighbour who had died.

"Bernadette! Hallo, Bernadette!" she cries.

No answer. The kneeling girl has not heard. Now Jeanne Abadie calls out:

"Come now, none of your silly tricks!"

No answer. The kneeling girl has not heard. Terror seizes Marie. Her mouth is contorted. Her voice trembles. "Oh, maybe she is dead. . . . O Blessed Virgin, surely the athma has killed her!"

"Nonsense," the experienced Jeanne Abadie declares inferentially. "If she were dead, she'd be lying flat. Who ever saw a dead person kneeling?"

Nevertheless, the younger sister sobs: "O Jesus and Mary, suppose she is dead for all that!"

"We'll waken her. See if she's not just making fools of us!"

She picks up a few pebbles and begins to throw them at Bernadette. At last one of the missiles strikes the girl's left breast. She raises her head and looks about her. Slowly the colour of life returns to her cheeks. She takes a deep breath. She asks: "What is the matter?"

Between the impact of the pebble and the utterance of her first words there pass but a few seconds, but these seconds signify a way so long that it cannot be measured by the divisions of time. When Bernadette felt the sudden little stone against her breast the lady was no longer there. The girl could not say in what manner she had vanished. She did not melt into nothingness or dissolve in the light about her. And in fact how could that be, since she seems in the most vivid manner to be of flesh and blood and clothed in the most precious fabrics? But neither did she visibly walk away or withdraw into the darkened niche. The likeliest thing was that out of the delicacy of her heart she who brought so much happiness had rocked her to whom she brought it into a mild unconsciousness before she left her lonely. Bernadette's well-being was so new to her and so blissful that there was in it no hint of any parting.

But for this well-being she has now to pay—now, after her return to the accustomed state of consciousness. First comes an eerie astonishment, mixed with revulsion, at all she sees. This leaves her only very gradually. She can think of no word for it. Almost it is a nausea of astonishment at the strangeness of the world about her. Is this stone a stone? And what manner of thing is a stone? And this foot, is it my foot, this remote, unfeeling object? Bernadette had first to grope her way painfully back from all sides into the ordinariness of things before she could ask: "What is the matter?"

"What the matter is? That's what we're asking you," Jeanne scolds. "Have you gone quite crazy? Praying here in Massabielle where the hogs root! You're not so devout in church. . . ."

Bernadette is quite herself again, a schoolgirl who will not have another be saucy to her. "That's none of your business. That's my own. . . ."

"Goodness, how you scared me, Bernadette!" Marie complains. "I began to think your asthma had killed you. . . ."

A fleeting pity for her sister comes over Bernadette. "I'm coming to you," she calls out. Quickly she strips off the other stocking too. As she stands there now it seems to her as though through her encounter with the lady she had grown half a head taller and had become more vigorous and sinewy as well as prettier. The nausea of astonishment at the strangeness of the world now yields to the intrepid feeling of a convalescent who has the sensation of being new-born. Bernadette ties the stockings about her neck, picks up her wooden shoes, and wades with firm, light step through the icy water of the brook. Midstream, where the water reaches her knee, she stops and expresses her wonder: "What cheats you two are! This brook is as warm as dish-water. . . ."

Angrily Marie shakes her head. "Jeanne is right. There must be bats in your belfry. My legs still sting from that dish-water. You'd better come and help us!"

Bernadette joins them without paying attention to her wet feet. They divide the bones into three lots. Of the thorny pile of wood and brush they make three bundles, which they tie up with thin, firm withes. It is no easy task. Bernadette is the quickest and ablest of the three now. While she is finishing her bundle she asks suddenly: "Didn't you see anything?" In her language the words sounded thus: "*Aouet bis a rè?*"

Marie regards her sister sidewise. She seems changed, so firm of purpose, so much older than half an hour ago. On the round child's face there is an almost imperious expression. "Why, did you see anything?" Marie asks.

The eager eyes of Jeanne Abadie are agleam with curiosity. "Was anyone with you in the grotto?"

"*Labets, a rè,*" Bernadette curtly ends the conversation. For these words mean: "No, no, nothing at all."

She sits down and quickly puts her stockings on. Then at a single bound she lifts the biggest of the bundles and places it on her head in the manner in which countrywomen hereabouts carry burdens. The other two girls have all they can do merely to lift their bundles.

"We'll go back to the city across the mountain; it's the shortest way," Bernadette decides.

"Not for anything in the world would I go through that water again," Jeanne confesses.

"But it's such a steep path," Marie objects fearfully.

Bernadette pays no attention. With great strides she passes over the rubble, sending no parting glance up at either the cave or the niche. A few yards behind Massabielle begins the wretched path which leads across the ridge of the Montagne des Espélugues down to the neighbourhood of the Pont Vieux. Bernadette leads the way. At a distance behind her Jeanne follows. Marie walks last. The girls are silent. Their burdens are heavy and the path is not only steep but narrowly skirts the abyss here and there. Worst is the last declivity before the peak is reached. There a ridge is to be passed over, and the naked rock is worn smooth by the rain. Wooden shoes are hardly the right gear here.

"God have mercy," Marie pants before the last climb, "I can't make it."

Bernadette, who has reached the peak, puts her bundle down, and runs back over the bad piece of road to help her sister.

Without a word she relieves Marie of her bundle and with elastic strides carries it to the summit.

"What do you think you're doing?" Marie cries. "I'm the stronger of us."

Jeanne Abadie laughs under her burden. "She's turned into a corporal of the Nemours barracks, and a minute ago she was scared of a bit of chilly water. . . ."

When the top of the wooded hill is reached, Bernadette, who walks on ahead, sets a quicker pace for her companions.

"Why do you run like that, silly?" Marie cries. "You won't be able to get any breath at all afterward. . . ."

Bernadette is silent. She thinks no longer of her "athma." A conflict is taking place within her. Her soul is one boundless yearning to speak of the lady. She is like a lover who languishes because he must keep his love secret. But in the depth of her heart she knows exactly that unpredictable things will happen if she yields to this temptation and opens her lips. I'll say nothing, nothing, she assures herself under her breath.

"What are you whispering to yourself?" Jeanne Abadie asks.

Bernadette stops and holds her breath. "I'd like to tell you something, but you must swear not to give me away. Mother mustn't hear of it. She'd take a stick after me. . . . Not a word at home! Do you swear, Marie?"

"I swear! You know that I always hold my tongue about everything."

"But Jeanne wished me in hell today. Did you really mean that, Jeanne?"

"Stupid! That's just a way of talking. It doesn't mean anything."

"All right. But first you must swear that you'll say nothing, not at your house nor at mine nor in school."

"I give you my word. But I won't swear. Swearing like that about some little thing, that's a mortal sin. You don't want to make me sin just a few months before my first communion? Come on! What happened at the cavern?"

Bernadette takes as deep a breath as she can. Her voice shakes. Inexpressible is the sweetness of revealing for the first time the mystery of that encounter.

"I saw a lady all in white with a blue girdle and a golden rose upon each foot. . . ."

In ecstasy she listens to her own words—poor words which hold and clasp the ineffable. Her heart seems to be throbbing in her very head. But Marie is seized with rage against her. She throws down her bundle. "Don't I know you? You want to scare us while we're still in the woods here and it's dim. But you won't scare me today with your silly lady in white. . . ."

She takes a hazelnut twig from her bundle and taps Bernadette's hand with it. The latter seems not to feel the blow.

"Why do you strike her?" Jeanne Abadie asks thoughtfully. "Maybe there was a lady there."

"Yes, and I wanted to make the sign of the cross and I couldn't. But later I was able to make the same sign of the cross as the lady. . . ." She stops suddenly and walks faster. She refuses to answer any of Jeanne's prying questions. At the eastern foot of the hill, where there is a view of Lafite's magnificent saw-mill, she suddenly throws herself into the grass.

"I'm so frightfully tired! Let's rest!" She presses her head into the very dampness of the earth. Let the cold come and the cough and the aching head and throat and the lack of breath. It is all one to her. She could almost wish herself ill. The other two sit down next to her and watch her impassioned face in astonishment. After a while words are wrung from her.

"Hold me tight, tight! I want to go back to Massabielle. . . ."

Jeanne Abadie winks. "Maybe you believe that that lady of yours is waiting for you there?"

"I know she is," Bernadette says.

CHAPTER NINE

Madame Soubirous Is beside Herself

MOTHER SOUBIROUS has had no easy day on this eleventh of February. For more than an hour she had to stay with her neighbour Croisine Bouhouhorts. The same old story, of course. Inexplicable why kind Heaven doesn't take pity on this miserable creature which cannot possibly survive. To be sure, this two-year-old boy is Croisine's only child and, like all unfortunate mothers, she screams and seeks to ward off death instead of resigning herself to God's will. The child will never be normal. Its legs are no thicker than a man's thumbs, and deformed too. Every three or four weeks the child is attacked by a dreadful convulsion, such as today's. The convulsions proceed from the brain. Then the child draws up its knees almost to the chin and rolls its eyes and loses consciousness.

Louise Soubirous, like all the Casterot sisters (above all the clever one, Bernarde), enjoys a reputation for uncommon medical ability. Not only Croisine calls upon her help but many another woman in the Rue des Petites Fossées. Croisine, at all events, neither very vigorous nor experienced, would hardly know what to do without Louise's help. She loses her head easily. Mother Soubirous zealously applies her proven medicament. Poor though she is, she does not spare her medicinal oil but embrocates the child's whole body with it. Then she wraps the child tightly in hot cloths and gives him a few drops of a certain tea. Finally she takes him and fairly dances with him up and down the room for half an hour, shaking his rigid little body in order to make the blood circulate again.

This treatment causes little Juste to vomit and soil her dress. But at this moment of catastrophe the convulsion is over.

Bathed in sweat and out of breath, Louise Soubirous returns to the Cachot. To her extreme annoyance she observes that all her birds have flown. Jean Marie and Justin, street-urchins both, have shamelessly contemned her strict injunction and stolen out of the house. She is even more infuriated by the fact that François has sneaked off and not awaited her return. Probably he has "just dropped in" at Papa Babou's, despite the oath of abstinence which had been his splendid Christmas gift to her. Exhausted, Louise sinks into a chair and sighs forth unconsciously the song of her life, which it is her wont to repeat so often each day: *"Praoubo de jou*—poor woman that I am. . . ."

But almost at once she puts on her kerchief again, for it occurs to her that Madame Millet has the habit of occasionally either cancelling or changing wash-day at her house. Wash-day at Madame Millet's is a sacrosanct ceremony which proceeds under the supervision of the exacting and devout widow. But toward the end of the week Madame Millet sometimes goes to Argelès to visit the Latapies. Élise Latapie, who died a few months ago, her adored adopted daughter, belonged to a branch of this extensive clan. Whenever Madame Millet goes to Argelès, wash-day is omitted. This means that Louise Soubirous loses thirty sous, her warm midday meal, her afternoon tea, and sundry culinary subventions which mistress or cook wraps up for the Soubirous children. Louise has the definite feeling that today is a day of ill omen. Everything is going wrong and the cancellation of Friday's work at Madame Millet's will probably ensue.

She slams the heavy door of the Cachot behind her. Uncle Sajou, stonemason and house-owner, is squatting on the stair landing and solemnly smoking his cheap tobacco. Unlike the

Soubirous, who are permitted to inhabit the former prison merely as a matter of charity, the Sajou family actually owns three small rooms, of which one, called the salon and filled with inherited furniture, is carefully kept and honoured as the sanctuary of bourgeois status.

"Dear Cousin André," says the badly beset woman, "I'm just running over to Madame Millet's for a couple of minutes. . . . Back right off, eh?"

Wearily André Sajou crooks his left index-finger to show that he understands. Your stonemason's trade is a silent one. Are not granite and marble, especially when hewn into gravestones, held to be the very symbols of silence? But toward the Soubirous, Uncle Sajou's silence is almost exaggerated. To be sure, they are kin. But in Lourdes everybody is kin, and failure in life is to be guarded against like an infection. You do your Christian duty but try to keep your distance, so as not to be implicated in others' misery.

Madame Millet's house is situated at the corner of the Rue Bartayrès. It is one of the most impressive houses in Lourdes. When Monseigneur Bertrand Sévère Laurence, bishop of Tarbes, stopped at Lourdes during his last diocesan inspection, he took up lodging neither in the parsonage of Dean Peyramale nor in the convent of the Sisters of Nevers but in the house of the wealthy widow, where, since that occasion, a suite is dedicated to his use. Madame Millet deserves this distinction conferred by clerical authority, for she is not only a devout but a militant Catholic. Monseigneur, an acutely practical man, does indeed find the rooms of Madame Millet, with their plethora of curtains, drapes, slip-covers, lace coverlets, not a little stuffy. The beds are like biers and get on one's nerves. They seem ravenous to serve as death-beds. Even the thick candle on the bedside table is ecclesiastical. Moreover, according to the taste of this prince of the Church, Madame

Millet's curiosity concerning the things of the hereafter is at once too pertly prying and too superficial. It is really a kind of ghost-mongering. After the death of her niece, whom she had loved as a daughter, this preoccupation surpassed the permissible. On the other hand—and this is the decisive consideration, to Monseigneur's mind—so and so many organizations actually subsist on the support of the wealthy and independent lady. One has to think only of the Sodality of the Children of Mary, to which are due, in addition to the magnificent annual festivals, numerous works of charity, and this organization is but one out of seven.

With trepidation Louise Soubirous uses the old-fashioned door knocker. The venerable Philippe, Madame Millet's servant, opens the door in person. The aspect of this macabre personage, the dark antechamber with its reek of naphthalene and death, always fill Louise with a grisly reverence. As in all the rooms of this house, there prevails here a *horror nudi*, a horror of bareness. All the wall-space is hidden behind very dark pictures and all objects are covered with innumerable yellowish lace doilies. Louise knows them from the washtub. They get yellower and yellower.

"My good woman," Philippe begins in the tone of a very lofty but correspondingly condescending prelate, "it's very sensible of you to have come. You relieve me of the errand. We have put off wash-day until next week. We will be with the relations in Argelès tomorrow. Since the passing of our blessed Mademoiselle Élise, we attend all the Masses for the repose of her soul in Argelès. We will summon you in due time. . . ."

At the mention of the dead, Louise assumes the appropriate expression of a condoler. At the same time fright thunders in her ear. Her worst fear is realized. The weekend budget is upset. She is really at the end of her rope. On the way home she tries to get a bit of bacon, a piece of soap, and a handful of rice on account at Lacaze's grocery. She doesn't dare show the twelve sous she still has. They would be taken from her as payment against former indebtedness. Lacaze refuses flatly. She is too much in the red. At the Cachot's gate André Sajou's creaking voice is heard. He is indignant. "My dear Cousin, it's a mother's duty to see to it that her brats aren't a nuisance to the neighbours. But look at your fine sons! They've been climbing around in the yard like reckless burglars. This time they fell into the soft mud; next time they'll break their bones. . . ."

"I was just running after the cat, Mamma," screeches Justin, the younger.

"And I only wanted to help Justin get out of the dung-heap," Jean Marie, dry-eyed, defends himself. Without a word Louise thrusts the two thoroughly dung-smeared sinners back into the room. She is far two horrified and disgusted to have strength left for punishment. A single thought weighs on her: the boys have nothing to wear except what they have on. She strips them. Luckily there is hot water left in the copper kettle. She pours it into the washtub. Wildly she scrubs and rinses, as though she would wash the poor soul out of her body. For Jean Marie and Justin this is a new adventure, to race around in the cold half naked.

Such is the scene that meets the eyes of François Soubirous as he re-enters. Loftily sombre, he remains on the threshold. He does not deign to glance at his sons. "I will not have you wear yourself out in this fashion!" His voice is vibrant. "You're a Casterot and I'm only a Soubirous. Who are the Nicolaus? You must not lose your confidence in me. . . ."

Without interrupting her work she examines him with a glance. He steps up behind her. "I saw Maisongrosse and Cazenave and Cabizos."

"And Babou too," she says.

"I am ill," he moans, "I am very ill. . . . God grant that I die. . . . Oh, you poor things. . . ."

On the wash-line which stretches from the fireplace to the smaller window Louise is hanging up the wet garments, which still give off a penetrating odour. Soubirous's plaint that he is ill has left her not wholly unmoved. The man, in truth, looks piteous. Who would recognize in him the intrepid journeyman miller of the 1830's? He has not had a decent meal for days. And even as he feels guilty toward her, so does she feel toward him. Suppose he did pour down a few drinks of the hell-broth at Babou's! Whether someone treated him or he got it on account, his conscience ached just the same. And undernourished as he is, who can blame him? And his digestion has gone back on him too. Louise, though sorely tried, is still partisan as a wife. She will defend her man against everyone, including herself. If only he is not really ill! That would be the last straw.

"The best thing you can do, Soubirous, is to go back to bed."

"Yes, you are right. That would be best." His tone is as full of delight as though the magic of her clever suggestion had chased all care away. And again he stretches himself out, released from his repentance by her absolution. From a paper bag she takes dried linden blossoms and heats water in a tin pot. After a while she puts a cup of the reliable infusion to her patient's lips. It is her experience that this unsweetened drink is the most efficacious remedy for the particular ill from which Soubirous suffers. He resists a little, like one whom grief has robbed of the will to recover. Sternly she forces him to drink the hot brew. Soubirous lies there with the expression of a man who has overcome the worst. Louise knows, too, that a weak man needs to have his courage raised.

"There will be no washing at Millet's on Friday," she tells

him. "But I'll hustle tomorrow. Something will turn up—maybe at Madame Rives's, the judge's wife."

"Tomorrow!" Soubirous groans ironically. "Cazenave won't even have dung to cart tomorrow. . . . *En garde, mon capitaine.* . . ."

She smooths his covers and waits for him to fall asleep. He is uncommonly gifted in the matter of sleeping and she need not wait long. After a while she lets her hands droop into her lap. She recalls that he was in a similar condition when, a year ago, he came home unexpectedly from his imprisonment on remand. He had luminously established his innocence of the malicious accusation. It had not been he who had stolen the oaken beams from Lafite's factory. Such nonsense! What could he have done with those huge beams? Yet in spite of having fully established his innocence before Police Commissioner Jacomet, Judge Rives, and the imperial prosecutor Dutour, the man had been broken for days, limp as a wet stocking and overcome by sleep. Odd how little pertinacity and sense men show when luck turns against them. Oh, when all is well and the twenty-sou pieces jingle in their pockets, then there is no end of boasting and talking and showing off. They will stand treat round after round. But when bread is lacking and honour is lost, they drink by themselves and go to bed and sleep. Then it is the poor wife who has to strive and struggle to keep the family from utter ruin.

"Shut your mouths, you miserable brats!" she hisses. "Don't disturb your sick papa when he sleeps."

She throws the last log on the fire lest the sufferer be cold. Then she picks up the two tin pails to fetch water. The nearest well is five houses up the street in the yard of Babou's. The men meet over brandy and the women over water. (Which is not to say that most women do not have a bottle of the demon in their cupboards, not to speak of the wine, which is not

alcohol in the sight of God.) At the well, Louise hears several
items of news that are not printed in the paper. Madame
Lacadé and her daughter have been in Pau for several weeks.
When a young girl is not seen in so long the reason must be
embarrassing. The dressmaker Antoinette Peyret gets one
hundred-franc note after another out of the rich widow Millet.
Not for nothing is she a bailiff's daughter. The widow, round
as a butter-ball, is having three black silk dresses made. Best of
all: Monsieur de Lafite, the uncanny cousin from Paris, a
Freemason if not the devil himself, ran after the fourteen-year-
old Cathérine Mengot the whole length of the Rue Basse the
other day and had the impudence not only to accost the girl
but to caress and pet her. "Cathérine, you are the one sweet
nymph in this filthy hole. . . ." Pig! But all men are like that,
brutal and selfish. Yesterday the most reverend Dean Peyramale literally kicked out Madeleine, who had been his cook
for years. And that irascible hot-head preaches against yielding
to the passions.

Burdened with this knowledge and with the water-pails,
Louise drags herself home. She leaves the pails at the door.
The girls can bring them in later. Three o'clock strikes. Where
in the world can Bernadette and Marie be? They ought to
have come back long ago. Louise is angry and anxious at once.
She thinks of Cathérine Mengot and the cousin from Paris.
Ruin lurks everywhere. Her daughters, too, are pretty and
stupid. This thought is pushed aside by the wretched problem
of what she is to prepare for tonight's supper.

The girls were delayed on account of the bones, for Gramont's shop was at the other end of the town and the heavy
bundles on their heads made them slower than usual. The
ragpicker gave two sous to each of the sisters and to Jeanne
Abadie. Unlike Jeanne, Bernadette and Marie decide not to
buy sweets but bread for their share. The loaf of bread and the

great bundles of firewood soothe Madame Soubirous somewhat when the two girls arrive at last and drop their burdens at the door.

"Where have you been all this time?" she asks angrily. "Two big girls like you, and you let me do all the work alone. Poor people have no time to take walks. Fetch in the pails of water!"

Obediently Bernadette and Marie bring in the pails. Obediently they peel the turnips and potatoes for which Mother Soubirous sacrificed some of her twenty sous today. The father's snores sound reproachful. "He's sick," the mother says. There is silence. From time to time Bernadette looks at her sister with large and searching eyes. Each time Marie lowers her head and compresses her lips convulsively. The grimace shows that she is threatened by defeat in the conflict within her.

The mother seeks to make use of the last gleam of daylight which enters the Cachot from the yard. "Come to the window so that I can comb your hair! You first, Marie!"

This combing of her daughters' hair is a daily practice. As well as she can, dwelling in this abandoned prison, Louise is strict in the matter of cleanliness. She is a true Casterot. The two boys are scrubbed with a hard brush every night before going to bed. In like manner she is careful of her daughters' hair. In the Rue des Petites Fossées lice, unluckily, are apt to travel from house to house. Yet cleanliness is the last mark of human dignity which may be preserved when all else is lost. Marie offers the more difficult object to Louise's maternal care. Her hair is very thick and stubborn; Bernadette has inherited her father's soft, black hair. While the mother combs out her younger daughter's hair she sends the older one to fetch home the boys, who have long since sneaked out along the passage. The mother has drawn a footstool to the window. Marie kneels on it with her back to the room. The thick hair crackles under the energetic strokes of the comb. "Ouch, ouch—" Marie mutters.

"Not so touchy, please," Louise mocks.

After a little Marie repeats her muttering.

"Listen, have you got a sore throat?"

"No, I have no sore throat, Mamma. . . ."

But when the girl utters her ominous throaty sounds for the third time her mother becomes suspicious. "What makes you buzz like a fly against a window?"

"I'd like to tell you something, Mamma. . . . It's about Bernadette. . . ."

"What's the matter with Bernadette again?"

"Ah, Mamma, Bernadette saw a young lady dressed all in white and with a sky-blue girdle in the Massabielle cave . . . and she had naked feet with golden roses on them. . . ."

"*Praoubo de jou!* What are you babbling about, you wretched child?"

"And at first Bernadette just couldn't make the sign of the cross. But afterwards she could when the lady let her. . . ."

Marie takes a deep breath, not as though she had broken her word, but as though she had accomplished a difficult task. And as Bernadette enters at that moment, her mother turns upon her with sudden anger. "What did you see, you imbecile?"

"You told on me! . . . Oh, why did you do that?" Bernadette asks with a long glance at her sister. Yet in her voice is no reproach, rather the breathing of a great relief. She takes two steps toward her mother and spreads her fingers as though she held out her hands toward a warming flame. And her heart melts in ecstasy because she may now utter her secret. "Oh, yes, Mamma, I did see a most, most beautiful lady there at Massabielle. . . ."

These rapturous words make the sorely tried woman's cup of woe run over; her painfully nursed equanimity is shattered.

At the end of a day of hopeless effort and disappointment she is subjected to the nonsense that these worthless gadabouts bring home. What chiefly arouses her indignation is the rosily glowing face of Bernadette. It is the radiant face of one who loves and who is ready to make every sacrifice, stubbornly and militantly, for the object of that love. Louise Soubirous's voice rises to so piercing a shriek that the Sajous upstairs prick up their ears.

"What did you see? Nothing—that's what! No most, most beautiful lady, but some piece of white stone. . . . You two see wonderfully beautiful ladies. But I work my fingers to the bone for you here and no one dreams of making things easier for me. O Blessed Virgin, what good-for-nothing children I have! They steal church candles; they fall into the dung; they don't know their catechism; and now they have visions of wonderful ladies too! I'll fix you!"

She grasps the flexible cane with which she beats the bedding into smoothness. The first blow falls across Bernadette's back. Marie tries to hide. That infuriates the woman wholly. She follows her younger daughter till she, too, gets her share. The two boys, deservedly enough, do not escape.

"You see," Marie howls, "now Mamma beats me on your account."

Louise throws the cane aside. She knows that she has forgotten herself and caused this horrible row. She has not considered her poor, sick, sleeping husband. But it needed not the noise to awaken the latter. For some time he has been standing up.

"I heard it all," he says.

Soubirous is tall and slender. His worldly ill luck and his weakness of character have robbed him of everything save the unassuming distinction of his figure. His authority over his children has remained intact precisely because he has left all executive action, whether of punishment or of penitence, wholly to his more vigorous wife. She uses him as a last court of appeal hidden behind clouds and pretends secretly to invoke the decisions of this court before translating them into action. This time, however, Soubirous himself walks up to his daughter with heavy tread and catches hold of her by the collar of her smock. The brief slumber has reduced him to the most melancholy depths of sobriety.

"I heard it all," he says for the second time. "So you are already beginning to commit follies, eh? Look, you're fourteen and over. Many a one at that age earns his livelihood and helps his parents. You see how it is with us. I can't feed you to the end of time. And you begin to commit follies. I understand why. Showing off—wanting to be important! That begins with stories and fairy-tales, making up something about a lady with golden roses on her bare feet. What will be the end of that, young woman? We are respectable miller-folk, your mother and I, and have always been modest, God knows. And I perform the most menial tasks for you, God knows that. But if you're going to see beautiful ladies in caverns and invent lying stories, you don't belong among respectable people; you belong among the jugglers and tricksters and tight-rope walkers and Spanish gipsies on the marketplaces. If you're that kind, young woman, then you needn't stay here; you'd better join the jugglers and the gipsies!"

Soubirous has spoken calmly in a deep tone of voice. It is the longest speech of a pedagogical nature that Bernadette has ever heard her father utter. And she looks at him quite blankly. What would he have of her? Firmly and yet apathetically her eyes are fixed on him. She presses both hands against her bosom. "Oh, Papa," she says, "I really and truly saw the lady, truly. . . ."

CHAPTER TEN

Dreaming Is Forbidden

Briefly after this domestic scene there take place several modest events which seem to point to a favourable turn in the fate of the Soubirous family. Aunt Sajou is a kindly creature. The ear-splitting tones of Louise frightened her. Usually the Soubirous, if you do not happen to think of the boys, are very quiet people. If Louise Casterot, who thinks so much of what is due her good blood, loses control in that fashion, things must be very bad indeed. Madame Sajou possesses a very well-stocked larder. She opens the cupboards with a sigh which is a tribute to her own goodness of heart. In God's name, then! She takes a pat of butter out of a huge tub and cuts a slice from a side of bacon. But since there is a pang of sensuous pleasure not only in the act of charity but in the conquest of avarice she adds six slices of good country sausage, one slice each, to the plate she is preparing. Holding these gifts, she knocks at the heavy door of the Cachot.

Louise, who stands by the hearth, is so astonished that she drops her wooden spoon into the watery soup she has put on to cook.

"Oh, my dear Cousin, the Blessed Virgin herself sends you this because I've prayed to her with all my might today. . . ." And since the fire burns very merrily and Madame Sajou is moved by her own goodness, she calls out to her husband to bring an armful of the driest logs. But before her spouse, who is so sparing of speech that he never contradicts his old woman, can carry out her command, another gift falls, as from the sky, into the Cachot. Croisine Bouhouhorts has had a visitor from the village of Viger in the person of an old peasant aunt who annually in the Carnival season brings her a present. Two dozen eggs this time. No sooner is the aunt gone than Croisine takes the egg-basket and runs straight to the Soubirous'. As usual she is breathless with haste and worry. "You must make me happy, dear neighbour, by accepting these eggs. For you really did save my baby's life today. . . ."

Louise does not stand on much ceremony. She is equally convinced that without her shaking him Croisine's poor little brat wouldn't be alive now. While she washes her hands and takes the basket with appropriate thanks, she calculates with ten eggs and the butter she can prepare a really magnificent omelet fortified with pieces of bacon. Tears of wild hungry yearning come to her at the thought of at last having something like decent food in one's stomach again. It is even possible that her children get into mischief and have silly notions of seeing dream ladies only because for days and days they have been in a state of perpetual hunger. But the law of accumulating accidents is such that to these fleeting benefits there is now added a more lasting improvement in the family's destiny. And this lasting improvement enters in the bodily shape of Louis Bouriette.

Louis Bouriette, like François Soubirous, is an unemployed day labourer nowadays. Once he was a stonemason, like Uncle Sajou. Unlike the latter he did not prosper. He attributes this to the splinter which once injured the cornea of his right eye and left it sightless. He is a self-conscious invalid. Twenty times a day he says: "I am a blind man. What can you expect of me?" Postmaster Cazenave gives him, too, occasional employment as messenger or letter-carrier. Now Cazenave has sent Bouriette to Soubirous for the following reason. The coachman Cascarde, who drives the omnibus to Tarbes, has been seriously injured in an accident. His position now belongs logically to the groom Doutreloux. Hence the job of groom and assistant coachman is free for Soubirous to take. According to Cazenave's experience a miller is always good at handling horses. For this job the postmaster pays two francs a day and lunch. If Soubirous agrees, he may report for work at five o'clock tomorrow morning. Louise folds her hands. The father of the family stands there, tall and dignified and deeply pondering, as it were, the pros and cons of this surprising offer.

"It was agreed between Cazenave and myself," he says at last with conscious deliberation, "that he would engage me if he had a vacancy. We are, after all, former comrades in arms. A miller like myself is used to other kinds of work, that is certain. But when one has as many children as I, one has no choice left nowadays. I shall be there promptly in the morning. . . ."

And he wipes from his forehead the sweat which, despite his faultlessly casual attitude, he could not prevent. Next he winks. A sly gaiety spreads over his features. The Frenchman of the South awakens. A noble, large, and boastful gesture is his due.

"Our kinspeople and friends here, who overwhelm us with their gifts, must honour us with their presence at a modest dinner this evening. A succulent omelet will be prepared, if I know my wife. . . ."

General protestations in which Louise would like to join. On one evening the silly spendthrift sacrifices the eggs which would feed his family for three days. But Louise has always been weak toward her husband's weaknesses. She has let him prevail over her own sounder instincts again and again. Without his pompous inattention to details they might not have lost the Boly mill or the Escobé or finally the Bandeau. For the sake of being the superior and generous one he used to serve

the stingiest customers wine and food. The consequence was
that these peasants and bakers, accustomed to turn over every
sou thirty times, became suspicious of the spendthrift miller.
It is not good to deal with frivolous people. Unluckily Louise
is not only weak toward her husband's weaknesses but has a
distinct weakness of her own for many of them. When at the
slightest bit of luck he shakes off misery in an instant, as a dog
shakes off drops of water, and stands up adventurously as now,
a gentleman and generous host, she likes him, the fine journeyman miller of their youth, and she laughs with glee even after
such a day as this. (From whom did Bernadette inherit her
gift of making up stories?) And so Louise seconds her husband's invitation, not haltingly but in well-set phrases, as befits
her acknowledged good breeding: "Surely you're not going to
insult me by refusing my omelet? You will at least taste of it.
Even people like ourselves need to celebrate the Carnival a
bit. . . ."

Her invitation to "taste of" the omelet builds a bridge. He
who merely tastes does not expect to satisfy his hunger. André
Sajou suggests to his wife that they add their resources for a
common evening meal. The stonemason, whose children are
grown and long away from home, is glad to spend an evening
in company, though it be only in the Cachot. He places a great
jug of his own wine on the table. Meanwhile fragrance begins
to arise from the huge omelet. While Louise turns it over in
the pan she sends up a prayer of thanks to the Virgin for
saving her and hers from hunger during weeks to come.
Bouriette, the messenger of good fortune, is about to take his
leave. With both arms Soubirous restrains him. The grown-ups
crowd around the table as best they can. The hungry children
huddle together on the narrow bench in the niche between
fireplace and window. The mother refuses to forgo the joy of
serving the children first: a portion of omelet, soup, and

sausage on their bread. Aunt Sajou brings to each of them a glass of the good, dark wine. It is indeed a feast.

But conversation lags at table. The province of Bigorre and the Pyrenean valleys are lands of poverty. The people are silent and have a vivid consciousness of physical enjoyment. The peasants in the hills and the workers in the towns are afraid of losing the good and pleasure of God's gifts if they wag their tongues while eating. Hence words are limited now to the just praise of the plenteous meal.

A brief social hour follows the meal. The men smoke their weed, which blends with the wood-smoke to form a suffocating cloud. Everybody is used to that. Bernadette alone has to leave the room twice in order to catch her breath. Political conversation rises no higher than abuse of the government, that is to say, of the two representatives of power, Mayor Lacadé and Police Commissioner Jacomet. The latter had recently issued an oral proclamation through the town-crier that wood from the municipal forest could be obtained only upon written request to the mayor's office. Unauthorized wood-gathering would be considered theft, in accordance with paragraph such and such of the criminal code. Thus the noose is drawn tighter about one's neck from year to year. Where are the goodly years when all things were to be had for the asking, years rich and cheap, before the Lapaca brook ran dry?

It occurs to Louise that her husband must get up at half-past four in the morning. She wants to bring the gathering to an end. In the Pyrenees the women are wont to tell their beads once more after the evening meal in order to bring the day to a worthy and pious close. Usually one of the women acts as precentor, the while the others murmur after her. Louise does not know why on this evening she decides that Bernadette shall lead the praying. Bernadette stands by the door at a distance from the others. Obediently she draws forth the little rosary which she had held up with outstretched hand today to the marvellous lady. Tonelessly she begins the first Ave. The mechanical murmur of the women accompanies her voice. The fire in the hearth flares upward. Otherwise there is no light save that of the pine-torch on the table, placed there by Aunt Sajou. Quickly the prayer runs down like a wheel. At its end Louise whispers: "Mary, conceived without sin, pray for us whose refuge thou art. . . ."

At the words, "Mary, conceived without sin . . ." Bernadette totters and has to lean against the door to keep from falling. Her face turns as dead white as it was when Jeanne and Marie found her by the brookside.

"Bernadette is fainting!" cries Croisine Bouhouhorts. All eyes turn to the girl.

"Are you sick, Bernadette?" Aunt Sajou asks. "Drink a little more wine."

Bernadette shakes her head. She stammers: "Oh, no, no . . . I'm not sick . . . it's nothing at all. . . ."

And now against her own will the frightened mother babblingly gives away the thing for which she beat her daughters a few hours before. "Oh, that Bernadette. It's all because she saw a wondrously beautiful young lady, dressed all in white, out at Massabielle. . . ."

"Be silent," Soubirous irritatedly interrupts her. "That's sheer nonsense. . . . Unhappily Bernadette has trouble with her heart. We had Dr. Dozous examine her. She can't stand the wood-smoke which fills this place day and night. What we need is a new chimney, my dear André. . . ."

An hour later the Sajou couple, dressed for sleep with pointed nightcap and headkerchief, lie in their broad bed.

"What's that Louise told about Bernadette and a young lady?" he asks.

"Oh, Bernadette saw a wondrously beautiful young lady,

dressed all in white, out at Massabielle." Madame had taken the trouble to remember the exact words.

"Who could it have been?" he ponders. "What beautiful young ladies are there hereabouts? . . . Lafite's daughters aren't in Lourdes. . . . Might be one of the Cénacs or Lacrampes. . . . Most likely just a Carnival joke. . . ."

This time Madame is the silent one. She makes no reply and seems asleep. Sajou ends his reflections with this yawning prophecy: "That Bernadette won't make old bones. I can see her carried out of the Cachot in a coffin right now. . . ."

Madame Sajou determines at the same time to consult sundry friends of hers on the morrow concerning the nature of the lady whom Bernadette saw at Massabielle. And Madame Bou-houhorts harbours the same purpose at this hour, while she bends anxiously over her ailing child.

Thus this eleventh of February draws circularly to its close. The concerted snoring of the Soubirous family, led by the father, fills the smoke-drenched air of the Cachot. The well-replenished fire throws its dancing flame-images and shadow-patterns tirelessly upon the walls. Sleeplessly Bernadette stares at these naked walls. Tonight, as never before, she fails to see forms and visions rise from flame and shadow. It is as though her encounter with the lady had exhausted the fear-born shaping vision of her eyes. She takes up as little room as possible in the narrow bed so as to avoid touching her sister with any limb. A residue of that revulsion from all fleshly things which pre-ceded and followed her communion with that most lovely lady makes her shudder now too whenever her hand or foot chances to touch her sister, who sleeps sweating and snoring like a young animal. It is still more strange that touching her own delicate body fills her with fright. She is not at one with it.

Next to her lies her body, a strange object, hardly more hers than that of her sister.

What has happened to her? She does not know. She knows only that it is a portentous thing. From above and from all sides it presses in upon her like the consciousness of an inescapable duty to which she is unequal, which she has neither sought nor can escape. To free herself from this pressure Bernadette fixes all her imaginative power upon the lady. She closes her lids tightly in order to recover her vision of all details of that gracious beauty: the whiteness of the garment, the blueness of the girdle, the faint gleam of the throat, the loose ringlets under the magnificent veil; the bright, comradely smile of ineffably mutual understanding; the waxen, bloodless glimmer of the naked feet with the golden roses. . . .

Whenever Bernadette thinks she has approached her inner image of the lady a maelstrom of black emptiness tears her away. It is not permitted her to see with the mind's eye the reality which her bodily eyes had beheld. But perhaps it will be granted her to dream of the lady. To bring this to pass she tries with all her might to fall asleep. She tries to think of utterly different things. She thinks of the village of Bartrès and seeks to recall all objects in the peasant house in which she lived so long—the birth-stool of the Laguèses, the cradle, the spinning-wheel. She counts the tin utensils on their stand; she calls the animals she shepherded by the names she gave them. She conjures up the dog, of whom she was fond and who has long been dead. She thinks of the meadows of Bartrès and of the hills of Orincles in snow and rain and sun. She gathers all the memories she has in her little head. Sometimes sleep overwhelms her, but for only a few minutes at a time. She awakens. Nothing has come to her. The lady will not come to her in sleep. She seems to want especially to prove (in order not to be mistaken for what she is not) that she is made of utterly other stuff than of the stuff of dreams. It is going on eleven o'clock when Marie is awakened as her hand accidentally touches a wet spot on the pillow. She turns to her sister and recognizes what is happening.

"Mamma, Mamma," she whispers in that tone, at once persuasive and fearful, with which one seeks to awaken those who are asleep. Louise sleeps the shallow sleep of the anxious mother. She starts up at once. "What is the matter here? Who calls?"

"Bernadette is crying, Mamma."

"What are you saying? . . . Bernadette is crying?"

Marie's nocturnal whisper seems to draw the words out in length. "Oh, Mamma, Bernadette is crying so hard . . . the whole pillow is soaked. . . ."

Carefully Louise Soubirous slips out of bed and gets up softly. She gropes toward Bernadette's face. "Can't you breathe, my lamb?"

Bernadette digs her knuckles into her eyes and shakes her head. The mother tries to calm her. "Get up if you want to, and you and I can chat a bit. . . ."

She throws faggots and two big logs on the dying fire. She draws a chair up to the flames. Bernadette kneels before her and buries her head in her mother's lap. Louise silently strokes the child's hair for a long time. Then she bends down to her. "Are you afraid, my child?"

Bernadette nods with all her might.

"Are you frightened of that lady of Massabielle?"

With equal vigour the child shakes her head.

"Well, then, you see it was all just a waking dream. . . ."

Bernadette raises her tear-stained face. She gives her mother a frightened look and shakes her head more violently than before. Louise's heart aches deeply for her daughter. "My poor lamb, I understand you. I passed through it at your age. Girls in that period often see things that don't exist. But it passes. . . . Just put it out of your mind. Life is far too hard to bother with things like that. You're a big girl now and have begun to be a woman, and in another year or two you may find a man and have children, just as I did. . . . Life goes so fast—it's hard to believe how fast, my poor child."

Bernadette keeps her head hidden and betrays no more of what is within her. But Louise Soubirous, despite her wise, consoling words, is firmly determined to go to confession not later than tomorrow and to request the opinion of Father Pomian or Father Penès or Father Sempet concerning this matter of the lady of Massabielle.

Would You Have the Kindness?...

A Stone Hurtles Down

IN THE school kept by the Sisters of Nevers there was a group of seven or eight girls not only devoted to the clever and energetic Jeanne Abadie, but wholly subject to her influence. Among these girls was Annette, the red-haired daughter of the mayor's secretary Courrèges; further Cathérine Mengot, she whom Hyacinthe de Lafite called "nymph of this filthy hole"; and finally Madeleine Hillot, a pale child with freckles and long limbs, who possessed a thin but really lovely voice and hence was made to serve as soloist on all kinds of occasions, secular as well as religious. Jeanne was the first to appear in the schoolroom on this morning. As her followers gathered about her, she winked at them.

"If you girls knew what happened yesterday you'd be astonished. But I daren't tell. . . ."

"Then why do you make our mouths water?" the realistic Cathérine asked. "Maybe somebody accosted you!"

"It's not about myself but about Bernadette Soubirous. . . ."

Cathérine shrugged her shoulders. "In that case it can't be very exciting. She's a silly goose."

Jeanne Abadie raised the curiosity of her friends to the point of torture. "I gave Bernadette my word. But I didn't swear. I had too much sense for that. . . ."

"Well, if you didn't swear . . ." Annette Courrèges insinuated.

"Well, if you didn't swear . . ." the girls repeated in chorus, emphasizing the rhythm of the sentence.

"Yes, if you didn't swear," Madeleine Hillot declared with decision, "you're not committing a sin."

Jeanne lowered her voice to the pitch of a sharp whisper. "Come close. I don't want the others to hear. Yesterday in the Massabielle cavern Bernadette saw a beautiful young lady, all dressed in white, with a sky-blue girdle. And the lady had naked feet with golden roses on them. . . . We were gathering wood, Marie Soubirous and I, and when we came back, there was Bernadette kneeling by the brook. She didn't hear us and she looked awfully strange. . . ."

"And you didn't see the lady?" the girls asked in a small babble of voices.

"Marie and I didn't even know she was there while we were gathering wood."

"Golden roses on her feet . . . how funny! Can't imagine who that could be!"

"Do you suppose I know? Holy Virgin Mary, I tortured myself thinking about it all night. . . ."

"Oh, maybe Bernadette just made a fool of you, Jeanne," Cathérine Mengot suggested. But the secretary's red-haired daughter made a gesture of contempt. "Bah, Bernadette isn't smart enough to lie and deceive. . . ."

"No, Bernadette doesn't lie," Jeanne admitted thoughtfully. "Let's try to get to the root of the matter. . . ."

Eager for sensation, the girls agreed to this proposal. They planned to visit Massabielle together, to try to find the strange young lady with the naked feet.

"But will the lady be there when we arrive?" asked Toinette Gazalas, daughter of the chandler.

"Whatever Bernadette could see we can see as well. Our eyes are as good as hers." Such was the judgment of Cathérine Mengot.

Jeanne Abadie became speculative. "But she'll have to come

with us when we go. If she's not there, the lady might stay away."

When, rather late that day, Bernadette and Marie entered the schoolroom Jeanne's followers surrounded and almost assailed Bernadette. "What is this story of a lady? Tell us, describe her exactly. Where did she stand? How did you happen to notice her? Did she call out to you? Did she move? . . ."

Bernadette tried to catch Jeanne's eyes. "Why, why did you give that away, Jeanne?"

Yet again there was relief rather than reproach in her voice. For now a number of people had come to know about the lady who really belonged to her alone: Marie, Jeanne, her parents, Uncle and Aunt Sajou, Madame Bouhouhorts, Uncle Bouriette, and now this crowd of girls who chattered away, as full of curiosity as though the lady were the most ordinary lady in the world! As from the very beginning, even so now Bernadette was assailed by two sharply contradictory feelings. She would have loved to keep her lady to herself alone, now and for ever, to her last breath, and share her ecstatic secret with no one. And at the same time she yearned to cry out her secret to all she knew and to bring all men before the countenance of the lovely one in order that they might rejoice in it no less than she herself. Perhaps this second desire was even more powerful than the contrary one.

"I told," Jeanne justified herself, "because I didn't swear and because it's an important matter. We've all decided to go to Massabielle and take a look at the lady."

"Do you believe we'll see her too?" Madeleine Hillot inquired.

"You'll probably see her," Bernadette replied. "Of course, I can't be sure."

"But Mamma doesn't want Bernadette to go back to Massabielle," Marie interposed fearfully. "She even beat us. And

Papa was very stern and said that if Bernadette sees ladies like that she'd better go join the tricksters and tumblers and gipsies. . . ."

Jeanne Abadie looked sharply at Bernadette. "But you are going back to Massabielle, aren't you?"

Bernadette lowered her head a little and did not answer.

"Did the lady speak to you?" Cathérine asked.

Bernadette did not raise her eyes. "No, she spoke no word. . . . But she is the most, most beautiful thing in the whole world. . . ."

"If she's so very beautiful, maybe she's not so very, very good." This doubt came from the pale singer Madeleine Hillot.

"I had that idea during the night too," the prudent Jeanne declared. "It may very well be that the lady is something evil. And so I've made a plan. Sunday, after High Mass, we'll take a little bottle of holy water from church. And when the lady appears in the cavern Bernadette must sprinkle her and say to her: 'If you are of God, Madame, approach. But if you are of the devil, Madame, betake yourself hence.' That's the right way to do. I believe that this is a sensible proposal and will help us find out the truth."

"Ugh, you make me shudder!" said Annette Courrèges. "But maybe the lady is neither evil nor good but a real honest-to-God lady. . . ."

"Oh, she is as real as real can be!" Bernadette agreed with the utmost passion.

"Ducks in a pond!" The teacher's voice was heard. "And all listen to the wisdom of our most learned Bernadette."

Sunday. High Mass was drawing to a close. The flat tones of the small-town chimes announced the miracle of transubstantiation. Under the guidance of Sister Vauzous, Bernadette and

Marie and the whole catechism class were attending the service.
François Soubirous was busy in Cazenave's stables until noon.
Jean Marie and Justin had begged to be allowed to play outside.
Louise Soubirous was sitting at home alone, idle for once, that
is, busily knitting. She had attended early Mass at seven. She
was not fond of attending High Mass, at which appeared the
people who are "in better circumstances" and who are well
dressed and rested. She had nothing to wear and so felt that she
belonged to the lowest class and to the dim morning church
where one of the chaplains—Pomian, Penès, or Sempet—celebrated a quiet Mass. This was an act of genuine renunciation
on Louise's part, for High Mass is more than a religious service;
it is the one great and precious thing the small town offered its
people after the crushing monotony of the week. The thunder
of the organ, like a great spiritual fire, warmed the chill soul.
People saw and saluted one another. And Dean Peyramale was
a priest of power and his nobly harsh voice went to the very
heart when, after the reading from the Gospel, he addressed
the faithful. Louise renounced attending High Mass chiefly because she did not wish to meet her more fortunate sisters. For
the widow Tarbès, formerly Bernarde Casterot, and Lucille,
the withered old maid, both had Sunday frocks. And Louise
was far too proud to appear beside these two luckier ones as
the black sheep of the family, as a Casterot shamed by having
drawn a blank in life's lottery. Toward her sister Bernarde her
attitude was a mixture of almost reverential respect and sharp
irritation.

But on this blessed Sunday morning she was truly contented
in her loneliness, not annoyed by her sons or irritated by her
daughters, not anxious about her husband, who, she knew, was
not wasting time at Babou's or some other bar but who was
performing the reputable duties of a "postal official," as he was
now designating himself. Cazenave paid ten francs on account.

Thus the most pressing debts had been met. After many weeks of privation there was once more a bit of meat in the house. A *pot-au-feu* with tender vegetables and little onions was already spreading its aroma through the room.

Her soul, too, had been contemplatively at peace since yesterday when she took counsel of Father Sempet in the confessional. Frankly, she had been quite disturbed about the matter of Bernadette and that lady. What was one to think of such odd and eerie things? But Father Sempet, a very superior person who did not know Bernadette at all, had smiled most kindly and said: "My dear daughter, those are harmless phenomena of childhood, with which mature people needn't bother their heads at all." That concluded the matter for Louise Soubirous. Nevertheless, she was a bit frightened when half an hour later Bernadette appeared in the Cachot surrounded by a crowd of schoolgirls and begged permission to take her friends to the beautiful lady of Massabielle.

"Have you all gone crazy?" Louise asked in sudden anger. "Bernadette is going to stay right here."

Jeanne curtsied, the very soul of reasonableness. "But, dear Madame, we just want to make sure whether there is anything to this tale of a lady. . . ."

These words put a clever thought into Louise's head: since, according to the priest, the whole thing was childish and unworthy of adult attention, the crowd of green girls would see exactly nothing and Bernadette would be thoroughly laughed at. That would shame her and cure her completely. But Louise, not wanting to withdraw her command at once, let the girls plead a little while. Then, according to a well-tested method, she invoked the putative authority of the head of the house. "If Sunday is a time for such follies, you may go to Massabielle for all I care, provided Papa permits it. Let Bernadette ask him. I'm only her mother. It depends on his opinion. . . ."

To lose no time, the crowd of girls now fairly ran to the post-office. Respectable people taking their sedate Sunday walks looked with amazement at this horde of girls seemingly in pursuit of some wild prank or pleasure. In the great yard of the post-office several men were standing about a horse with melancholy drooping head. The men were Cazenave, in riding-boots as always and with a visored cap; Doutreloux, the groom advanced to the job of coachman; the vet; and finally Soubirous, who had led the horse up by the halter. The vet passed his fingers along the mare's back and found a pressure under the collar. He was about to take his pot of ointment from his leather satchel when the girls stormed in. Including the Soubirous children, there were nine in all. Jeanne Abadie formulated the general request in well-rounded sentences and consequently put Cazenave, Doutreloux, and the vet, who had heard nothing, in possession of the remarkable matter under investigation. Soubirous was tempted to put his hand over her mouth. A dull, angry discomfort rose in his throat. He felt painfully embarrassed before Cazenave and the other men by this silly tale of Bernadette. Here he was with a job and an assured wage. Out of the depth of unemployment he had climbed the first rung of the ladder of respectability! And here came his own child to destroy his new position as a man of sense and worth among his equals with irregular, equivocal, irritating follies. He frowned and without paying attention to the others growled at his daughter: "What business have you here? Get home, both of you! And let me hear no more of the matter!"

Cazenave laughed. "Come, come, old man. Why do you want to rob those nice children of their Sunday prank? There's nothing to it. Children are like that. Let them go look for that lady of theirs. . . ."

The girlish chorus renewed its request. Bernadette alone was silent.

"What did your lady have in her hand?" Cazenave asked. "A rosary, eh?"

"Yes, Monsieur, a very long one with large white pearls. . . ."

Cazenave was vastly amused. "Look, Soubirous, if the lady carries a rosary like all the other ladies of Lourdes, there's nothing against your little daughter's associating with her. . . ."

The bread-giver's word had to be accepted. Soubirous was helpless. "But see to it that you're back in half an hour." His face was sombre.

"That's quite impossible, Monsieur Soubirous," Jeanne declared. "It's a long way."

The father, beaten and forced to retreat, growled: "We won't wait dinner. . . ."

The girls rose and fluttered off as a flock of partridges rises from a field. The vet smeared black salve on the horse's sore back. A few minutes later Soubirous took the sick horse back to its stable. As he was bedding the horse on fresh straw he observed that there were tears in his eyes. In his astonishment he could not tell whether these tears were due to the defeat of his paternal authority or were the harbingers of the mischief which his heavy heart felt to be approaching.

At the Pont Vieux a sharp altercation arose among the girls. Jeanne Abadie insisted that they choose the shorter way by the Chalet Isle and cross Nicolau's little bridge to reach the farther bank of the Savy brook.

"It's been doing nothing but raining and snowing for two days," Bernadette objected. "The lock will be open and the bridge under water. We've got to cross the mountain. . . ."

"Look," Jeanne mocked. "The egg's trying to be smarter than the hen. Would you kindly rely on me?"

But Bernadette remained firm. Thus two factions arose. The

majority, of course, sided with Jeanne Abadie, the acknowledged leader. Only Marie, Madeleine Hillot, and Toinette
Gazalas adhered to Bernadette. Behind the bridge the paths of
the two factions diverged.

"We'll see who gets there first!" cried Jeanne, with her usual
ambition and assurance, to the hostile group. Bernadette fairly
flew ahead; the others could scarcely follow her. A whirlwind
seemed to bear her toward Massabielle. Usually, running brought
on one of her attacks. On this day it was as though she had
never been afflicted. Marie tried to restrain her. She heard nothing. Not for a moment did she doubt that the lady was waiting
for her, standing with those pale, naked feet on the edge of the
niche. Perhaps she was actually impatient. Bernadette was so
long in coming. Perhaps the damp and cold made her suffer,
for clouds of fog were rolling through the valleys. And Bernadette's jealously cherishing care brooded over the physical and
spiritual well-being of the lady. She hardly noticed her companions. It was not important to her whether that loveliest one
would permit the girls to see her or not, for Bernadette had
not the slightest desire to convince anyone of the realness of
her lady. To her the reality was absolute. The girls panted and
cried out behind her. But she was as unconditionally solitary
as are only those whom an utterly compelling love fills to the
brim. She raced over the path on the ridge of the mountain of
caverns and reached the breakneck path which leads along the
upper rim of the cavern. With half-closed eyes she leaped, nay,
floated from stone to stone. One more leap and she was below.
In the midst of the rubble of the cavern floor she paused and
took a deep breath and gathered herself together, her hand
upon her heart. Then she raised her eyes to the niche.

The three girls who had painfully climbed down the last
steep stretch of the way heard her cry: "She is here! Yes, she
is here. . . ."

They found Bernadette with head thrown back and eyes wide open staring into the empty oval of the niche and whispering again and again: "She is here . . . she is here . . . she is here . . ."

The girls crowded about her, whispering now too from constricted throats: "Where is she? . . . Where do you see her? . . ."

"Up there! She is come. . . . Do you not see her greeting?"

And Bernadette returned the greeting in her zealous, awkward schoolgirl fashion.

"All I see up there is a black hole," said Toinette Gazalas. "Behind the hole is a big stone. No one could get through there."

"And I don't see anything at all," said Marie, blinking with all her might.

"She sees you; she sees you," Bernadette whispered. "She nodded in salutation to you. You must return her greeting."

"Hadn't we better go nearer?" Marie whispered.

Horrified, Bernadette spread out her arms. "No, no, for the love of God! No nearer. Not a step!"

She who was blessed felt herself all too near the blessing one. It was not now as on that first occasion. Then there had been a distance between them—the whole width of the brook. In wave after wave of gradualness the lady had had to reveal and offer her countenance to her chosen one. Today she was near enough to touch. Bernadette would have had only to leap up on one of the boulders by the wall of rock and stretch out her arms. Then she could almost have touched the naked feet with their golden roses. But she stood utterly still. She would not, such was her feeling, burden the lady with her rude and common presence. The latter, to Bernadette's profound satisfaction, had not changed her garments, although so distinguished a lady doubtless possessed an inexhaustible wardrobe. In soft folds the snow-white mysterious velvet clung to the delicate limbs. The transparent veil fell from the shoulders. It rejoiced the heart to see today's mild wind toying with it. The lady seemed to be eternally a bride and for ever as such before the altar, never doffing her bridal veil. And it was strange that for all her radiance she showed no least displeasure because Bernadette had not come alone to seek her out but with this swarm of silly, whispering girls. Indeed, it seemed as though she had found Bernadette's indiscretion right worthy of praise. In any case, she took no umbrage at the company in which she found herself, and now and then threw a friendly and encouraging glance at Marie and Madeleine and Toinette. Behind her Bernadette heard the whispering of the Hillot girl. "Now take that and sprinkle her and say what we agreed to say."

Bernadette held in her hand the vial of consecrated water which Madeleine Hillot had filled from the font in church. Yielding rather to the girls than from any impulse of her own, she did the thing that had been planned, sprinkling a little water uncertainly up toward the niche and then shyly and mechanically saying: "If you are of God, Madame, will you please come nearer? . . ."

She stopped, frightened. Never could she have ended that horrid sentence about the devil and "betake yourself hence." The lady would apparently not have taken even that in ill part. She seemed amused at the formula of exorcism, and her smile was almost a laughter that comes from the very heart. And now indeed she stepped forth obediently far out of her rocky oval, on her inviolate feet. A heavier creature could not have sustained its equilibrium there. But she stretched out her hands in an embracing gesture, and Bernadette felt coming over her once more that piercingly sweet sense of well-being, that boundless somnolence from which awakening is an awakening into a gruesome and an alien world. She feared this awakening even before her knees gave way. . . .

It was at this moment that Jeanne Abadie with her five friends appeared on the path by the sharp edge of the cavern. Holding fast by a bush, she bent over to see whether her adversaries were at work. This time Jeanne had had no luck. The little bridge, as Bernadette had foretold, proved impassable. The group had to turn tail and follow in the others' wake. Jeanne was enraged because Bernadette had proved herself the wiser. She was willing to be Bernadette Soubirous's friend, but only on condition that she could look down on Bernadette and pity her—as the clever pities the stupid, the apt pities the awkward, and the worldly wise the helpless. But since Thursday this relationship had been reversed. Bernadette had slipped from her power. Jeanne's arrogant will was impotent against her. And now there arose the sugary voice of Madeleine Hillot bawling one Ave after another, probably at Bernadette's behest. At that Jeanne flared up in such revengefulness and despair as she had never known. She did not know what she was doing.

"I'll scare you good and proper!" she screamed and lifting up a boulder, the size and form of a human skull, she hurled it into the depth. The stone landed a hair's breadth from where Bernadette was kneeling on the rubble. The girls cried out. Bernadette alone remained unmoved as though she had not noticed.

"Did it hit you? Are you hurt?" Marie wailed and shook her kneeling sister, who did not reply. And only now as they leaped up and faced her did the girls recognize the fact that the face of Bernadette Soubirous was no longer the face they knew as hers. The rounded form was still the same; so were the smooth forehead and the gentle, half-open mouth. Yet it was a being strange and other and not the sister of Marie who stared up at the niche with those insatiable eyes. Those eyes had forgotten the lowering of the lids. They would not darken even for a twinkling the image they beheld. The pupils were enlarged and

darker than their wont; the whites more shining. The skin of
the face was so taut that the cheek-bones and temple-bones
stood out. It was no longer the face of a child or that of a
young woman, but rather the face of an apotheosized sufferer
which had absorbed into itself all the sorrows of the world
before, like a light, it is extinguished. And yet the face's expression was not one of suffering but of both devotion and with-
drawal to a higher vantage-point. What frightened Marie most
violently, however, was again that face's death-like pallor and
utter bloodlessness, which nevertheless lent it a new and dreadful beauty.

"You've killed my sister!" Marie shrilled to Jeanne, who now
rushed down with her companions. Wailing, they surrounded
the unmoving girl but kept at a fairly safe distance, since no
one dared to touch her.

Jeanne Abadie had turned pale. She managed to say: "She's
not hurt. It's all the fault of the lady. Get some water. She'll
come to. . . ."

But the sprinkling with water from the brook failed to
awaken Bernadette from her trance. And now the girls lost
their heads. They ran hither and thither and cried like creatures possessed. Marie howled: "Mamma . . . Mamma," and
raced off to tell her mother. Jeanne Abadie and Cathérine Mengot ran to the Savy mill to fetch help. The others tried to talk
to Bernadette, without approaching her too closely. They were
afraid of her and her condition. Two heavily burdened peasant
women on their way from Aspin-les-Angles joined the group
and from random interjections learned, with much shaking of
their heads, the story of Bernadette and the lady. Who, who
could the lady be? The peasant women looked at each other
out of large earnest eyes.

At long last arrived Mother Nicolau and Antoine, the miller.
The woman, hearing that someone had fainted, had brought

chopped onions with her which she held under Bernadette's nose. The girl merely turned her head a little without changing the direction of her vision. Antoine now also bent over the kneeling girl, who seemed to him absorbed in prayer.

"Come on, Bernadette," he said with tender persuasiveness. "That's enough now; let's go home."

Since he received no answer, he tried to cover the girl's eyes with his large hand. But that huge awkward paw could more easily have covered the light of a lamp than the crystalline eyes which continued to see unhindered. With a sudden decisive movement Antoine Nicolau now lifted Bernadette high in his arms and carried her to the mill. Along the entire way she did not lose that fixed smile by which, beyond and through the miller's kindly face, she remained bound to the lady.

Nicolau with Bernadette in his arms, behind him the frantic schoolgirls, the peasant women with their packs, the breathlessly tripping Mother Nicolau—this strange procession sufficed to attract from all directions people who were taking their Sunday walks in the vicinity. Before the Savy mill was reached, a small crowd had gathered. There were questions on all sides; there was astonishment and argument. A few laughed. A consensus was soon established: the Soubirous girl had lost her mind. Antoine had placed Bernadette in a large armchair close to the fire. The room was filled with strangers. Mother Nicolau brought a wooden cup of milk with which to revive the fainting girl. But Bernadette's condition had no resemblance whatever to a swoon. Her consciousness was not at all extinguished. It was fixed with superhuman intensity upon the beauty of the lady, so that it perceived all other things only in the form of a far and utterly indifferent rumour.

Her rapture did not vanish gradually but came to a sudden end. It was as though that sublime woman's countenance which

had absorbed into itself all the woes of the world was suddenly consumed by a swift invisible fire and left behind it the
accustomed child-like face of Bernadette, ignorant, a little dull,
with apathetic eyes.

"Thank you very much, Madame," Bernadette said quietly.
She refused the proffered milk. "I don't need anything. . . ."

Now they overwhelmed her with questions: "What was the
matter? . . . What happened? . . . What did you see?"

"Oh, nothing," Bernadette answered rather tranquilly. "Only
the lady was there a long time. . . ."

These words marked a development which had taken place
between Bernadette and the lady. The relationship had become
intimate and, in a certain sense, an old one. The first intoxication
of astonished rapture had yielded to the urgency toward steady
devotion. To Bernadette the lady was no longer a unique
miracle that fades into nothingness but a permanent possession.
She looked at the people about her and let them talk and hardly
opened her mouth. Antoine, who had scarcely taken his eyes
from her face, came to her rescue. "Don't you see how tired
she is? Can't you leave her in peace?"

But Bernadette was not tired at all. The reason for her silence
was to be sought in a feeling of guilt which weighed upon her
more and more. It was guilt toward her parents. Was she not
betraying them by loving the lady more? What would her
mother say to her behaviour?

Louise Soubirous and Marie began running as fast as their
legs could carry them over the long distance from the Cachot
to Massabielle. But before they reached the saw-mill they met
the Piguno woman, who knew all there was to know. Bernadette was in the Savy mill and was hale and hearty. Quite a
girl! First she adored some pretty but invisible lady in the dirty
cavern and next she let Antoine, who isn't so bad either, carry

her off, all without a murmur. "So be calm, dear Cousin," she ended her encouraging account. "People aren't responsible for their children. . . ."

Louise's face became contorted. From Marie's confused talk she had inferred that Bernadette was dead or in mortal danger. Now she heard of the shameless behaviour of her oldest child. And for this she had let the *pot-au-feu*—their first nourishing meal in she didn't know how long—burn and spoil. And for this her poor François, returning from his weary toil, would have to suffer terror and be contented with a piece of bread.

"Oh, wait, wait! I'll show you," she moaned and hastened her pace.

All the strangers who surrounded the Savy mill made her blush with shame. And when she entered the living-room and saw Bernadette, enthroned on the armchair like a princess whose favour is sought by all, her temper gave way wholly. She shrieked at Bernadette: "You rouse the whole world, don't you, you fool?"

"I asked no one to come along," Bernadette defended herself strictly according to the truth.

This was an answer well calculated to enrage teachers and parents. "You make a laughing-stock of us before the whole world!" Louise howled and lifted her arm to administer a hearty box on Bernadette's ear.

But Mother Nicolau caught the up-raised arm. "Why, for the love of Christ, would you strike the child?" she cried. "She is a very angel of God. Look, look. . . ."

"An angel? What kind of an angel?" Louise gnashed her teeth.

"You didn't see her a while ago," Antoine interposed. "She was really like, oh, like. . . ." And because the right comparison for the beauty of Bernadette in her state of rapture did not occur to his awkward mind he chose a word easy to misunderstand, a word that floated above the sudden silence: ". . . like one who has died. . . ."

Louise, a vacillating soul, ever torn by conflicting emotions, felt this word pierce her very heart. In truth, she had not hastened here to punish her daughter, but in very fear for her life. Now this fear overwhelmed her again. She dropped on a bench and wept. "Father in Heaven, preserve my child. . . ."

Bernadette arose now and went calmly up to her mother and touched her arm. "Come, Mamma. Maybe we can get home before Papa. . . ."

But by this time Soubirous and his dinner no longer interested Louise. "I won't budge from this place," she whimpered with ugly obduracy, "if Bernadette doesn't promise me before all these people never to go to Massabielle again . . . never again."

"Promise your mother," Mother Nicolau admonished Bernadette. "Such excitement is very bad for you. You're sure to be sick from it."

Convulsively Bernadette folded her still icy hands. "I promise you, Mamma," she said, "never to go to Massabielle again. . . ." But with all the desperate cunning of love she added a forensic condition: "Unless you yourself give me permission. . . ."

The Nicolaus, mother and son, were alone now. Antoine lit a Sunday cigar. "What do you think of it all, Mother?"

"I don't like that nice child's condition at all," the woman said, sighing. "Things like that bode no good. . . . And her parents are healthy people and tough ones too. . . ."

The son arose from his seat, paced up and down the room, and threw a quite unnecessary log upon the fire. As he did so he said: "Never have I seen anything more beautiful than the face of that kneeling girl, Mother, and never will I live to see anything more beautiful. . . ." The thought that he had held Bernadette in his arms almost frightened him: "One ought not even to touch a being like that," he said.

CHAPTER TWELVE

The First Words

AND SO it was decided that the matter of Bernadette's lady
was done with and for ever buried. The silence in the Cachot
was positively zealous. Although the town rang with the schoolgirls' exaggerated tale, Father Soubirous acted as if he belonged
among the few who had heard nothing of the exciting event
that centred in his daughter. Despite his release from pressing
care in the matter of a livelihood, his disposition seemed notably perturbed. He came and went, greeting no one. At night
he sat with defiant elbows on the table before him. In sleep—
to which, as we have seen, he was given even by day—his very
snoring sounded hurt and quarrelsome. The purpose of all
these emphatic manifestations of depression was radically to
suppress in Bernadette any inclination to backsliding. Soubirous gave the impression of a stern and solid citizen angry at
fate, which had slipped a cuckoo's egg among the normal contents of his respectable nest.

Mother Soubirous, on the other hand, contrary to her quick-
tempered, bristling nature, treated Bernadette with tender patience and attentiveness. She brought the girl small gifts and
consoled her with every word, yet without touching the
wound, for she was fully aware of the sacrifice that Bernadette
was making for her family. She even let her stay away from
school this week. She hoped that all this loving-kindness would
cause the lady gradually to fade from the deeply stirred soul
of her child.

Bernadette seemed to observe neither her mother's tender–

ness nor her father's hurt taciturnity nor, above all, the shy
curiosity manifested by her small brothers. She was equable
and kindly and readier than usual to help in household tasks.
But she avoided any contact with the neighbours and seldom
spoke at all. Once when Marie made a veiled allusion to the
lady of the grotto, Bernadette not only did not answer but left
the room. Her heart, however, bled by day and by night, not
so much because she herself must be deprived of seeing the
lady but at the thought that the gracious and lovely one, un-
shod and thinly garmented, was waiting for her in vain through
the cold February hours. She suffered the torments of a faithful lover whom the might of external circumstances prevents
from keeping a longed-for rendezvous. Her only hope was that
her own state of compulsion was not unknown to a being so
distinguished and aware as her lady. Her lacerated soul attained the self-conquest of the further and terrible hope that
the lady would not keep troth with her too long but, weary of
the vain manifestations of her favor, come wholly to forget her
little friend Bernadette.

But the realization of this hope was carefully prevented by
Madame Millet and Mademoiselle Antoinette Peyret. The widow
Millet had come home from Argelès Sunday night. Immediately she heard from Philippe and from her cook of the strange
happening in the cavern. The little Soubirous girl, daughter of
her assistant washerwoman, had seen in vision a young girl
with naked feet. By virtue of this vision *la petite voyante*, the
little seeress, had been transported into a trance such as one
sees delineated on religious pictures. It had taken nearly an
hour before Bernadette had awakened from her ecstasy and
returned to life.

This astonishing bit of news was grist for the metaphysical
mill of Madame Millet, who, though a rigid Catholic, had caused
uneasiness among the clerics of her acquaintance both high and

low by her pert interest in the world of ghosts and spirits. Madame had not slept all that night. She constantly saw the image of her niece Élise Latapie, a sweet and gentle girl whom she had loved and cared for as though she were her own and who had died in the bloom of youth at twenty-seven. Since then how empty had been the all too spacious house which the late Millet, hoping in vain for a brood of descendants, had built forty years ago. Madame Millet made a passionate cult of the girl's memory. Her room was kept intact, so that she might return to life and home at any moment. Small and large objects were in their wonted places—her childhood dolls, her little sewing-kit, her embroidery frames, two boxes of sweets turned to stone, and, above all, the cupboard with her linen, shoes, and frocks. During that sleepless night the corpulent widow, wrapped in a fur coat, passed a full hour in Élise's unheated room. Her hope was fixed upon some rosy communication that might on the one hand assure her of her foster-child's well-being in the beyond and on the other hand hold out the certain promise of a happy though not too early reunion with the departed. She succeeded in point of fact in recalling Élise Latapie in livelier colours than usual and in summoning up in the mind's eye the image of the dead girl in the garb that she used to wear on festive occasions as president of the Sodality of the Children of Mary. It was a magnificent dress of white satin with a rope-like girdle woven of blue silk. Antoinette Peyret, the dressmaker, had fashioned it after a Parisian pattern, and in friendship for her mate of the sodality charged only forty francs. Just for her labour. Toward morning, therefore, it became perfectly clear to Madame Millet that the girl whom the little seeress had seen could be none other than her beloved niece in her costume as president of the sodality.

It was an odd circumstance that in the course of Monday Antoinette Peyret reached the identical conclusion. Late in the afternoon she hastened to her patroness and customer. She was far from old, but ill favoured and a little deformed. Out of her longish face the inquisitive eyes blinked tirelessly. As the daughter of a bailiff she had been early acquainted with all the naked miseries of life and man. Quicker than Madame Millet, she had elaborated the theory more accurately. What was the meaning of the naked feet in the vision? They pointed clearly to the state of penitence which is the lot of all mortals who have left the world, even of the pure soul of Élise, the child of Mary. Penitents always walk barefoot. There are probably neither shoes nor pattens in purgatory. The niece of the rich Madame Millet was, then, a poor soul in need of special prayers by her relatives and friends to shorten her melancholy sojourn in purgatory. That is why she appeared in vision to the Soubirous girl and appeared in a spot that might well be thought of as the mouth of an infernal region. And who could tell, furthermore, whether Élise Latapie did not desire to transmit personal wishes and communications first of all to her kind aunt, but also, possibly, to her modest friend Antoinette! Madame Millet and Mademoiselle Peyret proceeded to lock themselves up in the dead girl's room to hold a consultation concerning the theory and to determine what action to take. The servingman Philippe, who had been accustomed for a decade to use the plural of majesty, found himself much astonished by the secret conference.

Wednesday around four o'clock, when, as luck would have it, no one was at home except Louise Soubirous and her daughter Bernadette, distinguished visitors made their appearance in the Cachot. First came Philippe. He placed on the table a basket in which two roasted chickens and two bottles of sweet wine were elegantly packed. Next he bowed to Louise as though she were a great lady, and announced the immediate arrival of his mistress. Louise stared in some trepidation both at the man and at the gift. Two minutes later the rich, high-bosomed widow rustled into the room, which even as a prison could hardly have held her, and behind her slipped in Peyret of the crooked shoulder. Madame Millet was painfully impressed by the darkness and poverty before her.

"My dear Louise," she began, "I thought I ought to look in on you. And you mustn't thank me for these trifles, either. . . . I wanted also to ask you to come over and help us every Wednesday and Saturday, not only with the washing. My house is, alas, so very large!"

Louise did not know what to make of this extravagant benevolence. As a rule, Madame Millet was not stingy; but she was precise. What extra work, good heavens, could there be in that house in which slip-covers and doilies prevented even a speck of dust from settling on the furniture? Two days' work a week would amount to four francs; that meant sixteen francs a month —quite a small fortune. And it was offered without preliminaries! What could be behind it? Obsequious and yet distrustful, Louise silently wiped off the seats of two wooden chairs and offered them to the company. Bernadette stood at the little window. Her face was wholly in the shadow, yet her dark hair had a reddish-golden gleam, for the wintry sun had emerged from the clouds before its setting and penetrated even the gloom of the Cachot.

"You have a darling child there, my good woman," Madame Millet sighed, "as well as a most remarkable one. . . . You must be very happy."

"Do say good day to the ladies," Louise beckoned to Bernadette.

Without a word Bernadette shook hands with each of the visitors and went back at once to her observation post.

Madame Millet drew out a lace handkerchief and touched

her eyes with it. "I had a child too—not my own, yet even dearer. But you know. And Élise died a truly holy death, the death of a brave sufferer, so that Dean Peyramale was impelled to write a special letter concerning this death to His Grace the Bishop of Tarbes, in order that the example of it might not be lost."

"And it is for this reason that we have come, Madame Soubirous," the practical Peyret interrupted her weeping patroness.

"Yes, dear Peyret." The widow, short of breath, nodded. "You explain. I can hardly bear to. . . ."

Whereupon the bailiff's daughter in her business-like way set forth the complete theory concerning Bernadette's lady. No doubt was admissible. The naked feet and the identity of the dress, which she herself had made, proved that the lady could be none other than the recently departed Élise Latapie in the painful situation of a soul in purgatory. Élise had chosen Bernadette Soubirous to be her messenger, as it were, from the world beyond to this, in order to communicate to her loving aunt and foster-mother words and wishes of great import. Such was the manifest meaning of Bernadette's vision. Madame Soubirous was therefore requested to permit her daughter to complete her mission by interpreting truly the wishes of Élise in order that that poor little soul might find its repose.

Thunderstruck, Louise sat there, scarcely daring to raise her head. "But all that sounds kind of crazy . . ." she stammered.

"It is indeed enough to drive one mad," the Millet woman sobbed out loud.

Before the visitors had come, strange silent things had taken place between mother and daughter. Mamma Soubirous, whose own throat ached at Bernadette's quiet depression, was about to offer the child permission to go secretly to the grotto next Sunday; and Bernadette had been at the point of throwing herself at her mother's feet and crying out: "Let me go! Oh, let me go!" But now fear and horror once more invaded the mother's heart.

"It would have to be quite soon, of course," the dressmaker insisted.

Louise thought of the sixteen francs a month. She thought of the mortal danger to which she believed her daughter would be subjected by a repetition of the trance-like condition. She fought for delay. "It wouldn't be possible before Sunday next. . . ."

"I take that as your assent, then," Madame Millet interrupted her quickly.

"No, no, no, because my husband would never consent. . . ."

"It's not a man's business; men don't understand such things." The widow spoke from long experience.

Antoinette laughed. "The idea of telling a man everything right away!"

"Mesdames, I really can't permit it. Just think; I'm the child's mother and I'm asked to risk her being made ill and a laughing-stock both. I can't; I just can't."

The fat widow arose in her pride. "I, too, am a mother—oh, more than a mother. I, also, have a beloved child that is in great misery. When I think of the pain that child must have endured to find the long, long way back to this earth, my very bones freeze. . . . I cannot force you to consent, Madame Soubirous; but once that door of yours has been closed behind me, the whole responsibility will be for you to bear."

"My head swims," Louise moaned. "This is too much for me."

"And what is the opinion of our dear Bernadette?" the dressmaker said persuasively.

Bernadette had not moved out of the afterglow which set her hair on fire. There was a tension in her as though she stood

on tiptoe. She was like one poised for a great leap. Of what
account was that fat woman or the ugly dressmaker or the poor
stupid ghost from purgatory and all this nonsense? She knew
one thing only: her magnificent lady wanted to see her. And
maybe she could be clever and was trying to make possible a
meeting between them. For no other reason would she have
sent these fat women here. Hence Bernadette replied in a light,
musical, and yet triumphant voice: "Let my mamma decide."

The encounter on this Thursday took a new and different
course. Firstly, Bernadette was not free, as she had been before:
Madame Millet had burdened her with a commission. Thus she
had not the time to steep herself wholly in the lady's boundless
beauty. At the very beginning of this great love the world intruded disturbingly into a relationship that needed to exclude
every irrelevancy. The lady was already there, although it was
only six o'clock in the morning. (Louise Soubirous had made
the condition that Bernadette must go at dawn, so that no attention be aroused.) And, oh, the tender considerateness that
she who blessed always awaited her who was to be blessed, seeing that the world's way is quite the contrary. Bernadette
kneeled on a flat white stone, less to adore than to confess.
Words struggled breathlessly up from her heart, but her lips
remained mute.

Do, pray, forgive me for not having come in so long. But
I had to promise Mamma at the Savy mill never to come again.
It was terrible for me, Madame, to know you were waiting in
this bad weather. . . .

The lady's gesture was calming, almost disdainful, as if to
say: It's nothing, my child. I'm used to waiting for my own in
all weathers.

Bernadette's silent speech came again in a flood: I'm not all
alone today, Madame. Forgive me for that. Madame Millet and

Mademoiselle Peyret, the dressmaker, you know, are coming along. You see, it was only on account of Millet that Mamma let me come to you. She thinks the lady will let her earn four francs a week. And since Papa was made a postal official last Friday we'll be able to live much better. I ran ahead to tell you all this first. Madame Millet is old and fat. Oh, you know all about it, Madame. She couldn't keep up with me. Oh, dear, there they are now! They've caught up something so silly. But please forgive me! I know very well that you're not Élise Latapie and didn't come from purgatory.

The lady nodded and smiled as though to signify: Don't worry. We're a match for Madame and Mademoiselle. The main thing is that they got you your mother's consent.

Now the voice of Peyret was heard: "Careful, dear lady! Hold fast to my hand. One little step more and then one more and we're here. That's it. We've made it."

Bernadette heard behind her the old woman's wheezing. "The lady is standing up there," she whispered to her without taking her own eyes from the niche. "She just bowed to you in salutation. . . ."

"Ah, my poor, sweet Élise," Madame Millet stammered, "I don't see you! Why don't I see you? How do you fare where you are?"

With stiff fingers she lighted the consecrated Michaelmas candle that she had brought with her. This was the first candle to burn at Massabielle.

Hard as it was for her, Madame Millet let herself fall on both knees, raised her folded hands high, and sang in a frosty quaver: "Speak to me, Élise. Say one word, one only. . . ."

Antoinette Peyret was seized by doubt. They had told her that at the sight of the lady the face of the Soubirous girl became so supernaturally beautiful that it could not be recognized. Nothing of the kind was happening. Bernadette's face was as earthly and ordinary as ever. Thus the dressmaker poked the back of Bernadette, who was kneeling in front of her, with her sharp knuckles: "Be sure to tell the truth, do you hear me? Nothing but the truth. You'll be punished afterward if you don't."

Bernadette said without turning: "I have said nothing that is untrue."

"Hush," Peyret commanded, "and tell your beads."

Obediently Bernadette took out her rosary. But she was troubled and could pray only mechanically. But after a few Aves the bailiff's daughter drew forth a small inkwell and pen and a sheet of legal stationery. She liked to make sure and meant to take a document back with her, something black on white. "So, and now go up to your lady," she whispered acridly, "and request her to write real plain a list of her desires and complaints and how many Masses she needs said. Her dear Aunt Millet will do everything in her power. . . ."

Obediently Bernadette took pen and ink and approached closely the rock on which the lady stood. She mounted on a boulder and with outstretched hands held the writing-material up toward the niche. In this posture she remained for a space, and her gesture was so impressive, so utterly veracious, that fright shook the two women. They might be deemed worthy of beholding with their eyes a miracle such as the world had never witnessed. Now the Millet woman was possessed by a steady need of revelations and wonders from the beyond. But at the immediate possibility of one her heart almost failed and icy horror drove shivers down her spine. Followed by Peyret, she fled from the grotto and, far from the possible miracle, fell to her knees at the side of the brook. Bathed in tears she clucked into empty space: "Write it all down, Élise. . . . I won't be stingy with you!"

After a while Bernadette returned from the grotto with a

bright matter-of-fact expression. She gave ink and pen and paper back.

"But the paper is blank!" the dressmaker declared in the tone of a police magistrate who has got to the bottom of something.

"And what did the lady say?" Madame Millet asked, relieved and yet saddened.

"She shook her head and laughed," replied Bernadette.

"The lady laughed?"

"Yes, she laughed a little."

"Very interesting," Peyret observed pointedly. "So the lady can laugh! I don't believe the poor souls in purgatory can laugh. Run back now and ask her her name."

Still obedient, Bernadette returned to the grotto. She was sorely embarrassed to have to annoy the lady with such silly things today. Yet the lady seemed to possess a patience that was inexhaustible, for despite the grey February day she stood moveless within her own radiance. Only the golden roses on her feet grew faint and dim at moments. Bravely Bernadette approached the rock again.

"Please forgive me, Madame, but the two women would know your name."

A reflective absent-mindedness appeared on the lady's countenance, such as might show on the face of a princely personage who has been subjected to an error in tact. Bernadette fell to her knees and took out her rosary. After she had prayed she saw again the old smile on the lady's face. And now for the first time there sounded in the ear of Bernadette a voice, a voice almost too maternally deep in view of the lady's youthful and girlish grace: "Will you render me the grace," the lady said, "of coming here each day for fifteen days?"

She did not speak these words in good French, but in the dialect of the provinces of Béarn and Bigorre as Bernadette and her people spoke it. Accurately translated, she did not say kindness, *boutentat*, but grace, *grazia*. "Would you grace me by coming . . . ?"—such were her words. And after a long silence she added in a much softer voice: "I cannot promise to make you happy in this world, only in the next. . . ."

When after this decisive colloquy Bernadette issued forth from the grotto a little crowd had gathered about Madame Millet and her candle. There were the Nicolaus—mother and son—Marie, Jeanne Abadie, Madeleine Hillot, and, above all, a few peasants and their wives from the valley of Batsuguère, where the rumour of the visions at Massabielle had aroused much attention. More and more country people joined these, for this was Thursday and they were taking their farm products to market in Lourdes.

"Did she tell her name?" Peyret called out to Bernadette.

"Oh, no, she didn't do that. . . ."

"Did you even ask her?"

"I did as you asked me to do, Mademoiselle. . . ."

"Aren't you making fools of us? I watched you closely. You didn't so much as open your mouth."

"When I speak with the lady," Bernadette replied, "I speak here. . . ." At the word "here" she laid a finger on her heart.

"Aha," smirked the inquisitor. "And does the lady also speak 'here' to you?"

"No, today the lady *really* spoke to me."

"So she even has a voice?"

"Yes, and her voice is just the way she is herself. . . ." And Bernadette gave an exact account of everything.

That convinced Antoinette that she had trapped the girl. "You're trying to tell sensible people," she jeered, "that a lady, a soul from the beyond, perhaps even a blessed angel, uses the polite, grown-up form to a silly brat like you and says: '*Voudriez-vous me faire la bonté*' or, if you like, '*la grâce*,' eh?"

Bernadette's face brightened with astonishment and rapturous delight. "Yes, it is comical that the lady said *vous* and not *tu*."

This examination to which Peyret subjected Bernadette had quite unexpected consequences. To begin with, the dressmaker had harboured no particular doubts of the girl's sincerity. Genuine belief in a hereafter, curiosity, the instinct of the time-server, lustfulness for the unheard-of—such had been the mixed motives which caused her to persuade her patroness to engage in this adventure. Only in the grotto had the free demeanour of Bernadette incited her to suspicion. The girl's sober and unaffected answers in a supernatural matter served, however, to engage the hearts of the onlookers on the side of Bernadette against her malicious adversary. Bernadette had spoken of her vision with a clarity and precision rare enough among men when they speak of the humblest realities. Those who heard her were wrought upon to believe in the absurd against their will.

"You are a blessed creature," said one of the peasant women. "Who shall say whose visitation you receive?"

Madame Millet had almost given up the hope of identifying the lady with her niece. The words reported by Bernadette gave no ground for it. Nevertheless, she was not disappointed. She embraced Bernadette. "Grace has been granted you, *ma petite voyante*. I thank you. I am an old sick woman. But I shall make the pilgrimage to the grotto with you daily for the next fifteen days. . . . I don't believe, Antoinette, that you will want to miss a single day, either."

"Not a single one," the Peyret woman declared, swiftly forced to change her tactics against her will. "I am sure we'll learn many a truth from Bernadette."

The widow, worn out though she was, added: "I feel uplifted and calmed. I'm going to take Philippe along, too. It will do him good."

That also left Jeanne Abadie no choice but to acknowledge Bernadette's superiority and leadership, although she was the best pupil in their class and her friend the poorest. "I'm coming every day, too," she said. "After all, I was the first to hear about the lady."

"How are you the first?" Marie excitedly asked. "I am the first, since I am her sister."

Antoine Nicolau stroked his moustache, as was his habit in moments of embarrassment. "What do you say, dear Mother," he said in apparently careless tones, "about inviting Mademoiselle Bernadette to be our guest for the next fifteen days? The upstairs room is cold, to be sure, but she'd be so much nearer Massabielle."

"It would be a great joy to me," Madame Nicolau answered noncommittally. "But I don't want to get mixed up in anything. It is for her parents to decide what is to be done about her."

"It is I who will request the pleasure of having Bernadette as my guest," Madame Millet announced majestically.

Bernadette hardly knew what was happening to her. People were suddenly using such high-flown, cultivated, almost affected speech. What would they have of her? She did not in the least understand why the grace which the lady had shown her should at one stroke alter her position among men. "We must certainly go home now," she said.

The Pont Vieux was crowded with people going to market. Not a few of these joined the strange procession which, led by Bernadette and Madame Millet, who still held her lighted candle in her hand, moved on toward the Cachot. The news travelled from mouth to mouth.

"That young girl appeared in the grotto again. . . . For the

third time today, Thursday. . . . Of all people, it happens to
the Soubirous brat. . . . Not quite right in her upper story, that
one. . . . How that family has gone to the dogs. . . . Don't let
an imbecile sell you a gold brick like that. . . . Can you imagine? The rich Millet woman is mixed up in it. . . . Well, if you
have as much money as that you've got to *look* for trouble. . . ."

As they entered the town itself the jeers flew faster. Yet the
crowd had increased to a hundred persons at the corner of the
Rue des Petites Fossées. The policeman Callet, who had just
come from Babou's bar, was astonished by this "demonstration" and considered whether it was not his duty "to restore
order." For the regime of Louis Napoléon, which had itself
risen to power through street-riots, entertained a corresponding
fear of the mob. Callet ran straight to Mayor Lacadé and then
to Police Commissioner Jacomet in order to report, for those
were the two civil authorities whose executive functions the
former rural guard united in his modest self. Louise Soubirous
rushed from the Cachot with horrified eyes and tousled
hair.

"My God, what's up again?"

Marie beckoned to her reassuringly. "Bernadette is perfectly
well today. The lady spoke to her—ever so politely—and said:
'Would you have the kindness to come here every day for fifteen days?'"

"This thing is going to kill me," Louise moaned. "I'm going
to lose my child."

The crowd thronged the gateway. Madame Millet, Mademoiselle Peyret, the Nicolaus, and the girls entered the dim room.
"My dear Madame Soubirous," the rich woman began, no
longer condescendingly now but as equal to equal, "I am grateful to God for having given us your Bernadette. I shall join
her in the daily pilgrimage to Massabielle. My swollen feet will
make that a goodly act of penitence. But I beg you to let me

give the child bed and board during this period. I trust this offer will not be an unwelcome one. . . ."

It was not, of course, unwelcome. Her sickly Bernadette would sleep in a soft little bed and have food five times a day, at least a roasted chicken-wing. She scratched her head with the handle of her wooden spoon. "Let me catch my breath, Madame Millet; I'm overcome. . . ."

But Madame Millet let herself be carried further and further by her emotions. "Bernadette shall occupy the lovely room of my blessed departed. You know that that room has been like a sanctuary to me. Yet, though I don't know whether the lady of Massabielle is my poor Élise or not, none but Bernadette shall sleep in her bed. . . ."

This forced Peyret to seek to shine with equal magnanimity in the eyes of her patroness. "What an absurd smock you are wearing, dear Bernadette! I'll present you with a dear little white dress so that the lady may take pleasure in you. . . ."

"Did you ever hear of fool's luck?" Jeanne Abadie whispered and nudged Madeleine Hillot.

"Mesdames," Louise said imploringly, "do please permit me to take counsel with my husband and with my sister Bernarde Casterot. I can't assume the responsibility for these fifteen days alone. And look at all those people! Blessed Virgin, how will this end?"

"Take counsel with your family, Madame Soubirous," Madame Millet said with majestic grace. "But Bernadette had better come with us at once. Besides, dear Peyret, you can make over Élise's sodality dress. She wasn't much larger. . . ."

Bernadette, as was her wont, showed little interest. Amid these favours showered upon her she reflected concerning the words of the lady: "I cannot promise to make you happy in this world." She could not promise it and yet seemed to be performing it on this very day.

Toward four o'clock on that afternoon there appeared in the Cachot the family oracle, Louise's clever sister and Bernadette's godmother, Bernarde Casterot. She was respectfully welcomed by the Soubirous. She was accompanied by her youngest sister Lucille, the old maid whose subservience made her seem her sister's menial. It had always been the habit of the family oracle to spend several hours in picking to pieces and then putting together again whatever question was submitted to her wise adjudication. Having pronounced sentence, she brooked no appeal. Bernarde Casterot, the widow Tarbès, had in fact a very acute brain in her peasant skull, differing markedly from her sisters, whom she held to be hopelessly confused and feeble of mind. She owed it exclusively to her own strong sense that the fortune of the late Tarbès, instead of being frittered away, had been increased by various astute transactions. She stood alone in the world but squarely on her own two feet. A very few years ago she had flatly refused an offer of marriage. She was too well versed in the irresoluteness of the male, his universal frivolousness and lack of healthy realism.

Disapprovingly she looked about her. Louise, once the prettiest of the Casterot sisters, deserved better of fate. But that happens when girls take things into their own hands and marry for love, forgetful of the practical and serious side of marriage. Love picks a handsome man, as Soubirous was in his day. But if men in general are good-for-nothings, handsome men are without exception unmitigated scamps. A glance at the marriage bed instructed Bernarde that it had been hastily put to rights, because her sister had succeeded in rousing her handsome husband just a few minutes before.

"Where is Bernadette?" the godmother inquired.

"She is staying with Madame Millet," Louise answered nervously. "She's invited there for the fifteen days."

"Mistake number one!" thundered Bernarde Casterot.

"Why a mistake, Sister?"

"Because you can't see farther than your own nose."

Angrily Soubirous began to pace up and down. To show his marital prowess he was accustomed to taking sides with his sister-in-law. "A mistake! I told her so! I did! But she does as she thinks best. Doesn't even ask my advice. A bad business, letting the child go. What will people say?"

Bernarde's laugh had a sharp edge. "I can tell you exactly what people will say. They will say the Soubirous are making a mighty good thing out of Bernadette and her lady."

"You're right, undoubtedly right," Soubirous growled angrily. "I can hear them now."

"They'll say more than that. They'll say that Bernadette invented the whole business in order to become Millet's heiress."

"Of course they will!" Rage flamed from Soubirous toward his wife. "The whole thing's a disgrace. Mud will be thrown at us."

Pitilessly Bernarde threw water on his noble rage. "Well, it's no special honour to live in this place."

"All right. But have I always been an honest man? And have I always given more than I've taken?" Soubirous was deeply self-convinced. "Even you will grant me that, Sister. But now I am through with this whole business. I will hear no more of it. This is the end. Bernadette will be shipped off to Bartrès. . . ."

Bernarde nodded. "Brainless. Men. It all comes back to me. I haven't much time, Brother-in-Law. Kindly sit down on your behind. The rest of you, too. About time you let me talk. You called me in, didn't you? So don't interrupt me."

Obediently they sat down. Bernarde alone remained standing sturdily before them. She had taken off neither her headkerchief nor her black cape. "Bernadette," she began her summing up, "is a dear child, without cunning, without much sense even, which is no wonder. I've often looked at the girl and wondered what's the matter with her. I'll stake my life on it that this business with the lady is no mere fooling as far as Bernadette is concerned. She hasn't the cunning to invent anything so crazy or so astute. She sees the lady. Nobody else does. Our grandmother used to tell us children a tale about a girl she knew who once saw our dear Saviour in a dark hallway, alive and near enough to touch. Things like that happened often in the old days. The lady may well be a heavenly creature. Yet she may be spawn of hell, though nothing points to that except her choice of such a filthy place to appear in. It's a wild enough story and I don't know what its end will be, though I took five whole hours to think about it. For your sake I hope the whole thing will die down. But Bernadette will go to the grotto for fifteen days. She must. The lady has desired it, and the lady may be from heaven. No one can dare to prevent the girl from fulfilling the lady's wish. That is my opinion. . . . But my advice is this: a daughter belongs in her mother's house. The mother can't hide her head in the sand and act as though her daughter were up to some harmless mischief that doesn't concern her. You've acted foolishly hitherto, Sister. From now on you are to stand daily beside your child at Massabielle. The thing is no joke. Consider what it means to Bernadette. And if you stand by her, people will not feel like jeering. And not you alone. All the women of the family must take their stand at her side. Lucille and I will go daily with Bernadette to the grotto right after early Mass. That's what I've decided for myself. The rest of you can do as you like. . . ."

The voluble oracle had spoken. The Soubirous couple sank into a subdued silence. Louise felt guilty in that it had taken her sister to remind her of her maternal duties. François, not wholly convinced by the logic of his sister-in-law, felt that he was not strong enough to oppose fate; and so he determined for his part to continue to nurse his paternal indignation and avoid the whole matter as long as possible.

CHAPTER THIRTEEN

Heralds of Science

"AFTER ALL, we're living in the second half of the nineteenth century," the coffee-house owner Duran observed with a sigh the while he brought the pedagogue Clarens his black coffee, the revenue officer Estrade a cup of chocolate, the writer Lafite a glass of bitters, and the imperial prosecutor, who had a bad head cold, a steaming glass of mulled wine. It was past four and the Café Français was beginning to fill up.

"Did you gentlemen read today's *Intérêt Public* of Tarbes?" he asked. "It contains the following notice, verbatim: 'The Blessed Virgin Mary appears to a schoolgirl of Lourdes.' The penny-a-liner has the audacity to print that in the second half of the nineteenth century."

"Don't overestimate this century or its mental maturity," old Clarens said with a smile. "Our earth is probably millions of years old. But we think nineteen shabby centuries a mighty space. I always tell my boys in history class: Have no illusions. Mankind is in its swaddling-clothes."

Duran is not the man to be staggered by well-rounded sentences. In his mind danced and hummed all the editorials in all the papers for whose opinions he paid so much money. "Are we to have suffered in vain?" he asked in his declamatory manner, his right hand raised in false theatrical style. "Have the bonds of dogma been burst only that reactionaries may again feed us on their stale clerical messes?"

Hyacinthe de Lafite stared at his glass of bitters. "Personally

I find it a very pretty fairy-tale," he said. "You're quite right, Clarens. We are living at the dawn of some antiquity. Then why the devil shouldn't one of the heavenly beings, the goddess Diana, say, or the Virgin Mary or even a water nymph appear near a crumbling cave to some poor shepherd's or broom-maker's child? It's positively Homeric. I wouldn't exchange it for seven hundred scenes from modern novels in which red-haired bankers' wives deceive their husbands with the footmen or in which upstarts *à la* Balzac or Stendhal think they're blowing up the social order when they've got an aristocratic country wench with child. . . ."

J. B. Estrade regarded the poet with astonishment. "Did I understand you correctly, Lafite? Are you a believer?"

"A believer? I am the one genuine unbeliever of my acquaintance because, my dear man, I pray neither to the rosary *nor* to mathematical and chemical formulæ. I regard religion as an ethnological form antecedent to poetry. Don't look at me so sourly, Clarens. My definition is wholly irrefutable. Art is religion secularized. Consequently art *is* the religion of the nineteenth century."

The revenue officer pushed his chocolate from him with a frightened gesture. "What you say may be valid enough in Paris, but not among simple countryfolk like ourselves. As a good Catholic, which I am, I confess that I regard this story of the vision at Massabielle as troublesome and thoroughly objectionable."

"I have no doubt," the intolerant Lafite replied. "The reason is that all that is called religion today is mechanical repetition, empty convention, and political factionalism. So when an original human creature really experiences the presence of its divinities and sees the invisible in visible form in the manner of ages that were truly religious, then, of course, the conventional imitators are filled with moral discomfort. For nothing so irritates an age of faint and servile copying as the appearance of an authentic thing."

"But, Messieurs, Messieurs!" Duran besought them, gazing uncomprehendingly from one to another. "What are you talking about? The whole thing is an out-and-out piece of trickery. You know that a travelling circus from Pau has been in and around the neighbourhood for some time. It's easy to imagine some pretty equestrienne playing this trick on a poor stupid country child. . . ."

Lafite laughed. "That's a hypothesis, to be sure. It would be interesting to hear the hypotheses of you other gentlemen. What's yours, for instance, Monsieur le Receveur Principal des Contributions Indirectes?"

"Hypotheses of that kind come within the purview of the imperial prosecutor's office," Estrade replied with a bow toward the bald-headed Vital Dutour.

"You're in error, gentlemen," Dutour declared, speaking over his cold. "The authority of the State does not deal with hypotheses. All preliminary investigations are in the hands of the police." Thereupon he shook hands with Jacomet, who had just come to the table. "Anything new?"

The police officer wiped his forehead—mighty waves of heat were coming from Duran's monumental oven. "It's a raging madness." He shook his head. "I've received several reports. Callet reports a demonstration which took place in front of the Cachot. My daughter tells me that tomorrow half the town intends to accompany the Soubirous girl to Massabielle. And the brigadier of gendarmes, d'Angla, reports violent excitement in Omex, Viguès, Lezignan, and other villages."

"And all that," Duran wailed again, "in the middle of the nineteenth century. In our entire enlightened country Lourdes will fall into hopeless disrepute. What will they write in *Le*

Siècle, in *Le Journal des Débats*, and especially in *La Petite République?*"

"They will write nothing," Lafite said. "Don't overrate your importance. Only *Le Lavedan*, which is behind time again, will write about the affair."

"But we can't tolerate public demonstrations," the police officer remarked ponderingly. "What's the opinion of the imperial prosecutor on that point?"

Vital Dutour had to fight down a fit of coughing before he spoke. "The key question for the judiciary is this: *Cui bono?* Who is benefited? Coming to this present case, who is benefited politically? For don't forget that in our time every raised eyebrow has political significance. If the Virgin Mary appears to a day labourer's child today, a definite political motive must be attributed to her too. Her act is calculated to stir up the Church, hence the power of the hierarchy, hence the royalist party, which *is* the party of the Church even though the clericals appear today, as a matter of tactics, to be supporting the liberal regime. Hence the visions at Massabielle serve the restoration of the Bourbons, which is the avowed ambition of the French clergy. As representative of the imperial government I must therefore reckon this phenomenon among the effects of those incitements to treasonable action which have recently been quite seriously on the increase. According to the principle of *Cui bono?* it is logical to assume that behind this affair stand certain priests who are determined to kindle flames of fanaticism among the ignorant and discontented population in order to weaken the imperial government. Such, Messieurs, is my well-considered and far from hypothetical point of view. I beg you to give me another glass of mulled wine, my dear Duran. You've got a rotten climate here, in every respect. . . ."

Clarens smiled. "You're breaking butterflies on wheels, aren't you?"

The police officer expressed his agreement with the prosecutor. "Very clear and correctly reasoned."

But Estrade was most unpleasantly impressed. "The imaginings of a child are not religion," he replied. "Nor can you identify religion with the Church, or the Church with its clerical. These are by no means royalist as a body. I personally know priests with sincere republican leanings."

Hyacinthe de Lafite gaily rubbed his hands. "Hold on, gentlemen. Let's stick to the matter in hand. We've now heard two theories of a criminalistic character. Our friend Duran supposes a very pretty bareback rider who, dressed up as the Madonna, makes her daily appearances to the girl. And the imperial prosecutor believes that some priest, say our own Peyramale, dons the Virgin's costume and evokes these visions."

Dutour was sour. "I can't say that your humour is particularly hilarious. I didn't say that a priest is *in* this phenomenon but *behind* it."

"You gentlemen can't agree, eh?" said Dr. Dozous, having caught the last words. Shaking a shower of drops from his raincoat, which he did not take off, he sat down tentatively. "It's distressing, but I have just five minutes. . . . Unless I err, this cultured circle is discussing the same subject that everybody else is discussing."

"Right, and we are waiting for science to explain the wonder to us," Lafite said with a nod toward the physician.

"I know, Monsieur Lafite, that your scepticism embraces science, too, as you explained to me the other day between the Pont Vieux and the Place Marcadale. Here is a case, however, where science is really in its proper place, I mean that utterly unprejudiced, critical science which recognizes the existence of all phenomena, however incredible, and brings them under the observation of its microscope. . . . For myself, I have never yet had occasion to observe a case of genuine hallucination. I fully intend, however, to send a report on it to Voisin at the Salpêtrière."

"And you really intend to mingle with the rabble at the grotto?" Estrade asked in amazement.

"Oh, don't do that," warned Duran, approaching with fresh drinks. "That isn't worthy of a physician of your standing."

"I'm not, don't forget, just your local sawbones." A distrustful melancholy shadow flitted over Dozous's pale and still youthful face. "I've written a few things, and last autumn the University of Montpellier offered me a chair of neurology. You gentlemen probably know the high standing of Montpellier in the medical world. I refused because it seemed to me that I've gone pretty badly to seed here—not so badly by a long way, however, as to take no interest in a rare pathological case."

"Your opinion then, is, that we're dealing with a case of mental disease?" Dutour asked tensely.

"I have no right to make a diagnosis," the physician answered cautiously. "To be sure, the asylums are full of paranoiacs who see visions. But since I recall this little asthma patient quite clearly, I am unwilling lightly to assume a crass derangement of this kind."

Dutour pressed his inquiry. "Would you, then, be willing to speak of catalepsy, mesmerism, or hysteria?"

"Those are hard-and-fast words for very fluid facts and states, my dear friend. First of all we must observe the patient carefully during one of her attacks. I am told the daily pilgrimage to Massabielle will extend over two weeks."

The imperial prosecutor made a memorandum in his notebook. "I'd be deeply obliged to you, dear Doctor, if I could obtain an authentic account of your investigation."

"Why not?" Dozous asked, on the point of leaving. "I turn up here daily, if only for a moment, and I shall make no secret of my opinion."

Hyacinthe de Lafite had long been silent, staring the while into Duran's ultramodern kerosene lamps. Suddenly he said: "I find that all you gentlemen miss the essential point. The true problem is offered not so much by the little visionary as by the great crowd that follows her. . . ."

By four o'clock Antoinette Peyret came to deliver Élise's festive frock, refitted for Bernadette's use. And now for the first time in her life Bernadette faced her own life-sized image in a long mirror. Beside her knelt Antoinette, draping the satin into proper folds.

"I didn't know you could look so pretty," she said from out of a self-conquest of her critical nature.

Madame Millet, however, was openly enthusiastic at this transformation of a beggar's child into a child of Mary, for which she could claim the credit. "Pretty as a picture!" she exclaimed. "Our little seeress certainly makes a picture. A lithograph should be made of her."

Bernadette, blushing furiously, gazed as though she were seeing a mirage. She was so excited because until this hour she had not known how she looked. In the Cachot there was a broken bit of looking-glass but no real mirror. Hence Bernadette knew the figure, face, and garment of the lady far more exactly and in detail than she had known herself. It could have been said that the lovely one in the niche was far less a "vision" to her than her own image in the mirror. Penetrated by a wholly unknown sense of worthiness, her heart beat high. She felt a frightened rapture and an exquisite festiveness. For the first time tomorrow she would face that beloved being with some worth of her own. Would the lady notice the festive garment, the veil of tulle, the blue string belt, the homage which the imitation offered? Oh, the lady is always aware of everything; but will she be pleased with this outfit? Bernadette would have liked to run at once to Massabielle to show herself. She radiated the enjoyment of satisfied girlish vanity. Never again would she don her old smock and her faded *capulet*. These garments now disgusted her. And what will her mother say, and Marie and Jeanne Abadie and the Nicolaus, when to-morrow this new Bernadette appears among them?

From one of her innumerable neatly packed pasteboard boxes Madame Millet produced a white artificial rose and pinned it with a golden pin to the girl's breast. Bernadette uttered a little cry; the thing was so new and unaccustomed. She did not move away from the mirror. Darkness alone brought to an end the joys of this fitting.

Thereupon, again for the first time in her life, Bernadette sat in a proper dining-room at a white-decked table to eat a proper dinner. Philippe, wearing gloves, served an exquisite soup, brook trout with drawn-butter sauce, and a foamy sweet dessert, the like of which Bernadette had never tasted. The drink was a white Burgundy which titillated the tongue. Like many souls who have but meagrely satisfied the shyer appetences for joy Madame Millet insisted on a good cuisine. Antoinette Peyret, whose tirelessly busy tongue had got her an invitation to stay to dinner, was sharply watchful of Bernadette's table manners. She quite expected the ill-bred brat to loll vulgarly in her chair and to be unaccustomed to the uses of knife and fork. But since Bernadette's demeanour was faultless; since, frankly watching her hostess, she followed the latter's example and, to the astonishment of Philippe, helped herself to the prof-fered dishes with the neatness of a courtly lady, the dress-maker found the suspicion of the morning awake in her again: the girl was a hardened and thoroughgoing swindler who had thought out a gigantic fraud and was wearing this sleepy and indifferent air the better to hide her criminal talents. She, Antoinette Peyret, a bailiff's daughter, after all, had taken two years to learn how to behave herself with seemly freedom in the elegant houses of Lafite, Millet, Cénac, and this confounded brat took to it all from one minute to the next.

"Where did you get your good manners from, Bernadette?" she asked maliciously. Frost seemed to shake her and her crooked left shoulder rose almost to her ear.

"God teaches His beloved, dear Peyret," the hostess said. Whereupon the dressmaker determined hereafter to keep both her suspicions and her hostile feelings to herself. Millet, an idle, childish old woman, was evidently besotted about the little female sharper. Antoinette knew her patroness well enough to understand that, to keep her favour, one had to seem to share her boundless enthusiasms. Luckily, however, Madame Millet was also moody and forgetful.

At last Bernadette was permitted to go to bed. Madame Millet conducted her personally into the room of the idolized niece, lighted an extravagant number of candles, showed her the things there and explained them as in a museum, placed a box of sweets on the table, and finally embraced her with tears. And now Bernadette was alone, for the first time in her life too, in a room, an enclosed space. It seemed to her at once that this aloneness was the happiest privilege of wealth. She felt as though a heavy burden had been lifted from her back. She hastened immediately to Élise Latapie's tall mirror in order to gaze her fill upon herself in the festive frock. She took a long, long time for this enjoyment. Then and then only did she take up the little white bag which she always carried with her and the contents of which she counted and checked jealously every night. A knitted stocking was in the bag, two lit-

tle books—a primer and a catechism—a few bits of gaily
coloured silk which Madeleine Hillot had once given her, a
piece of brown rock-candy, a dry crust of bread, three glass
balls, and a tiny figure in tragacanth representing a miller's ass
with pack on back. Her earliest recollections went back to the
Boly mill. Such were the treasures which she kept and guarded.
Nothing was missing. With lost eyes she now peered about the
room, which was much larger than the Cachot in which six
human beings had to live. What a tiring room that was!
Here were no splotches of damp on the wall, but silken hangings with wreaths and flower arrangements upon them, pictures themselves and needing not her eyes' creative sight. The
very ceiling was painted with little angels. Here one would
have to stay in bed till ten o'clock merely to do justice to the
walls and ceiling. While Bernadette was putting out, one after
another, the magnificent candles provided here, leaving lit but
a single one on her bedside table, she suddenly caught sight
in a vitrine of the collection of tiny dolls which Élise Latapie
had gathered there. She and her sister Marie had never owned
any dolls, neither big nor little ones, except a single many-
coloured jumping-jack which Papa once, when he was still a
miller, had brought them from a weekly fair held at Saint-Pé de
Bigorre. But it had not been a sympathetic jumping-jack with a
nut-cracker face and screaming patches. He somehow bore a
relation to the he-goat Orphide and thus to that realm of the diabolic which seemed so often to pursue her. Élise Latapie's gay
little dolls came straight from fairyland. Breathlessly Bernadette
regarded them. She took a very special fancy to a little Tirolese
with a small flat green hat and a red bodice. It required all her
self-control to obey her mother's warning never to touch other
people's things. She was strongly tempted to put the green-
and-red little peasant doll into her bag. But she remembered

her father, who had been called for one fine morning by the policeman Callet on account of a piece of oakwood which he had not even seen.

With infinite care Bernadette took off the festive dress, the veil, the artificial flower, the white silk stockings, and the shoes. Slowly she felt herself becoming herself again. But this old self of hers now seemed far coarser to her than it had ever done. It felt to her almost as though she were some brown animal of the forest which, frightened and awkward, had to make its lair of this horribly soft and ice-cold bed. She even missed the hot, sleeping body of her sister, from which she had shrunk since last Thursday. But she was so weary that she fell asleep quickly despite the uncanny canopied bed.

When next morning at six the mistress of the house, Antoinette Peyret, and Philippe all came to wake her she was fully dressed. To their perplexity they observed that the girl had not put on her beautiful festive dress but her old smock, her *capulet*, her wooden shoes.

"What do you mean by doing this?" Antoinette cried. "Why didn't you put on your lovely dress?"

"I did put it on. But then I took it off again. . . ."

"Why did you take it off again?"

"I don't know, Mademoiselle. . . ."

"What sort of an answer is that?"

"I had to do as I did. . . ."

"Did someone bid you do that? The lady perhaps? . . ."

"No, no one bade me, and the lady isn't here. She's at Massabielle."

"You *are* a confusing creature."

Madame Millet was radiant. "I think I understand our little seeress. The frock of the sodality president didn't seem humble enough for her to appear in before the lady. Isn't that so, my child?"

Bernadette tried painfully to consider that explanation adequate. "I can't say exactly, Madame. It was just a feeling. . . ."

"Just hardened and pig-headed," murmured the dressmaker, who found it difficult to stick to her good resolutions.

In front of the Millet house in the Rue Bartayrès several hundred people were already waiting. In this crowd there were men, too—Uncle Sajou, Bouriette, Antoine Nicolau (who had made the trip to town for the purpose of being in at the start), and many others. Madame Millet scrutinized the assemblage to see whether it contained a single priest from either town or country, seeing that this strange matter fell well within the province of the Church. No soutane was to be seen. Mother Soubirous approached Bernadette in so subdued a way as though the child had already wholly escaped from her keeping. Only her sister Bernarde Casterot, who was visibly unimpressed by the rich Millet's pomp, gave her a bit of courage. Like many other women, Bernarde and Lucille were carrying candles. Upon Bernadette, too, a candle was half forced.

"Let's start!" the oldest of the Casterot sisters urged. Mother and aunts clung to Bernadette's heel. Next came the neighbour women of the Rue des Petites Fossées. There arose a deep, expectant murmuring. Bernadette spoke no word, saluted no one, was wholly unconcerned. She hurried forward, as though there were no one with her, as though this numerous following of mature and sober people were a quite subordinate and rather troublesome accident. And once again Antoinette Peyret could not restrain a rancorous sense of annoyance over the independent behaviour of Bernadette, inconsiderate and unchecked. Jeanne Abadie, no less, who with her schoolmates had been ordered from the front lines, hissed into Cathérine Mengot's ear: "She has to be first, of course!"

In truth, Bernadette did desire to reach the grotto first. The people were all so indifferent to her that it seemed to her most improper, and not unlikely to disturb the lady, were she to appear in the midst of this confused mob. Her eternally vigilant sensitiveness knew that association with the most gracious of beings was a matter so delicate as to have its own rules, which could be perceived only in the very depth of the soul and any slightest breach of which turned those very rules into sudden pangs of conscience. Even as she trembled for the lady's well-being, so she trembled with an equal fear of arousing her displeasure. Hence she leaped across obstacles of the way and, far ahead of all, raced down the last, steep path. Madame Millet stopped, struggling for breath. "She flies like a swallow," she panted, "like a leaf in the wind."

When the crowd with its burning candles, which made the whole place smell of molten wax, at last arrived on the natural platform facing the grotto, Bernadette had long been kneeling and had sunk into a state of rapture. The lady's benevolence at today's meeting had been intenser than ever before. She had shown more than benevolence, rather a deep-hearted joy which with its glow irradiated the countenance, the garment, even the eternally pallid hands and feet. She from whom blessing proceeded acted for the first time today as though she, too, were being blessed and as though she were not only giver but receiver; and this was so perhaps because through the fulfilment of her wish an important and far-reaching plan was beginning to be realized. She had come nearer Bernadette than ever; she had almost crossed the extreme edge of the rock; she had bowed so low that her long, delicate fingers seemed almost to touch the girl. Bernadette's consciousness, which hitherto despite an immeasurable desire therefor had offered a fear-tinged resistance to the state of utter rapture, had yielded this time on the instant.

"She is dying! Help!" It was Bernarde Casterot, the clever one, who uttered this soft cry, not otherwise than the stupid

schoolgirls had done on the Sunday before. And Louise Soubirous stared with horrified eyes at this creature, who had
issued from her womb but who now resembled one dying in a
state of bliss because she had conquered all earthly sorrow and
suffering, or rather like one dead, with nose already thin and
pointed, who yet smiled incomprehensibly because she was
redeemed from the long road of her martyrdom. Uninterruptedly Louise shook her head and moved her toneless lips. "It
isn't she . . . it isn't Bernadette. . . . I don't know my own
child any more. . . ."

A deep emotion had no less overcome the throng which,
densely packed, knelt beside the banks of the Savy and the
Gave. Now every human assemblage creates a personality of
its own and in some respects possesses other, more delicate
and less sense-conditioned perceptory nerves than the individual. These nerves were now aware in the empty hollow of the
rock of a presence—no indefinite one, but one of the sharpest
particularity of character. And even as a human head will
leave the impress of its form upon a pillow, or as any form
leaves its lineaments upon the plasticity of clay, so the felt
and highly characteristic presence in the grotto expressed itself through the bearing of the rapt girl which did not remain
rigid but like the image in a mirror repeated and gave back
what it beheld: the nodding, the smiling, the beckoning, the
folding or outspreading of the lady's hands. Bernadette was, as
it were, the perfect photographic negative of the invisible,
which thereby was brought for the onlookers to the boundary
of the visible. There were assembled on this spot many souls
prepared to believe, a few mockers, and a majority of the
merely curious. But all gazed breathlessly from the niche in
the rock to the mediatrix and from the mediatrix to the niche.
Their expectancy was satisfied. For the unexpected had become a presence. It evoked no emotions of celestial well-being,

but a shivering of the diaphragm and a devotion of unexampled power. The shivering of the diaphragm was most keenly felt by the mockers. For in every individual of this race which is man there lives an inborn inclination toward the suprasensual. Where it is most deeply buried it will, when invoked, be transmuted into a correspondingly deep discomfort. Suddenly a woman began the first Ave of prayer. Resonantly a chorus joined her in order to establish a kind of equilibrium with the invisible through the thunderous rising of many voices.

Bernadette seemed to hear nothing. A quite other noise sounded in her ears. Once more the Gave seemed in rebellious spate. Once more a rout in panic terror seemed to race across the river, comparable to the echo of galloping horses and rattling vehicles; once more the piercing cries arose: Flee, flee. . . . Avaunt from here! Fearfully Bernadette raised her arms toward the lady, whose countenance for the first time was stern and proud, as though her pilgrimage also was not at an end, as though she too had still to wage battles and vanquish her enemies. With wrinkled brow she looked attentively at the river, as though to tame it with her eyes' radiant blue. The uproar yielded at once. The hoarse voices crashed into silence. The immemorial rumbling and foaming of the Gave came to the lady's heel like a daunted wolf.

Of a sudden Bernadette arose and was the girl of every day. Beholding her mother's desperate face she threw her arms about her. Then many wept. . . .

Sunday morning the hour of the *apéritif* at the Café Français was always moved forward to ten o'clock. The place was crowded to the doors, for the rumour had spread that today Dr. Dozous would report the results of his investigation to the gentlemen at his table. The prosecutor Vital Dutour and the police commissioner Jacomet were already watching the clock with impatience. Both gentlemen had been invited to a secret conference in the mayor's office at eleven. During the past three days the happenings at the grotto of Massabielle had assumed proportions that forbade the authorities merely to look idly on. This very morning, for instance, a mob of more than two thousand people had gathered and had taken possession of the whole region on both sides of the waters. Above all had the surrounding villagers streamed thither in great masses. Thus it was high time to decide on whatever measures were to be taken. From the point of view of the public authorities the whole business was unbelievably delicate and difficult to manage. There were statutes enough to justify proceedings against any breach of the peace. But what kind of breach of the peace could be said to include the hypothetical appearance of the Blessed Virgin Mary as a fact not only accepted in all faith by a considerable part of both the rural and the urban populations, but ardently welcomed and acclaimed? Vital Dutour and Jacomet were both genuinely nervous, especially the imperial prosecutor, whose influenza should have kept him in bed and who was shivering with fever. Both hoped that the report of the municipal physician would point out some path to pursue. Precisely today Dozous had to be late. Another herald of science was present, namely the historian Clarens, who on the afternoon before had thoroughly examined the cave of Massabielle from both a geological and an archæological point of view. Clarens reported that the limestone of the grotto had a very odd habit of sweating. His words were exactly as follows: "Especially on the right hand, immediately below the niche with the thorn-bush, thick drops of sweat trickle across the stone."

Hyacinthe de Lafite refused to admit the comparison. "Why do you call the drops sweat? Why not tears? Are you, too, influenced by the dirt-grubbers of the realistic school? . . ."

"If tears seem more appropriate to you, my friend, let them be tears. *Saxa loquuntur*. In very truth! In this age the stones have reason enough not only to speak but to weep."

"All that's not important, Messieurs," Vital Dutour interrupted them. He was always irritated when those two gave vent to their glittering subtleties. "Did you discover nothing else?"

According to his own opinion Clarens had, in fact, made a discovery of some import concerning the niche in the rock. He was convinced that in immemorial ages it had been the scene of the practices of a heathen cult. The whitestone behind the niche's portal had probably been a sacrificial altar upon which the fruits of the field had been offered up to some primitive divinity. His researches had long since taught him that the whole mount of caverns had been not a profane but an archaic sacral region. The ill-repute of Massabielle fitted in wholly with this theory. The soul of Christianized humanity habitually retains dark memories of the scenes of pre-Christian cults, and fears them. The fear of the ancient gods is transformed into fear of the devil, for old gods who are forced to give place to new ones always become demons. Hence it had ever been the custom of the Church to redeem the old places of sacrifice by building basilicas on their sites.

Hyacinthe de Lafite was delighted. "Your theory confirms what I've been saying right along, namely, that this whole region of Bigorre is pre-Christian in character and that therefore the goddess Diana or some native water nymph might very well appear to a child of shepherds or broom-makers. For there's probably no fundamental mental or psychic difference between the peasant children of 100 B.C. and those of 1858 A.D."

Vital Dutour spoke out of his depth of suffering: "Gentlemen, these interesting and learned discussions get us nowhere at all and you've no idea how troublesome this mad business can become."

"If this business goes on," the police commissioner agreed with a glance at his powerful, useless fists, "we'll have to ask for military assistance against the demonstrations. No well-ordered regime can tolerate daily popular gatherings of this size. The calling-down which I expect from the prefecture won't be any laughing matter. Baron Massy's sense of humour is limited."

"It's a scandal," Duran wailed. "It cries to Heaven. Even the *Mémorial des Pyrénées* had two whole columns yesterday on what it entitled 'The Apparition at Lourdes,' and the last *Lavedan* printed a curiously weak-kneed article. The rumour is that Father Penès wrote it anonymously at the instigation of Peyramale in order to prevent worse consequences."

Vital Dutour glanced about him and lowered his hoarse voice to a whisper: "The phenomena in question are directed personally against the Emperor."

The astonished question was heard: "Why do you say that? Eugénie is bigoted enough. . . ."

"From the vantage-point of my position I probably know the masses better than you do, Messieurs. The Emperor governs at present by the suspension of law due to the national security enactment. But we Frenchmen are anarchists, all of us. If we can strike a blow at the ruling authorities, we despise no means. Well, both socialism and republicanism are old stuff by now. Let's try mysticism for a change. . . . But there's the doctor. . . . Where do you stand, Dozous?"

Today the physician carefully took off his top-coat and hung it on a rack. Then he sat down for once not fidgeting to go. His mood seemed far from gay.

Vital Dutour went for him without delay. "Did you conduct your investigations?"

"So far as it was possible," Dozous admitted tersely.

"And the result?"

"Not very considerable."

"Did you find a clinically tenable case of derangement?"

"I consider the girl no crazier than you or I."

"That is to say, she's a swindler?"

"There's not the slightest evidence for such an assumption."

"According to that I must presume, dear Doctor, that you have joined the ranks of believers in a miracle."

"O God Almighty!" cried Duran in horror and struck his hands together.

Dozous bowed slightly in the direction of the public prosecutor. "My name is Dozous. I contribute to the *Courrier Médical* and am a corresponding member of learned scientific societies. I reckon it an honour to be a scientist who makes no prejudgments. . . ."

Vital Dutour became zealously forensic. "Since you assume neither madness nor deception, your conclusion must be that the phenomena are genuine."

"Phenomena can be perfectly genuine subjectively without objective reality. . . ."

"Anyone who sees things that have no objective reality is just plain crazy. . . ."

"According to that, Shakespeare and Michelangelo were crazy, too," Lafite threw in.

Dozous took out of his inner coat-pocket three little sheets covered with handwriting. "I jotted down a brief memo on what I witnessed this morning. I'll probably send it to Voisin in Paris. It may be best if, in place of further discussion, I just read you the little that I have here."

The physician took off his nose-glasses, held his notes close to his near-sighted eyes, and, hesitating often and in a soft, indifferent voice, deciphered his notes. He paid little attention to his auditors.

" 'February 21, 1858. 7:10 a.m.

" 'I arrived at the grotto simultaneously with the crowd. Nevertheless, I succeeded in catching up with Bernadette Soubirous, who had arrived before the others. Behind the girl knelt her kinspeople, holding burning candles. She carried one too. She made a continuous series of courteous gestures, extremely graceful and reverential at once, toward the niche in the wall of the rock. These gestures were both droll and moving, since there was no visible object to which they were directed. She held her rosary in her hand but seemed not to be praying. Soon her face underwent the changes which had been reported to me. These changes mirrored faithfully the vision which the girl saw in the rock. . . .' "

At this point Jacomet cleared his throat with emphatic incredulity. Dozous, undisturbed thereby, continued the colourless reading of his notes.

" 'The observer almost had the impression that he saw what the child saw. There was an interchange of salutations, an eager smiling and rapt listening, a nod of deeply understanding assent —all this so vital in its verisimilitude that the greatest actor could not equal it. Gradually the child's face turned pale as white marble and the skin became so taut that the structure of the skull appeared clearly marked at the temples. I have observed the same transformations in T.B. patients in the last stages. There now seemed to supervene the state of mesmerization which has recently come to be called a trance. I bent over our patient for purposes of examination. I took her arm and felt her pulse at the radial artery. It was normal, scarcely too rapid. I counted sixty-eight beats per minute. The blood pressure, so far as palpation served, was neither too high nor too low, as it would be in an advanced case of cerebral anæmia, quite aside from a flattening and emptying of the pulse. Hence the pallor and the tautness of the facial epidermis could not be attributed to a violent circulatory disturbance. I have had frequent occasion to examine cataleptic patients during attacks at Montpeilier. In every instance the entire nervous system, including the pulse and blood pressure, was markedly affected. Hence in the case of Bernadette Soubirous we are not dealing with an affection of the nervous system, such as catalepsy or hysteria. In order to ascertain all possible symptoms I also examined, as far as I could, the eye reflexes. No anomaly here, either. The pupils were slightly enlarged, the iris somewhat contracted, and the whites gleaming and moist. But this is normal in anyone who fixes his vision intensely upon a definite object. Bernadette's trance, in fact, seemed upon the whole less a loss of normal consciousness than an enormous concentration of attention. She kept her burning candle in her hand. It was rather windy, and now and then a gust of wind would blow out the flame. She observed this each time it happened and without turning her face aside from the rock handed the candle to someone behind her to have it re-lit. During my examination I had the distinct impression that she knew exactly what was going on. . . .' "

"That, by God, is my impression, too," Dutour observed. But Dozous paid no attention to the interruption.

" 'Not till I was through did she arise and take a few steps forward over the rubble toward the niche. Close beside her I heard twice in succession a long-drawn-out "yes" wrung from her very depths. When she now turned toward us, her expression was wholly changed. Hitherto it had been one of a somewhat rigid joy; now it was a tragic mask of suffering and sorrow. Great tears rolled down her cheeks. . . . A few minutes later the vision had apparently vanished. Bernadette, normally pink and white again, herself announced the fact by a gesture. I asked her: "Why did you cry just now?" She replied at once most unaffectedly: "Because the lady wouldn't look at me any more but gazed beyond the people toward the Chalet Isle and the city. And she seemed suddenly so filled with grief and she said to me: 'Do pray for all sinners!'" Since I wanted to test her mental abilities I put the question to her: "Do you yourself know what a sinner is?" She answered without hesitation: "Certainly I know, Monsieur. A sinner is one who loves evil." That was quite a good answer. What pleased me was that she said "loves" not "does." After this, at all events, a diagnosis of feeble-mindedness was out of the question. The crowd about us had watched the foregoing scene like an exotic religious service, with the most acute attention. After a while it gave vent to an elemental storm of applause which oppressed me strangely, like a catastrophe of nature. But Bernadette paid no attention at all to the words of praise or benediction that descended upon her from all sides. She seemed not to have the faintest awareness of the significance which she had for these masses of people. She urged her followers to scatter quickly in order to escape from the annoyance of them.' Well, that's about all. . . ."

Dr. Dozous had read his rather confused notations painfully and with many pauses. He now folded the little sheets. There was silence. Even Duran, that enlightened but uncomplicated soul, did not know what comment to make. After a longish interval the imperial prosecutor lifted up his voice: "If I have correctly understood the report of science, it is this: Science excludes fraud; it excludes mental disease and a miraculous occurrence, too. I venture, then, to ask science: What is left?"

Thoughtfully Dr. Dozous repeated the question: "Yes, what *is* left? . . ."

CHAPTER FOURTEEN

An Interrupted Secret Session

MAYOR LACADÉ was walking restlessly up and down in his office in the Rue du Bourg. He wore the long morning coat in which he had officiated at a festive ceremony half an hour earlier, adorned by the tricoloured sash. As always, the rosette of the Legion of Honour burned in his buttonhole. But his brow was clouded. His clean-shaven sagging cheeks, below which the iron-grey beard protruded like a stone, were a deeper purple than usual. The cause of his rasped temper lay on the green table, at which was seated his aide Courrèges, father of red-haired Annette, who formed part of the group of girls about Jeanne Abadie. The object on the green table was an official communication from Argelès bearing the personal signature of the sub-prefect Duboë: "The Mayor of Lourdes is herewith requested to render at the earliest possible moment a report concerning the breaches of the peace known to have taken place there, as well as to communicate the nature of the measures taken by himself to quell the hereinbefore-mentioned riotous assemblages."

"Am I to send the Most Blessed Virgin to jail?" Lacadé fairly roared. "That's hardly my function. It seems rather the office of the imperial prosecutor. He may have her remanded for examination by the imperial gendarmerie. The State is the State, the civic community is only the civic community. I represent the latter. The distinction has evidently escaped the worthy sub-prefect. . . ."

"But, look, we've got to do something too, Monsieur le Maire," Courrèges warned him.

"Who knows that better than I?" Enraged, he pulled a heap of press-cuttings out of a drawer. "The whole provincial press is raking us over the coals; and as for the laughter of Paris, it won't seem funny to us. . . ."

Courrèges, who had been throwing glances at the door, cleared his throat. "I believe the gentlemen are waiting. . . ."

Lacadé pulled himself together and began to worry his beard with a pocket comb. "All right, ask them in. It's a secret session. Just the same, you stay in the anteroom in case I need a witness." With both hands outstretched, Lacadé received the prosecutor and the police commissioner. "I disliked breaking in upon your Sunday rest, Messieurs," he welcomed them in his sonorous oratorical voice, "but as the chief magistrate of our city I can no longer dispense with the support of the civil authorities. I've already received an official inquiry from the subprefect. Of course it exaggerates when it speaks of breaches of the peace. However, the entire liberal press is doing the same thing and is having a wonderful time at the expense of our city. We're beginning to offer a most regrettable subject of universal interest. I confess that I'd rather face a revolt of the slate-miners or the lumbermen than these disturbances which simply make no sense. We'd be less subject to ridicule. I've done everything in my power to work toward a modernization of our town, and see all my plans in ruins. Do you suppose that the railroad connexion will be granted us after this scandalous business? Like hell it will! And the new waterworks? We might as well forget about them. And the tourist trade from Paris and the medicinal springs that science was to discover? Everything gone to the devil. What Parisian is going to venture into a hole where there are no sanatoria but instead dirty caverns in which spooks perform their medieval antics? We're dealing with something more important than the babble of a little swindler or imbecile. . . ."

"I suggest," the bald-headed Dutour broke in upon the mayor's jeremiad, "that we begin by examining the legal situation."

"That's your office, Monsieur," the mayor sighed. He leaned back in his armchair, closed his eyes, and folded his hands over his softish belly.

With that voracity for striking inferences which fills every good jurist with lively satisfaction even in the throes of grippe and fever, Vital Dutour began his exposition: "The bare facts, Messieurs, are as follows: a fourteen-year-old girl of lowly origin and less than normal understanding asserts that she has visions of the supernatural. According to the criminal code, there is nothing in this situation that constitutes either misdemeanour or a felony which would empower us to take any steps. If the girl had characterized the subject of her vision as the Virgin Mary or the Mother of God one might, at least constructively, trump up a charge of an outrage against public religious sensibilities. But the Soubirous girl, according to my information, speaks persistently of 'the lady' or 'the young lady' or 'the beautiful lady.' Now, irritating as these expressions may be to a truly devout nature because of their naïve— I am tempted to say, impudently naïve—character, they cannot be interpreted as blasphemous in the sense of the law. A beautiful young lady is nothing but a beautiful young lady. The bare facts, consequently, give us no handle for any legal action."

With appropriate modesty Jacomet begged to be heard: "The imperial prosecutor will permit me to observe that the facts of the case would justify arresting the girl if a suspicion of either fraud or madness could be adequately supported. . . ."

"But, my very dear Jacomet," Vital Dutour observed with annoyance, "we've gone into all that. Didn't you just fifteen minutes ago hear with your own ears the report of our city physician Dozous? He flatly rejects both suppositions. I don't deny that the attitude of this representative of science got quite badly on my nerves. . . ."

The mayor indulged in a look of deep weariness. "You gentlemen persist in regarding the visions as the facts of the case. But these visions interest neither the State nor the municipality. It might not be a bad plan to forbid certain kinds of vision. But the most absolute type of regime possesses no means of doing so. I'm no jurist but a simple citizen of the land. Common sense tells me that the incriminating circumstances are not the visions but the incomprehensible mass agitations which they engender."

"If I hadn't been interrupted," Dutour said with emphatic boredom, "I would have reached that second point almost at once. Perhaps I regard this mass agitation and movement even more seriously than does the mayor. I clearly recognize its subversive, anti-governmental tendency. Now let us, however, regard the legal situation from the angle of the assemblages in question. What do all these people do? They call for the Soubirous child at her home; they escort her to the mount of caverns; carrying burning candles, they kneel before the grotto, they tell their beads; they give full utterance to their approbation and finally they disperse voluntarily. . . . Can that be forbidden?"

"It must be forbidden!" Lacadé cried with great bitterness.

"But how, my dear Mayor? Do you know any paragraph of any statute which would justify such action?"

"I don't suppose there is one," the mayor said hesitatingly.

The imperial prosecutor indulged in an ironical pause. "In point of fact, Mr. Mayor, there are two. The first of them you ought to know better than I. You'll find it in the Royal Ordinances concerning the Practice of Communal Administrations, issued on July 18, 1837."

"I'll have Courrèges look it up immediately!"

"Don't bother; I know the paragraph. It empowers any mayoral office to close to public traffic all streets, roads, bridges, fields, and any other localities of any kind whatsoever, on or in which the life or health of the inhabitants is likely to be endangered."

"By God, Monsieur le Procureur, you are a first-class lawyer!" Lacadé nodded. "Where was my head? This legal right to close streets and roads to traffic suffices for all purposes. And as a matter of fact the unfenced forest path across that mountain is dangerous to life and limb. I sincerely believe that, and I'm going to have the town-crier proclaim an ordinance to the desired effect this very day. . . ."

The imperial prosecutor had to fight down a long spell of coughing and sneezing. "I'd most strongly advise against any such thing at this moment!"

"I thought you were recommending it! And now . . . ?"

Vital Dutour fixed his eyes upon a portrait of Napoléon III. Nothing was visible in the wintry light except the blue-white sash of a decoration across the bosom of the formal evening coat. "My guiding star in the treatment of political questions has been this," he confessed, "never must any authority be guilty of a measure whose aim is too transparent. If you close the approach to Massabielle the believers will say that we're afraid of the Blessed Virgin; and the unbelievers will say exactly the same. We'll be the laughing-stock of both. Moreover, there remain three other approaches which cannot be said to constitute any danger. . . . The alternative legal possibility of which I spoke might be taken into more serious consideration. Maybe you know what I'm thinking of, Jacomet?"

"Good Lord, I'm just a plain policeman, Monsieur!"

Vital Dutour had taken off his signet ring. He now tapped with it on the table. "You gentlemen must know that the Imperial French government has established a concordat with the Holy See. I took the trouble to study this instrument yesterday. Article Nine provides that the Church may not open any new place of prayer without the formal consent of the Imperial Ministry of Culture. . . . Am I making myself clear?"

"You think this article can be employed by us?" Lacadé asked cautiously, not willing to expose his ignorance again.

"Yes and no. It depends exclusively on the Church."

"I smell the clericals behind the whole business," Jacomet declared.

"I hope you're right, my good man," said the prosecutor. "But Peyramale is very far from being a fool."

Adolphe Lacadé laughed heartily. "Just think of all the people this idiot child is drawing in! The Emperor and the Pope both personally signed that concordat."

Just then Courrèges was seen thrusting his head nervously in. "Did you make another appointment, Your Honour?"

"What a question! You know my appointment schedule better than I. . . ."

"Someone wants to speak to you. He insists. . . ."

"Now why this roundabout way? I have no secrets. . . ."

"There is a caller here," Courrèges burst out. "It's the Reverend Dean Peyramale himself."

Fast as his age, dignity, and weight permitted him Lacadé rushed into the anteroom, whence could be heard the warmest tones of his voice.

The priest named Marie Dominique Peyramale was an uncommonly tall and substantial gentleman of forty-seven. His strangely fiery countenance was furrowed and grooved beyond his years. He wore a fur overcoat and an astrakhan cap and hence at this moment looked more like an Arctic explorer than like the cantonal vicar of Lourdes. Between the clergy and the civil authorities of the South of France there frequently existed a state of tension. This was due to the well-tested policy of the insecure imperial regime of playing opposing forces off against each other in order to keep all in check. The South of France was ultra-Catholic; the people were but little influenced by modern nihilistic tendencies. Consequently many offices were given to the "disciples of Voltaire," as the elegant phrase ran.

The dean of Lourdes was by no means the man to fear these "disciples of Voltaire" or to let them make him nervous. Unlike most of those young civil servants, he had really read the great sceptic. Fear and shyness were not his predominant qualities, anyhow. Occasionally when, chilled to the marrow, he returned from his pastoral visitations, he would even drop in for a little glass of Calvados at the Café Progrès, that very den of liberalism. On such occasions it was amusing to see the lions of liberalism surround this Daniel, to be honoured by shaking his hand. Peyramale was of that conspicuous tolerance which is achieved only by those whose intolerance is bone-deep. By which is meant this, that he who still wavers and can still be shaken in his convictions must needs be publicly intolerant in his own defence. But a personality which, like Peyramale's, has been forged in the extremist fires can no longer be confused by contradictory views. He knew the truth to be true and in his fairly long clerical career he had not lazily accepted this truth but had won through to it in honourable battle. He was among those who had not just blindly and stubbornly turned away from the doubts of the age. But all that lay in the remote past now. The lions no longer made him shudder; rather, certain lamb-like creatures among his own colleagues who shivered at every cold draught. Under certain circumstances, moreover, Peyramale could become a high explosive. That happened if anyone, even a superior in the hierarchy, sought to interfere with his conduct of his sacred office or with his care of the poor. The latter function had been not a little criticized by the great world, as that world was represented by the Lafite family. The dean's preference for the very common people did not need—this was the point of the criticism—to be combined with such outspoken rudeness toward the better classes, even though he himself was admittedly the scion of a family of admirable scholars. He did not beg the rich for alms; he exacted tribute. Father Pomian, the aphoristic wit of Lourdes, once called him a *pétroleur* of mercy.

"Your Reverence will catch cold," Lacadé warned the dean, who refused to take off his furs. "Look at our poor prosecutor's condition."

The dean had a deep voice whose metallic resonance was always veiled by a slight hoarseness. This voice was the delight of the women of Lourdes. With its somewhat roughened mellifluence it now filled the mayor's office. "What I have to say can be briefly said. I know you gentlemen have a hard nut to crack. My purpose in being here is to help you. You are not to fall into the gross error of thinking that my chaplains and I attribute any religious significance to the so-called visions of Massabielle."

"I understand Your Reverence, then, to deny the possibility of a supernatural phenomenon?" Vital Dutour interrupted him.

"One moment, Monsieur. Not for an instant do I deny such a possibility. I simply do not regard it as probable that God Almighty should show us the grace of miracles. If the supernatural is to draw its veil aside, the necessary condition is a universal openness of soul. We are far enough from any such state. Hence I would refrain from using the exalted word miracle in this connexion at all. If this business at Massabielle is not pure fraud, as I assume, it is to be placed within the province of spiritism, animism, occultism, ghost-conjuring, and similar vain superstitions from which the Church averts its face in horror."

"How interesting and how refreshing!" Lacadé nodded his approval. "Does Your Reverence know the Soubirous girl?"

"I do not know her, nor have I the wish to know her."

"But wouldn't it be advisable," the imperial prosecutor asked, "if Your Reverence himself were to lay down the law to the girl in person?"

"I have no such intention, Messieurs. Please leave me out of it! It's the business of the authorities to deal with a minor who is either a criminal or a psychopathic patient."

"I thought Your Reverence had come to help us out!" Jacomet pleaded.

"I have done so in that I have instructed the cantonal clergy not to set foot in the grotto and to ignore the whole matter. I have reported to the bishop to the same effect. Furthermore, the teaching sisters, above all Sister Vauzous, have been insistently admonished to use an extreme degree of strictness to put an end to the mischief. That is all I can do."

"Your Reverence has an enormous power over the people here." Lacadé tried flattery. "You are a very apostle of the poor. Wouldn't it be appropriate for you to raise your voice?"

"I haven't any intention of adding further importance to this Shrovetide turmoil."

Peyramale clapped his fur cap on his huge head. "I wish you gentlemen an agreeable Sunday."

The mayor accompanied Peyramale to the head of the stairs. Returning, he asked: "Well, how about applying Article Nine of the concordat now?"

"The damned paradox is this," Dutour growled angrily, "by siding with us the old fox has stopped up that hole. A conflict with the ecclesiastical authorities would be much more to our purpose than this harmony. He's blandly shoved off on us the whole responsibility."

"Confound it!" Lacadé groaned. "Today there were two thousand people, tomorrow there will be three thousand, and next day five, and all we have are Callet and a couple of rural guards."

"I would like in all humility to make a suggestion," Jacomet made himself heard. "I don't know much about higher politics. But a man like me comes into daily contact with all kinds of shifty individuals—burglars, thieves, vagrants, drunkards, scamps of all kinds. That teaches you, in a way, how to scare people and how to apply pressure to them. Now, wouldn't it be the devil and all if I couldn't find a means of putting the fear of God into the Soubirous brat this very day and making her quit the whole tomfoolery? And if the girl is too scared to go to the grotto, why, this whole ghost business will fade out by tomorrow. So I'm asking you gentlemen to turn the case over to me for a bit."

"Not a bad idea, my dear fellow," Dutour said after a moment's reflection. "Not bad. And it's quite proper too, since you are the officer of first resort. However, I'd like to form my own opinion of the child, too. I'll examine her before you do quite informally in my house. Will you see about that? Agreed, Your Honour?"

Lacadé was on pins and needles. Noon was striking and he had a bad taste in his mouth. Bernadette had already cheated him of his forenoon glass of Malvasier.

"Act promptly, Messieurs!" he cried and grabbed his soft felt hat. "It depends on you whether Lourdes gets railroad connexions or not."

CHAPTER FIFTEEN

Open War

THE DRESSMAKER Antoinette Peyret had hoped that the moody widow Millet would before long have her fill of Bernadette and would sooner or later give the girl her walking-papers. Like many of the low-born she could not endure that another no better than herself should share her hunting-preserves, above all through her own fault. Had she had the faintest idea of the consequences, she would never have expressed her notion concerning the poor soul in purgatory. Unhappily Madame Millet continued to be foolishly fond of her little seeress and even Peyret, who knew her patroness thoroughly, could not foretell when a reaction and an end of the matter might occur. To Peyret's extreme astonishment a reversal of roles took place: it was not Madame who showed Bernadette the door; it was Bernadette who gave notice of departure. This thing happened on Saturday in the forenoon just before luncheon, to which Peyret had not been invited. Bernadette, who had just had a brief conference with her aunt Bernarde, approached her hostess with a deep curtsy.

"I thank you a thousand times for all your kindness, Madame, but I believe it would be better for me to return to my parents."

Madame was so shocked that her double chin began to quiver. "For Heaven's sake, my dear child! Don't you feel well and comfortable here?"

"Not any longer," Bernadette confessed quite frankly, adding at once, however: "But it's all my fault."

"Aren't you pleased? Isn't it lovely here?"

"It's far too lovely, Madame."

The eyelids of Peyret, who was present, went up and down, up and down. She expected an outburst of rage, such as she herself had often experienced. Again things were topsy-turvy. Madame Millet sniffed up a few tears. "You are a blessed child, Bernadette, and I must respect your decisions. We'll meet tomorrow at the grotto." She took both of the girl's hands, as though she couldn't bear the parting. "But do stay and eat with us. We're having rabbit stew. . . ."

"Rabbit stew," repeated Antoinette, her mouth watering.

"Thank you, Madame. But I think I'd better go right away," Bernadette pleaded. "May I say good-bye to Monsieur Philippe?"

After the girl was gone, Madame waved Antoinette away. "Better leave me alone today, my good woman. I need no company at meals."

On the way home her aunt Bernarde said to Bernadette: "I'd love to have had you at my house, not only because you're my godchild. You could have slept with your aunt Lucille in the attic. But the right thing for you to do is to go home to your family. The world has a very evil tongue. Everybody is lying in ambush, so to speak. Don't let it go to your head."

That warning was quite unnecessary. There was no danger of Bernadette's fame going to her head. She did not grasp its existence. What troubled her far more was that in the Cachot the old natural familiarity seemed hard to re-establish. Her mother acted paralysed, went about her tasks in silence and had tears in her eyes whenever she looked at her daughter. Father Soubirous acted extremely subdued, was as silent as Mamma, and his slightly emphatic show of being injured had given place to an entirely unemphatic embarrassment which choked Bernadette. It was horribly oppressive to see that Soubirous was ashamed of yielding to his favourite habit of going to bed by day. Maybe his daughter was a seeress; maybe she was something even different, as the old wives were whispering; God knew why she should be that. What was a master-miller's mind to do with stuff like that? It was certainly pleasanter to sit in a quiet corner in Babou's bar than to be the whole time in the presence of so superior a being.

Her sister Marie, too, most cosily intimate of all, behaved affectedly. Talking to Bernadette, she acted refined by mixing French phrases learned at school with the native dialect. Jean Marie and Justin simply avoided her as much as they could. There was something uncanny about their sister. Worst of all, there was company at the Cachot all day. Aside from the close neighbours, such as the Sajous and the Bouhouhorts, even Cazenave had to stick in his nose one day, and there came Maisongrosse, the baker, and Joséphine Ourous and Germaine Raval, and even so wealthy a woman as Madame Louise Baup, who brought her lady's maid Rosalie because the latter occasionally saw visions, too. And the venerable shoemaker Barringue, whose old hands trembled like aspen leaves, knocked at the door. He brought Bernadette a leather girdle which he had made with those trembling hands. On the porcelain clasp of that girdle was a picture of the Madonna. "There is your lady," said Barringue.

"No, that's not my lady at all," declared Bernadette to the artist's discomfiture.

Under these circumstances the family was happy that the Sajous let Bernadette sleep in a tiny chamber under the roof. And Bernadette was equally happy that she had privacy in which to reflect that of the fifteen days of the radiance of her great love only three had elapsed. Twelve more, twelve more, she kept repeating to herself. On this Sunday Louise had surpassed herself. She had exquisitely seasoned with garlic the saddle of lamb which the butcher Gozos had urged her to take for next to nothing. They were just sitting down to eat this sumptuous meal when the policeman Callet, old messenger of ill, appeared at the door. "Your young daughter there is to come along with me," he grunted, letting his pipe continue to hang in the left corner of his mouth.

"I knew it," Soubirous moaned out loud. "I knew it would come." He saw the same angel of judgment who had dragged him to prison by reason of a false informant's lie.

"Don't be scared," Callet laughed. "No order to arrest, this time. The imperial prosecutor would just like to take a bit of a look at your girl. . . ."

"Won't you let her finish eating?" Louise implored. At this moment it seemed to her of supreme importance that her child be not robbed of this rare repast.

"No need for hurry," the guardian of public order agreed. "People ought to eat slowly and enjoy their food. The court can wait."

In spite of his good-natured tolerance he was surprised that, contrary to all experience, the supposititious delinquent cleaned her plate not only calmly but almost with a certain sloth.

Vital Dutour, still thoroughly miserable with his cold, had had nothing but a cup of hot broth. Interrupting himself he went into his study the moment that Bernadette was announced. The light in this room was dim. But in the fireplace the flames danced and crackled about four logs of larch wood bigger than any Bernadette had ever seen. The State furnished its servants with excellent fuel as extra compensation. Since he had caught this heavy cold Dutour had had his desk moved nearer the fire. His back to the window, he now observed the delinquent through his lorgnon. He bade her approach the desk. His first impression was: perfectly normal. A proletarian child of this region, like a hundred others. Next he was struck by the poverty of Bernadette's garments and by the fact that her not ungraceful little figure seemed less clothed than swathed. First there was this queer *capulet*. Dutour, who had come to this region but recently and had no knowledge of the costumes of the peasantry, took it for a shawl such as was worn by the women of Madras. Yet this shawl was so faded that the ornaments on the hem were no longer recognizable. By throwing the round face into deep shadow the garment seemed to lend it a great charm. The formless smock fell to the very feet in their tiny wooden shoes. The whole figure was like a sculptor's work which the artist has put aside half finished. Every fold of the garment, the interplay of light and shade, all made the impression of something begun, uncompleted, indicated merely. The eyes, to be sure, those large, dark, hooded eyes, were anything but tentative in character. Despite himself the prosecutor recognized them as the eyes of a woman harbouring a great love. Not rarely had he met such women's eyes in the courtroom, clear, alert eyes, eyes sharply on guard to defend a possession of the heart.

"Do you know who I am, my child?" the bald-headed man began the interview, nervously pulling his stiff cuffs forth from his sleeves.

"Oh, yes," Bernadette answered slowly. "Monsieur Callet told me that you were the imperial prosecutor."

"And do you know what kind of man that is?"

Bernadette leaned gently against the desk and looked at Dutour attentively. "Not quite, no."

"Let me explain to you, my dear child. His Majesty the Emperor of the French, who is the sovereign of us all, has placed me here to see to it that any wrong done be discovered and expiated, such, for instance, as lies and fraud which someone may perpetrate against his neighbour. . . . Now do you quite understand who I am?"

"Oh, yes, you're much the same as Monsieur Jacomet."

"A good deal more. I'm his superior officer. He hunts down the criminals and swindlers. Then he sends them to me that I may turn them over to the courts and the penitentiary. You will be examined by Monsieur Jacomet on this very day. I've summoned you here, however, not because I'm Monsieur Jacomet's superior officer, but because I'm sorry for you and desire to warn and to help you. If, in fact, you tell me the whole truth and act sensibly, I may be able to spare you the examination by Monsieur Jacomet. Let us see what can be done for you."

The girl's eyes, intent upon defending a great love, looked very guardedly at the man's face. He lowered his voice a little.

"A great tumult has been caused by your small self in this town. Doesn't it fill you with any fear and dread? I ask you in all seriousness, Bernadette: do you intend to go to Massabielle again tomorrow morning?"

Bernadette did not prevent her eyes, so tranquil as a rule, from sudden flaming. "Of course, I must go twelve times more to the grotto," she answered immediately. "The lady desires it, and I have promised."

"Now there you go with this lady," Dutour said in a disappointed tone, as though he had expected better of the girl. "You'll admit, my child, that you're not clever and very ignorant. You're the worst pupil in the whole school. The court, you see, is informed. You can't deny that all your schoolmates, even far younger ones, excel you in reading, writing, arithmetic, and even in religion."

"That is true, Monsieur. I am very stupid."

"You admit, then, that your schoolmates are brighter than you. Now reflect, my child. How is it about the grown-ups? And how is it especially about those among the grown-ups who have spent years in studying and possess whatever knowledge is to be had in this world? I'm thinking of people like Father Pomian and myself, for instance. Now we, who ought to know, assure you that this lady whom you say you see is a childish bit of imagination and an absurd dream. . . ."

"The first time I saw the lady," Bernadette said, "I thought too that it must be a dream. . . ."

"There you are, my girl. That wasn't so stupid. But now you reject the advice of old and learned men!"

Bernadette smiled her deep womanly smile. "Once you can mistake a dream for reality, not six times."

Vital Dutour listened sharply. What a striking answer! Hallucinations differ from dreams, evidently. He, who was no great dreamer before the Lord, had to venture out into unknown territory. "It happens that one has the same dream repeatedly."

"But I do not dream," Bernadette declared vividly. "This very morning I saw the lady exactly as one sees other people. And I spoke with her exactly as one speaks with others."

"Let's drop that for a moment," Dutour parried. In this matter of the supernatural he felt at a distinct disadvantage before the delinquent. "Tell me how you people live at home; I mean, how things are going with you."

Bernadette gave her account with the frankness of the simple poor, uninhibited by middle-class pride or reticence. "Till ten days ago it was very bad, Monsieur. We had nothing to eat except corn-mush. But now Mamma works for Madame Millet three times a week and Papa has a job with Monsieur Cazenave. . . ."

The prosecutor gave evidence of great satisfaction at this account. "So this lady of yours seems to have her practical side. What is this story about Madame Millet?"

Bernadette gave him a long look before she replied: "I don't know what you mean, Monsieur."

"Oh, yes, you do, my child. Remember, the court knows everything, everything. You're concealing the fact that you're living with Madame Millet."

"That is not true. I don't live there any longer. I slept there only two nights, last Thursday and Friday."

"Nevertheless, you were a guest in one of the richest and most luxurious houses in Lourdes. You would never have entered it without your lady."

Bernadette made so vigorous a gesture that her hood fell and revealed her dark hair. "Madame Millet called for me and begged Mamma to let me be her guest. I did it to give her pleasure, not myself. It was no great pleasure to me."

"How about the white silk dress?" the prosecutor asked sharply.

"I never wore it. It's in Mademoiselle Latapie's clothes closet."

The imperial prosecutor arose and pushed back his armchair. "Be careful, Bernadette. You see that the court knows everything. The court knows about the presents which everybody sends you and your parents. If the court were to conclude that your lady represents an excellent and profitable business scheme, you would be lost, destroyed. . . . But I offer you my hand in helpfulness. I'm willing to save you even the examination by Jacomet, which is the first step toward imprisonment. What I ask is simple enough. I am not asking you to abjure or retract anything. Promise that you will obey me, for I represent the court by whose pursuit you are threatened."

"If I can do so, Monsieur, I will obey you," Bernadette said, unperturbed.

"Then put your hand in mine and promise that you will go to the grotto no more."

Bernadette withdrew her hand, as though she had touched fire. "That I cannot promise, Monsieur. I must fulfil the lady's wish."

Vital Dutour's nether lip shot out. "So you reject my help. Consider well. This is my last warning."

Bernadette's head drooped a little. Her face flushed slightly. "I must go twelve times more to the grotto," she whispered.

To his own astonishment, Dutour found it hard to keep his self-control. "We're through, then!" he almost roared. "I need keep you no longer. You are intent upon your own destruction. . . ."

Left alone, he felt thoroughly ashamed. Court practice had accustomed him to cheap victories through his position of antecedent advantage. There he had dealt with contrite and broken souls who whined for mercy. "I am stretching out my hand to you to save you." That was a prosecuting attorney's standing phrase which never failed of its effect. Usually the accused would reply to it with flattered tears. The girl had shed no tear. In spite of the proffered poisoned mixture of threats and helpfulness, tried innumerable times and never known to have failed, the girl had remained obdurate. Worse, worse, instead of his having shaken the girl in her assurance, she had shaken him out of his. Thus the result of this examination was a flat moral aftertaste which applied to his own life. For several minutes he knew with complete awareness that the reproach of opportunism which he had hurled at this poor starveling applied overwhelmingly to himself. What was his entire so-called career but a pliant betting on whatever tendency seemed to prevail? Strange how this girl really had something to defend, though it was but a phantom of her mind. By that, by virtue of that mere phantom, she was securer of moral quality than he. What he defended meant nothing to him. Today its name was

Napoléon; yesterday it had been called Louis Philippe; tomorrow it might bear the name of Bourbon or even of some intriguing lawyer. The State with a capital S. Ha ha. . . .

Frightened, he faced his mirror. A subaltern face grinned back, a morose paper face with a red and swollen nose in the middle. And so it actually happened that the imperial prosecutor really poked out his tongue in derision at his own mirrored image. Then he consoled himself: Jacomet will manage the matter; Jacomet is a tougher customer than I.

With this hope in his heart he swallowed his medicine and went to bed.

After this first successful skirmish with the power of the State, Bernadette took refuge in the church. Hidden in a dark corner, she felt securer than at home. She was badly afraid of Jacomet, who in her father's case had played the part of so implacable a persecutor. The commissioner, however, knew where to find her. He had taken it upon himself to watch her in person. When, after vespers, Bernadette slipped out of the portal amid the crowd of worshippers, Jacomet met her with an extremely friendly air and gave her shoulder a paternal pat. "I've got to trouble you to come over with me for a minute, dear child. It won't take long."

It was no arrest, but a kindly invitation. Nevertheless, a crowd at once surrounded the couple. Bernadette appeared to be quite calm. She told her aunt Lucille, who stood next to her, to inform her parents. The crowd, however, took up arms, as it were, against the commissioner. Mocking cries arose: "Pretty big fellows to arrest children! You're not so big when it comes to their starving, eh?" Other voices muttered: "Careful, Bernadette! Don't say nothin'! They want to get somethin' on you!"

The office and dwelling of Jacomet were on the ground

floor of the house of the Cénac family, who, like the Lafites, Millets, Lacrampes, and Baups, belonged to the patrician group of Lourdes. The house was situated on the Place Marcadale. The floor above Jacomet was occupied by the tax-collector J. B. Estrade, who lived there with his sister, an elderly maiden lady. Estrade had begged his neighbour to permit him to be present at Bernadette's examination. Dozous's account, as well as the enthusiasm of his sister, who had joined the last pilgrimage to the grotto, had aroused his interest, even though his strong aversion to the matter persisted; for, both as an economist and as a student of sound literature, he had little patience with occult extravagances. He was already waiting in the big armchair with its white-buttoned cover of black oilcloth when Jacomet, accompanied by his victim, entered the office. This was a room with but one window. The furnishings consisted of the armchair, Jacomet's desk, two file cabinets, a wastepaper basket, and a cuspidor. There were only two chairs. Hence Bernadette had to remain standing. After Jacomet had sharpened a pencil and placed a sheet of legal paper in proper position he began according to formula: "Well, now, what's your name?"

"But you know my name." Bernadette was immediately frightened by her own answer. She had begun to perceive the effect of these formal constatations. Hence she added at once: "My name is Soubirous, Bernadette. . . ."

Jacomet put down his pencil and continued in a fatherly tone. "My dear Bernadette, you probably haven't a clear notion as to what is now going on. Look, with this pencil I'm going to write down everything you say. These things that you say will add up to what is known as a deposition and this deposition will form part of a dossier or file of information marked with your name. Now to have a police dossier bear your name isn't a very pleasant circumstance, my poor child. Decent people, especially young girls, don't have such things happen to them. But I'm not through yet. I'm sending your answers this very evening to His Excellency the imperial prefect at Tarbes. His name is Baron Massy and he is a very powerful and a very stern gentleman with whom it is better to have no dealings, if possible. I hope you understand now what we're doing. All right. Now tell me how old you are."

"I'm fourteen, Monsieur."

Jacomet's pencil remained poised in air.

"You don't say so. Sure you're not exaggerating?"

"Oh, no, I'm going on fifteen."

"And you're not through school yet!" Jacomet sighed. "Your parents certainly have a hard time with you. You ought to try to be a help to them. What do you do at home?"

"Oh, nothing special. I wash dishes, I peel potatoes; often I keep an eye on my little brothers."

Jacomet pushed his chair back from his desk and squarely faced the delinquent. "And now, my child, give me a full account of your experiences at Massabielle."

Bernadette crossed her hands over her stomach, as peasant women and women of the people do the world over when they stand at their gates and gossip about the happenings of the day. She inclined her head slightly toward her left shoulder and fixed her eyes on Jacomet's sheet of paper, which he rapidly covered with writing as her narrative proceeded. It was a curious circumstance that by dint of much repetition her tale had come to sound smooth and almost mechanical.

"Pretty crazy story," Jacomet said at the end with appreciative emphasis. "Do you know who the lady is?"

Bernadette's eyes opened wide. "No, naturally I don't."

"Pretty quaint sort of lady. Elegant as everything and hangs out where Leyrisse herds the swine. . . . How old would you say she is?"

"Sixteen or seventeen."

"And you say she's very good to look at!"

Convulsively Bernadette pressed her folded hand against her heart. "She is more beautiful than anything else in the whole world."

"Listen, Bernadette, you remember Mademoiselle Lafite who got married a few weeks ago. Is the lady better-looking than she?"

The comparison amused Bernadette. She laughed. "You just can't compare the two, Monsieur."

"Well, anyhow, your lady stands quite still, doesn't she, like a statue in church?"

"Oh, no, she doesn't at all." Bernadette was hurt. "She's ever so natural; she moves and comes nearer and talks to me; she greets the people and even laughs. Oh, indeed, she can even laugh."

Jacomet scrawled a five-pointed star on his official paper. Without lifting his eyes from this idle exercise he changed his tone a trifle. "There are people who say the lady entrusted you with mysterious secrets."

Bernadette fell silent for a space. Then she said softly: "True. She told me something that was meant for me alone and that I must not repeat."

"Not even to me or to the imperial prosecutor?"

"Not even to you or the imperial prosecutor."

"But suppose Sister Vauzous or Father Pomian were to ask you?"

"I couldn't tell them, either."

"But suppose our Holy Father in Rome were to command you?"

"Not even then. But the Holy Father in Rome would not do that."

Jacomet grinned over at Estrade, who sat very still, his

shiny hat on his knees, his cane in his hand. "Stubborn little thing, eh? . . . Tell me, little one, what do your parents say to all this business? Do they believe it?"

Bernadette considered at far greater length than she had yet done. "I do not believe that my parents believe," she declared hesitatingly.

"There you have it." Jacomet's smile retained its paternal quality. "And you ask me to believe if your very parents don't? If your lady were a real lady, wouldn't other people see her too? Why, anyone might come along and say that every day at dusk he saw a mysterious chimneysweep who whispered secrets to him that he couldn't tell anybody else! Well, that would impress stupid people just as much. Am I right? Admit it, Bernadette."

Bernadette sank into apathetic silence at the policeman's wit. The latter was now determined to take the offensive with the tried and tested tricks and stratagems used against petty offenders. "Now pay attention, Bernadette," Jacomet admonished her. "I'm going to read your answers back to you, so that you can confirm their correctness. Then I'll send them to the prefect. Ready?"

Bernadette came closer to the desk in order that no word might escape her. Jacomet began to read off his notes in his most indifferent official tone. He came to the description of the lady: " 'Bernadette Soubirous declares that the lady wears a blue veil and a white girdle.' "

"A white veil and a blue girdle," she interrupted him at once.

"Impossible!" cried Jacomet. "You're contradicting yourself! Admit that you spoke of a white girdle."

"You made a mistake in writing it down, Monsieur," Bernadette asserted calmly.

But the police officer had been far too successful in the use of this flypaper method, as it were, to recede from his position. The game continued at a great rate. The delinquent listened tensely.

" 'Bernadette Soubirous declares that the lady is about twenty.' "

"I declared no such thing. The lady isn't quite seventeen."

"Not seventeen! How do you know? Who told you?"

"Who should have told me? I saw it for myself."

Jacomet glanced at Bernadette. After a lengthy passage of correct notation he tried his luck for the third time. " 'Bernadette Soubirous declares that the lady exactly resembles the statue of the Blessed Virgin in the parish church.' "

Anger now flared up in her and she stamped her foot. "I said nothing so silly! That's a lie. The lady has nothing to do with the Blessed Virgin in the church!"

At this point Jacomet sprang up. It was time to proceed to the second degree of torture applied to petty offenders. "That's enough!" he roared. "Don't imagine that you can play a game with me. God help you if you lie! Nothing but a complete confession can save you. Tell me the names of all persons who are in league with you. I know them, you know."

Bernadette recoiled and turned pale. Never had any human being roared at her like that. There was a deep amazement in her calm voice. "I don't understand the things you are saying, Monsieur. . . ."

Jacomet unleashed his planned and official rage. "Oh, you don't? Well, it takes me to tell you. Certain persons, whose identity is known to me, have put you up to circulating this disgusting story about your visions. They trained you, stupid as you are, down to the smallest detail, and now you go around reeling off by rote what they taught you to say. Hell, didn't I hear with my own ears just now that you'd got the whole story by rote?"

Bernadette had recovered her self-possession. "Ask Jeanne Abadie whether anyone put me up to it. She was there the first time. . . ."

"Well, of course, it's nothing to me whether you confess or go to jail," said Jacomet. He took the girl's hand and drew her to the window. "Tell me what you see out there?"

"A great many people are standing in front of your house, Monsieur."

"Well, all those people won't help you and can't help you. Because three gendarmes are out there too. See yonder! That's the brigadier d'Angla, with Belhache and Pays. They're waiting for me to order them to take you to jail. Don't be your own worst enemy. Monsieur Dutour, the prosecutor, ordered you not to go to Massabielle any more. Before Monsieur Estrade here as witness, declare that you will obey."

Bernadette whispered: "I must keep my promise."

For the first and only time Estrade intervened. "My dear child," he admonished Bernadette, "the commissioner really has your welfare at heart. Heed him, and promise."

Bernadette gave the stranger a brief glance. It convinced her that he had no mandate to interfere in her dreadful conflict. Hence she disdained to answer him, and Estrade felt an access of shame, as though someone had reprimanded him.

"You want me to call the gendarmes?" asked Jacomet.

Convulsively Bernadette's fingers clasped her little bag. "If the gendarmes take me away, I can't help it."

"That's not the end of it." Jacomet continued to apply pressure. "I'll have your father and mother thrown in jail too. Not my business if the rest of the family starves. Don't forget that your father was in jail before and he wasn't suspected of any such gigantic fraud as this."

Bernadette bowed her head so low that her face could not be seen. A long, long silence. This had been the third degree and took time for its full effect. Instead of an answer from the girl there was heard a repeated soft rapping at the door.

"Come in!" The commissioner's tone was rasping. He needed relief. In the frame of the door appeared the tall form of Soubirous. He stood there, uncertain of himself, stripped of his usual dignity, twisting his cap in his fingers. In the expression of his eyes there alternated humble fear and lightning-like anger. Probably he had drunk to give himself courage, but had not drunk enough.

"What the devil are you doing here, Soubirous?" Jacomet fairly screamed.

Soubirous, breathing heavily, stretched out his arms toward Bernadette. "My child, my poor child—that's what I want."

Jacomet suddenly decided to be civil again. "Listen, Soubirous. This damned business at the grotto has got to come to an end. I won't stand it any longer. Tomorrow, by God. Get me?"

With all his might François Soubirous beat his breast with both fists. "So help me God, Chief, that's all I want! It's got to stop. It's destroying my wife and me."

Jacomet gathered up his papers. "The girl is a minor," he grunted. "You're her father and responsible to me. You've got to forbid her to go out except to school. If necessary, lock her up at home. Otherwise I'll lock you all up, the whole bunch, I swear to you. I've got good grounds. And I'll have you watched night and day. Now you can go, with my blessing. But God help you if I have to summon you again!"

Out of the Cénac house Bernadette came with her father, her head still bowed. She gritted her teeth. She did not want to cry here, not till she got home to her little room under the roof. The square was black with people. A dark murmuring came to her: "Don't give in, Bernadette. . . . You've held your own bravely. . . . There's nothing they can do to you. . . ."

But all that Bernadette heard was her father's self-pitying voice: "Look at this scandal, my child. We owe it all to you."

Only the most faithful followed her to the Rue des Petites Fossées. At their head marched Antoine Nicolau, swinging a club. "I would have come to fetch you, by my faith, Bernadette. . . ."

She scarcely noticed her knight. She had to struggle for her breath, which came harder and harder.

The police commissioner turned to the imperial tax-collector. "Well, neighbour, what do you make of it?"

Estrade rubbed his forehead as though to soothe an ache behind it. "The girl didn't lie," he said briefly after a pause.

Jacomet laughed a deep self-satisfied laugh. "There you have the naïveté of the layman. Among the most hard-boiled customers I don't recall a single one more astute or keen-witted or stronger-willed than this young girl. Didn't you observe how subtly she formulated her answers; how she calculated every move and didn't walk into a single trap? She didn't, by God, give in till the very end. And if her old man hadn't come in, I don't know now just how I would have managed."

Estrade shrugged his shoulders. "What good would it do her to go on with a swindle as dangerous as this?"

"It's the intoxication of success, my dear man; it's the applause; it's the very playing of the part, not to mention the gift. The human soul doesn't present much of a problem to us who are in police work. . . . And do you imagine that saints, if actually under police examination, would behave as hard-boiled as this little practitioner of a sort of celestial imposture?"

"Come, come, my dear friend. Who's talking of saints or heaven? I am convinced that the girl does not actually reflect concerning the odd and eerie character of her experience.

She accepts it as given. It fascinates her and hence she exerts a fascination upon others. Yes, that's what I felt as I listened to her. . . ."

Jacomet's smile was one of indulgence. "My dear sir, taxes are your specialty and police work is mine. You have a deep insight into the conduct of financial affairs and I have some modest skill in analysing the souls of the plain people. In this department of psychology you can keep your shirt on and rely on good old Jacomet."

CHAPTER SIXTEEN

The Lady and the Gendarmes

Sister Marie Thérèse Vauzous stood facing her class. Her delicately moulded countenance, meant by nature to be beautiful, was more haggard than ever. The eyes were deep in their hollows and the lips narrow and tight. The very children could see how miserable their teacher looked. It was all due to the nocturnal vigil which Sister Marie Thérèse had kept from last night until this morning.

Dean Peyramale had commissioned Chaplain Pomian to act in a certain matter. The catechist, however, called suddenly to Saint-Pé, had delegated the task to the teacher. Not easy, this task of which Pomian had rid himself. The nun Vauzous passed the night poring over difficult books which seemed to throw no light on her problem. What the dean demanded was merely this, that in the presence of all her fellow-pupils Bernadette be told in appropriate terms that it was, at best, a shameless piece of arrogance for a young girl who had not yet even made her first communion to assert blandly that she was having intimate personal intercourse with the Most Blessed Virgin. Peyramale had literally insisted, moreover, that stress be laid upon the comical side of this example of youthful muddle-headedness. The whole thing had started among schoolgirls. He nursed the hope that it would be buried under the jeering laughter of these very girls. The deadliest weapon against extravagance is ridicule. In choosing Pomian, Peyramale had used good judgment. For Pomian was quite a humorist, if not so vigorous and popular a one as the dean himself. Sister Marie Thérèse, unluckily, had not a spark of humour. She came of the strictest French society, which is on principle averse to taking anything as a joke. Her father was a royalist general who had once taught at Saint-Cyr and been pensioned off by the Emperor. Her mother's father had been so conservative a professor of political science that the famous de Maistre was in comparison a noisy rebel. Military and professorial scrupulousness were in Sister Vauzous's very blood. Thus it came to pass that during the night of preparation for her task she had read many sublime and dense and difficult pages concerning the problems of grace, freedom, sin, merit, and had, in truth, got into deep waters. Especially the problem of grace had weighed upon her mind. Hence at this hour Sister Marie Thérèse was deeply stirred and weary and peaceless. What her mind had never permitted her to doubt had suddenly become questionable to her burdened heart, namely, the quality of the sacrifice of her own life. For the ambition of a powerful spirit does not stop at intermediate or penultimate aims. Do strictness, prayer, work, extrication from humanity, mortification of the flesh, humiliation of the mind, as she practised them, suffice to attain the ultimate goal?

She cast a glance at the left corner seat on the sixth bench of the centre row. Bernadette was present after a whole week's absence. While all the girls chattered in their usual way she sat in silence with eyes lowered upon her desk. The girl seemed extremely crest-fallen after the authorities had yesterday, Sunday, put a stop to her wild goings-on. Thus the nun reflected.

"Soubirous, Bernadette," she called out. "Come forward and stand before the class."

Bernadette slunk past the acrid whispering of the class and stood, as she had often done, in the place of trial and testing.

Sister Marie Thérèse paid no attention to her, but turned to the class.

"My dear children! We shall discuss a matter today that doesn't belong to our studies and is not mentioned in the catechism. The catechist will not question you concerning it, nor need you learn it. But you mustn't chatter, either, but pay attention and really try to understand, for it is important. You girls know, and indeed I've told you so many, many times, that all human beings are sinners, one a greater and one a less, but all, all. If, as our holy religion demands of you, you were veraciously to search your consciences, what would you find? Untruth toward your parents and toward others too, in which you have indulged during nearly every waking hour. Perhaps even covetousness of other's possessions. In any event, there is inattention during Holy Mass, careless saying of the rosary, laziness, insincerity, pertness, evil thoughts, not to speak of all your habitual small naughtiness. There, for instance, Cathérine Mengot is biting her nails again! Now listen carefully. The Lord didn't make us all alike. Some have a heavier burden of sins and faults to bear and some a lighter. Perhaps in our very city there are a few less afflicted with faults than their fellows. But if there are such, they are not among us here. Did you follow me, Bernadette Soubirous?"

"Yes, Sister," Bernadette replied in a tone of complete indifference.

"Or are you of the opinion that there is one among us who is worthier than her fellows?"

With some surprise Bernadette looked at the nun out of eyes that also showed the weariness left by a sleepless night. "No, Sister," she said mechanically.

"I appreciate your humility, Soubirous." The nun nodded. She had honestly earned the class's laughter. "Silence! Let's go on. In His infinite goodness God has in the course of the ages caused to appear on earth a very few exceptions in human form, that is, men and women, such as we do not know, who committed almost no sins or faults, who neither lied nor coveted what was not theirs, nor prayed spiritlessly, nor were insincere or lazy or impudent, nor scratched their heads in so ill-bred a way as Annette Courrèges is doing this moment! These exceptional people who were all but sinless you have come to know in sacred history. Who can name one of them? Soubirous!"

Bernadette did not open her lips. Already the hand of Jeanne Abadie was wildly waving.

"Well, Abadie, whom can you mention?"

"Saint Joseph," fairly burst from the girl.

"I don't know why you should be thinking of Saint Joseph," the nun said, wondering. "Be that as it may. Let's go on. Even in later ages such wondrous people appeared, though they had a harder time than the earlier ones of sacred history. . . . I am speaking of the intercessors whom we invoke in our litanies. I'll tell you something of these chosen ones. They were mostly men dedicated to God, solitaries, hermits of both sexes, monks and nuns. They went into the wilderness, into barren and many-clefted mountains, such as our Pyrenees. There they lived on roots, wild honey, and a daily mouthful of water. Often they took no nourishment, but fasted for days and days. They kept vigil through the nights in order to pray in succession all the prayers in the world. Many invented new prayers. There were those who scourged themselves with leather whips. Others wore iron girdles with rusty spikes that penetrated their flesh under their coarse cowls. Do you know why they did that? In order to subdue their evil thoughts and wishes, even though there were but few traces of sinfulness left in them. They did it in order to drive off the devil, who, jealous of their consecrated lives, sought to tempt and assail them again and again. The practice of these saintly people is known as asceticism, dear girls. Remember that word. For when amid infinite travail and torture they had so far advanced in asceticism that all the devil's wiles and temptations were overcome, then it came to pass that a few of them were enabled to see with the eyes of the body things which we lowly and ordinary people can never see. They saw the glorified and transfigured, such as the holy angels who are roundabout us. They saw visions. The Saviour Himself appeared to them wreathed in radiance with His crown of thorns and His wounds. Or else the Most Blessed Virgin, her naked heart transfixed by swords, her hands folded, her tearful or transfigured glance raised high to heaven. . . . Soubirous, did you understand?"

Bernadette gave a violent start. She had heard nothing, nor understood anything. With unbearable heartache she had thought of the lovely lady who was waiting for her in vain. Dull and silent, she looked at the teacher. The latter shook her head. "She doesn't even understand all that."

Ready to jeer aloud, the girls stirred in their seats.

"And you want to pretend to be like these most consecrated beings in the whole world?"

"No, Sister."

"Maybe you deserved to have these visions on account of all the rock-candy you've sucked?"

"No, Sister."

That answer unleashed the mocking laughter. Even the witnesses of Massabielle roared; even Marie could not repress a sourish grin. Sister Vauzous let the uproar die down.

"You see, Soubirous, even your schoolmates cannot but laugh at your goings-on. Instead of doing some serious work, you think up this silly and crazy fraud in order to attain a cheap importance. Till now I thought you were stupid. But

you're not; you're something much worse. I didn't expect
much of you ever. But I did not think that you would make
a vulgar jest of the most holy things and play the clown for
the benefit of dull and idle people. . . . Now go back to your
seat and be ashamed for having so impudently disturbed the
holy Lenten season with your belated Shrovetide pranks."

That afternoon Bernadette crept back to school. Ineffable
sorrow weighed her down. She went alone. She avoided everyone. She could not endure even Marie's companionship today.
Half-way, Peyret met her and shadowed her for a space, her
head trembling with indignation.

"You are a faithless creature, Bernadette. Faithless to the
lady, faithless to your benefactress Madame Millet. We waited
at Massabielle this morning, Madame Millet and I and many,
many others. And Madame Millet said: 'I'd wager a hundred
francs that Bernadette will not be faithless.'"

"But they have forbidden it," the girl groaned.

The dressmaker, who liked her plots as sensational as possible, jeered and hounded: "Bah, forbidden! Who can forbid
you to go where you choose? Don't let Jacomet make a fool
of you. He only wanted to scare you. He can't really do anything to you when you've not been guilty of anything. And
if they do lock you up, you must just let them. Duty is duty."

"But they threaten to lock up Mamma and Papa too, and
then my little brothers would starve."

"Can't be helped, just can't!" Peyret's zeal was extreme.
"Even if they lock up your parents, you just can't break your
word and neglect your duty."

Bernadette began running, merely to get rid of the woman.
She said no farewell. She was afraid of being late at school
too. The clock in the tower of the hospital was striking two.
She now approached a viaduct which spanned a low-lying
part of the town on the way to school. She was just about

to set foot on it when she found that she could not do so and had to remain standing and fighting for breath. An invisible obstacle lay across her path. It seemed to be in the nature of a huge beam of wood which, despite her utmost efforts, she could not surmount. At the same moment a power, like a strong and pitiless hand, seemed to take her by the shoulders and force her to turn around. Slowly she trotted back the way by which she had come. But before she reached the Place Marcadale she heard the resounding clicking of four hobnailed boots behind her. She was being followed. It was the two gendarmes Pays and Belhache, who had been instructed to shadow her. The two enormous fellows, in shining uniforms with trailing swords and feathered hats, appeared, as though casually, one on either side of her.

"What's eating you, sweetie?" the black-bearded Belhache asked. "You were told to go to school, weren't you, not to play hooky?"

"I meant to go," Bernadette informed him veraciously. "But on the viaduct there's such a huge beam of air that you can't get across."

"Now what kind of nonsense is that—a beam of air!" This came from the withered Pays, father of five daughters. "You can't make a damned fool of me that way."

"And now, my sweetie, you're going to be a good girl and go home, eh?" asked the younger and milder Belhache, whose avocation was chasing women.

"No," Bernadette said thoughtfully. "I'm not going home; I'm going to the grotto."

"Oh, you are, are you, sweetie? Hey there, Pays, run and fetch the brigadier!"

Three minutes later Pays returned with the gorgeous d'Angla, who was buckling on his sword-belt on the run and chewing a thick slice of salami. His mouth full of food, he repeated: "A beam of air—that's the latest, a beam of air!"

"Do let me go to the grotto," the girl implored them.

"On your own responsibility you can go," the brigadier decided, stroking his blond side-whiskers. "But we're coming along, the three of us."

Callet, not to be left out, soon joined this armed escort.

The Soubirous girl with four policemen made a parade to rouse the town. Piguno had seen it and had rushed first to Aunt Bernarde, next to the Cachot. All windows flew open. At every door appeared curious women, wiping their hands on their aprons. By the time the Rue Basse was reached, eighty to ninety people were trotting behind Bernadette. Today, however, she did not fly like a swallow, like a leaf in the wind. Her legs seemed leaden.

Arrived at the grotto, she fell on her knees, dropped like a beaten creature, and stretched out imploring arms toward the niche. But the niche was dark, the niche was empty, as nothing in all the world had ever been empty. The one rose-bush branch above the thorn-tree stirred morosely in the river wind. The river itself murmured indifferently. Rain began to fall, too, so that the grotto was nothing but a prosaic shelter for a crowd of people.

A cry of utmost horror came from Bernadette: "I don't see her . . . not today . . . I cannot see her!. . ."

She took out her rosary and held it convulsively up toward the niche. The oval remained a deadly void filled with a comfortless brown twilight, all that this twenty-second day of February had left to give. Only the stone behind the portal glimmered like a whitish bone. The hole in the rock was a mere hole in the rock, and that the lady had ever issued forth therefrom seemed now indeed either a lie or the product of a sick fancy. And Bernadette was shaken by an immeasurably tragic remorse, by the despair of the lover who has guiltlessly lost his beloved because the powers of earth have prevented him from keeping his troth. The lady had been bitterly disappointed and had withdrawn from the inhospitable grotto to her worthier and habitual dwelling-place. Bernadette's wordless heart cried out toward the grotto: Did you not know that Monsieur Jacomet would send me and Papa and Mamma to the penitentiary if I came to you? And yet I have come. Could you not have waited just a little while before putting an end to everything?

Suddenly a thought came to Bernadette to which she rushed as to a last refuge. "Of course, I can't see the lady," she wailed piercingly. "She is hiding because there are so many gendarmes around me. . . ."

This disillusioning reason roused the crowd to laughter. Voices were heard: "You must see now that she's a fool. . . . But they say she almost got the better of Jacomet yesterday. . . . Don't be taken in. She's a poor unfortunate. . . ."

A practical joker lifted up the black-bearded gendarme. "Here's Belhache. He looks like the devil. That explains everything."

Belhache stroked his formidable beard. In his association with sharp-tongued slate-miners, road-menders, vagabonds, innkeepers, and bar companions in the land of Bigorre he had sharpened his wit and tongue. "Of course, I look like the devil and I am he. Unluckily I'm only a poor devil whom the Blessed Virgin should help to make a bit of cash instead of running away from me."

The joke soon made the round of the town. An hour later Duran of the Café Progrès was able to greet his guests with the question: "Do you know that the Most Blessed Virgin will simply have nothing to do with the gendarmerie?"

Dutour and Jacomet were among the guests. Although the contempt with which their commands had been treated was embarrassing, they were not ill content with this turn of affairs. The acrid antidote of ridicule desired by Dean Peyramale had luckily been found. Nothing could be better than to have the lady give up the game herself. Thus the imperial authority was in a position to instruct Jacomet to continue to supervise the Soubirous family, but not to interfere with Bernadette's next visit to the grotto. After today's fiasco, people would soon tire of the performance.

Bernadette, her mother, and her aunts as well as sundry other persons were at this time in the Savy mill. The child was crushed. She had to be lifted onto Madame Nicolau's bed. She lay there ashen-grey, with closed eyes, struggling for breath. If there was an expression which could be thought of as the antithesis of rapture, such was the expression on her features. The skin was not taut but slack; the struggling lips were swollen. Antoine had put a wet kerchief across her forehead. Mademoiselle Estrade, who had witnessed the scene at the grotto, turned to a pale and careworn woman who stood beside the bed:

"Do you happen to know the child well?"

"How should I not?" Louise Soubirous moaned. "Am I not her unhappy mother? This thing has now been going on for eleven days. Some people laugh at us, others pity us. Crowds follow and confuse us till our heads swim. And the police threaten us with the penitentiary. O Holy Virgin, why are we tortured so? Look at the girl yourself, Mademoiselle! She's a very sick girl. . . ."

Uncontrolled, Louise Soubirous flung herself across the bed, sobbing: "Speak, my child! Say one little word!"

Since Bernadette did not recover from her despair or break her silence, Antoine hurried to the post-office to fetch Soubirous. And now her father sat at her bedside too, irresolute, tender-hearted, for the first time wholly overwhelmed by his child's suffering. With his rough hands he caressed her knees while tears coursed down his cheeks. "Poor little one, what have they done to you?" he stammered. "You didn't mind them. What of it? . . . You're my child and I love you. . . . I'll protect you. . . . Tell me what you want, my baby. . . ."

Bernadette neither opened her eyes nor spoke. Not until Antoine proposed sending for Dr. Dozous did she stir and say: "If I see her no more, I shall die."

Soubirous took Bernadette's hands and drew her up tenderly. "You shall see her, my lamb. I give you my word. No one shall prevent you. If they lock me up—well, they've done it before. But you shall see her."

But on the very way home François Soubirous was sorely depressed by the fact that pity for his child had wrung from him so rash a promise. The better to cover his sore inner discomfort he slunk past the Cachot and went to Babou's.

CHAPTER SEVENTEEN

Monsieur Estrade's Return

ON THE morning after this tragic Monday Bernadette was granted an incomparable reunion with the lady. It seemed to her as though she had been separated from her adored one not for a day but for a stretch of time that could be measured solely by the measures of wretchedness and privation. But the lady, too, seemed deeply moved by this reunion with her favourite. Although her raiment was the same, yet did she seem to have garbed herself in beauty and graciousness as never before. Her cheeks were more blooming; her light-brown ringlets struggled farther forth from beneath the veil; the golden roses upon the pallid feet burned as with fire. The power and the grace of the blue eyes were so intense that Bernadette immediately fell into a trance and remained thus for a full hour.

Not more than two hundred persons had assembled, those of the inner circle, so to speak, among whom were, of course, the dressmaker and Madame Millet, who had not permitted the failure of the vision or the horse-play of the gendarmes to shake her faith. The gendarmerie was represented today solely by the brigadier d'Angla, who had been detailed to this post. D'Angla had hoped to earn the esteem of his superiors by reporting to them today the final failure of the whole farce. He was intensely annoyed to observe that today's performance promised to be very far from a failure. As always, when ecstasy transformed the countenance of Bernadette and she performed her strange and naïve rites, a shiver like an electric current passed through the bodies of the kneeling women. Fickle as was the crowd and ever ready at any sign of failure to laugh or jeer, it could never escape the spell when Bernadette mirrored in her countenance and bearing the reality of the lady's presence. The brigadier, one of Duran's friends and customers, was green and blue with rage at what he saw. Now the whole messy business begins over again—such was his thought. Dutour and Jacomet, moreover, were weaklings. They did not give him permission to put a stop to this nonsense as they usually did in the case of political meetings. And so the very devil provoked d'Angla to make an extremely false move. He cried at the top of his voice: "To think of there being so many idiots left in the nineteenth century!"

An uprush of rage came from the crowd. A voice began in answer to intone one of the best-known hymns in praise of Mary. A chorus took it up:

> "*Nous voulons Dieu! Vierge Marie,*
> *Prête l'oreille à nos accents;*
> *Nous t'implorons, Mère chérie,*
> *Bénis, ô tendre Mère,*
> *Ce cri de notre foi. . . .*"

Bernadette was wholly untouched by these incidents. While she curtsied, knelt, rose, listened with open lips, took fright, was soothed, took fright again, she seemed to herself to be carrying on an interchange of loving words beyond the boundaries of time. For true womanly love is self-consumed in the constant effort to grasp the beloved object's strange and other being, not out of curiosity but for the sake of achieving a more triumphant devotion. By this time Bernadette had come to know many of the lady's sharply marked characteristics. She knew that the lady was extremely sparing of words and would say nothing that had not a precise purpose. She knew, too—and this was grievous—that the lady had come to her not merely to inflame her but on account of a deeply considered end of which Bernadette was ignorant and with which she herself had nothing to do. She had the impression that it was not at all easy for the lady to come on this daily journey to the grotto, that it required, in fact, a large measure of self-conquest. With the profound acuteness of love's sensibility she knew also that despite the serenity of her salutations and assenting bows and smiles, there was something the lady hid, perhaps a slight revulsion at all she had to see. Bernadette suspected this from her own experience. Every time that she had awakened from her loving converse she had known this revulsion as well as that astonishment at the world's alien ways. Probably, she suspected as well, the lady is a thousand times more disgusted at her, as she herself was at her sister's body on a certain night. Thence arose, too, certain inclinations and disinclinations of the lady. She did not, for instance, like to be approached too closely. Only at the highest moments did she summon Bernadette to approach the rock and herself come to the uttermost edge and bend forward. Thus one had to beware of importunity. Nor did she like having her behaviour considered a thing foreseen or to be taken for granted. Freedom sat upon her, never obligation. Self-determined, she came and went according to her will. Therefore Bernadette ventured no word of reproach concerning yesterday's absence. The lady was never uncertain of herself and knew her own value. Therefore the appropriate posture in her presence was on one's knees, if possible with a burning taper in one's hand. If ever one moved to and fro in the grotto, or, still worse, turned one's back, an expression of nervous suffering would tarnish the radiance of her countenance. If, on the other hand, one did a painful thing—Bernadette knew this well—such as sliding on one's knees over the jagged rubble toward the rock, then was she transfigured with joy. These matters were in all likelihood allied to that word which several times the lady had whispered as if to herself, the word penitence. Although Sister Marie Thérèse had mentioned this concept in class, Bernadette had not too clear a notion of its meaning. Her restless zeal to please the lady, and this alone, began to clarify the significance a little for her. Penitence seemed to consist of every voluntary mortification, of incurring pain and weariness against one's sloth and love of ease. If the jagged rubble made the knees bleed, then an act of penitence had been accomplished. When that happened the lady made a strange gesture. She acted as though with her hollow hands she were dipping water from a well, the invisible water of penitence, and were then holding it high as an offering and in proof of her not desiring to keep it for herself. Bernadette's tireless efforts, born of love, to discover the lady's wishes had given her insights even more acute. Doubtless the word penitence had to do with that slight revulsion which was at times mirrored in those lovely features. Several days ago the lady had uttered the command: "Pray for sinners," and had then added almost inaudibly and to herself: "For the sick world." At these words she seemed to behold things which intensified that revulsion to the point of pallor. Sin is the thing that is evil, bad. So much Bernadette had already known. By fathoming her beloved lady's attitudes she had now come to learn—and this knowledge harmonized with her own instincts—that the evil and bad was none other than the ugly which aroused the feeling of disgust visible in her, the ever beautiful. But penitence eased the disgust of the ever beautiful and perhaps rendered even its causes less hateful. . . .

Upon this day the lady was impelled to ask Bernadette to urge those present to the practice of penitence. With tears in her eyes the rapt girl turned to the people and thrice whispered the word penitence. This was the first of the events which set this Tuesday apart. The second was an unpardonable attack upon the lady which made Bernadette shake with horror and indignation. A nameless man went about in the grotto whistling softly and tapping the walls with his stick. Bernadette had by now become so accustomed to her state of trance that from within it little escaped her, even though she gave no evidence of this. The whistling man on his round of exploration approached the wall that held the niche. He began to poke with his stick into the branches of the thornbush. Bernadette's heart stood still, for now the stick of the shameless one was tapping against the delicate feet of the lady, who recoiled.

"Go away!" Bernadette's voice was piercing. "You are hurting the lady. And her feelings too."

Meanwhile Antoine and two other lads had captured the miscreant and brought him forth from the grotto.

"If there's any more violence," d'Angla called out in a stentorian voice, "I'll order the locality cleared!"

Instantly the crowd intoned another hymn in Mary's praise:

> "Ô ma reine, ô Vierge Marie,
> Je vous donne mon cœur,
> Je vous consacre pour la vie
> Mes peines, mon bonheur."

The third event of this day weighed most heavily upon Bernadette and filled her with far keener fear than a renewed confrontation with Dutour or Jacomet would have done. For the first time the lady assigned a practical task to her. While hitherto she had had to suffer only for the bliss with which she had been graced, she was now being condemned to an activity which made her tremble. After the lady had recovered from the attack of the man with the long stick, she bade Bernadette approach. Her voice had a solemn sound. "Please go to the priests and tell them that a chapel is to be built here. . . ." More indistinctly and softly she added: "Let processions come hither."

Monsieur J. B. Estrade, the tax-collector, had let his sister persuade him to be present at the grotto today. He had had to overcome very violent inner resistance. Even last Sunday, when he witnessed Jacomet's examination, he had been strongly fascinated by what he had himself called Bernadette's state of being fascinated. The little creature seemed to him to harbour a decisiveness and a power of conviction against which Estrade's cool good sense had not quite prevailed. He was afraid of his own impressionableness. That is why his sister had to work so hard to get him to witness the performance with his own eyes. Not otherwise than Dutour or Jacomet, he tacitly hoped that Bernadette would fail.

Estrade was what is known as a practising Catholic. He was consciously allied to the Church and obeyed her usual and common behests. Since this Church had been the spiritual home of his parents and of his forefathers he, a modest man with a mediocre career, harbouring no extravagant notions, saw absolutely no reason for departing from the ancestral pattern. To him, as to so many, loyalty to the Church of Rome meant a beneficently definite patriotism within the least definite of life's provinces, that of eternity. There was the added factor that his melancholy but comfort-loving temperament impelled him to political conservatism, a fact which enhanced his loyalty to the most conservative of human institutions. In addition, however, Estrade was a man who both reflected and read. Consequently his rather secretive mind was sensitive to all the attacks of historical criticism, as were the minds of all thoughtful and well-read people during this period. He possessed, however, the strength or, if one prefers, the weakness of repelling all uncomfortable elements, that of genuine doubt as well as that of ardent belief, so he dwelt in an inviolable middle region and considered himself a good citizen and Catholic.

Not for a moment did he credit the objective reality of Bernadette's lady. Nor did he do so now as he turned his back to the grotto and went without taking leave of his sister. He chose the wilder path along the brookside in order not to join the crowd returning to town. A great disquietude had undeniably taken hold of him. He remembered certain distant days of his youth on which what he called the divine had overwhelmed him with world-embracing emotion. This, whatever it was, had seemed unfriendly to mature years. In youth, indeed, it seemed to soar with rushing wing upon the soul and fly away again with sudden presences and long delays. Then a mysterious current quickened the soul and brought the tears of an assurance of eternity to the burning eye. What is that thing's nature? Estrade was not a little astonished that today his eyes burned and were moist.

It was, evidently, the sight of this little hysterical female that had so astonishingly caused his conventional rigidness to begin to melt. He saw before him the sign of the cross that Bernadette had repeatedly made, a cross that slowly enveloped her whole face. If there is Heaven, Estrade meditated, and if the spirits made perfect salute each other, this must be the slow and distinguished manner of their salutations. Incomprehensible the strange power with which this dim-brained child of the Pyrenees was able vividly to communicate by glance, gait, gesture, a thing which was not. How, for instance, Bernadette had looked up questioningly, not seeming to understand the lady clearly; how she had strained to listen with desperate tension, and then, understanding at last, had suddenly glowed with child-like happiness and kissed the earth! This thing had constituted a ceremonial so full of an ineffable and vital sense of the presence of divinity that, in comparison, the most solemn of High Masses assumed the aspect of an empty, pompous show.

So deeply was Estrade absorbed in his unquiet meditations that he did not immediately recognize one who, out for a walk, met him near the saw-mill. It was Hyacinthe de Lafite, wrapped in his voluminous cape. Certain gentlemen—Lacadé, Dutour, and even Dozous—had been known to criticize the wearing of this outmoded garment as a piece of affectation. Certain women, on the other hand, thought it most becoming and sighed at the poet's appearance in it: "Poor Lafite, what sufferings of love he must have known!" For women do not believe in a melancholy that springs from purely intellectual sources.

"You are up early," Lafite addressed the tax-collector.

"I might return the compliment, my dear fellow. I thought you, of all people, would still be abed."

"I am badly misunderstood. I never go to bed before nine o'clock."

"So early in the evening?"

"Oh, no, nine in the morning, my friend. Night is my divine patroness who redoubles my intellectual powers. I work and study. Tonight, for instance, some verses came to me of which even I do not disapprove. Incomparable, after a night of vigil, are the morning hours between five and seven. Then and then only can man cross the boundary into the realm of utter clarity."

"I can't say that that was my experience this morning," Estrade grumbled. "I've just been to the grotto. . . ."

"Everybody goes." Lafite smiled. "First Dozous, now you.

Clarens will be next. Lacadé and Duran will form the tail end."

"I didn't dream that what is to be seen there would be unforgettable."

"I know, I know. The shepherd girl out of the antique world who in the year 1858 sees the guardian nymph of the spring and redeems her from two thousand years of boredom."

"I rather think, dear friend, you'd stop joking if ever you were to witness this remarkable ecstasy. As a poet, it's really your duty."

"Wait, Estrade," Lafite said very seriously and held his friend's arm. "If I'm not mistaken it is written in the Gospel of John: 'Blessed are they that have not seen and yet have believed.' I apply that to literature. They are mere tyros who need to have seen something in order to represent it. I reject with contempt the notion that personal experience is necessary to the understanding of a thing."

"Imagination cannot take the place of some experiences," Estrade observed.

Lafite stood still and inhaled the pure air. It was the first fair morning in weeks. After a brief pause he gathered himself for the onslaught. "None of you can quite get over the remnants of the illusion of religion. That's your trouble! But in our century the gods die. And it takes not a little power to survive the death of the gods without being taken in by idols. Such periods, as history shows us, are hard and evil. Look at the Church in today's world, the Catholic Church, not to speak of others. What does it amount to? It's Christianity at reduced prices; it's the great clearance sale of God. Nor can it be otherwise, since the foundation itself has crumbled. An all-powerful, omniscient, omnipresent God, who causes Himself to be reborn of a Virgin herself immaculately conceived in order to redeem a world, which stands in need of redemption only because He didn't choose to do a better job when He was creating it—well, you must admit, that's no more worthy of credence than that the panoplied Minerva sprang from the head of Jove. But even in his mysticism man is a creature of habit. The ancients found it as hard to get rid of their Minerva as we do to get rid of the Virgin. The ruin of faith totters on undetermined foundations and all kinds of deistic scaffoldings have been erected to keep it from falling. All of you sway hither and yon somewhere on these scaffoldings. Don't think, my friend, that I'm a mere dupe of the Enlightenment. I know perfectly well that mysticism is one of the noblest qualities of man and can never wholly perish. But when from your uncertain scaffoldings you seem to see a bit of it, immediately dizziness seizes upon you; for you are not yet strong enough to bear the vision of emptiness without tottering and losing the little mind you have."

"You're right about that, Lafite; I did get dizzy at Massabielle this morning. I don't know why. I don't even know if what I've seen has anything to do with religion. At all events, Bernadette transported me back into a realm of feeling and aspiration which, thank God, I haven't entirely lost."

Silently, side by side, they went as far as the Pont Vieux. The river was dashing against the piers of the bridge. At last Estrade, unable to master the emotion in his voice, asked: "Do you nourish no hope, Lafite, of finding home at last?"

"Whither and where?" cried Hyacinthe de Lafite and waved his hat in farewell. "I wish you a very good morning, Estrade. I am going home to sleep. For my only home is sleep and the undeceiving void. . . ."

CHAPTER EIGHTEEN

The Dean Demands a Miracle

THE DAY was almost spring-like. In two or three weeks one could hope in this land for the conquest of winter. The great garden of the parsonage of Lourdes was a sight to be seen. Expectantly it lay between its enclosing walls. It was like a dwelling hastily being prepared for a new tenant. The brown lawn had been dug up here and there, the red soil of the beds had been well spaded, the laburnum and lilac-bushes had been pruned. The withered leaves had been swept into heaps and pyramids of river sand waited to be strewn on crunching paths. The rose-trellis was not yet, to be sure, exposed to the February air. These roses were Marie Dominique Peyramale's pride and joy. The dean was examining each of the bushes, those wrapped in straw and the more delicate ones wrapped in sackcloth. His right hand stroked the wrappings as though it could tell whether the hidden slumbering life beneath were on the point of awakening. Thus employed, Peyramale's right hand had indeed forgotten what his left was doing. For this left hand was firmly holding a letter. And it was an important letter, written by no less a personage than Monseigneur Bertrand Sévère Laurence, bishop of Tarbes.

Not until Peyramale had completed his inspection of a part of the rose-bushes did he break the episcopal seal on the letter which the morning post had brought. The epistle was in answer to his report and respectful request for directions concerning the recent events at Lourdes. As the dean had expected, the bishop shared his point of view entirely. For the present, the so-called "apparitions at Massabielle" required no taking of a definite stand and certainly no action by the ecclesiastical authorities. The canon law demanded direct interference only in case of "proven heresy, harmful superstition, and incitement to serious popular unrest concerning matters of faith." No such matters were in evidence. There was nothing to go upon except the assertion, incapable of proof or disproof, that a fourteen-year-old girl was having visions of an unnamed and unknown lady. Hence the attitude taken by the dean of Lourdes—these were His Lordship's appreciative words—corresponded harmoniously with the interests of the diocese. Hence the clergy in question was to continue publicly to ignore the aforementioned apparitions. The dean was therefore to continue to instruct the clergy in the strictest terms not to join the processions at Massabielle. If questions of conscience arose in the confessional, an answer of somewhat the following character might be employed as a model: "It is at all times possible that messengers from Heaven appear upon earth and that miracles take place. But nothing warrants the assumption that any such thing has happened at Massabielle."

The bishop of Tarbes, however, was by no means inclined to take the unhappy affair too lightly. He reminded the dean of a painful precedent case: some years earlier a certain Rose Tamisier had played a comparable comedy in Avignon and hypocritically feigned to have meetings with the Most Blessed Virgin. The then vicar general of that diocese, a man of less good sense than generous enthusiasms, had permitted himself to be most embarrassingly cornered by this ambitious candidate for sainthood. The consequence of the exposure of the fraud had been a baleful diminution of ecclesiastical authority, a flaring-up of atheism all through Provence, and a political triumph of anti-clerical forces all along the line. Hence the utmost vigilance was to be used—thus the bishop ended his epistle—accompanied by constant prayer for enlightenment from above and for the prevention of similar hurts.

Peyramale folded the letter. Although it contained praise of himself, the letter left him in a disgruntled mood. It is so easy for these princes of the Church to use caution and tact. They are like the generals at headquarters whither no bullet ever penetrates. Life with its harshness comes to them in the guise of black marks on white paper. A man like himself sat with his own behind in the dung.

Moreover, Peyramale, a judge of human nature, had a very specific suspicion. In the matter of this disgusting nonsense he hadn't a doubt that certain rich ladies had their finger in the pie. The *pétroleur* of mercy had a keen understanding of the pietistic and ultradevout ladies of the stripe of Baup and Millet. These good-for-nothing females regarded the Church as their salon or club. It existed to serve their thirst for power and lust for gossip and sensations, all in a splendid setting of candle-light and incense. When it came to active fulfilment of the command to love one's neighbour or a practical alleviation of the unendurable physical and spiritual misery of the Pyrenean regions, they closed their pockets and wailed over the money they had already spent on the annual feast of Saint Anne or on the decoration of sundry altars. They would be only too pleased, on the contrary, to give a leg up to supernatural powers and to arrange a little miracle to their own higher distinction. The dean had been informed concerning the odd relationship between Bernadette and Madame Millet. The bishop had been quite right to recall the precedent offered by the fraudulent Rose Tamisier.

Once more the dean turned to a La France rose-bush. He was afraid it had not survived the severe winter. He was just about to scratch the stalk with a knife to see if it was green when he was startled by the dull, many-voiced rumour of crowds in the street. The sounds approached the gate of his garden. He knew at once: that is Bernadette Soubirous and her followers. And it happened that this fearless man was unable to subdue a certain excitement due to this absurd child. As though caught in mischief, he felt in his pocket for his breviary. A clerical gentleman ought not to be discovered with idle eyes and empty hands. Peyramale was furious with himself for taking out his breviary. Nevertheless, apparently absorbed, he began to pace up and down the avenue of acacias which led from the garden gate to the door of the house.

It was her clever aunt Bernarde who interpreted the lady's words, "Please go to the priests," as pointing to none other than the dean. Fathers Pomian, Penès, and Sempet were certainly not meant by the lady, since these gentlemen, though easier of approach, were after all only the chaplains and assistants of the vicar. The lady's parsimonious use of words unluckily rendered her meanings general and vague. She never, for example, named names, neither her own nor another's. Bernadette was never addressed as Bernadette, but always in such courteous, indefinite phrases as: "I beg of you," or "I would request you." Perhaps the lady simply could not remember the difficult names used hereabouts. It could be argued, on the other hand, that she had as thoroughly mastered the fluent use of the dialect of Bigorre as a stranger or an educated person had ever done. Perhaps it was forbidden her to name the names of persons who would be too exalted by this mark of distinction.

It would, at all events, have been an immense relief to Bernadette had her aunt's interpretation pointed to the three chaplains rather than to the dean. To Bernadette, Peyramale embodied all the terrors of her childhood. She knew him only from seeing him in the pulpit or on the street. Terror had shaken her each time that, accompanied by her schoolmates, she had been obliged to hear the veiled thunder of his homiletic voice. Very early in her life she had been inspired by reverential fear at Peyramale's huge figure, his long-paced, quite unclerical storming through the streets. Briefly, the worthy Peyramale was too big for little Bernadette. He was her special bogyman. And him she was to meet as her lady's ambassadress. Her heart sank abysmally. She felt like turning back. But the energetic Aunt Bernàrde Casterot was not one to joke with when once she had taken a matter in hand. And she had now, readier of faith than the child's mother, taken in hand the matter of the lady. Pitilessly she gave her niece a nudge which propelled the girl across the stone threshold of the garden of the vicarage.

There, at the end of the avenue, the giant stood in all his might, reading his breviary. His back was turned to Bernadette. If only he would never turn around, she prayed, her mouth horribly dry. With small steps she worked her way toward the monster. It seemed to her that this was more like wading through the icy Gave than any common walk. She took care to make as little noise with her shoes as possible. Oh, these wooden shoes! It were better to walk barefoot. Still at a great distance from Peyramale, she stopped and listened to her throbbing heart.

The dean swung suddenly on his heel. Thunder and lightning were on his countenance. She had expected nothing else. He drew himself up, as though he were not already too terribly big. "What are you doing here? Who are you?" His tone was arrogant and hard.

"I am Bernadette Soubirous," she stammered with short little breaths.

"What an honour!" Peyramale jeered. "The latest celebrity comes calling. Do your courtiers and servants always follow you?"

Silently Bernadette stared at the ground. The dean roared:

"If any of that crowd dares to enter my garden, I'll have him arrested! There will be no monkey-shines here!"

Without turning or inviting his visitor to enter, the dean with huge paces went into the house. Pale and lost, Bernadette followed him. The reception hall of the vicarage was large and chill even though a sumptuous fire burned in the hearth. The full-blooded dean seemed impervious to cold. His face was red with rage and his powerful lips were pouting. He towered above the child as though to crush her.

"So you're the shameless street-brat that goes through these delightful antics, eh?"

Since Bernadette remained silent, his next roar made the rafters ring. "Talk! Open your mouth! What do you want of me?"

Tears choking her, the girl began: "The lady told me . . ."

Brutally he interrupted her: "What do you mean? What lady?"

"The lady of Massabielle. . . ."

"Don't know any such person. . . ."

"But it's that most beautiful lady who always comes to me. . . ."

"Is she a Lourdes lady? Did you ever know her?"

"No, the lady is not from Lourdes. I never knew her."

"Have you asked her her name?"

"Oh, yes, I've asked her her name. But she gives no answer."

"Perhaps the lady is deaf and dumb?"

"No, she is not. She speaks to me."

"What does the lady say to you?"

Bernadette grasped her opportunity and said quickly: "This morning the lady said to me: 'Please go to the priests and tell them that a chapel is to be built here. . . .'" She breathed with relief. Thank Heaven, the words had been spoken and the commission executed.

Peyramale drew up a chair and spread his huge form upon it while with his fiery eyes he devoured the intimidated girl.

"Priests? What does that mean? Your lady seems a confirmed heathen. The very cannibals have priests. We Catholics have religious, each bearing a specific title. . . ."

"But the lady did say 'priests,'" Bernadette declared. She felt a trifle easier, having communicated the message to the right man.

"Well, you've come to the wrong address, anyhow," Peyramale thundered. "Have *you* any money with which to build a chapel?"

"Oh, no, I have no money at all."

"Well, then, tell your lady from me she'd better first of all provide the money for her chapel. Will you do that?"

"Yes, Your Reverence, I'll tell her that," Bernadette replied with pleasing promptness and in all seriousness.

Incredulously he stared in wonder at the simple-mindedness of this creature. "Nonsense!" he cried and jumped up. "Tell your lady the following: The dean of Lourdes is not accustomed to accept commissions from unknown ladies who refuse to give their names. Moreover, he doesn't consider it very fitting for a lady to climb barefoot on rocks and send immature adolescents with messages. Finally, the dean of Lourdes requests the lady once and for all to leave him in peace. That is all. Do you understand?"

"Oh, yes, I'll tell her everything." Bernadette nodded vigorously. For to her the lady alone was important and not the lady's affairs in the world. Faint with fear and excitement, she was not at all aware of the dean's rude rejection of her most gracious and lovely one.

He, however, pointed to a big broom which his housekeeper had left in a corner. "Do you see that broom?" His thunderous rage reached its very peak. "With that very broom in my own

hands I'll sweep you out of the temple if you dare to annoy me
ever again."

The thunderous tumult overwhelmed Bernadette. Sobbing
loudly, she dashed out.

It was not in any way the dean's good day. On close observation it turned out that six of his oldest rose-bushes had died, a
loss hard to make up. Years of care and culture were required
by one of those slender stalks before a sturdy trunk developed
to bud and bloom with endless fragrance from April to November. And now he might as well feed the fire with them. But
other things troubled him. He was definitely oppressed by his
behaviour to Bernadette Soubirous. True, she was a little swindler or, more accurately, the misused tool of Millet and other
ambitious women. Yet that was no reason for the dean of
Lourdes to act toward this feeble child like a regular ogre or
like the devil in the puppet shows. When she ran off yowling,
he had been tempted to call her back and console her with a
fatherly nudge and a little saint's picture. For he knew that
she belonged to the poorest of the poor. Yet, God knows,
tenderness gets you nowhere at all in dealing with this rabble,
whose low cunning he knew to the last fibre.

But there came still other reflections to weigh upon him.
With the street-girl's visit his inner security in respect of the
whole affair has been impaired. Through the mediation of
Bernadette the lady has succeeded in making a place for herself in his brain. He thought of the many visitations of the
Virgin in ages past, proven and confirmed in the ecclesiastical
chronicles of this land. For example, was Anglèse de Sagazan,
the shepherd girl of Gascony who in the valley of Garaison had
been repeatedly favoured by the Most Blessed One, so very
different from Bernadette Soubirous? And how about Cathérine Labourde of Saint-Sévérin? And Mélanie, the girl of La

Salette, that hamlet lost on an Alpine peak of Dauphiné? The Church had acknowledged the visions of La Salette as authentic and highly conducive to faith. Oddly enough, too, these phenomena had occurred in quite recent times, not more than twenty-one or twenty-two years ago. Hence there was not only the case of Rose Tamisier but the far more alarming case of Mélanie of La Salette. The bishop had ordered the extremest caution to be used. Marie Dominique Peyramale determined to weave into tomorrow morning's early Mass a prayer for the "discovery of the truth" concerning Massabielle and was immensely irritated to reflect that this harmless little witch with her few words had, after all, moved him, the immovable, to retreat to that extent from his position.

Bernadette felt even wretcheder than the dean. Hardly had she, still sobbing, gone a hundred paces between her aunts when sudden terror struck her because she had been guilty of a frightful omission. She had not given the lady's entire message but forgotten the second part: "Let processions come hither."

Oracularly, Aunt Bernarde decided that this second part was not now obligatory, seeing that the dean had rejected with ill-natured jeering the very condition for processions, namely, the chapel itself. But Bernadette was not so clever or so agile in reasoning as her aunt. Her lady, so tacit by habit, knew what she wanted. She demanded processions. It was necessary to convey this wish instantly if at tomorrow's meeting Bernadette were to have an unburdened heart. The lady's actions were unpredictable. If she were to be disappointed in Bernadette, the misfortune might happen that she would withdraw herself for several days or even, horrible to contemplate, for ever.

The way to the dean's house, so few hours after her expulsion, was not much more comfortable than going to be executed. The giant would foam with rage and, true to his promise, drive Bernadette out with the broomstick. He might even beat her. Yet what could she do but grit her teeth and be prepared for the worst? Bernadette besought her good-natured aunt Lucille not to desert her, bravely to enter the garden with her, and at a proper distance witness the catastrophe. They all decided to postpone the dreadful visit until later in the afternoon. Toward sundown, they thought and hoped, even the most irascible man is a little weary and less prone to accesses of rage.

At the time appointed, Peyramale was again surveying his rose-bushes and grimly reckoning up the winter damage. This time Bernadette surprised him. Suddenly she stood before him, a little bundle of terror with dark eyes, like those of a sacrificial lamb, searchingly upon him. Aunt Lucille had ventured only a few steps beyond the garden's threshold.

"I must say you have courage," the veiled voice said angrily.

"Monsieur le Curé, I'm sorry to trouble you. It's my own fault. I forgot something," she said, trembling.

The dean had leather mitts on and was holding his pruning-shears, which made him seem the more formidable. As though pursued by furies, Bernadette reeled off the second part of her message: "The lady said: 'Let processions come hither.'"

"Processions?" Peyramale laughed. "That's the best yet. Processions? What does she need processions for? Don't you provide her with those daily? We'll present you with a big pitch-torch, so that you can organize and lead your processions when and as you like. What need have you of a poor religious? From what I hear, you're your own bishop and Pope, and conduct such mad services at Massabielle that people laugh and weep." Against his better judgment Peyramale had become a prey of his own irascibility again. He fell back on mockery. "Maybe the lady would like the processions to begin tomorrow?"

Bernadette nodded with the utmost sincerity.

"I can well believe it."

Carefully curtsying, she was about to withdraw. "I do truly beg your pardon. I've given all the messages now," she barely breathed.

"One moment, there," he called out. "It is I who decide here when you are to go. Do you recall my message which you are to deliver to the lady?"

"Oh, yes, I do indeed."

"It isn't all. I've got another message for you to give," he growled, with eyes upon his wrapped rose-bushes. "Did the lady never give you any indication as to who she is?"

"No, never, truly not."

"But if she is what people say she is, she ought to know something about roses."

That was more than Bernadette could grasp. Peyramale now proceeded to inquire, in a voice which was grim with either earnestness or jeering, concerning the exact place of the lady's appearance.

"They tell me that in the grotto a wild rose-vine grows against the rock. Is that true?"

"Yes, that is true," Bernadette assured him, happy over what she felt to be a change of moral atmosphere. "Right under the niche, where the lady always stands, there's a long hedge-rose. . . ."

"Splendid coincidence." Peyramale nodded, visibly pleased. "Now listen hard, my girl, and tell the lady this: the dean of Lourdes, Madame, urges you to perform a little miracle by letting the wild rose-bush bloom now at winter's end. It won't be hard for you to fulfil this modest wish of the dean of Lourdes. . . . Did you grasp that, girl?"

"Oh, yes, I did indeed."

"Then repeat what I said."

Faultlessly and with soul relieved, Bernadette repeated the message of Peyramale to the lady.

CHAPTER NINETEEN

Vexation

THE WHOLE town buzzed with the dean's message to the lady. Once more Marie Dominique Peyramale had proved his masterly ability to meet the most difficult situations. The liberals and anti-clericals looked upon his demand as a juicy joke. They laughed, though not without some confusion, seeing that it was not so simple now to assert that the Church favoured the visions or was actually responsible for them. The dean's message, on the other hand, filled believers of every degree with intense excitement. If this were in very truth the Most Blessed Virgin, then she was queen of the rosary and of roses. Would she, then, miss the opportunity of performing this modest miracle of the rose, which, with March at the door, might still admit of a normal explanation? Was it really asking too much of Heaven to grant Its adherents this small support toward an improved position in a godless world? The dean of Lourdes was a sly fellow. No one could help admitting that.

The coffee-house owner Duran welcomed his guests with repeated winks. "Would you like to bet that we'll be treated to a neat little miracle? Don't forget—the weather is fine, the sun shines at noon, in four days we'll have March. Certain ladies will attend to what's still wanting. A nice big brazier under the hole in the rock, for instance, or a few hot-water bottles stuck in the shrubbery! Cazenave tried it in his winter garden and had handsome carnations and gladioli for Christmas. I'll take on any bet." Thus the presiding spirit of the Café Progrès built up an anticipatory defence.

A miracle of quite another kind was the great yearning cry after a miracle which arose throughout all the extent of the Pyrenean countryside, after rumour swift as lightning had carried the substance of the dean's conference with Bernadette to the remotest mountain villages. All these heavy-handed peasants, shepherds, cottars, road-menders, lumbermen, slate-miners seemed suddenly overwhelmed by the dread-fraught recognition of man's shipwrecked and outcast estate upon this earth. For once they refused to accept the curse of suffering and torment like oxen at the plough. Like the literally ship-wrecked, their souls demanded to see amid the endless fogs of mortality a heavenly flag of rescue—a miracle, the February blooming of the rose.

The one who seemed least concerned over the miracle was Bernadette herself. On the very next day, instantly upon her arrival at the grotto, she hastened to deliver the dean's messages. She could not, as always before, sink deep into her rapture of seeing and hearing. Touched with dread, the byplay of the world stood between her and the lady. With toneless monotony she poured out Peyramale's messages, hardly daring to utter them, arrogant or condescending or inappropriate as they were. Was it possible to address the lady thus: "The dean of Lourdes said that you are to furnish the money for the chapel yourself. The dean of Lourdes said that he does not accept commissions from unknown ladies. The dean of Lourdes desires you to leave him in peace hereafter. The dean of Lourdes desires you to cause the hedge-rose beneath your feet to bloom"? The lady listened calmly to all these impertinences. Not once did she show upon her countenance that pallor of discomfort which unsuitable acts or words were wont to call forth. Now and then she smiled faintly and rather inattentively at Bernadette's hasty report. Nothing but a shadowy glance at the wild rose proved that she had heard the dean's demand.

She seemed distraught. She did not lean down toward her favourite. Her crystalline blue eyes painfully sought some far horizon. She, of whom it was said that she was but an empty vision, seemed herself beset by visions—visions of torment and horror, for again and again her lips pronounced the word "penitence." Her revulsion was very great, and Bernadette did her best to ease, by penitential acts, the lady's presence in this revolting world. Repeatedly the girl kissed the earth; she slid about on her knees until they bled; she was not satisfied until the palms of her hands were sore and wounded. She tried to incite the crowd to imitate her penitential practices. Her success was small. Few understood her. Nearly all would rather witness a miracle than make themselves uncomfortable in order to diminish the sufferings of the lady. The lady shivered despite the fairness of the day. The roses at her feet were very faint. At the end of twenty minutes she withdrew, and people reported that today Bernadette's face had undergone almost no change.

The faithful regarded this Thursday, the twenty-fifth of February, as the testing day of the miracle of the rose. Inclusive of the eleventh, the first day on which Bernadette had seen the lady, this was the third Thursday since the beginning of the visions. The passion of those who, desirous of a miracle, so boldly forecast the behaviour of the lady, was easy to understand. Not only the peasant women of the Batsuguère valley but also Madame Millet, Aunt Bernarde, the Bouhouhorts, the Nicolaus, the Sajous, and many others were convinced that something great would come to pass today or never.

Violent scenes had taken place between the mayor and the imperial prosecutor on the one hand and the prosecutor and the commissioner of police on the other. Each sought to saddle the other with the responsibility for the pitiful situation into which the authorities had manœuvred themselves. Above all did the devil himself seem to have got into the Parisian press. Dutour's political instinct had not led him astray. The great dailies utilized this silly and harmless story in order to make hypocritical attacks from ambush on that absolutist imperial regime which had owed its existence to conspiracy and sudden riot. "With the brilliancy of lightning," thus wrote the *Journal des Débats*, "do these sorry phenomena at Lourdes illuminate the material and mental depths to which the people of our southern provinces have been condemned. What has been done during the last decade to help this gifted population to integrate itself with the currents of modern life? Nothing and less than nothing, as a matter of cold calculation. A group the education of whose children is largely in the hands of monks and nuns can hardly be expected to attain to that height of untrammelled thought which alone can put an end to tyranny. The unleashing of the instincts of religious fanaticism is the surest means of diverting mankind from its highest aims, the conquest and organization of the earth. We desire the Imperial Minister of Education and Culture, Monsieur Roulland, to take these lines to heart."

Monsieur Roulland, in point of fact, took the lines so much to heart that he adjured his chief of staff with hair on end: "Rid me of this crazy business!" Unluckily he gave no specific directions as to how that end was to be accomplished. Hence his chief of staff turned wailing to the Ministry of the Interior and to the Minister of Justice, Delangle. So the Ministry of the Interior composed highly seasoned official questions which finally made their way to Baron Massy, the prefect of Tarbes. Similarly Delangle passionately demanded of the chief imperial prosecutor, Monsieur Falconnet, at Pau that *he* set matters to right immediately. That highly embittered gentleman now began to pelt with ever-angrier demands the sub-prefect Duboë at Argelès and the commissioner of police at Lourdes. Simultaneously the chief prosecutor Falconnet demanded of the imperial prosecutor Dutour an accounting for these incriminating events. Thus on this bureaucratic Jacob's ladder mounted and descended official questions and replies without arriving at any decision, not to mention a plan of action. And since not even the highest competent authority, the Ministry of Culture, ventured a decisive step, the lower officials were mired in uncertainty. Intrusions of the beyond into the actual world seemed safe from any provision of the legal code. To save face, everybody agreed that careful watch over the Soubirous family was to be continued, as well as over the girl Bernadette and the irregularities provoked by her. But since in affairs of state as in the world in general it is always the weakest who is made to suffer, the whole vial of everyone's wrath was finally emptied over the head of the poor policeman Jacomet. The lady's pertinacity became an actual threat to his job. If this thing went on, he would be discharged with a beggarly pension. He lived through evil hours. He was bitter and scared at the same time. Nothing could save him except that determination which all his superiors seemed to lack. Hence on the Thursday in question he was prepared to set an example. He summoned not only the entire constabulary of Lourdes—seven men plus Callet—but called on Argelès for assistance. The brigade stationed there sent three more men. Hence at six o'clock on that morning there were eleven armed men at Massabielle in order to put the fear of God into the lady, Bernadette, and the latter's adherents.

But Jacomet had not reckoned with the fact that on this day of testing five thousand souls from all parts of the land would assemble here. From the roads they pressed forward in throngs across the mountain of caverns, the Chalet Isle, the Saillet woods, toward the grotto. Jacomet ordered his subordinates to rope off the grotto in order to keep the masses from immediate access to it. Only Bernadette and her closest adherents, besides Dr. Dozous, Estrade and his sister, and a very few other important personages, were to be admitted within the lines. Jacomet roughly turned back the miller Antoine Nicolau, the earliest male adherent of Massabielle. Whereupon Antoine knelt down immediately in front of the brigadier d'Angla and intoned, harshly and stubbornly, a hymn to Mary. A large part of the crowd at once followed his example. Jacomet's orders, far from hurting the lady, tended to serve her. The portal of the grotto was of about the size of a theatre's proscenium arch. By virtue of the fact that today the thronging spectators formed a wide semi-circle about the stage, their front rows kneeling, their back rows standing, more people were enabled to see more and more clearly than ever before. Jacomet, intending to do no such thing, had happily created order for the detested performance.

On this day Bernadette found a lady of again quite different aspect. (Oh, never could her yearning love wholly fathom her beloved!) Nor was it the lady's intention today to lead her favourite into blissfulness. Hence Bernadette did not today fall into that profound ecstasy from within which she made the invisible to be visible. Yet had the lady never been so solemn as on this Thursday. Or rather it may be said that she was solemn for the first time on this day. Her ineffable charm was touched with sternness and determination. Even her smiling and the salutation of her nod, these heart-warming ceremonies of each new meeting, were restrained, official, symbolic only, as it were. The folds of the garment were rigid; the hem of the veil was unstirred by any wind; the ringlets which were wont to stray over the forehead were carefully hidden.

Bernadette was at once aware that she must do more than her utmost on this day. In the course of long nights she had carefully considered by what means, if need were, she could approach more closely the oval opening in the rock. Boulders enough fronted the rocky wall. Over these one could easily clamber at least to the bush of thorns which hemmed the portal like a beard grown wild. The lady made her first sign of the cross and Bernadette followed her example. Thereupon she beckoned with her index-finger and at once Bernadette, mounting the nearest boulder, climbed so high that her face was on a level with the thorn. She would never have ventured upon this closer approach without the lady's expressed desire. For now her head was but an inch or two distant from those pallid feet on which the golden roses flamed. In an access of passionate devotion which was to her also an act of sacrificial penitence, Bernadette thrust her head into the bush of thorns and kissed it. Luckily her cheeks were not badly scratched, and only two or three drops of blood appeared. From the human mass came the uprush of a mighty murmur. Even the agile grace with which the girl in the faded little cape had swung herself nearer the oval had been admired. Her contempt of pain in performing the ceremony of the bush of thorns seemed to point immediately to the miracle which could not now delay. The impassioned crowd anticipated the event. The eyes of the imaginative already saw the wild rose-bush, fed at its root by the blood of the little seeress, break abundantly into brilliant rosy bud. It was the highest moment hitherto in what Peyramale had called Bernadette's "mad services."

But the lady seemed to pay no great attention to these improvisations. She had other purposes. Insistently, enunciating each syllable clearly, like one giving important orders to a child, in her perfect yet by virtue of its distinction slightly foreign use of the dialect, she now said: "*Annat héoué en a houn b'y-laoua!*" And these words meant: "Go to the spring yonder and drink and wash yourself."

With two leaps, but without averting her face from the lady, Bernadette was once more below. Spring? she reflected. But where is there a spring? For the moment she was puzzled. Then it occurred to her that perhaps the lady's command of the dialect was not so complete but that she might confuse the words for spring and for brook. Bernadette dropped to her knees at once and began swiftly to slide on them—for she had by now become mistress of this form of locomotion—in the direction of the mill-stream. Already far advanced, she turned her face back toward the niche. With well-defined impatience the lady shook her head. Ah, the girl thought, it is not from the brook that I am to drink but from the Gave. Swiftly she changed her direction toward the river, which was about thirty feet distant. But the lady's voice called her back: "Not to the Gave, please!"

In these five words and in their tone of warning there was a certain condemnation of the Gave, as not fit for the lady's purposes. Although the choleric, racing river, possessed of time and transitoriness, was said by Clarens to enclose an eternal Ave in its name, its waters seemed to be the playground of hostile forces. Whither now? Bernadette wondered and, openmouthed, turned back toward the niche. The lady condescended to repeat the sentence concerning the spring and also, as though to help the girl, added the following: "*Annat minguia aquero hierbo que troubéret aquiou!*" And these words meant: "Go eat of the plants which you will find yonder!"

Bernadette surveyed the grotto for a long time until in the right corner she perceived a place without sand or rubble. A handful of grass grew there and a few miserable herbs, among them the little flower *dorine*, which is also called saxifrage because its humble pertinacity is powerful enough to cause it to force its way through rocks to the light of day. Thither Bernadette hastened to slide. She fulfilled the second part of the command by cropping a few blades of grass and herbs and swallowing them. This act revived a memory of her childhood. Once when her parents had come to visit her at Bartrès she had led her sheep to pasture, and her papa, in those days still a miller conscious of his worth, had lain beside her in the grass. Some of the grazing animals had had greenish spots on their backs. "Look, Bernadette," Soubirous had said in jest yet with a sombre expression, "the poor beasts are so fed up with the nasty grass that its green oozes out of their backs." Bernadette, who had never understood any pleasantry and had always taken things literally, had been seized by a great compassion for the sheep and had burst into tears. And in this hour there came to her the recollection of those green backs of the sheep and of her own tears, seeing that the lady bade her herself to eat of the bitter herbs.

But worse was to come, since Bernadette had yet to carry out the first and more important part of the command: "Go to the spring yonder and drink and wash yourself." Since the lady had spoken of a spring, there must be a spring hereabouts. Of that much Bernadette was sure. And if the spring was not above the earth it must needs be beneath it. The girl stared at the barren bit of earth of which she had just tasted the bitter green. Therefore she began to scratch up the earth with her bare hands, to burrow into it like a very mole. Against the back of the grotto were leaning the spades and tongs of the road-menders. It did not occur to Bernadette to take one of the spades to ease her toil. In wild zeal she continued to scratch and dig, fearful lest the lady grow impatient at her listless and unsuccessful effort. But even at this moment, busy executing the incomprehensible order of seeking a spring that did not exist, she never thought of questioning the lady's intentions. Sensitively as she sought to fathom the nature of the bond between her lonely self and the lonely self of the lady, she never took thought concerning the lady's secret purposes. Her obedience was blind and unconscious because of the extremity of her passion. She was all woman in this respect, too, that the creative plan of the beloved was indifferent to her except as it offered her room for the exercise of devotion.

When Bernadette had hollowed out a hole of the breadth and depth of a milk bowl, she came upon muddy earth. The next lumps of earth came easier from the small hollow. She took a deep breath and paused because her work had tired her. Then she beheld water gathering at the bottom of the hollow, no more than would half fill a wineglass. This tiny puddle would have sufficed to moisten lips and cheeks and forehead. Doubtless the lady's behest signified a symbolic action of this kind. To be sure, she had an easier time with symbols than did poor Bernadette, for symbols were native to that distinguished world from which the lady doubtless came. But in the world of the Soubirous all things were taken in their plain and literal sense. The girl would have considered it a sheer fraud not in all reality to drink and lave herself.

Therefore she dug a little deeper and now the puddle of water, doubtless a remnant of the last flood, seemed lost and seeped into the mud. So nothing was left for Bernadette to do but to take a particularly moist lump of earth and smear it over her face and to take another and seek to choke it down. This effort was so desperate and nauseating that the girl's mud-smeared face was contorted by strain and disgust. But scarcely had her spasmodic and violent efforts forced the earth down her œsophagus when her empty stomach rebelled against this nourishment of the dead, and a frightful urge to vomit shook her. In the presence of five thousand miracle-seekers she had to yield to this urge, and it was long before the lump of earth came up.

Her mother, Aunt Bernarde, and Aunt Lucille hastened to

her aid. Water was brought from the stream. The face and hands and garment of the girl were cleansed. All were ashamed. Only Bernadette, weary to death in her mother's arms, had not the strength to be ashamed. She was too feeble even to observe that the lady had abandoned her.

What, however, had the crowd seen, not having heard the commands of the lady concerning drinking and washing and eating herbs? First they had seen Bernadette, careless of the thorns, thrust her face into the bush. This ascetic kiss had aroused the enthusiasm of the spectators. The miracle was about to be. This had, however, been followed by an un-paralleled anti-climax. With face confused, Bernadette had slid toward the crowd—she who had hitherto, like the priest at the altar, turned her back to the audience and faced it, again like the priest, only to communicate the words of the invisible. And now she had not known whither to turn. Now it was hither and now it was yon, the while her glances at the niche had been full of doubt and uncertainty. And her face had been the everyday face of a child of the Soubirous. And finally she had crept into a corner of the grotto and there devoured grass and with her own claws scratched up the earth and smeared her forehead and cheeks with the filthy mud, of which she had lastly tried to devour a lump and then had had to vomit it up again. Whereupon members of her family had hastened to the poor filthy creature and with moist rags restored her to the semblance of humanity.

The spectators saw and understood only these gestures. What they beheld was a repulsive aspect of mental derange-ment, such as even asylums but rarely afford. And that was to be their miracle! Not only the enthusiasm and the rage of a mass of humanity, but its disappointment, too, has the power of the elemental. A crabbed deathly stillness had reigned up to the moment when the mother and the aunts had approached the

exhausted child. Next had arisen long and subdued laughter
that brought neither relief nor release. The crowd's laughter
was meant less for Bernadette than for itself, its stupidity and
easy credulity. By virtue of an unaccountable intoxication
thousands had hoped that here in Lourdes a thing would come
to pass that would lend meaning to the meaninglessness of life
and demonstrate their undemonstrable faith. Now common-
ness and flatness prevailed again and no miracle of roses had
pierced the greyness of reality. Bernadette was evidently a poor
crazy creature, and the lady a figment of her sick brain. Now
it was clear that priests and policemen were people of sober
good sense and that one had better stick to them.

Bernadette's most faithful followers now said: "Crazy as
they come. We certainly didn't suspect that!"

Jacomet was aware of his opportunity. Now if ever he could
succeed in trampling out this mischief like a smouldering fire.
What the ministries and the prefectural and sub-prefectural
offices and the imperial prosecutors and the mayor had failed
to accomplish, he, the mere subaltern, would bring about.
Praised by his superiors in office, honoured by the whole of
enlightened France, recipient of the gratitude of the relieved
clergy, he would be able to read of himself in the papers to
which Duran subscribed: "A modest police official tears out
the fangs of the Hydra of superstition." Surrounded by his
armed minions, Jacomet chose the highest spot available as a
platform and let his most cutting official voice resound.

"My dear people, you now see plain as day how you've been
made fools of. Confidence men, whom we'll discover yet, have
had a good laugh at you and your muddle-headedness. You've
at last seen with your own eyes that the poor Soubirous child
is a mental patient, who will soon have to be taken away and
securely locked up in a suitable institution. This business with
the Most Blessed Virgin is over and done with. She probably

has something better to do, anyhow, than to keep people from their work on an ordinary, shabby Thursday in February. She's certainly too much your friend to want you to lose time and money. She's perfectly satisfied to have you tell your beads, and that's the opinion of all the religious too. The Blessed Virgin doesn't care about the police having unnecessary trouble or expense, either. Look at the gendarmes! On your account we've had to get three extra ones from Argelès. These men's branch of the service is hard. They're busy night and day and you've put an extra burden on them. All these useless expenses caused by you could have been used for some worthy purpose. So I ask you please to use your good sound sense. You don't get miracles on ordinary weekdays; you don't even get them on Sundays. The Lord God won't stand for irregularities in nature any more than His Majesty the Emperor will stand for irregularities or disorders in the State. I hope you've all understood me and that by tomorrow order will have been restored in our entire region."

After this pithy and folksy and humorous address the crowd began to scatter, silent and subdued. Most of them pretended always to have known that the whole business was fraud and folly. Others were quite silent because they found it not so easy to get over their disappointment and disgrace. Between the grotto and the brook sat Madame Millet on a camp-stool which she always brought with her of late. Madame Baup, the dressmaker Peyret, Mademoiselle Estrade, and another lady of good social standing surrounded her. The latter's name was Elfriede Lacrampe and she was the niece of a much-esteemed physician. Millet did not seek to restrain her tears. "I feel as though I had lost a beloved child," she sobbed.

"It's not my fault, dear Madame Millet. I've always warned you of the girl," Peyret of the crooked shoulder insisted.

But Madame Lacrampe raised her pale eyes to heaven. "You

shouldn't have persuaded me to come along, dear friend," she sighed, facing the widow. "You know how fragile my faith is at best. This affair has certainly inflicted another hurt upon it."

Dr. Dozous and Monsieur Estrade strolled back to town together. They did not converse. At last, when they reached the saw-mill, Estrade opened his lips. "Odd, how even people like you and me are not impervious to the influences of mass psychology. . . ."

CHAPTER TWENTY

Sheet Lightning

Bᴇʀɴᴀᴅᴇᴛᴛᴇ's ʙᴇʜᴀᴠɪᴏᴜʀ after this catastrophe was once
more incomprehensible and amazing. The lady's failure to appear on Monday had made her want to die of despair, though
it had in no wise alienated from her the hearts of the faithful.
On this other day of incomparable shame, when she had been
forced to vomit in the presence of the largest public of her
career, she was calm, equable, even—it must be admitted—hopeful and serene.

None understood Bernadette because all, high or low, were
accustomed to estimate life by the sole measure of success. Now
it had happened that by virtue of the rather mad integration
of a living legend with the long-repressed yearning of the humble, this child named Soubirous had become the centre of interest in town and country and the subject of daily talk and
controversy in every house. She had become a star, as every
ruler, conqueror, hero, discoverer, artist must needs become a
star when once the brilliancy of success sets him in relief. Success forces him automatically to play himself, to assume his
own life-role, wherefore the term "star" is a very apt one. Who
does not lose the spontaneity of nature once he knows that a
hundred thousand eyes are fixed on him?

Bernadette did not lose it. Her innocence in this matter of
success was, to be sure, so great and so astonishing that her
preservation of her spontaneity was no merit in her. People did
not understand her, but neither did she understand them. What
did it profit these thousands to lie in wait and watch her deal-

ings with the lady? It would have been far better had no one ever come. Neither the dean nor the prosecutor nor the chief of police would then have troubled her. Followers had brought her nothing but vexation and anguish. Love was the important thing, that and the loveliest of beings and nothing else at all. In the very depths of her being Bernadette had not the faintest need of convincing anyone that the lady was real and no figment. It was brute force alone that had made her engage in controversy on this point. What could she do when clerical and lay authorities cross-examined her? Tell the simple truth, that was all. Could she have denied the lady for the sake of peace? Again and again people talked about the Blessed Virgin. Whoever the lady might be, to Bernadette she was above all *the* lady, and this simple word had more substance and meaning to her than the holiest name would have had. Bernadette knew very well that at the bottom of all the confusions that had come about were the lady's additional plans, messages, and commands. Had the most gracious one's interest been concentrated on her alone, how simple everything would have been. But Bernadette, who in her hours of rapture had experienced such overflowings of bliss, was not immodest enough to grumble at these plans of the lady, despite the unhappy confusion in the matter of the spring. Her path lay straight ahead. Whatever people might say, the lady's commands had to be exactly carried out.

The Cachot had been overcrowded all day. The heavy handle of the prison door had not been idle a moment. People sat on beds, on the table, even on the floor, which Louise Soubirous scrubbed daily. But not as hitherto did there obtain a mood of felicitation to veil the Soubirous as with incense. "How happy you must be to have a child like that!" "Who would have dreamed of such an angel coming out of the Cachot?" Today the visitors' eyes were sad and reproachful, as though a scandalous changeling had issued forth from here, of whose appearance the Soubirous family was far from guiltless. It was an evil sign that Aunt Bernarde and the serviceable Lucille had taken leave so soon! Aunt Sajou shook her head. "That oughtn't to have happened. . . . Nothing like that!"

Aunt Piguno cornered the Soubirous. "You know, good people, what Madame Lacrampe said? And she has more experience than anybody else, because her feeble-minded daughter is in the asylum! She said everything might go on this way a few months longer; then the eye-twitching will set in, and next paralysis, and then the power of speech fails. That's the way and it's a great misfortune, but you oughtn't to wait to reserve a place in the asylum at Tarbes. And you mustn't lose your composure, though I know how you must be feeling."

"*Praoubo de jou!*" Louise's choked voice cried ever and again.

Meanwhile Peyret had turned up and, in front of the assembled company, had let loose at Bernadette: "Oh, poor Madame Millet has the worst sick headache she's had in months. Two doctors had to be called in, Peyrus and Dozous. . . . But how could you have behaved like that—eating grass, eating mud, and then vomiting!"

Simply and unaffectedly Bernadette stood before her and replied: "But the lady told me to go to the spring and drink and wash. She pointed to that far corner. But there was no spring. So I had to dig, and I did find a little water. But I couldn't swallow that without swallowing the sand too."

The dressmaker gave a start as though a viper had bitten her. "You're trying to tell us that the Blessed Virgin wanted you to act like a beast of the field! Listen, everybody! This stubborn brat is trying to make us believe that the Mother of God behaved like a demon and told her to devour grass and mud.

That goes beyond everything. The dean ought to be informed of such blasphemy."

"The things you're saying are not true, Mademoiselle," Bernadette declared with the utmost calm and then added, repeating this statement for the hundredth time: "I do not know who the lady is."

"All I know is that you're a sly piece!" said Peyret, with a side-glance.

Piguno cast a sorrowful look at Mother Soubirous. "Sly? Dear God, that poor, poor creature . . ."

Soberly Bernadette concluded the defence of her lady: "And the lady didn't tell me to eat earth but to drink of the spring."

Uncle Sajou lighted his pipe, a thing he had not done here for some days out of respect. Clearing his throat, he asserted in his creaking voice: "Spring? Since there is no spring, the lady lied."

"That's a fact—she lied," others opined.

Bernadette's eyes flashed. "The lady does not lie."

The cobbler Barringue, so stirred by the scandal that his head had joined his hands in shaking, said: "In the hills the springs always come from above not from below, as every child knows. Below, you find nothing but stagnant water."

Nevertheless, Bernadette's answers succeeded in making her dismay of the morning seem less inexplicable. As always, she was convincing through the sober simplicity with which she represented the lady as a being of human character whose wishes and commands, however eccentric and even troublesome, must be fulfilled to the letter. Her logic, based upon the power of love to command conviction, was more than a match for the critical abilities of these small minds. Without their knowledge she forced them anew to admit the truth of her premise, namely, that the most beautiful of beings was an overwhelmingly real one, wholly guided by sound reason and incapa-

ble of harbouring a treacherous or delusive plan. She seemed
not in the least concerned over the spring that could not be
found. Her face had a healthier glow than for the past two
weeks. A rosy flush was spread over the cheeks which the thorns
had scratched. The tear-worn eyes of Louise Soubirous clung
fearfully to her child. Piguno's evil prophecy can't, just can't
be true, that Bernadette will be paralysed and bereft of speech
within a few weeks. Piguno was a beastly witch, that was all;
and it was, strangely enough, in this hour of great disappointment that the mother began to believe that it was truly the
Blessed Virgin who had appeared to her child in the guise of
this lovely and self-willed lady.

There was one who on this forenoon had yet spoken no
word. It was Soubirous, the father of the family. Now he rose
to the occasion in a manner that none would have expected of
his irresolute character and his subjection to the judgments of
the world. He showed the whole company the door. He did it,
of course, in his own dignified manner, bowing to all sides, his
hand upon his heart. "I am a poor man, and as though that were
not enough God has sent me this trial. I can't get on the inside
of my child's mind. I can't tell whether Bernadette is touched
in the head or not. All I know is this: she is not pretending. But
what am I to do? We've got to go on living. And we can't live
like this. There isn't very much air in this room, dear neighbours and kinsmen, and my family numbers six. I therefore beg
of you not to take it in ill part if I ask you to go now and not
to come back."

These words were so clearly wrung from the depth of a suffering spirit that the unbidden guests vanished and took no
umbrage. Peyret and Piguno, to be sure, hastened to spread
their poisonous gossip from door to door. The last to go was
Louis Bouriette, the one-eyed, also a helper at the post-office.
Him Soubirous requested to report himself as ill to Cazenave.

Thereupon for the first time in many days he went to bed while a faint wintry sunshine glimmered through the two little windows of the Cachot.

Marie, wanting to console Bernadette, sat down close beside her at the table and opened the catechism. The girls studied as though nothing had happened. Jean Marie and Justin, however, whom all these events had liberated from the usual restraints, sneaked out on some voyage of discovery of their own.

It is not rare for great ideas to appear in the world through the mediation of quite small minds.

Bouriette, the former stonemason, was not quite blind in his right eye. Had it been quite blind it would, in the sense of the Gospel, have "offended" him less. As it was, it offended him constantly by itching and burning and being inflamed. Also the dark-grey shadow which never left the right eye seemed to impair the clearness of the left. Bouriette had made of this infirmity the very centre of his life. It brought him the pity of others; it enabled him to pity himself and to cultivate an agreeable self-satisfaction. "What can you expect of a blind man?" may be recalled as this invalid's favourite phrase. Thus Bouriette did indeed demand little of himself. In his best years he had given up his difficult craft to get along, as best he could, on odd jobs. It was more comfortable thus and his excuse in the face of both his family and the world was a good one.

Although the mending of his infirmity could bring him no practical advantage, nevertheless an uncommon thought came to him on the way from Soubirous to Cazenave. Like all who are afflicted by a steady discomfort he considered any medicament that was harmless to be of some use. He therefore returned to the Rue des Petites Fossées where he lived. At his door he met his little six-year-old daughter.

"Listen, baby. You know the grotto of Massabielle where Bernadette Soubirous always has her visions?"

The child was a little hurt, like one whose frequentations were not duly esteemed. "Why, Papa, I've been there three whole times!"

"Then listen, darling. Go to your mother and tell her to give you a big piece of sackcloth. Wrap up in it a lump of the moist earth dug up in the right corner at the very back of the grotto. Don't forget! All the way back in the right corner. Then bring it to me at the post-office. Understand?"

Half an hour later, equipped with the wrapped lump of earth which by now had the consistency of porridge, Bouriette hid in the darkest corner of Cazenave's stables. There he sat down on the straw of an empty stall with his back against the bricks of the wall. He pressed the cloth with the moist earth firmly over his right eye. Water began to trickle down his face. Believing that the effect would take some time to show, he stayed in his dark hiding-place until the clock of Saint Pierre's struck two.

When at last he stepped out into the day he staggered back, overcome by excess of light. Convulsively he closed his good eye. The steady dark grey of the other's vision had turned into a tumultuous milk-white brightness. The grim fog had yielded to a transparent cloud-like veil, shot through by fiery sheets of lightning. Through this bright feathery veil Bouriette could see the outlines of things with precision. An immense excitement seized upon him, less on account of his eye than on account of his discovery. He raced across the Place Marcadale to see Dr. Dozous.

It was during the physician's office-hours and the waiting-room was crowded. Unabashed and without knocking, Bouriette insisted on bursting into the doctor's sanctum.

"That's no way to act, Bouriette," the doctor reprimanded him. "Go back and wait your turn."

"I can't wait!" The man was beside himself. "I've got back

the sight of my right eye. I treated it with mud from the grotto, and now I can see. It's a miracle!"

"You're all in such a hurry with your miracles," the doctor growled. Then he darkened the room and lighted a lamp with a powerful reflector and examined Bouriette's eye.

"Four serious scars on the cornea. Retina partly detached. Still you can see a little, can't you? Sometimes more, sometimes less."

"That's right," Bouriette echoed, "sometimes more, sometimes less." Like all patients with eye-trouble, he could easily be made uncertain concerning the degree of vision.

"And today it's better, eh?"

"Oh, much better, Doctor. It's like sheet lightning and I can see everything by it."

"That's not properly seeing. You pressed against the eyeball for hours and irritated the optic nerve."

Dozous turned the lamp and threw sharp light upon the chart against the wall.

"Can you read those letters with the right eye, Bouriette?"

"No, Doctor, I can't."

"How about the left eye?"

"No, I can't, Doctor."

"The devil you say! Well, how about both eyes?"

"No good, Doctor. You see, I don't know how to read."

Dozous pulled up the curtains. "Come back tomorrow when you're calmer, Bouriette."

Withdrawing, the invalid murmured stubbornly: "It's a miracle just the same."

Dr. Dozous did not know whether this case came under ophthalmology or psychiatry.

The Spring

CHAPTER TWENTY-ONE

Vexation's Aftermath

Louise Soubirous had definitely determined to take her daughter's part. Not for the lady's sake—to her she was not too well inclined; she had alienated if not robbed the mother of her favourite child. Who could deny that since the eleventh of the month Bernadette was no longer Bernadette? If nowadays life in the Cachot was not quite so care-ridden, that was meagre enough compensation for the anguish, danger, annoyance to which one was exposed. Above all, Mother Soubirous was angry at the lady on account of the uncanny sentence spoken during her third appearance: "I cannot promise to make you happy in this world, only in the next."

Not that Louise was a Christian of little faith and underestimated the importance of happiness in that other world, for the good reason that that other world is incomparably more enduring than this. Her sound motto would have been: a little happiness in this world and a little also in the next world, neither too little nor too much, but nicely balanced. What she would chiefly have prayed for was that there be no too catastrophic changes in the temperature of well-being either here or yonder. Of what avail that her little Bernadette be tortured on earth by need, asthma, court proceedings, mockery, and unjust suspicion, only to be permitted to lead above a life so special and distinguished as she was neither used to nor desired? That did not seem an equitable arrangement to Louise. Both her husband and herself had been fighting for years for one thing: their excellent right to a middle station. They desired neither stark want nor yet pheasants and Burgundy. The utmost limit of their dreams was the possession of a little mill, more or less like the former Boly mill.

But since the voice of fame had sounded in the Cachot, one altogether new note had been added to the gamut of Louise Soubirous's modest emotions: the note of vanity. She had become not unlike the mother of a musical child prodigy who exhibits her virtuosity day by day. While Bernadette, totally absorbed by her visions, remained indifferent to public approval, her mother distrustfully lay in wait for the public, jealously made estimates of the increasing or diminishing number of attendants and of the volume of applause. Hence Thursday's unfavourable reaction was a blow to her. Like all mothers of child prodigies, she was most intolerant of the inner circle of devotees. These constituted, as it were, a band of apostles whose duty lay in unconditional enthusiasm. She was most bitter against the Bouhouhorts woman. That good-for-nothing creature, who didn't know how to handle her half-dead brat and so continually wasted *her* good time and strength, had had the cheek to make a grimace of disgust when Bernadette had tried to swallow the lump of earth. She'd show her. Just let her come again begging for help. And the fat, stuck-up Millet woman with her sick headache! And her own sister Bernarde Casterot! That was so bitter a pill that she handed her wooden spoon to Marie, put on her kerchief, and before the midday meal hurried to her sister. With uncommon lack of respect she assailed the family oracle. "So you've gone back on my Bernadette, too, eh?"

"Why do you holler so, you fool?" Bernarde asked loftily.

Louise was beside herself. "Nothing, nothing, nothing can pry me away from my child's side. You can all stay home. I'm going to the grotto tomorrow!"

The widow Tarbès, formerly Bernarde Casterot, laughed

contemptuously. "Empty-headed. No change there. You're the mother; I'm only the aunt. Who stood beside your child when you still buried your weak head in the blankets?"

Undeniable. Louise at once lost her self-assurance in face of her sister's old superiority. The sturdy Casterot planted herself with oppressive firmness in front of Louise. "Goose! Naturally going to the grotto continues. Nine times more. As the lady said. And I only hope all those chicken-minded creatures will stay home and quit their scratching and clucking. Of course, that wouldn't suit you!"

Friday saw the fulfilment of Bernarde's hopes. The crowd was thin. Among the bare hundred who showed up there were many of the malicious, the jealous, the doubters, who expected today to intensify yesterday's fiasco. Neither Peyret nor Piguno was absent, nor a little group of schoolgirls under the leadership of Jeanne Abadie. Madame Millet could not leave her bed. Of the most faithful only Mother Nicolau and her son turned up. Bernadette was glad. She was more at her ease than when the presence of hundreds and thousands seemed to scorch her back.

She knelt facing the niche and took out her rosary, although the lady was not there. She knew at once that the lady would not come today. But it was not the stunning blow of the past Monday to know that there would be no meeting today. Bernadette had made great strides in her knowledge concerning the lady. She knew that the lady was not so wholly self-directing as she herself had assumed. The lady doubtless had other obligations, appointments, duties, and was probably also bound by some well-defined rule and order which it was not for her to overstep. She simply could not keep the engagement every time. Other duties made it impossible. Despite the absence of the gracious one today Bernadette was no longer in an agony of suspicion that the lady might be faithless and leave her for ever without a farewell. Her love had gained in assurance. Deep inside her heart she was sure that the cause of the lady's absence today was simply weariness. It did not seem too unlikely that the lady might have a sick headache. Was that not a common affliction of distinguished ladies? Bernadette had no clear notion of its character. What she was quite clear about was the high degree of self-denial demanded of the lady whenever she condescended to make the trip to Massabielle. Quietly Bernadette told her beads. Then she arose and turned to the assembly with a confident smile.

"The lady did not come today." After a brief pause she was impelled to explain. "Yesterday must have been very fatiguing. . . ."

This was one of those remarks that enabled Bernadette to render the invisible so warmly human and bring it near to the hearts of men. Whoever had heard one of those sentences and looked into those dark-brown, tranquil eyes could no longer resist or entertain a doubt of the girl's sincerity. Suddenly yesterday's antics no longer seemed so humiliating. God knows what definite but incomprehensible thing the lady had had in mind which had confused even her mediatrix. Better wait and see. Several women could not restrain their tears. Bernadette's words were repeated from mouth to mouth. None paid attention to the moist bit of earth in the right-hand corner of the grotto.

The sheet lightning had disappeared from before Bouriette's eye. But the feathery cloud that had taken the place of the dark-grey fog remained. Through it he could see objects quite clearly. And he was convinced that the moist earth of Massabielle had been the source of his healing. He did not, however, go back to the doctor. The latter might shake his faith and thus hinder the completion of the cure. Bouriette was firmly

determined to continue the treatment. He had already told a
few people of the partial regaining of his sight. Most of them
had laughed him to scorn. Oddly enough, he had found a
measure of belief among two or three of his former colleagues.
The guild of the stonemasons and road-menders had a spirit of
loyalty. They were mostly poor men, old before their time.
But if one of them—as had happened recently—won a prize in
the lottery he would treat the others to so many rounds that
soon his winnings would be dissipated. Nor were the members
of this guild more pious than other inhabitants of Bigorre. But
if an honest-to-God miracle were to happen to any, the rest
would welcome it as a handsome feather in the whole group's
cap. Thus when the invalid had related his elevating experience his old comrades had exchanged appreciative glances.

Around three o'clock Louis Bouriette went to Massabielle
for a fresh bag of earth. Arrived at the grotto, he met a small
group of women bending over a thin trickle or rill of water
which, starting at the moist patch of earth in the grotto, was
making a tiny channel for itself through the sand to the Savy
brook. This rill was not much more than a narrow thread of
water which a swift summer rain might cause to purl along a
garden path. Yet it had a lively and purposeful way of running that seemed to point to a plenteous source.

"Well, what's that?" Bouriette asked in amazement.

"We were telling our beads," one of the women explained,
"when suddenly the water began to run. We didn't notice it
before."

"The devil!" Bouriette whistled. "That doesn't look like
stagnant water. It's a real little spring."

The eyes of the old peasant woman of Omex were triumphant. "The Most Blessed Virgin told Bernadette to go to the
spring and drink and wash. There is the spring. . . ."

"As God lives, that's spring-water!" cried Bouriette and ran to the Savy mill to inform Antoine Nicolau of the event. Now, a good miller has a sound knowledge of three things—of grain, of horses and donkeys, and, not least, of water. If need be, an able miller can dam a brook, row a boat, provide a basin for a spring. With an expert air Nicolau bent over the thread of water and with his finger tried to trace it to its source. "There's something to every single thing that Bernadette says," he finally declared. "This vein comes straight from the rock."

"So the Most Blessed One did perform a miracle!" one of the women cried contentiously.

"It's not easy to catch a spring," the miller said instructively, "and I'm no expert at it. It commonly appears in the form of so and so many rills which must be united. The rills can be lost in the sand and your spring will stop flowing. It wouldn't be a bad plan for you women to hold your tongues."

Nicolau and Bouriette took brief counsel with each other. Then they went over to the road from Tarbes which crossed the ridges on the other side of the mountain of caverns. There the masons and road-menders were busy breaking stones. Bouriette's former comrades, grateful to the Virgin, consented to help. After working-hours they went with their tools to the grotto. Most of the men proceeded to mend the steep path that descended so dangerously from the edge of the rock and to provide it with a wooden railing.

Before dark set in wholly, Antoine Nicolau sent to his mill for pitch-torches. By their flickering light he went expertly about his delicate task. He succeeded beyond all hope. He had followed the rill to the depth of but a few feet into the rock when a stream of water of the thickness of a child's arm suddenly gushed forth. Swiftly the hollow was filled with water to its brim. Now the men began to build a round basin of stone no bigger than the baptismal font in church. They chose for this purpose round well-worn stones. They fitted these together with great precision and filled the gaps with mortar. They made a stone floor for the basin, leaving open only the source at the point where Antoine seemed to be holding the spring even as one holds a restive horse by the halter. Clear and pure water rose in the basin. All drank greedily of it. There was no aftertaste to the good, plain mountain water. Later Nicolau and Bouriette returned to the mill once more to fetch armfuls of wooden gutters, such as every miller has in store. These served as pipes to drain off the overflow, and the new spring, visibly happy at its birth, plashed swiftly through them. Not till the work was completed did Antoine dash into the Cachot to convey the victorious news to Bernadette.

That evening Lafite and Clarens were taking a walk on the Chalet Isle. February was ending and spring lay in the air. A massive full moon stood in the heavens. As the gentlemen came forth from the gate of the park they saw the red glow of torches gleaming from Massabielle.

"You'll see," Clarens observed, "there will be no peace until . . ."

"Until what?" Lafite asked and received no answer.

They chose the path to the grotto, Lafite for the first time. Clarens had already witnessed the vexatious antics of the day before. They came upon the men who had just finished their work and were now looking at it with satisfaction.

"What are you fellows doing there?" Clarens asked.

"Behold the spring!" Bouriette replied with the gesture of a successful prestidigitator.

Antoine dipped his arm into the water up to the elbow. "Bernadette promised us a spring. Here it is. And what a spring! It yields at least a hundred litres of water a minute."

Lafite tapped Clarens's shoulder. "Well, my friend, how do you like my power of divination? Three weeks ago I spoke, you remember, not of an oread or dryad but of a water nymph."

Clarens turned to the men. "Who ordered you to do this work and who is paying you?"

"Oh, Monsieur," one of the road-menders said, "we worked a few hours overtime for the lady. She's our employer. She'll pay us some day. . . ."

From amid the laughter rose the miller's voice: "Well, here's a real miracle which we owe to Bernadette. And yesterday they mocked her."

"Not so fast, dear Nicolau," Clarens interrupted him. "Where is your miracle? Is a spring a miracle? Wasn't it always within the mountain? Bernadette didn't produce it by magic, but only discovered it."

With a grandiose gesture the poet pointed to the skies. "And yonder moon, gentlemen? Is Luna, the dead satellite that circles for evermore around us, not a miracle? Because you have no eyes for the great miracles you need the little ones."

This pantheistic observation was most ill received. Ironically a grey-haired road-mender shook his head. "What is it you say, Monsieur? You want us to take the moon for a miracle? We all know the moon very well. She's always there. Whatever is always there, is no miracle."

The two gentlemen returned to the Chalet.

"Our authors nowadays," said the pedagogue, "have unfortunately forgotten how to speak to the simple."

"You may be right, dear friend," Lafite replied. "I find it hard to communicate my meanings even to you. God knows what's happened to all of you. I'll soon fade out of the picture. I gladly give ground both to the lady of the grotto and to my dear relatives who have apprised me of their return."

CHAPTER TWENTY-TWO

Exchange of Rosaries

THE FORMATION of the spring of Massabielle was more than a triumph for Bernadette. It was a victory of the people of Bigorre over the powers of both the Empire and the Church. Not only in the morning now did pilgrims by the thousand seek the grotto in order to be stirred and shaken by a child's making visible the divinely invisible. By evening, too, long processions with tapers and torches of pine and pitch made their way to Massabielle. Thus was fulfilled as a matter of course the lady's desire for processions which the priests had bluntly refused.

Although the mere appearance of a hitherto unknown spring could never be acknowledged as a miracle by the theological authorities, the whole world spoke of a miracle. Even sober and cultivated people such as Estrade, Clarens, and Dozous could not help admitting that the coincidences which led to the discovery of the spring were strange and mysterious. The masses, who as recently as Thursday had condemned Bernadette as a repulsive lunatic, were now impelled by their feeling of guilt to intensify their enthusiasm. The wavering, the suspicious, the hostile now vied with one another in proclaiming their faith. Antoinette Peyret, for instance, appeared morning after morning at the door of the Cachot and by kneeling in the street paid homage to the dwelling of her wonder-worker. This gained her the increased favour of Madame Millet, who, having been the first to believe, considered herself, as it were, the mother of the miracle itself. Piguno, suddenly of an extreme humility, begged Louise Soubirous to permit her daughter to bless her rosary by touching it. Bernadette refused angrily. Jeanne Abadie, too, who had thrown the first stone, sought in vain to kiss her friend's hand. The common people, especially the Pyrenean peasantry, experienced days as from lost and forgotten centuries, such as the most daring imagination would not have ventured to introduce in any modern period. It was as though in this countryside of Lourdes there vibrated volcanic strata of the supernatural which now burst through long-sealed scoria into living flame. These people were like people everywhere. The poorest were perhaps somewhat poorer than in the rest of France. In the country they lived in shaky cottages. They slept with their domestic animals. Rarely did they see a franc. The thoughts of the men revolved about how these twenty-sou pieces were to be obtained. The women were preoccupied with the daily corn-mush, a bit of butter or lard, a piece of red or white flannel for a new *capulet*. Not wealth but poverty is the last refuge of materialism. Need and want are condemned to overestimate the value of common material things.

By the favour of incomprehensible powers Bernadette Soubirous had performed a greater miracle than the discovery of a spring. Without her knowledge or desire Bernadette communicated to the downtrodden something of that compassionate consolation which flooded her own being whenever she saw the lady again. Inexplicably she transferred to masses of men a portion in the heaven of her love. Through Bernadette's mediation they came to feel that behind the forms and words and rites used by the clergy there lay not a vague possibility but an almost tangible reality. No longer were mortal need and sorrow mere granite loads to be dragged from meaningless birth to equally meaningless death. The granite had grown porous and strangely light. Even the dull mind of the swineherd Leyrisse was touched by the dance-like consciousness of life's twofold and festive character which filled the souls of all. He had long since ceased taking his swine to Massabielle. But his choked voice blared all day from his throat the folk-songs of his native hills. And all existence, with its hatred, enmity, greed, envy, fear, suspicion, jealousy, lost no small portion of its heaviness. Morning after morning the lady appeared, to prove that the universe held more than this mere mortal misery. No need, therefore, to agonize over the daily bite of bread like a hungry dog. Work was tinged by a spirit of play. The she-goats were milked as they had not been and the linen washed. And expectancy lifted all hearts: What will happen in the grotto tomorrow?

From its centre at Lourdes the earthquake sent its vibrations to every corner of France. That country had gone through three revolutions whose aim had been to secure the freedom of the mind against misuse of the cross, which the propertied classes carried in front of them to secure their privileges. And this country rose in rebellion against what it held to be a relapse to conquered states of mind. As Clarens was accustomed to tell his students, mankind was just beginning its history. The earth had not yet been subdued. Industry with its new machines would provide happiness and comfort for all. There was no more important task than the conquest of this planet for the good of all. He who retarded the execution of this task by metaphysical fantasies was an enemy of man's higher development and so of man and society themselves. Thus thought Monsieur Duran with due consideration of the great Parisian press; thus thought the great Parisian press with due consideration of Monsieur Duran. That press did not even follow Lafite's flight toward the moon as a miracle. Nothing aroused its wonder save such reactionary thinking as would not see that the organization of nature was a relatively simple thing. Heaven is empty and rigid space dotted by some billions of sidereal systems. Nature is equivalent to this heaven. In the immeasurable voids between the globes of fire there was evidently no place for the so-called supernatural. On a minor satellite of one of the least of those sidereal systems there vegetates an ape-like creature called man. The notion that a male of this animal species, above all one of its wretched females, could be the image of beings who rule (rule, itself an anthropomorphic fallacy) the universe, this could be but the ideology of such primitive savages as had not yet won man's first, if not also his final, victory—the renunciation of wishful dreams. Not until this sad and intentional stupidity at the basis of all illusionism was overcome; not until man had liberated himself from the immemorial emotional delusion that he and his earth were the centre of things and his mind something other than a purposeful function of matter determined by necessity; to sum up, not until he resigns himself to see his life in its true colours of a physico-chemico-biological mechanism, not until then will he begin at last to be a human being instead of a semi-animal haunted by demonic dreams. This evolution toward a truly human status will inevitably issue in tolerance, the rule of reason, and the annihilation of all dark and aggressive instincts. And it was for this reason that the affair of Lourdes was considered to be no negligible mishap. It blocked with the oldest kind of rubbish man's clear path to his earthly redemption from poverty, prejudice, and ignorance. Now neither *Le Siècle* nor even *La Petite République* dared to speak quite so frankly. The power of the Church had still to be reckoned with, as well as troublesome suits for blasphemy. But the little paper *Lavedan* printed a very gay article called "The Spring" which had probably been inspired by Mayor Lacadé. The point of the article was that the ground of Lourdes and its vicinity was full of mineral and curative springs which needed no wondrous lady for their discovery and utilization.

But in addition to the France of these militant editorials there was still another France, not necessarily that of the believers or of the hierarchy, but a France of souls easily charmed and delighted to be deeply stirred, a France predominantly of women. These listened breathlessly to the daily reports from Lourdes. The tale of the shepherd girl and the lady, a very French tale, filled them with very happy emotions. And so Bernadette found defenders who also had access to certain papers. The controversy flamed and the "apparitions of Lourdes" became a national affair of broadest import.

A national affair! Precisely that. The imperial regime would have expected an attack from any political faction rather than from that of Heaven itself. Had the Socialists or the Jacobins, the Freemasons, the royalists, or the adherents of the house of Orléans, sought to trip up the regime on the occasion of a political trial or a case of bribery, it would have been no difficult matter to resist them by ordinary means. But in the inner ministerial group, where twice already the matter of Lourdes had been on the agenda, the same joke was cracked in which Lacadé had indulged two weeks before: We can't be asked to send the Blessed Virgin to jail.

Meanwhile the chancellery of the imperial cabinet had insisted on a full report from the Ministry of Culture. Monsieur Roulland did furnish an extensive report which closed with a frank and yet malicious appeal for a gracious expression of the imperial will. When this expression seeped down the bureaucratic slope it amounted to no more than that an end be put as soon as possible to the phenomena of Massabielle and the dissensions proceeding therefrom. The order was rendered even feebler by the admonition that no harshness be practised and that extreme considerateness be shown for the religious sensibilities of the affected regions. Minister Roulland exploded with mocking laughter when in the handsome but turgidly composed official document he recognized unmistakably the style of his master, Napoléon the Less. Now let the press rage. His back was covered. Thus all the authorities of the world, from the Emperor to Jacomet, were united by a single bond, that of hopeless embarrassment.

At once Roulland hastened to gladden the heart of Baron Massy, prefect of the Hautes-Pyrénées, by communicating to him the equivocal imperial decision. Of Massy none could ever say anything except that he was a gentleman who knew how to behave. He was always dressed in seemly black and wore patent-leather shoes and kid gloves even in his office. His high wing collar was frantic with adherence to the conventional. He was a scion of one of the most proper of French families, had received all the proper orders and decorations due to his rank, including the Vatican's Order of Saint George, and beyond that looked like the very embodiment of the rubber-stamp of passports: "Special characteristics: None." Now, the province which Massy administered happened to be considered in the private tradition of governmental circles as the springboard, no one knew why, to the prefecture of the province of the Seine, in which Paris is situated. Hence from Tarbes there stretched a direct road to one of the highest offices in the Empire. The baron knew precisely what he had at stake. If he did not succeed in forcing an issue to the affair of Lourdes satisfactory to his superiors and agreeable to all parties, Paris and his further career had gone to hell.

No sooner had he glanced over the long dispatch from the ministry than he threw himself into his carriage. The way from the prefectural to the episcopal palace was of the shortest, but on principle the prefect was averse to appearing as a pedestrian among his subjects. The relations between himself and the prince of the Church at Tarbes were not exactly strained; they were definitely chill. Consequently His Lordship Bertrand Sévère Laurence, who knew precisely what o'clock it was, had no objection to keeping His Excellency waiting fully fifteen minutes. The message he sent was that he happened to be in his private chapel. His Lordship was anything rather than a proper gentleman and scion of a proper family. Quite the contrary. He was a plebeian, a proletarian, who had arrived. His father had been a road-mender somewhere in Béarn. His friends whispered that His Lordship had been virtually illiterate to the age of fifteen. Not until then had this gifted ignoramus, impelled by the compensatory passion of the low-born, rushed, with brilliant distinction in all branches, through the seminary of Aire and through the university. Massy was indignant beyond measure at being kept waiting. This trickiest of old foxes, his thoughts ran. Then he started, having almost crushed the high silk hat between his knees. When finally the tall peasant figure of His Lordship stood before him, he somehow broke and would have kissed the episcopal ring had not a mild gesture prevented that.

"Monseigneur," the Baron began, "I implore your assistance. This business in Lourdes assumes the proportion of an uprising. You alone can save us from the necessity of using severe measures."

The corners of the bishop's mouth were made by nature to droop. Hence his habitual expression was both sarcastic and proud.

"By all means use severe measures, Your Excellency." He sighed sympathetically. "The only thing desirable . . ."

"I am fighting for the honour of our holy religion, Monseigneur. It is seriously threatened by this unworthy comedy."

The bishop raised his bushy white eyebrows. "The clergy

of the canton of Lourdes have been strictly forbidden by the dean to become witnesses of this comedy, as you are pleased to call it."

"It's not enough, Monseigneur. You should forbid the comedy itself. You should forestall the ridicule to which these so-called appearances subject the faith before believers and unbelievers at once."

Bertrand Sévère leaned back in his armchair, his labourer's hand upon the ivory crook of his cane. "Suppose these appearances contain a kernel of the supernatural," he said very slowly.

The proper Baron Massy felt his proper collar choking him. "A kernel of the supernatural. Who is to render decision?"

"A single institution." The old bishop smiled faintly. "Holy Church."

Massy decided to loosen his tight cravat a trifle. "It was my impression, Monseigneur, that you entertained no faith in a supernatural kernel and condemned the whole farce even as we do."

"It may be; it may be, dear Baron." Again that impenetrable smile. "But you'll admit that the bishop is the very last man to block the road to a possible miracle. And a miracle, a revelation of the supramundane, is possible everywhere and always, even in my modest diocese. Therefore my function can be but to exercise the utmost caution and reserve; of you, Your Excellency, we expect, as usual, the wise decisiveness of action." And almost humbly he inclined his white, priestly head in farewell before the authority of earth.

Returning from his futile errand, Massy at once dictated a circular dispatch to the sub-prefect, the police headquarters at Lourdes, and the prosecutor's and mayor's offices of that town. He demanded an intensified supervision of the Soubirous family, especially in respect of moneys received by that family. The unlicensed sale of consecrated objects (the blessing of

rosaries, perhaps, for money or its equivalent) might be interpreted as constituting a misdemeanour subject to arrest. Were
a single case of such practice to come to the knowledge of the
authorities the whole Soubirous family was to be taken into
custody. Massy closed his dispatch with the memorable directions that the gendarmes assigned to service at the grotto were
to appear on duty fully armed and wearing gloves. These
gloves (of yellow washable leather, according to official prescription) obtruded themselves on Massy's proper mind because it seemed to him that nothing less would convince the
airy lady that he, personification of the power of the State,
was about to take the matter seriously. But such is the complicated malice of circumstance that ultimately these gloves did
not assume the character of a threat but rather of a gesture of
reverence toward the lady.

March had begun. Four times more, Bernadette thought,
then my fifteen days will be over. It will be the last Thursday
and I'll return no more. But would she not? She had not promised not to come at the end of the fifteen days. Again this was
merely the rigid assertion of her aunt Bernarde. But Bernarde
was a strong-minded woman and, like many of her kind, inclined to pessimism. In contrast to Father and Mother Soubirous she had a decided preference for the disagreeable. Thus
Bernadette was torn between deadly terror and boundless hope.
Was it not at least possible that the lady might remain true to
her her whole life long? Could not the lady grow old and
older, along with herself, there at Massabielle from day to day?
People would get used to the whole thing and come no more.
She herself would do a full day's work, like everybody. Monsieur Philippe was getting quite old. Perhaps Madame Millet
would need a serving-maid. She herself would shrink from no
kind of work. If only the lady would appear to her every

morning, she would be glad to wash soiled linen, a thing she abhorred most. Passionately she clung to the dream that the unitedness demanded by her love could last her life. The other possibility, namely, that next Thursday would see the end of all, seemed to her so monstrous that her imagination could not envisage it. Could life go on without this daily grace of love? These urgent questions threw into trivial shadow the wondrous deed of the finding of the spring. Bernadette strained to hold fast to each hour of her swiftly fleeting days of grace. Her speechless heart pleaded each morning at the grotto: "Stay long, Madame—long, long today."

And the lady with a friendly smile nodded assent. But her stay, which never extended beyond three or at most four quarter-hours, always fell short of Bernadette's desire. The lady probably knew what could be demanded of Bernadette's endurance and what not. If it was so exhausting for her who brought it to evoke the ecstasy, how much more so must it be for her who endured it.

Sundry rites had now been added to the ceremonies at the grotto. Daily upon her appearance the lady demanded that Bernadette eat of the herbs, drink of the spring, and lave herself therein. It was odd that the auditors, who during the last visions had become ever more accustomed to imitating the young visionary's gestures and repeating her spasmodic words, disdained to use the new and ever more merrily plashing spring. Although Bouriette's experience had made the round of Lourdes, none credited it. Bouriette had called himself a blind man for long. Well, he had never been really blind but full of sly and desirous glances at the world. His case was too equivocal to prove a miracle. Thus it happened that the spring was considered merely as the lady's ready answer to the dean's demand for a miracle of roses. The lady was no sexton to follow literally a parson's bidding. She had her own notions and was not dependent on those of an irascible quarreller. So you want to test my powers by asking for roses in February? Wait, my friend! I won't cheapen myself by just producing roses. I'll produce something that neither you nor the rest dreamed of. Will you at last admit my superiority? Thus the spring was taken as the triumphant reply of the living lady to the abstemious and hostile clergy. Except Bouriette, no one ascribed a practical purpose to her. He, however, had held his tongue for several days. The jealous notion had come to him that the curative property of the well might grow less if shared by other sufferers.

Morning after morning thousands now witnessed how at the beginning of her ecstasy Bernadette obeyed the command of the most gracious one to wash in the spring and drink of its water from her cupped hands. They attributed to this only a ritualistic or mystic significance. Bernadette seemed to them to be celebrating a strange communion with the lady. It occurred to no one that the lady had called forth the spring for a sober and objective reason. Nor did any comprehend that the lady repeated her command daily in order to lead the people along the right way through imitation of the girl. Bernadette alone, gifted with the insight of love, had fathomed the circumstance that it was not always possible for the lady to communicate her will directly. Just as she could not bear to name names, so she could not bear to say crudely: Act thus and so, and the following will come to pass. Some element of royal, courtly reticence demanded of her these roundabout mysterious methods. Yet Bernadette's mind was not concerned with the world but only with the lady. Therefore she too failed to ponder on the nature and purpose of the spring. Her obedience was of that perfect kind that asks no questions.

Yet was Bernadette not wholly free of a slight tinge of guile. Now and then she was tempted to use the unresting cunning of love to test her beloved. The rosary had come to be the most enchanting part of her communion. It was a tranquil blended lostness to the world when Bernadette murmured her Ave and dropped a black bead of her poor little string and when the lady with speechless lips but clear observing eyes imitated the girl's gesture and let another pearl of her long radiant rosary glide through her fingers. That meant more than prayer in common; it was a heart-intoxicating form of contact, such as befitted a love like this. For it was then as though each of the two held an end of the same invisible staff, through the substance of which flooded back and forth between them warmth as of blood and yearnings of the soul. All objects which Bernadette touched at the lady's bidding had a new and fresh and pristine significance as if they had only now come into being, even her old, shabby rosary.

The previous night the following thing had taken place: Antoinette Peyret had come to the Cachot with one of her young seamstresses whose name was Pauline Sans and who was only two years older than Bernadette. Peyret's eyes no longer gleamed with suspicious arrogance but with dismayed obsequiousness. She did not tire of praising Pauline as her best worker and dear friend, and besought Bernadette to fulfil the girl's wish. Pauline Sans blushed deeply and asked her who had been so blessed to exchange rosaries with her. She could not imagine anything more heavenly than to use in prayer the beads on which the lady's eyes had rested. Her own dearest possession was this rosary of hers, inherited from her mother, strung with large, blood-red, genuine corals. Profitable as this exchange would have been, Bernadette rejected it at once, not without violence. Later she grew thoughtful and changed her mind and declared that she would use Pauline's rosary next morning if the girl would stay quite near her.

When that morning the first salutations were over, as well

as the laving and drinking, and Bernadette, as every morning, knelt on a broad, flat stone facing the niche, she shyly and hesitantly drew from her bag the magnificent coral beads. Her heart beat in wild restlessness. Now she would come to know what she meant to the lady. For was not her poor little black rosary the only material bond of their love? Even in sleep she kept it under her pillow. And Bernadette was frightened at her own intrepidity in laying this snare for the lady. If she observes nothing, I am indifferent to her; if she observes, she loves me.

Then with the moving self-distrust of one who doubts his beloved's love she did not dare to set the trap so searchingly. She tried to give her happiness a chance. Therefore she swung the conspicuous corals up and down, so that the lady must see them. The lady hesitated at once, let her own rosary sink, and showed upon her countenance that faint dimness which Bernadette had come to know so well. Her lips moved. "That is not your rosary. . . ."

And Bernadette's quivering heart cried: "No, Madame, it is not mine. Mademoiselle Sans besought me to exchange my unbeautiful one for her beautiful one. I thought maybe you would rather have a beautiful one. . . ."

As though hurt, the lady receded a step. "Where is your own?"

Bernadette flung herself upon Pauline, who was behind her, and tore from her hands the black rosary. Triumphantly she held it high above her head. Again the crowd misunderstood the gesture and imitated it with enthusiasm. A very storm went through its ranks: The lady blesses our rosaries.

Thus once again what was a sacred ritual to the many was a sacred reality to Bernadette. Her whole being trembled: She loves me.

CHAPTER TWENTY-THREE

A Louis d'Or and a Box on the Ear

Vital Dutour, imperial prosecutor, was massaging his bald yellow head. Jacomet's proposal struck him as detestable, the typical product of a police brain. Odd, for Jacomet, though not bright, was a good-natured, honest chap. He had always fulfilled his duties to the entire satisfaction of his superiors, seeing that he had known how to make himself feared and yet remain popular. His private life was exemplary. Mademoiselle Jacomet, his daughter, was a veritable angel of the poor. All day long she knitted undershirts and neckerchiefs and distributed them in the streets. Jean Marie and Justin Soubirous, as the "poorest children in the town," had repeatedly benefited by these offerings of a benevolent heart. Father Pomian, to be sure, could not help observing that the wool of which the undergarments were knitted was genuine police wool, since they scratched much more than they warmed. But one knew what weight to attribute to Pomian's jests. In them pastoral gentleness was often sacrificed for the sake of a neat point. Marie Dominique Peyramale, no lamb in mildness himself, yet called Pomian to account more than once in the matter of his aphorisms. My dear fellow, he would say, the age is past in which colleagues of ours could be the parasites of the fashionable on the terms of Vauvenargues. . . .

Dutour, to sum up, considered Jacomet limited but decent. But the commissioner's latest notion was the reverse of decent. Now, it was no new thing in Dutour's experience that the mentality of the criminalist and that of the criminal are subterraneously allied. And the *agent provocateur* embodied, as it were, the centre of equilibrium between those two poles. Jacomet's idea was precisely to employ such a creature.

In his last dispatch the prefect of Tarbes had expressed the definite wish that a case be found to prove that the Soubirous abused the credulity of their fellows by deriving material benefits from the apparitions and their consequences. It would be a damned rare case of metaphysical corruption. But it would suffice, for men judge nothing with more implacable harshness than that which they are themselves utterly prepared to commit, namely, the selfish exploitation of a ready and willing simplicity of mind. On what other principle is the whole of commercial advertising based? If it could be proved against the Soubirous that their daughter's visions constituted a profitable business, Lourdes and all France would be healed at one stroke. Dutour had not required Massy to point that out to him. Nevertheless, he found it hard to accept Jacomet's crude proposal without hesitation. To be sure, great things were prophesied for the following Thursday, which would constitute the final triumph of Bernadette and the lady over public authority. Therefore a pitiless blow would have to be struck within the forty-eight hours which still divided that time from this.

Vital Dutour desired to try one last measure before he consented to let Jacomet have his way. Bernadette was said to have blessed many rosaries. Of course her smooth mind had thought of an alibi at once. The lady had demanded that she use her own rosary and she had only lifted up the other for a moment. Never mind. In cases where laymen blessed religious objects a well-disposed clergy could be made to see an offence against the practice of religious rites. To this might be added the fact that, at the expense of Madame Millet, a sort of altar with a crucifix, several images of the Madonna, and many candles had been erected in the grotto. The concordat, however, was known to forbid any new place of worship without the consent of the Ministry of Culture.

The imperial prosecutor did the same thing that the prefect had done: he visited the highest ecclesiastical authority within reach. The dean liked Dutour as little as the bishop liked the baron. The prosecutor explained to the dean at length that things had now developed so far that a preventive act on the part of the Church was not only advisable but had become unavoidable. The blessing of rosaries and the erection of altars by unconsecrated and unauthorized persons constituted an offence against the authorities of both Church and State. Peyramale had had Dutour, scarcely recovered from his severe influenza, shown into the icy reception hall. The prosecutor was at once afflicted by cold feet and terror of a relapse. The boorish priest did not even offer him a brandy. Vital's mood grew more and more sombre. He knew that Peyramale wished the Soubirous girl to the devil no less than did he or Lacadé. Also he knew that the vain priest, though he recognized his, Vital's, visit to be an act of self-humiliation, would take no step toward meeting him half-way. He did not, in fact, judge Peyramale's motives correctly. The dean had the boyish inclination of siding with the robbers when it came to a conflict between the hunted and the hunter. He was altogether sick of the goings-on concerning the lady. He still considered Bernadette a little swindler. (Yet, for reasons he could not fathom, it had given him quite a jolt when, reciting the Matutin of February 26, he had come upon the following words of the prophet: "I saw a stream of water flow forth from the temple on the right side and all to whom this water came were saved.") Nevertheless, it was going just a bit too far that courts and police should now ask him to pull their chestnuts out of the fire. Pitilessly out of his ravaged and furrowed explorer's face he looked up and down the imperial prosecutor, who was lifting his knees a little to keep his feet from touching the freezing floor.

"My dear sir," said Peyramale, "as far as an offence against religious worship is concerned, you are very wide of the mark. A little wooden table on which people place candles and holy pictures remains a little wooden table and is in no sense an altar. The erection of an altar demands quite definite conditions. Anybody may place a wooden table with candles, crosses, flowers, and so on, anywhere, at home or in public—the latter, to be sure, only if the public authority has no valid ground for objecting. The mayor's office or your own may sequestrate the table in the grotto. But I can be of no more help to you, if you choose to do it, than if the table were in the house of Madame Millet."

These unmistakable words decided the imperial prosecutor to drop all hesitation in respect of Jacomet's plan.

At eleven o'clock on Tuesday a new guest appeared in the Cachot. He was a stranger. In his suit of checked English weave, a plaid shawl over his arm, an umbrella in his hand, and a grey beaver on his head, the man gave the impression of an Englishman on tour, such as often came in summer to take the cure at Cauterets and Gavarnie. The presence of this personage of the large checks had not remained unremarked in Lourdes. The coachman Doutreloux, who had driven him over from Tarbes the day before, had been surprised that a rich gentleman like that with three diamond rings on his fingers should use the rickety common vehicle of the poor instead of renting a private landau, even if he did not travel across country in his own coach-and-four. Doutreloux, who was not one of your silent drivers, had permitted himself to express his astonishment in seemly phrases. He had been answered that Lourdes was now a place of pilgrimage and that pilgrims had better approach their shrines in humble fashion rather than with spanking horses and polished harness. Hearing the phrase "place of pilgrimage," Doutreloux had reflected that his friend Soubirous would not have minded giving Bernadette a good beating to diminish the "holy" worries she was causing him.

The stranger with the diamond rings found no one in the Cachot except Louise and François Soubirous. The latter had sent word again that he was ill. Marie was at school. Bernadette had been bidden to hunt up and bring home her two small brothers, who were indulging their lust for freedom beyond all measure. It was not the first time that curious travellers had sought out the Soubirous family. No wonder, seeing that the name of Soubirous was, as the former miller now said, "dragged" daily through the French press. These strangers gazed at the paternal dwelling of the wonder-worker sometimes with pitying, sometimes with astonished eyes. They wandered about in the Cachot not as though it were a dwelling-place of human beings but as though it were a museum in which was preserved for posterity an inventory of utmost human need. And as one often and harmfully fails to guard one's tongue in the presence of children, these curiosity-seekers often let fall remarks touching the wretchedness of this habitation, by which the proud Soubirous were impelled to the angry pretence that this place was purely provisional and was only to serve until a mill on the Lapaca brook was ready to receive them. Now and then these visitors would press a coin into Father or Mother Soubirous's hand. These coins were accepted without false delicacy. None could blame them for this. They had not stolen their time to use it to show off their poverty to idle folks.

The man in the checked suit seemed more persistent but also more genial than others of his stamp. He did not look down on the Cachot from the height of his wealth. He praised the orderliness and cleanliness he saw, and so won Louise's confidence at once. His vivid little eyes peered appreciatively into her pots. She and François were not even struck by the fact that this distinguished millionaire spoke the Pyrenean patois in its commonest and most authentic form. On the contrary, it served to gain their entire sympathy. In the course of the conversation the distinguished foreigner drew forth a straw-covered flask in which an old, amber-hued cognac glimmered. The master of the house well knew how to value this liquor, of which a beakerful was formally handed to him. At last the stranger came out with his request.

"Listen, good people! I've come over from Biarritz, where I own a house near the Emperor's villa. I've got a little daughter there just like your own. Ginette was fifteen last autumn. She's a sweet little thing, but always a little sad. Her lungs aren't too strong and she has just one wish, to own the rosary of the little seeress, of which there has been so much talk. There isn't any price I wouldn't pay for it."

"Bernadette will never sell her rosary," Soubirous declared gruffly.

"Then let her bless my daughter's rosary, which I've brought with me."

François pushed far from him the drink of temptation. "You're a distinguished gentleman," he said, "and have far more knowledge of the world than I. But one thing I do know: my wife and I are quite ordinary people and therefore my children can be none other than we are. Bernadette sees her lady. Well and good. People say one thing and another about the lady. But no one knows who she really is. Outside of that, my Bernadette is just a plain girl like any other. She's not a religious and doesn't wear a stole, and can't consecrate anything, either."

"Don't you believe him, Monsieur," Louise broke in. "My Bernadette isn't just a girl like any other. Even when I was pregnant with her I had strange dreams. My sister Bernarde Casterot knows about her too. And the Laguèses of Bartrès always said: 'That girl of yours, Louise, may have a slow mind, but things go on in her that nobody knows about.'"

The huge plebeian fist of the millionaire with sudden magic produced several large gold coins on the table. "Would that be enough to buy your daughter's blessing?"

With wide-open eyes François and Louise stared at the money. Soubirous had almost never seen louis d'or or napoléons d'or or ducats. To be handed a little heap of twenty-sou pieces had hitherto been to him the height of worldly well-being. This dizzying treasure would at one stroke alter the fortunes of the family. One could rent a decent and dignified dwelling; one could probably pay for the lease of a mill. Nor were Louise's thoughts less agitated. Her agitation made her sigh heavily.

"Oh, no, Bernadette will never bless the rosary."

"My daughter would be contented, Madame, if her rosary were made to touch some garment which your daughter wears next to her body. For that alone," the stranger said luringly, "I'd pay two louis d'or."

Louise looked at François and François looked at Louise. Suddenly Louise jumped up and took the rosary of this odd suppliant out of his hand and thrust it under Bernadette's pillow. "She always keeps her own rosary under her head when she sleeps," Louise whispered.

Well satisfied, the stranger pocketed the rosary thus consecrated. "I'm very much obliged to you, Madame Soubirous. My little daughter will be more than happy. According to to-day's rate two louis d'or equal fifty-two francs and forty centimes in silver. It would be nice of you, Soubirous, to make me out a little receipt on this slip of paper. It's better to have things straight."

"Don't take money, please, please!" cried Bernadette on the threshold. She had heard the last sentence. "The lady would be angry."

Then as though to beg pardon for her desperate interference, she curtsied to the stranger and reported to her mother: "The children will be here right away, Mamma."

What happened now was, as Louise said to herself, a characteristic Soubirous performance. The head of the house drew himself up to his full height and with a contemptuous gesture pushed back toward the fellow in the checked suit the money which, as though the sign of a completed bargain, lay in the middle of the table. He turned to Bernadette. "I had no share in this," he declared grandiosely. "Only your mother's heart weakened for an instant. She has too many mouths to feed with the few sous that my position at the post-office brings me. I thank you, Monsieur, for your kindness, even though I cannot accept it."

"A bargain is a bargain," the stranger argued shrilly, forgetful of his millionaire's role. "I've got the goods; you've got to take the money."

"We have no goods for sale," Soubirous declared, with Spanish grandeur.

"If two gold pieces aren't enough, take five!" roared the millionaire, wholly at variance with his script. "I owe it to my daughter and you to yours."

Bernadette, now beholding the man's bull-like neck, felt a violent nausea. The back of that neck was turkey-red and covered with scars and boils. The man at this moment took thought and changed his tone. "When all's said and done, Soubirous, you've given me what I need." He winked. "I shouldn't have been so frank."

The effect of this speech was lost in the ensuing confusion. The two small boys came in, Marie returned from school, and neighbours appeared on the threshold, drawn hither by the visit of the "English millionaire." The latter, in lieu of better results, had come to a decision. His commission had been simply to make sure that the whole or even a portion of the purchase money be actually left in the Cachot. Hence he took his leave with cordial hand-clasp and thanks to the Soubirous, pinched Bernadette's cheek paternally, gathered up his hat and shawl and umbrella, carefully left the cognac bottle on the table, and made his way out. Close by the door there was a little bench which served Mother Soubirous as a place to put miscellaneous objects. With the practised skill of a prestidigitator who can make objects appear and disappear with lightning speed, the stranger produced on the edge of this bench one of the luring louis d'or.

No one had observed this trick except little Jean Marie. The boy embodied whatever practical good sense the family had. He had proved that recently when he brought his mother the lump of consecrated wax from the church. He was no more thievish than anybody else when opportunity and security seem combined. If now, ignorant of its value, he slipped this glittering booty into his pocket, it was by no means with the intention of keeping it for himself. But he had definitely sensed the fact that, since the appearance of the lady, a high and mightiness of sentiment had taken hold of his family which often lost them practical advantage. The urchin slid the coin into his pocket to guard it from his family's dangerous idealism. He planned to give it triumphantly to his mother on the next day when he was alone with her and Bernadette was not watching. A few minutes later the stranger came back with profuse apologies to fetch his forgotten bottle. He forced a last drink on the head of the house. A swift glance at the little bench convinced him that his efforts had not been wholly wasted.

Near two o'clock that afternoon, on her way to school, Bernadette was arrested. A certain Léon Latarpe, a road-mender, who had been made an assistant constable, took her gently by the arm. "Little girl, you've got to come along to jail now."

Bernadette's eyes were bright and haughty. She knew that the lady loved her. What power against her had the world?

"Hold me tight, Monsieur," she laughed, "or I'll run away."

At the same time Callet took the Soubirous couple into custody and led them through two whispering rows of people to the provincial courthouse. By choosing this building as the scene of the trial Vital Dutour intended to prove that the matter was no longer a joke. Anyone who becomes involved with the examining magistracy does not get out as easily as from a mere police court. But Providence decreed that the protagonist of this lamentable comedy, the prosecutor's only examining magistrate, Monsieur Rives, was more than next door to being a fool. It was in his house that Louise Soubirous was often hired as a washerwoman.

The State had chosen a thoroughly indecent method for settling its score with the lady. But it is in the very nature of the State not to be fastidious in its choice of means when faced by real danger. And in an industrial age a miracle constitutes a real danger. It shakes to its foundations that social order which has shunted all metaphysical needs to the grass-grown railroad siding of religion in order that the great arteries of traffic be not blocked by them. There it is their function to wither nobly away as decorations for the three moving events of mortal life: baptism, marriage, death. Hence the apparitions of Massabielle represented an inexcusable ebullition of those vestiges of the suprasensory which no modern State can afford to tolerate. Neither Dutour nor Jacomet was really a wicked man. They were faithful and conscientious servants of the State.

They acted as they had to act. According to the Prophet Isaiah, God said: "My ways are not as your ways." Even so could the State say: "My morals are not as your morals." Deeds for which the State must drag its subjects to the gallows or to prison—murder, theft, fraud, blackmail, defamation—the State itself immemorially commits without a pang of conscience whenever it deems its stability threatened. Yet in justification of this most appalling aspect of its character the State could adduce the scriptural words of the High Priest: "Better that one man perish for a whole people than a whole people for one man. . . ."

For the coming Thursday a gathering of tens of thousands of souls had been announced. The State and its policy, embodied by Vital Dutour, was obliged to prevent this triumph of the lady. And its only means was to bind the visionary in chains. Time pressed. No means toward this end was too despicable. Yet the prosecutor was guilty of a gross error at the very outset. Fearing, like every bureaucrat, the reproof of encroaching on a colleague's functions, he turned the matter over entirely to the ungodly ass named Rives. The examining magistrate's cherished aim was to prove Bernadette and her parents' specific "guilt." He did not understand that this "guilt" was the feeblest and most trivial point in the whole lamentable business. The point and the purpose were to paralyse both Bernadette and so the lady for a considerable space before and subsequent to the dangerous Thursday. The law prescribed that the accused must be examined by the magistrate within twenty-four hours of his arrest. Had Rives had any sense he would have let Bernadette and her parents stew in jail until one o'clock on the following day. Then, by virtue of the tricks and feints familiar to every judge, he could have dragged out the examination to cover the necessary period. Instead he ordered Bernadette to be brought before him immediately.

He roared at her to intimidate her to the utmost. "Well, here you are, you shameless idle wench!"

"Yes, here I am, Monsieur," she replied with the utmost calm.

"Now you're going to jail, my little miss, and no god can save you from it. That grotto business is done with, once and for all. You can receive your lady behind lock and key from now on."

Bernadette smiled faintly and spoke these exact words: *"Que soi presto. Boutami, è qué sia soulido e piu ciabado e quem descaperei."* And that means: "I am ready. Take me to prison. But let it be strong and well barred, otherwise I'll escape."

The magistrate stiffened at so much self-assurance, which he took to be incomprehensible insolence. He leaped up and shook the girl. "Where have you got the louis d'or?"

Out of her veiled eyes Bernadette regarded him so innocently that he had to turn his glance aside. "What is a louis d'or, if you please?"

"The gold coin which the strange gentleman gave you people."

"We took nothing from him, neither I nor my parents," Bernadette said with utter tranquillity of soul.

This would have been the right moment at which to close the first hearing. But the imperial prosecutor had disdained guiding the proceedings himself and Bernadette succeeded in upsetting Rives's equilibrium. "You're sly enough to drive one mad!" he cried. He raised his bell high in his hand, rang it, and ordered the court attendant who appeared to bring in the Soubirous couple for the necessary confrontation. This was another unforgivable error, even as a matter of legal procedure. The two Soubirous bore themselves rather well. The natural dignity of the former miller put the magistrate out of countenance. All answers radiated unmistakable innocence. Thereupon Rives committed his grossest error. He gave away the court's shabby conspiracy and summoned the *agent provocateur*. The man in the checked suit cut so piteous a figure that it was clear even to the Soubirous' not too flexible understanding how grossly and stupidly they had been tricked. Rives was so ashamed that he was tempted to rush out. Privately he cursed Dutour in his rage. At last he cried out: "Someone must have the money! Who else was in the room with you?"

"My sister Marie and my two little brothers," Bernadette said slowly and thoughtfully.

"All right. Bring 'em all in!"

Jean Marie confessed at once. He took the coin out of his pocket and said in his childish whine: "I found it on the bench. I just wanted to save it for Mamma."

And now something happened which none would have expected of an ecstatic visionary. Bernadette flushed to her very hair. Her face was now as common and energetic as that of Bernarde Casterot herself. With strangely deliberate steps she went up to her little brother and boxed his ears so violently that he howled and staggered backward. She wrenched the gold coin from his grasp and flung it at the *agent provocateur* as though the act were an irrevocable sentence of death. Her action was so swift, so irresistible, so final, and so exalted that nothing remained for the judge to do but to put an end to the scene. "Get out—all of you!" he thundered. "Go to the devil!"

In front of the courthouse a great crowd awaited the Soubirous family and with cries of victory escorted it to the Cachot. The self-inflicted hurt of the authority of the State was beyond measure. When night set in, stones crashed through the windows of the imperial prosecutor, the police commissioner, and the examining magistrate. At four o'clock the post-coach left the Place Marcadale. The "English millionaire" and the baker Maisongrosse were the only passengers for Tarbes. On the road, exactly half-way between Lourdes and

Bartrès, Doutreloux brought his horses to a halt. Antoine Nicolau, Bouriette, and two mighty road-menders stood in wait. The man in the checked suit was lifted from the coach and expertly bedded face downward on a pile of broken stones. Antoine took off his broad belt and also tested a cudgel which he had brought with him as an extra precaution. The first blow was his right. Maisongrosse, a great lover of popular sportiveness, encouraged the men with cries of applause. Doutreloux, pipe in mouth, added bits of technical advice. The "Englishman" squeaked in a high-pitched voice: "I call your attention to the fact that this is a crime—it's felonious assault and homicide. . . ."

"We know all about your legal knowledge, Fatty," Antoine laughed, while one of the road-menders took a knife and sliced away the stranger's checked cloth until his back was naked. "But don't worry. We'll fix it all with the court." Then his leather belt whirred through the air.

After the job was thoroughly done, they lifted back into the coach the "millionaire," whose checked suit hung in strips. He was quiet now. But Antoine and his comrades were in their jolliest mood. No Dutour and no Jacomet would dare demand an accounting of them.

CHAPTER TWENTY-FOUR

The Bouhouhorts Child

In addition to Louis Bouriette there dwelt another man in Lourdes who could not tear his thoughts from the spring in the grotto. This was none other than Lacadé, the mayor. Unlike the officials of the State involved in the matter, Lacadé possessed the non-partisan far-sightedness of a truly business-like imagination. Not quite consciously the mayor found himself suddenly no longer unhappy over the repeated defeats of the higher authorities, even though these meant victories for the lady and so of a power no less disastrous to the city than to the State. But he had a hunch that the weakening of the higher authorities might at the right moment serve to fortify his own position. Lacadé was really taking a long view. He suffered from a combination of voracity with a feeble digestion which often condemned him to insomnia. In the course of long nights he proposed to himself the following question: Why does Tivrier, ever since the Emperor has been taking the Vichy cure, earn millions by exporting the mineral waters of the Vichy springs? Wherever springs of this kind arose, they probably amounted to the same thing. Who is going to tell the difference between Vichy, Gavarnie, and Cauterets? Pay the professors well enough, and they will furnish their expert certificates. Lacadé's acute eyes had surveyed the world for sixty years. He knew what was what. He knew, too, that, when need was, this much-vaunted science did not at all mind becoming the mistress of some profit-producing and enterprising spirit. Why should not the same thing that was possible in Vichy be possible in Lourdes? Professors would be found to produce expert opinions according to which the chemicals found in the waters of Lourdes would be pronounced efficacious in the cure of hyperacidity, rheumatism, gout, liver disorders, gallstones, and heart conditions. What a Tivrier could do, shall not a Lacadé accomplish? The keenly speculative spirit of the mayor rose to even greater heights. Properly presented, the matter of Bernadette might prove not at all useless to himself. Many of the oldest and most famous wateringplaces of Europe trace their renown to a legend. Lacadé began to dream of a prospectus to be distributed by the hundreds of thousands of copies. In it a facile pen, like that of Hyacinthe de Lafite, might write the touching tale of a simple maiden, possessor of a magic rod, who, guided thereto by inner voices and visions, struck the illustrious spring of Massabielle from the living rock. Next, science must give its blessing to the discovery. And thus what began as a simple dreamy superstition of the humble would end under the brightest blaze of enlightened progress. Neither Vichy nor Cauterets nor Gavarnie had anything so charmingly worth committing to print.

Like every good businessman Lacadé kept his plans strictly to himself. Least of all must the State have an inkling, since it had a legal influence upon the exploitation of curative waters. Luckily the mountain of caverns as well as the adjoining areas on both sides of the road to Tarbes was municipal property. The estates of old Lafite, no bad businessman himself, ended at the Chalet Isle, while the State lands did not begin till far beyond the Gave River. Lacadé could not think of any third competitor. The thing to do was to go slowly, to let the enthusiasm produced by the miracle recede with smiling tolerance, and, quite unlike Dutour and Jacomet, not take a single false step. Then in about a year one might, in conjunction with Cazenave and a few other straw-men, incorporate a company of the watering-place of Lourdes and issue shares.

Lacadé dispatched his two assistants, Courrèges and Capdeville, on a secret mission to the grotto to fill a few bottles with the newly discovered water. He was disappointed in its taste: no trace of the tingling carbonic acid content that might serve to make it a table water. The professors would have to interpret this lack as a virtue. Lacadé decided at once that charged waters were deleterious, giving rise to regurgitation and flatulence. The report obtained with equal secrecy from the head of the municipal waterworks was correspondingly heartening. The spring gave a hundred and twenty-two thousand litres a day. One could grow as rich here as Tivrier had grown in Vichy.

Now there flourished at this time on the faculty of the University of Toulouse a very great balneologist indeed. This was Professor Filhol. But Lacadé was not so simple as to employ a weapon of such calibre at this rather premature date. Before a Filhol is asked for his irrefutable pronouncement, the soundness of the business idea must be given a thorough test. The test could not, however, be made by the local apothecary Labayle. The latter happened to be a member of the municipal council and a man of considerable means who might come to harbour plans similar to the mayor's. But in the little town of Trie, near Tarbes, Lacadé had a good friend, also an apothecary, by the name of Latour. What is a friend for except to render favours? An expert opinion given as a friendly favour is cheap and not binding. Hence Monsieur Latour received a bottleful of the water of Massabielle with the request for an analysis in respect of its chemical composition and medicinal value.

While the prosecutor and the chief of police had angrily withdrawn from public sight since the breaking of their windows, the mayor could be seen on repeated daily promenades along the streets of Lourdes. He was more solemn and more condescending than ever. His soft hat, sole relic of his revolutionary past, described melodious circles in the air when he returned the salutations of his fellows. He had visions of a radiant future as father of his family and of his townsmen. He never dreamed, with all his long views, that his dangerous competitor would be neither the State nor Lafite nor Labayle but the lady.

According to ancient use and wont the neighbour women gathered in the room of the Bouhouhorts to sew the child's shroud against its need. And the need seemed immediate. It was destined that Mother Soubirous should be away from home on this day when the poor creature had the severest attack of convulsions it had ever suffered. Its mother had firm faith in the remedies and manipulations of Louise Soubirous and was bitterly angry at her friend on account of her absence in this hour of desperate need. For what did it avail her to use all Madame Soubirous's devices, the hot packs and the constant shaking of the convulsed and fevered little body? Though the child's mother, she lacked the happy touch. All was in vain. There the child lay, breathing in quick, small gurgles, only the whites of its eyes showing. In spite of the fever the little face had turned, a brownish yellow.

Beside the desperate woman stood her husband. Bouhouhorts was one of the slate-miners who work away from home and come in but once a week. His heart was gratefully happy that this misery was about to end and that he could look forward to coming home from his hard work unburdened at last by this heavy, hopeless care. Bouhouhorts was no monster and it was his own man-child that was dying; but a two-year-old child is no more than that. He was only twenty-eight and could beget as many sons and daughters as he wanted, if once his

woman were rid of this nightmare. But women are like that.
With the strength of lionesses they will cling to mere night-
mares. They are so taken by these that they repulse their own
husbands. Tenderly Bouhouhorts patted the back of his Croisine.
She moaned once more: "Go to Dozous again or to Peyrus.
Maybe one of them will come."

"What's the use?" He shrugged his shoulders. "Peyrus is out
in the country and Dozous has office-hours. Anyhow, look, it's
too late. That's the death-rattle. It's what's called being *in
extremis*. . . ."

Françoinette Gozos, one of the neighbours, the butcher's
daughter, raised her voice in conventional consolation: "Dear
Croisine, don't lament so. You should be happy. You don't
want your child to drag himself through life as a hopeless cripple, do you? He's baptized and without sin. You'll have an
angel waiting for you up above."

The mother pressed her head against the child's bed. It is
easy for these women to seek to console her. In this hour she
had no prayer more ardent than that her child be permitted
to drag himself through life as a cripple. If only he would
live! She had not the slightest desire for an angel to wait for
her above. Wild fancies beset her mind. One image haunted
her: Bernadette dipping her head into the basin of the spring.
Suddenly the lightning of cognition pierced the heart of
Croisine Bouhouhorts. This dipping and laving was no vague
and vain ceremony but a very purposeful mode of action
which the lady, through Bernadette, was constantly urging
upon others.

She leaped to her feet with a wild cry. Her mind was made
up. She snatched the child from the big basket that served him
as cradle, wrapped him in an apron, and rushed forth from the
house. The lightning of intuitive perception had been so powerful that she had not even stopped to wrap the child in a

warm covering. Jean Bouhouhorts and the women, convinced that grief had robbed Croisine of her understanding, followed her with loud cries. Leaping actually like a madwoman, she raced with her burden through the streets and soon brought the whole town to its feet. In her race with death she continued to gain; not even her husband could keep up with her. But a great crowd followed her in the direction of the grotto.

Bathed in sweat, she broke down at the rim of the spring's basin with just strength enough left to immerse the child in the water up to its neck. "Accept him or give him back to me, O Virgin," she stammered in her utter confusion. She paid no attention to the women who were saying to her: "You're killing the baby. . . . The water is ice-cold."

"If I can't save him, I'll kill him; what's the difference?" Croisine panted again and again. They tried to snatch the child from her. She bared her teeth and hissed. It was not safe to approach her. So they let her be, and a stillness as of death ensued. Naught was heard save the agonized rattle in the child's throat. Then that died too.

Suddenly one of the women beside the basin said: "Blessed Virgin, the child is crying out. . . ."

It was true. The thin squeak of a new-born infant's voice could be heard for several seconds. The people looked at one another and were pale. Croisine, having bathed her child for exactly fifteen minutes, wrapped it again in the apron, pressed it to her bosom, and raced off. When at last the heavily moving mass of men arrived at the Bouhouhorts dwelling next to the Cachot they saw Croisine with widespread arms of warning at the door. She whispered: "Quiet! He is sleeping . . . my child is sleeping. . . ."

The child continued to sleep all that day and the night following. Next morning it drank with unknown eagerness two glasses of milk. Thereupon Bouhouhorts went to work. A few minutes later Croisine went to Babou's well to fetch water. When she came back she saw the child sitting up in its basket for the first time in its life. She wanted to cry out but could not. The child laughed a laugh as of victory. Brief hoarse cries issued from the woman's breast, wails of bliss. The first healing, the first miracle, had happened. In Lourdes.

An hour later people by the hundreds streamed up and down the narrow Rue des Petites Fossées. At the bedside of the child stood two physicians. Dr. Dozous had asked Dr. Lacrampe to be with him, for they had not been able to reach Dr. Peyrus, who had at times treated the child. The Lacrampes belonged to the first families of Lourdes and the physician of that name, himself very wealthy, practised only sporadically. Dr. Dozous had brought with him his book of case histories. After both physicians had given the child a thorough examination the municipal physician opened his book and read: " 'Justin Marie Adolar Duconte Bouhouhorts, born February 1856. Pronounced case of rickets. Severe catarrh of the colon, March 1856. August 25, high temperature, violent convulsions, reflexes noticeable. Next day: reflexes absent, temperature normal. Tubercular meningitis? Progressive paralysis of lower extremities. Death a matter of hours.' (No entries for an extended period.) 'Diagnosis hesitates between meningitis and poliomyelitis. Complete paralysis of the legs. . . .'"

Dozous let the heavy book sink. "You see, Doctor, how complete my records are. That's because I report all interesting cases to our colleagues in Paris."

In the room of the Bouhouhorts about fifteen wide-eyed neighbours reverentially surrounded the two physicians. The latter paid no attention to the mere laity but in the consecrated Greek and Latin of their guild celebrated the services of science, which the laity for its part heard with the same shudder of awe that it felt in the presence of the offices of the Church.

"I examined this child for the last time three days ago," Dozous declared. "There was no change in the total paralysis of the thighs. You yourself observed the atrophies and contractions, my dear colleague. Meanwhile, however, a new innervation has doubtless set in. Palpation leaves little doubt of the fresh muscular substance. Satisfy yourself once more."

"If your diagnosis was correct," Lacrampe said, "these findings are inadmissible. Were the nerves of the motor-system really destroyed? Couldn't we assume a mere atrophy due to rickets?"

"Sorry, colleague. I am bound to stick to my diagnosis."

Lacrampe shrugged his shoulders. "Then we're face to face with a medical mystery. A cold bath produces nerve substance out of the void. Have you so much faith in hydrotherapy, my dear Dozous?"

A weary irony appeared on the face of the municipal physician. "I prescribe cold baths to fat people who don't feel well as an ascetic practice to correct gluttony and lassitude."

"Then would you assume a traumatic process here—healing through the shock of fright?"

"Ask me something easier, my dear colleague."

"Then what remains but to assume that in the water of Massabielle there is present an unknown and powerful therapeutic substance? . . ."

Dozous picked up his hat and gloves. "At all events, I'll report on this case immediately to both Charcot and Voisin."

Lacrampe was frightened. "Don't do that, my dear colleague. The gods of science would rock with Homeric laughter over the state of medicine in Lourdes. That wouldn't be an agreeable thing for us."

"It is *not* an agreeable thing for us," Dozous affirmed dryly. "I, too, am not accustomed to believe things I cannot see."

CHAPTER TWENTY-FIVE

You Are Playing with Fire,
O Bernadette

Duboë, the sub-prefect, came to Lourdes himself to give final directions for the Thursday which was to close the glorious fortnight of visions. All authorities were badly worried. The cure of the Bouhouhorts child would serve to double or treble the attendance. The brigades of the gendarmes of Saint-Pé de Bigorre, Aucun, Laruns, Eaux-Bonnes, Bagnères de Bigorre, Pierrefitte-Nestalas, Luz, to mention only the larger towns, announced that the entire populations were in readiness to start on Wednesday on the pilgrimage to Lourdes. Hence the maintenance of order had really become a technical problem of the first magnitude. Under the chairmanship of Duboë consultations took place in the mayor's office. The military commandant of the town was asked to be present. It was decided to hold the troops in readiness for the ominous day. Military action might be necessary. According to the directions of Baron Massy the soldiery, like the gendarmes, was to appear in full parade dress. No one noticed the fact that thus the lady might be said to have for the first time summoned to its ranks the French army.

At the same time the imperial prosecutor Dutour received a special delivery message from his superior, Falconnet, at Pau. The document was accompanied by a letter from Delangle, Minister of Justice, as well as by a number of newspaper cuttings. A part of the Parisian press expected mad surprises of the coming apparitions, for it was evident that there had arisen a fraud as gigantic as none had dared to stage since the days of the temples and fraudulent priests of Isis in decadent Rome. Hence the coming Thursday was bound to produce an incomparable *coup de théâtre*. Magic miracles would be shown to the credulous mountaineers. Electrical mechanisms showering sparks would be combined with a magic lantern so cleverly placed that the lady of Bernadette's vision would be rendered visible to the mass of fools who constituted her daily following. If anything were needed to prove the incompetence of the officials of Lourdes, it would be a crude theatrical imposture of this kind. Delangle, disturbed by these paragraphs in the papers, hurried angry commands through to his subordinates to be sure to confiscate in ample time all mechanical devices for the production of miracles. Nor was this all. Certain circumstances pointed to a conspiracy of long standing. The touching story of the innocent shepherd girl became on close inspection a decorative invention of propaganda. Bernadette Soubirous was no country girl at all, but an extremely astute city person originating in the lowest classes—thus wrote the *Courant* of Amsterdam—and afflicted with all the moral ailments native to the lees of society. The first hearing before the police had established the fact that she was a character of extreme cunning and avid exclusively of material gain. It was precisely for these reasons that she had been picked as the protagonist of the miracles, for which purpose she had been trained and rehearsed in a convent not far from Pau. A dress-rehearsal was known to have been staged exactly one month prior to the first "apparition."

Accordingly, Baron Massy sent a telegram directing that the grotto of Massabielle be watched and guarded day and night by the combined forces of the prosecutor's, the police commissioner's, and the mayor's offices. Sundry representatives of all the sources of authority were consequently obliged to crawl about in the grotto looking for hidden electrical devices and magic lanterns, a spectacle which aroused universal merriment.

At midnight the country people began to arrive. The cold was bitter. People from each village, knowing they would camp in the open for hours, gathered fuel and lighted fires. Soon the broad valley around the mountain of caverns on both shores of the Gave River had the aspect of an encamped army. One camp-fire after another blossomed hotly forth in the moonless night. The fires lit up the Chalet meadow, the meadow of Ribères, the Saillet woods, and all the land from the Pont Vieux to the heights of Bétharram. Whoever gazed down from the fortress or the slopes of Vicennes would have supposed the presence of a spreading conflagration. The grotto of Massabielle alone lay in utter darkness. In accordance with the prefect's orders Jacomet had confiscated not only Madame Millet's altar with its images and offerings but also the many candles that were wont to burn there day and night. The only lights that now and then gleamed in the grotto belonged to the lanterns of the gendarmes, who relieved each other from time to time in their nightlong vigilance against the introduction of magic apparatus. A few peripatetic hucksters had arrived from Lourdes. They sold salami, roasted chestnuts, almond cakes, rock-candy, herb-brandy, and wine. Their takings were so handsome that they exceeded those of the summer fairs and of local festivals. The crowd's mood was neither solemn nor mystic, rather one of anticipation of festive joy. This elevated but free and open temper was also to be attributed to the life-like naturalness of the lady according to Bernadette's representation of her. For the lady, who was now being investigated by the lanterns of the police like a traitor or other criminal, had long become the intimate friend of the common people of Bigorre. The most beautiful lady of Massabielle—people spoke of her not as of a mystic vision, but as of the loftiest queen in the world, whom the common run of mortals could not expect to meet, but the true image of whose personality all could describe and pass on. Little Bernadette had succeeded in an accomplishment usually reserved to the greatest poets alone. What the grace of Heaven had revealed to her eyes moved about among her people in the guise of reality.

Today, as on that other Thursday of the great vexation, the miracle-hungry were prepared to witness the mighty and monstrous. There were those who entertained the extravagant hope that the lady would unveil herself magnificently to all the people today. Everyone would be able to see her, to the jubilant joy of this generation and as an eternal symbol to the generations to come. Others were of the opinion that the day of farewell had come and that if nothing greater happened, then the wild rose would burst into bloom as a parting present. These peasant folk who kept arriving all night, group by group, were a marvellous conductor of the miraculous. Had they been able to melt and be reforged into a single personality, even as Bernadette was one, they would have seen with the eyes of the body. And yet, no more than on that other Thursday, were these people capable of disillusion. Their faith was no longer dependent on what would or would not happen today. Was not the healing of the Bouhouhorts child sufficient? The very times of the Gospel seemed reborn.

At the first break of dawn, around five o'clock, Jacomet estimated that seven to eight thousand had assembled. At six there were twelve thousand; at seven, more than twenty thousand. The whole valley was black or, rather, many-coloured with humanity. From hamlets on the Pyrenean peaks the mountain peasants and shepherds, wrapped in black cloaks, had climbed down, among them withered ancients whose iron-shod alpenstocks shook in their trembling hands. The maidens of Provence had come, serious and tranquil as the girls of the Roman Campagna and descended, indeed, from identical ancestors. Many bore earthen vessels on their heads to carry home the water of the spring of grace. The ploughman of Bigorre, round of head, thick of neck, resembled the Roman Cæsars, while the peasant of Béarn with his easily quickened profile spoke of the temper of Gaul. Among them sturdily stood the Basque, neither Gaul nor Roman, more antique and strange than either, moveless as a rock. For hours he could remain thus, his chest thrust forward, his pointed chin lifted, the stern eyes in the spare face fixed on a single point. Many Spaniards had crossed the frontier, singly and in groups. Swathed in the complicated rhythms of their brown cloak-like coverings they stood aside and proudly aloof. The red and white *capulets* of the women, the bright-blue caps of the men of Béarn, the dark ones of the Basques, the uniforms of the dragoons, all these, surveyed from the height, were like a meadow filled with human flowers in some springtide of God.

The police commissioner wore his best uniform and white kid gloves. Several brigades of gendarmes took their places in parade dress and gloves, as had been ordered. At the Pont Vieux a lieutenant had stationed half a company of the forty-second regiment of the line. He had, as it were, to defend the bridge-head of enlightenment against the lady. But enlightenment and progress had not failed to send their own curious messengers. Except Duran and Lafite, the whole Café Français had put in appearance. The only element unrepresented was the Church.

Some of the country people had arrived on horse or in wagons. The riders guided their horses into the river to be nearer the grotto. A few carts broke down under their too heavy loads. Men climbed trees and the very rock itself, yet only a very few could hope to catch even glimpses of what would go on. But the vast majority who could glimpse nothing were inexpressibly prepared to see the miracle through the eyes of the few.

When Bernadette approached, a storm of applause went from one end of the vast crowd to the other, such as would greet even an emperor only after a mighty battle won. The gendarmes of Lourdes, who under the command of d'Angla had been detailed to watch the girl, had involuntarily become the bodyguard of a princess. Jacomet, to his intense shame, was forced, as herald and major-domo of this fool who was making all France look like a fool, to clear her path to the stage of her antics. And this fool, to crown everything, was a fool so besotted that she did not even seem to enjoy her celebrity. Did ever a girl of fourteen since the beginning of things enjoy a day of homage such as this? "O thou most blessed one!" people cried and "O thou full of grace!" and cast themselves down before her and touched her wooden shoes or sought to touch her hands or the hem of her faded little cape. But her glance was full of care and her face twitched with oncoming tears when the throng pressed her too closely. O stern lady, why did you not grant your favourite a trace of the piercing delight of vanity?

Bernadette's heart was far too filled with fear to have room for any other emotion. Would this Thursday be the last day? Would the grace of love she had known come to an end so soon? She stood in an empty space with her immediate train. The gendarmes had given passes to only about fifty persons, the family, the near neighbours, Dozous, Estrade, Clarens, and so on. She fell upon her knees at once. The lady was there. As at an inaudible command the twenty thousand threw themselves upon their knees. Hesitantly the gendarmes, one by one, followed suit. The only one who remained standing was the police commissioner, a traffic-policeman in the realm of mystery, himself most uncomfortable. Bernadette saluted the lady and smiled and made the great sign of the cross. Then Jacomet slowly dropped to his knees too and heard a thin rattle of mocking laughter, as of rain on a roof.

Nothing occurred on this Thursday to satisfy the immense expectations of the crowd. The lady was as little given to histrionics as Bernadette herself, and could not be fired to the unusual by the expectations of an audience. As always she avoided the spectacular. The usual ceremonies ensued: the eating of the herbs, the laving, the drinking, the praying of the rosary, the salutations, smiles, expressions of fear and reassurance, the listening, the whispering. Half an hour saw the end of it all. The twenty thousand had hardly gathered the harvest of their yearning, yet was the storm of applause at the end no less than that at the beginning. Bernadette arose, her face radiant with bliss. Her mother, sister, aunts, Millet, Baup, Peyret, Jeanne Abadie, Madeleine Hillot, all assailed her with questions: "What did she say to you? . . . Will she come again? . . . Was it the last time? . . . Are you to return to the grotto? . . ."

Bernadette was glad to reply, as always: "Oh, yes, she'll come back. But I'm not to go to the grotto any more."

"Never any more?"

"Oh, yes; when she returns, I'm to go to the grotto again."

"And when will she return?"

"Oh, she will let me know," Bernadette said as though it were a matter of someone going on a brief journey who would write a postcard to announce her return.

"And how is she going to let you know?" asked Bernarde Casterot.

"That I don't know myself, Aunt."

But Bernadette's happiness was entire. The very leave of absence, taken and granted by the lady, filled her with a tranquillity which was none other than the contemplative enduring of joy fulfilled. The great fortnight had made inroads upon Bernadette's strength. It was clear that the lady granted her an interval in which to gather both her forces and the harvest of these days. Bernadette was aware of the goodness of this pause for her. The lady had other errands, and the many appearances had perhaps made her weary too. There are separations which even the fondest lovers welcome, seeing that they give love a chance to catch its breath.

The streets of Lourdes and the Place Marcadale resounded with the festivities of the twenty thousand. Food and drink were all but exhausted. Cazenave had to send a large truck to Tarbes to fetch a few barrels of wine and other supplies. Duran was forced to hire an extra waiter from the very street. Lines of the hungry and thirsty stood in front of the several inns. The businessmen of Lourdes, the progressive no less than the reactionary, began to develop a taste for the lady of Massabielle.

On the way home her closest friends and followers had had to surround Bernadette to protect her from the very violence of love of the Bigorre peasantry. All wanted to embrace and kiss her. With great difficulty she was finally spirited into the Cachot. Then at last she revealed the most important happening of the day, which had not seemed so very important to her.

Mother Nicolau inquired: "And the lady hasn't yet told you her name?"

Bernadette immediately grew thoughtful. Then she related: "I didn't ask out loud. But she felt me asking. Then her face flushed a little and she said, though I could hardly hear her . . ."

"Well, what? Come on! Surely you didn't forget it?"

"No, I repeated it to myself on the way home to learn it by heart. She said . . ."

"She said? Why do you hesitate?"

"She said: '*Què soy l'immaculada councepciou.*' "

"How did she say it? Tell us again. . . ."

" *'Què soy l'immaculada councepciou.'* "

"*L'immaculada councepciou. . . .*"

With burning eyes Madame Nicolau went out and told it to Germaine Raval, who was ironing clothes and who left her ironing and told her friend Joséphine Ourous, who was beating carpets. And Joséphine told Rosalie, the maid of Madame Baup, who herself had visions at the very moment when Rosalie was stealing jam from her mistress's cupboard. But Rosalie told her mistress Madame Baup, who hastened to Madame Millet's house, where it was determined to convey the news to Father Pomian without delay, whereupon dutifully Father Pomian set out to see Dean Peyramale.

"My father and my grandfather were physicians and research men," said Marie Dominique Peyramale, as he walked up and down in his comfortable study while Pomian warmed himself by the open fire. It was past five o'clock and the lamps were lit. "If I have reason to thank God for the grace of faith, I cannot but also thank my fathers for the critical intelligence which is my heritage from them. You and I, my dear Pomian, know very well that the critical intelligence is not a thing to be made light of."

"So what decisions have you arrived at?"

"Not any, my dear fellow. The little girl will be here any moment. I beg you to stay till I give you a signal. Then leave me alone with her."

Bernadette had not yet wholly conquered her fear of the dean. Her hands were icy and trembled when she was ushered into the study, which was, to be sure, less formidable than the frosty reception room downstairs. But when she saw the two priests she was startled and her heart beat fast.

"Approach, my dear child," said Peyramale, determined to be most friendly, though in the first stage of the interview the old, unmotivated rage still quivered in him. "Sit down by the fire. Would you like something to eat or drink?"

"Oh, no, thank you, Monsieur le Curé."

"Make yourself quite comfortable. Your catechist, here, and I would like to ask you a few questions. Will you answer them truthfully?"

"Oh, yes, Monsieur le Curé."

Peyramale brought his chair close to Bernadette, who sat stiffly beside the fire. He regarded her closely as a physician would a patient. "Now tell us what the lady said to you today."

"'*Què soy l'immaculada councepciou,*'" she replied with a visible effort to remember.

"And do you know what that means, 'I am the immaculate conception'?"

"Oh, no, I don't know that."

"Do you know what that word means, 'immaculate'?"

"Oh, yes, I know that. An immaculate thing is clean."

"Good! And 'conception'?"

Bernadette lowered her head and did not answer.

"Well, let's leave that," the dean shirked. "Can you tell me what you know of the Mother of God? Father Pomian must have tried to teach your class a good deal on that subject."

"Oh, yes," Bernadette stammered, cracking her knuckles with the air of a poor pupil who does not much trust her wooden head. "Oh, yes, the Mother of God brought the Christ child into the world. She lay on straw in the stable at Bethlehem. At her left the little ox eyed her, and at the right the little ass on which she had ridden into the stable. And the little ox snorted. And then came the shepherds and the three kings out of the East. And then the Mother of God had very bad luck all her life and seven swords through her heart because her son, the Saviour, had been nailed to the cross."

"Well, that's all correct enough, my child." The dean nodded.

"But didn't Father Pomian tell you anything else? Didn't he speak of the immaculate conception?"

At this point Pomian interposed. "I'm convinced that I never mentioned that dogma. It doesn't belong to the pedagogic material of an elementary class."

"Perhaps Sister Vauzous discussed it?"

"Practically out of the question." Pomian shook his head.

The dean looked almost sorrowfully into Bernadette's eyes. He remembered what Clarens had said to him earlier today, that Bernadette's chief power in conversation was her indifference. He leaned farther forward. "You must have heard the expression somewhere. Try to remember who told you about the immaculate conception. Or would you deny ever having heard about it?"

Bernadette closed her eyes in order to obey the dean and try to remember. After a while she said in an apologetic voice: "Maybe I've heard about it. But I don't remember."

Peyramale arose and stood behind her. "Then I will tell you of the nature of the immaculate conception. Four years ago, on December 8, the Holy Father, Pope Pius in Rome, proclaimed to the world the doctrine that the Most Blessed Virgin Mary, from the first instant of her conception, that is, of her presence in her mother's womb, had been preserved free from all stain of original sin, by a most singular privilege and grace granted by God on account of the merits of Jesus Christ. . . . Do you understand that, Bernadette?"

Slowly she shook her head. "How can I understand that, Monsieur le Curé?"

"I quite believe you, my child. How could you, indeed? It is not a matter for the world's understanding. Great scholars have racked their brains about it. But maybe you can grasp this one thing—if the Most Blessed Virgin were to speak, all she could say of herself would be: I am the fruit of the immaculate conception. She could not say: I am the immaculate conception. Birth and conception are events. But a person is not an event. No one could say of himself: I am the birth of my mother. Eh?"

Bernadette looked at Peyramale silently and indifferently. Behind the veiled roughness of his voice anger echoed faintly. "Therefore your lady was guilty of an inexcusable blunder. Will you admit that?"

Bernadette wrinkled her forehead under her hood. "The lady," she said after a minute's reflection, "is a stranger here. It seems to me sometimes as though she found it hard to express herself."

Pomian could not quite hide a smile at these words. The dean gave him a stealthy signal. Softly he withdrew. Bernadette wished that the familiar catechist had not gone. It was eerie to be alone with Peyramale. The latter sighed from his very depth. "This is a very serious moment, my dear child. Do understand that! In a few weeks from now you will for the first time approach the Lord's table. I am responsible for you. The care of your soul weighs heavily upon me. What am I to do with you? Your eye seems honest and your words sincere. Yet I cannot bring myself to believe you—today less than ever. You are a cause of anguish to me, Bernadette. I beseech you, therefore, as your confessor, quite as though I sat in the confessional: renounce this falsehood! Confess: 'Madame Millet, Madame Baup, Madame Cénac, or God knows who, by stealthy whispering, suggested that phrase concerning the immaculate conception to me in order that I might be important in men's eyes.'"

Bernadette was sad. "But I can't confess that. It isn't true. None of those ladies suggested anything to me."

The dean sank his eyes deep into the girl's apathetic ones. "They tell me that against my will old Father Ader, whom you used to know at Bartrès, called on you. Try to remember! Didn't he, though without knowing it, suggest this idea to you?"

Calmly Bernadette replied: "Father Ader wasn't alone with me. My parents were there and Aunt Bernarde and Aunt Lucille and Aunt Sajou; and no such matter was mentioned, anyhow."

Peyramale was silent. He sat down at his desk and began to turn the pages of a book. After a long interval there came from him a quite other voice, soft, faint, deep. "Have you ever thought about your life and what your future would be like, my dear little girl?"

"Like the future of all the girls hereabouts," Bernadette answered quickly and spontaneously.

Peyramale did not lift his eyes from the book as he continued: "You're a grown girl, a woman, then, as one might say. After first communion, girls may indulge in proper pleasures. They go to dances and get to know the young fellows and have real fun. Then, please God, they marry some good chap. You're a miller's child, so you might marry a miller. Then the children come. Think of your own mother. There's more trouble than joy. But such is our mortal lot and God has given us no other. Wouldn't you like to go to dances too? Wouldn't you like to be such a woman as your mother? Tell me yourself!"

Bernadette blushed and spoke vividly: "Of course I'd like to go dancing and have a husband some day like the other girls. . . ."

The giant Peyramale rose and went to the girl on his creaking shoes and laid his clenched fists on her shoulders. "Then wake up! Now! Else life is at an end for you. For you are playing with fire, O Bernadette!"

CHAPTER TWENTY-SIX

Apes of the Miracle

AFTER THAT Thursday Bernadette went to the grotto no more. But the women of Lourdes continued to go mornings and evenings. The devotional table confiscated by Jacomet had been stored in the mayor's carriage-shed. But by Friday it gleamed again, wreathed and bedecked with tapers, in the rocky niche of Massabielle. Jacomet had it confiscated once more. Next day it had been stolen and set up again. This game continued until the imperial prosecutor gave orders that the table be reduced to firewood. Whereupon Madame Millet brought suit on the ground that her property had been purloined and destroyed and at the same time donated a far more impressive table than the first. Mayor Lacadé, who, according to Dutour, had grown very lax in his conflict with the lady, advised the prosecutor to give up the policy of mere pin-pricks.

"If you're going to deal a blow," Lacadé declared, "it must be a decisive one. And we will strike such a blow, my dear Prosecutor. Depend upon it."

Dutour, amazed at such serenity of wisdom, began to suspect Lacadé of some private intrigue. But during the following days his attention was absorbed by new and most uncommon phenomena. As though Heaven had graced Lourdes too highly through the intervention of the lady, hell and its forces seemed understandably to desire to play their little part in public too. The result was an epidemic of mental derangement which broke out here and there. The whole countryside of Bigorre suddenly swarmed with visionaries, ecstatics, lunatics, and somnambulists.

It was not success alone that evoked these imitative phenomena. There has been from of old a deep alliance between the psychopathic and the diabolic. Belief in the divine is nothing other than the substantially convinced recognition of the fact that the world is meaningful, that is to say, a spiritual world. Madness is the completest denial of this meaningfulness. More than that, it is the symbol of the meaninglessness of creation embodied in a creature. Where the last vestige of the world's meaning is obliterated in a soul—a very rare occurrence—madness assumes mastery. Thence it comes that ages which deny the divine meaningfulness of the universe are smitten even to blood by collective madness, however reasonable and enlightened they may be in their own conceit.

The first of these apish phenomena happened to Bernadette's fellow-pupil Madeleine Hillot, the pale girl with the long limbs and the agreeable soprano who had once belonged to Jeanne Abadie's group. Madeleine was genuinely musical. The divine absorbs the whole being of him upon whom its grace falls. The demonic takes it easy and chooses our talents as its entering wedges. Such is the origin of the morbid vanity of the talented. In the case of Madeleine Hillot it chose her most sensitive organ, that of hearing. One afternoon the girl was kneeling in the grotto and telling her beads. Suddenly she felt bathed in the waves of a soft but angelic vocal choir. Her breath failed, so delicate and yet so resonant was the choiring, the like of which she had never even imagined. At first she did not reflect but yielded wholly to the delight of listening. As she awakened from this delight, a mad pride assailed her: now I, too, am among the chosen. Softly and stealthily she let her own voice blend with that heavenly choir. It did her little good, for during the very next measure strange cacophonies intruded upon the texture of the music—instruments that perfectly mimicked the grunting of swine, the screech of peacocks, the cawing of ravens. In the intervals tinny trumpets blared. The tranquil rhythm of the music changed into a syncopated dance, to which some percussion instrument of the African jungle beat the time. But the worst was that Madeleine, when she sprang up, was impelled to swing her legs in the measures of this dance. She fled, yelling. Now, Jacomet was a man of conscience. Neither he nor the State was averse to rival phenomena. Hence his records preserved an account of Madeleine Hillot's acoustic vision against the distant future.

Some days later a lad of Omex, walking along the bank of the Gave, saw a great, fiery balloon floating above the mountain of caverns. He made the sign of the cross and the balloon burst. The lad ran to police headquarters. But Vital Dutour deleted the fiery balloon from the records which Jacomet submitted to him. He was of the opinion that the case was probably not mental but had to do with the rare phenomenon of ball lightning. The records were, however, permitted to retain the account of a group of children who at the lonely hour of noon had seen the entire Holy Family gathered in the grotto. Questioned by Jacomet, these children gave vent to the most grotesque descriptions. The Madonna, dressed in stiff gold, had quite resembled a queen of cards. Saint Joseph had carried a pack on his back and a silver pitchfork in his hand. Guests of the Holy Family had been at table with it eating corn-mush—Saint Peter and Saint Paul. Why just those two? Well, it was they, all right, Monsieur.

Two other cases were a bit more uncanny. A little girl walking with her mother gazed into the Gave near Massabielle. She was so shockingly frightened by a thing visible to her alone that she fell into a convulsive rigor and could not speak for two hours. "*Laid*" was the first word she could stammer, that is to say, "demon."

An altogether classical example occurred in the house of

Cénac, where Jacomet and Estrade lodged. Modest lower-middle-class people residing there had an eleven-year-old son named Alex, of whom they were exceedingly proud. Alex was a model boy, always at the head of his class, excellent in all branches of study. His industry and scholarliness and neatness were all equal. He avoided the companionship of his fellows as too plebeian for him. In dress and demeanour he preferred the formal and the stiff and, asked after his aim in life, declared it to be a judgeship. This boy turned crazy without assignable reason and within the space of an hour. He attacked his mother and wounded her with his pocket-knife. Thereupon he barricaded himself in the kitchen and treated his fellow-dwellers in the house, who sought to soothe and to persuade him, to a flood of the filthiest language, of which the word *"merde,"* roared again and again, was quite the mildest. The parents protested with solemn oaths that their boy had never even heard such expressions. At last they got the better of him. He had to be tied to his bed with ropes. He foamed at the mouth, and from his eyes flamed such frightful hatred and madness that his poor parents could not endure the sight. Dr. Peyrus was on the point of ordering the boy's transfer to the asylum at Tarbes. The mother, as a last resort, ran to see a certain Father Beluze, a monk and friend of hers, who happened to be visiting Lourdes. Beluze performed the prescribed rites of formal exorcism with entire success. Only a few days later Alex returned to school, stiff, thoughtful, precise, the joy and pride of his parents.

During this whole period Bernadette had many imitators. Estrade to his annoyance and Jacomet to his satisfaction had occasion to observe several of these personally. They had all watched their prototype's demeanour closely and successfully: the curtsying, saluting, smiling, nodding, lifting of the arms. Yet it seemed their special mission to illustrate the immeasurable abyss that divided authenticity and imposture. When they pretended to see the lady the spectators felt the niche to be emptier than before. Yet among them there was a strange enough case. One morning at seven the rumour spread with the swiftness of wind that Bernadette was going to the grotto. A great crowd gathered in all haste. And in truth Bernadette, even as all knew her, was kneeling there, a burning taper in her hands. There was the white *capulet* shadowing her face, the long smock, the wooden shoes. With her back to the crowd, she washed in the spring, drank of its water, ate of the herbs, slid on her knees, uttered long quivering sighs, and whispered: "Penitence! Penitence!" The imitation was so perfect that almost none of the witnesses of the great fortnight was taken aback. Only the whole performance remained curiously ineffective, like a thing that had been and had been worn thin. At the end of ten minutes the figure leaped up and threw back the hood of the cape and revealed a merrily grinning, brown, pock-marked girl's face. She picked up her skirt and began to dance. Before she could be captured she escaped across the rock like a beast of these mountains. There were those who said it was a very young Spanish maid-servant whom Madame La-crampe had had to discharge on account of shameless thievery. Others recognized her as a member of a tribe of gipsies that had recently been ordered to vacate the neighbourhood. Noth-ing precise was ever known. Jacomet reported a case of "ritual profanation" to the prefect. Hyacinthe de Lafite found the episode to be fascinating: "One might compose a lyric dance-drama on the subject of the gipsy girl mocking sainthood, and our maestro Giacomo Meyerbeer might write the music in the style of his *Robert le Diable*. . . ."

Probably connected somehow with this opening of the abysses of the demoniacal, which continued to increase from the time of the lady's vacation, was François Soubirous's fall from grace. For fully two weeks Soubirous had not stepped into Babou's bar. He had several reasons. Firstly, Babou's bar had become the centre of mockers, the home of blasphemers, the debating-club of the unbelievers. On a lower plane it corresponded to the Café Français. Although Soubirous hardly fancied himself a champion of faith in the miraculous, he was the father of the first chosen of these earthly and heavenly irregularities. Shame and pride equally forbade his presence at brandy-soaked and tobacco-drenched verbal battles during which the sanity or the veracity of his own daughter was dragged through the mire. There was another more compelling reason: François Soubirous had made a tacit but energetic vow to abstain from imbibing liquor for the present; and to this vow he had now been true for many days with unexpected tenacity of will. It would at any time have been unjust to call Soubirous an ordinary drunkard. His genuine sense of dignity alone would have sufficed to keep him from unseemly behaviour. No fellow-citizen could say that he had ever seen the miller Soubirous losing control of either his mind or his members. The half-pint or so of the vinous demon which the visionary's father required to be content corresponded exactly to the measure of hollow misery with which he awoke each morning. Oddly enough, this hollowness of misery had tended not to decrease but to undergo noticeable expansion since those performances of Bernadette which had thrown so much light on her and hers. In spite of an element of frivolity in him Soubirous took life ponderously and hard and was given to seeing things in dark colours. The fame which for a month now had shone on the Cachot filled the man with disquietude and care and even more emphatically with a secret, dull jealousy of her who had brought it about. Deep within his heart he bitterly resented the arrogant glamour which his daughter had caused to be connected with the humble name of Soubirous. Some of the results of this glamour were, at the same time, undeniably pleasant. Quite a coil of emotions, it was clear. François Soubirous was of those obdurate ones who draw from lowliness a reproachful pride. Women are not so made, he reflected. They delight in being on the foolish filthy tongues of people.

To restore to him his wonted equilibrium would now have required more than the daily half-pint. But in strict adherence to his vow he drank not even a glass. It was a deadly conflict with himself that he waged. The purpose of the vow had been to persuade fate to turn the whole affair to good, that is, to have it fade into forgetfulness. At the same time François Soubirous knew what was owing to himself as the father of a miracle-worker. He went to church daily. This forced him to slink in front of Babou's and other bars several times a day and this meant sundry daily climaxes of the conflict raging within him.

On the second Sunday after the lady's vacation he turned the corner of the Rue des Petites Fossées. At Babou's very door fate overtook him in the form of the policeman Callet, the brigadier d'Angla, and the gendarme Belhache. These men of arms were all off duty that day. They too were enjoying the respite granted by the lady. At the sight of Soubirous these three men, without any previous consultation among them, had the same thought. Though in subordinate stations, they represented the cause of the State against the miracle no less than did Minister Roulland, Prefect Massy, Prosecutor Dutour, or Commissioner Jacomet. To reveal the father's moral weakness to the point of nakedness would be no bad contributory evidence in this case.

"Hey, big fellow, why so offish?" shouted the brigadier. "You're as elegant-looking as a bishop in mufti."

Soubirous was in fact wearing his formal black Sunday suit, which Cazenave had presented to him. He tried to get past the gendarmes with a courteous greeting. But d'Angla pinned him down: "Look, Soubirous, you can't really reproach us with having done you any harm?"

Soubirous stopped with a sombre countenance. "I can reproach you all with that little matter of the Englishman."

"All right," eagerly cried Belhache of the bandit's beard. "But who kept still and let Nicolau and Bouriette beat that fellow up? We did, in order that you might have your revenge."

"Gentlemen!" d'Angla admonished them. "It's going to rain in a minute. We'd better continue our discussion at Babou's."

"I'm going home," Soubirous said.

D'Angla took him by the shoulders in comradely fashion. "Home? What's there to do at home at half-past ten on Sunday morning? You're not going home when the gendarmerie invites you for a drink."

"Oh, yes, I am," Soubirous insisted, although the men had already towed him into the bar. Babou's two rooms were crowded to the last seat and had been so continuously ever since Lourdes had become the most famous town in France. But places were provided for such distinguished guests. D'Angla summoned the mighty Papa Babou: "None of your own stuff today! Something special, Babou, if it costs our whole extra pay. We're honouring our friend. . . ."

Babou puffed out his cheeks and kissed his fingertips. "I've got three bottles of the very best left in the cellar."

Now, lovers of brandy have since ancient times experienced the same thing: the first glass is easier to resist than the second, the second than the third, and so on. At the first glass Soubirous reflected: It isn't well to affront the authorities. At the second glass he thought of nothing but gave himself up to the long-missed rapture of the burnt wine that burns. At the third glass he decided to go on drinking but to guard his tongue. If he did that, nothing amiss could happen. About the table of the gendarmes men crowded in rows, eager and curious as though a game of chance for high stakes were being played.

D'Angla sang the praises of Soubirous. "By God, my friend, your behaviour is something to be proud of! Your name is all over every paper in the world, and you go on living in the Cachot. Don't think I'm butting in. But you could make all the money anybody would want. The rich bigoted women would throw it in your lap and no one could hold you responsible. But the authorities know now that you're not making any money, that you're the same poor devil you always were. That's something to respect, Soubirous!"

"A man does what he can," Soubirous said curtly.

Belhache, who had no high opinion of the incorruptibility of generals, ministers of state, prefects, and other people in power, whistled through his teeth. "Godamighty, the higher-ups are different from that! You don't have to throw money at them. They go after it themselves, never fear!"

"I'm not acquainted with any higher-ups," Soubirous said cautiously.

One of the surrounding crowd cried out: "You deserve a little mill, Soubirous, by God you do! At the Lapaca brook two are untenanted and there'll be water enough at the end of this winter. You ought to have somebody present you with a mill. Nobody could blame you. A miller, when all's said, works for the common good."

"I'm no worse miller than many another," Soubirous said, careful to preserve his taciturnity even though this subject made his heart sore.

Amid palavering so careful the first bottle was emptied. The guest, as a matter of courtesy, was given more than his share, and a satisfaction long yearned for filled to the very brim the soul of the breaker of his vow. They had come to the lees of the second bottle when d'Angla's innocently sincere bright glance sought his friend's eyes. "You're a great riddle, you are. You've got a daughter who has grace. Twenty thousand gathered at the grotto the other day. And you're almost never seen there. What are we to think of that? How do you account for it?"

"I'm an ignorant man and I owe no one an accounting."

"Don't try to wriggle out of it, Soubirous. Do you believe or don't you?"

Soubirous, whose courtesy excess of brandy had constantly increased, could no longer control his now heavy tongue. "You're all clever as hell," he jeered. "Because you ride on railroad trains and send telegrams all over Europe, you think the Blessed Virgin can't come to people like us. But it's to us that she comes, by my faith. And if she wills it, she can ride on railroads too."

"That was a good one!" roared the bystanders. "Why shouldn't the Blessed Virgin ride on a train? That'd be enough to make Dean Peyramale telegraph to the bishop of Tarbes."

Little Callet, of whom the liquor had first taken full hold, drummed on the table with his fists. "Not on a train," he growled lustily. "On a balloon. Yes, on a balloon, and she can bring with her the whole Holy Family."

Primitive blasphemies of this kind delight the heart of the little people. They need not be unbelievers. On the contrary, one who is saucy like that to the heavenly powers is a devil of a fellow and the expense is small. The smoke-filled room echoed with laughter. In the midst of this laughter the brigadier suddenly asked: "Say, Soubirous, how does it feel to belong to the Holy Family?"

"What's that? What yuh mean?" Soubirous stammered drunkenly.

"Well, you do belong to the Holy Family now."

"How d'yuh make that out?"

"Well, listen to me. You know what the Holy Family is, don't you? The Blessed Virgin and her Son and good old Saint Joseph."

"Saint Joseph!" someone cried. "He always reminds me of the Prince Consort Albert of England, the husband of Queen Victoria."

"No insults to the heads of friendly states," Callet crowed, "or I'll have to take action."

"Prince Albert can do a good deal that Saint Joseph couldn't," a knowing fellow observed.

The brigadier, scratching his side-whiskers, went on with great persistence. "If the Blessed Virgin visits your Bernadette she must do it for family reasons, that's clear. Or isn't it, by God? She must feel related to Bernadette, eh? You can't deny that."

"You can't deny that!" Callet repeated and then assailed Soubirous in the most cutting tones of officialdom: "Confess this instant that you belong to the Holy Family!"

Soubirous had just emptied that final and decisive glass which turns a mild intoxication into a witless feeling of tragic solemnity. Slowly he drew himself up to his full height and stammered with a sombre air: "I confess that I belong to the Holy Family."

Thunderous applause filled the room. But Callet's squeaking voice rose above it. "And in the presence of a member of the Holy Family there's to be no more belching and farting around here. Those are orders!"

"Silence!" d'Angla roared. He waited till he had been obeyed. Then across the table he brought his red face close to Soubirous's yellowish pale one. "And now tell me, Soubirous, and don't be ashamed, how is it to belong to the Holy Family?"

Soubirous looked about him with quenched eyes. Thick drops of sweat stood on his forehead. He never could stand much. He had been sober too long. He had drunk too fast. His mouth was almost paralysed. "If you belong to the Holy Family," he all but blubbered, "if you've got a Holy Family, that's . . . that's . . . that's a curse!"

He collapsed and hid his head in his arms. No one laughed now. Callet and the gendarmes went to the well in the yard and stuck their heads in cold water to sober them up and make a decent appearance in the street again. Half an hour later they took François Soubirous home.

This scene led to the stubborn rumour in Lourdes that the imperial prosecutor had once more ordered Bernadette's father to be taken into custody. D'Angla, Belhache, and Callet were after all so badly ashamed that, following a brief consultation, they could not bring themselves to report on this case of violent intoxication, even though their superior officers would doubtless have thanked them for it and even though the little local weekly paper *Le Lavedan* could then have printed a brief article which, half moralizing, half in a popularly scientific vein, could have borne the title "The Drunkard's Daughter."

CHAPTER TWENTY-SEVEN

The Fire Plays with You, O Bernadette

TWENTY WHOLE days passed by before the lady let it be known to Bernadette that she would return to Massabielle. During this period all vexations increased frighteningly. Especially were the children affected. What had got into these children no one could understand. One afternoon a great crowd of nine-to-twelve-year-olds proceeded to the grotto and there parodied the blessing of the rosary and the miracles of healing with such blasphemous mischievousness that the praying peasant women fled from the spot in horror. Dean Peyramale foamed at the mouth. He could have sworn that certain lions of the Café Français had instigated this mischief—probably on a secret understanding with the authorities. Since Peyramale could prove nothing against any adult, he fetched the two ring-leaders among the boys from school next day and punished them with his own hands. Next Sunday in a brief allocution he defended Bernadette, without naming her, against the vulgar malice of these mockers. The people pricked up their ears. Was the Church changing its attitude? No. Marie Dominique Peyramale did not yet wholly credit Bernadette's veracity or her soundness of mind; but the girl had cast a spell over him. Though he did not betray himself he was helplessly stirred to the heart. Without meaning to do so he threw his weight on the side of her whom he would have liked to shake off like the aftermath of a confusing dream.

Meanwhile Vital Dutour and Jacomet utilized to the utmost all these apish pranks. A long daily report was dispatched to

Massy and to the authorities in Pau. These recorded not only the mischievous goings-on of schoolboys, not only the various more or less serious imitations of Bernadette by sundry candidates of thaumaturgy, but also certain inexplicable individual phenomena such as the acute mental seizure of the model boy Alex and its rapid cure by Father Beluze. There were many additional cases of attacks, swoonings, and sudden derangements which occurred in the area of the grotto. All were duly reported. What was not mentioned was the assertions of a few ill persons who claimed to have been suddenly healed or at least improved by using the water of the spring. One could hardly blame the police commissioner for omitting these, for most of these cures seemed to rely on confused and confusing testimonies.

Minister Roulland was by no means dissatisfied with the reports from Lourdes. He was able to place very good material at the disposal of the subsidized press. It was his aim to lift the apparitions of Massabielle out of the realm of politico-religious debate and assign them to that indifferent twilight in which the press keeps tales of haunted houses, sea-serpents, vengeful mummies, psychic manifestations, and similar occult matters. In addition, a new note appeared in print. Firstly, Bernadette was an impostor. Secondly, she was afflicted with adolescent insanity. Thirdly, she undoubtedly saw a lady in the grotto. Nervous patients of that type have seen visions since the beginning of time. Occult phenomena have been recorded in all ages. They are unpleasant but inconsequential. They are spooks. They do not belong to the province of religion but to that of a pixyish twilight not yet illuminated by any ray of reason. The Church was, moreover, the keenest enemy of these twilight phenomena. As far as the lady was concerned, she was probably no different in character from the bogyman who frightens sensitive children when unwise mothers depict him too sharply. Such was the tenor of the government press, which desired in no wise to disturb the relations between Church and State, which were excellent through the direct influence of Louis Napoléon himself. At this tone the left-wing sheets were indignant. They refused to grant that twilight world any place in the life of the nineteenth century. Twilight was but a name for obscurantism, and if in the enlightened air of France spooks braved the light of day they were to be exterminated, root and branch. This again aroused the ire of the conservative and Catholic press, above all of so influential a paper as *L'Univers*, whose editor Louis Veuillot, to the horror of Roulland, proceeded in person to Lourdes and wrote a series of enthusiastic articles about Bernadette in order to render the lady of Massabielle fashionable in the most reactionary bourgeois circles. Thus tactics which had been meant to obliterate the affair from the consciousness of the nation served to revive controversy and to render the miraculous more familiar and at home in the willing or unwilling consciousness of all Frenchmen.

Roulland went to his colleague, Finance Minister Fould, who was the accustomed mediator between the Emperor and the government. Roulland, a historian by profession, declared in a declamatory manner: "Napoléon is Cæsar. Let Cæsar speak at last."

Two days later Fould returned Roulland's visit. "Dear colleague," he began, "you know yourself how superstitious the Emperor is."

"Does that imply that His Majesty believes in the lady?" Roulland asked acridly.

"Not a bit. The ladies in whom the Emperor believes are far less mysterious. But he believes that the lady in whom he does not believe might do him harm. There you have the psychology of superstition."

"And what does the Emperor deign to command?"

"He thinks that the gentlemen concerned should manage the affair themselves."

"Does that mean," Roulland asked with pricked-up ears, "that we are empowered to close the grotto?"

Fould smiled. "I'd go slow if I were you. Just now it is the Emperor's great desire not to offend the clericals. You know he dreams of being the liberator of Italy, like Bonaparte. He is constantly receiving letters from Cavour, who has offered him an alliance. If it were to come to war, the Papal States would constitute the most delicate problem. Dear Roulland, try to persuade the bishop of Ţarbes to effectuate a closing of the grotto. I am told that Monseigneur Laurence is a gentleman with a very clear head."

The consequence of this conversation was that Baron Massy, to his great distress, was directed to call on the bishop once more. And again, as his watch confirmed, he was kept waiting five minutes. Hence he was robbed of his normal conventional chill by the time the conversation got under way.

"In view of all that goes on I trust that Your Lordship will abandon your prudent reserve. The reports from the police of Lourdes simply make one's hair stand on end. Street-urchins consecrate water and bless rosaries. Loose women make fun of the Blessed Virgin. If these things go on, they will end by throwing all France into the arms of Protestants and atheists."

In his annoyance Massy had shot somewhat beyond the mark. Bertrand Sévère Laurence was quite unmoved. After a proper interval he nodded. "I've been kept informed. It's all very regrettable. But let us not exaggerate. Granted that some schoolboys have behaved very mischievously. But I am told that the dean took very proper care of them. I'm afraid, Baron, that the official zeal of your excellent subordinates errs on the side of excess."

The prefect, contrary to all use and wont, nearly lost his temper. He flared up. "My subordinates, Monseigneur, are trying to re-establish normal conditions while your clergy hides its head in the sand."

Almost imperceptibly the bishop's tragic and sarcastic mouth twitched. "The clergy acts according to its prescription. In view of the astonishing popular excitement, you will admit that it is not easy to act so."

"The silence of the clergy, Monseigneur, constitutes an ever-greater threat against peace and order. Either the phenomena of Lourdes are of a supernatural character in the strictly theological sense, in which case it is necessary that the Church acknowledge them, or they are impostures, in which case it is necessary that the Church reject them. But it is for the bishop to decide."

His Lordship's smile was an instructive one. "Sorry that I can't agree with your sharp antithesis, Baron. You seem also to misinterpret a bishop's role. Ah, if the line could be so sharply drawn between reality and fraud in supernatural matters! But such decisions are not easy even in affairs of mere nature and the world. Between your two contradictory theses there are a thousand scruples and shadings and we require the most conscientious research and unlimited time and, above all, the help of the Holy Spirit to penetrate through that misty world to where lies the truth."

"In other words, Monseigneur, there's no end to the matter."

The bishop laid his blunt-fingered hand upon the jewelled cross on his bosom. "You, sir," he said, "see only the objectionable mischief of the police reports. Other reports speak of far happier things. I may confide to you that in Lourdes and in my entire diocese very wholesome phenomena are being observed. Enemies are being reconciled in a truly Christian spirit; prayers are more ardent than they have been for decades. . . ."

Baron Massy nervously slipped his fingers into his black kid gloves. "Prayers are offered in an unconsecrated and illicit place."

"Prayer is good wherever offered, Your Excellency."

The baron was convinced that the moment for his trump card had come. "May I call to Your Lordship's attention the opinion of our most influential paper? *L'Ère Impériale* writes as follows: 'In order to establish a place of worship one should have better motives than the babbling of a hysterical child and should choose a more fitting site than the puddle in which she performs her ablutions. . . .' "

Bishop Bertrand Sévère Laurence treated this quotation with the most finished inattention. His farewell words were mild: "You are of course obliged to think in purely administrative terms. It is my duty not to think in such terms. It is for this reason, and to my sincere regret, that I cannot oblige you."

Bernadette Soubirous was oblivious of all these conversations, speeches, interventions of the great of this world. Nor would they have at all impressed her, since the outer effects of her love had nothing to do with this love in itself. During the days of her vacation Bernadette desired primarily to use her utmost efforts to bridge the gap which had come to yawn between her family and herself. She passed her entire days in the Cachot. She watched over her small brothers and helped her mother more diligently than ever. But she did play the truant as often as possible. On the eve of the last Thursday in March Bernadette was aware—ignorant of the how or why —that the lady was announcing her return. She was feverish with anticipation and happiness. She at once told her mother and her aunts Bernarde and Lucille. She did not sleep all that night.

On the morning of this last Thursday in March Dr. Dozous put in appearance at the vicarage at eleven o'clock. The dean and the municipal physician met rarely and only on official occasions. Despite the slightness of their contacts a warm fellow-feeling united the two men. Each knew that the other incurred the disapproval of their "betters" for the sake of the weary and heavy-laden.

The dean received the physician not without some surprise but with great cordiality. He went so far as to open a bottle of Burgundy.

"We haven't had much chance to chat, my dear Doctor."

"I haven't really come to chat or drink with you," replied the physician the while he dreamily held the purple vintage up against the light.

"Nothing would please me better than to be of some service to you," Peyramale said with his strangely incandescent eyes upon the doctor's bony face.

"I'm afraid, Your Reverence, that the only service you can render me is to listen. . . . I was at Massabielle this morning. . . ."

Peyramale lifted his head and withdrew silently into himself.

Dozous went on hesitantly. "It's not the first time that I've witnessed the appearances. What I saw today was—how shall I put it?—by far the most fantastic. . . ."

Tensely Peyramale regarded the physician without relaxing or speaking.

"I must begin at the beginning, Dean. You have heard that I examined the girl six weeks ago during one of her visions. I was convinced even then that neither catalepsy nor any mental malady could be assumed. . . ."

"Were you able to come to any sort of diagnostic conclusion?" the dean interrupted him.

"There has been little research into psychic conditions of this sort. There's a whole lot of literature and I sent for it all without being any the wiser in the end. Finally I found a kind of explanation to the effect that visionaries have actually been known to hypnotize themselves to the point of sleep by contemplating their own visions."

"Stop, Doctor. You mean to say that you regard Bernadette as an authentic visionary and that you exclude all grosser explanations?"

"Bernadette," Dozous replied, "is beyond question an authentic visionary. Visions, however, are not miraculous in my opinion so long as they produce no objective effects. Monsieur de Lafite declared that highly developed minds that are haunted by visions turn these visions into high and concrete works of the imagination. Such, he asserts, was the secret of Racine, Shakespeare, Michelangelo. These gigantic spirits are scarcely conscious of the visions as such. Gifted primitive minds, however, see their visions in clear embodiments such as, for instance, the lady of Massabielle. . . ."

Peyramale put his long pipe aside and sat without stirring. "Do you consider our Parisian's definition adequate?"

"I considered it adequate up to the moment when the spring appeared."

"Then is the appearance of the spring sufficient reason, according to you, for assuming a miracle?"

Dozous fidgeted. "I'm a natural scientist, dear and reverend friend. Belief in miracles is pretty far out of my line. A spring is but a spring. Science records the existence of hypersensitive natures who possess an extraordinary scent for subterranean waters and metals."

Peyramale repeated with emphasis the learned terms used by the doctor: " 'Primitive,' 'genius,' 'hypersensitive'! What do these terms explain?"

"They explained enough up to, well, up to the healing of the Bouhouhorts child. . . ."

"And does that cure force you to abdicate your scientific temper and to believe in a miracle?"

"Not wholly." Dozous hesitated. "My colleague Lacrampe is of the opinion that the water of Massabielle must contain unfamiliar curative substances. I can't entirely exclude this possibility."

Peyramale's veiled voice spoke very slowly: "The healing of a paralysed child by one immersion in the spring, that is a pretty amazing circumstance."

The physician nodded in agreement. "Most amazing. Remember, the cure was immediate. Yet I'm willing to grant Lacrampe the hypothesis that the immersion may have represented the culmination of a long self-curative process which escaped my observation, although the mother and all other witnesses agree that the child was *in extremis* precisely in the hour of its recovery. . . . But in regard to what happened today I cannot even make such a concession to doubt. For it is an irrefutable fact to which I myself was eye-witness."

Peyramale remained silent. His eyes, no longer fiery but strangely fixed, did not move from his guest's face. Dozous proceeded to relate that he had gone to the grotto today because he was interested as to how the reunion with the lady after so long a separation would mirror itself in the condition of the visionary. And Bernadette did seem to sink into a state of ecstasy deeper and more prolonged than ever before. The reunion overwhelmed her wholly. Nor had the strange transformation of the child's face into a radiantly beautiful death-mask ever been so amazing and moving as on this day. All women had wept and even many of the men present. Bernadette hardly stirred from her knees. The usual rites at the spring, even the salutation and whispering, were almost wholly omitted. Only the prayer of the rosary was retained. For the first time in the grotto Dozous had witnessed Bernadette in a state of trance which bordered on an entire loss of consciousness. He was surprised by the depth of her trance, for he had often observed that in her usual state of ecstasy Bernadette had been aware of all that happened around her. As always, she held her black rosary in her left hand, the burning taper in her right. Her hands did not move. From her slightly lifted left hand the rosary hung limply down between her outstretched fingers. Then it happened that her right hand, probably under the weight of the thick candle, inclined leftward and sank down, so that the flame began to lick the outstretched fingers of the other hand. Her relatives started toward her to snatch the candle from Bernadette's grasp. Then, according to Dozous's account, the experimental scientist sprang to life in him. With arms held out he barred the women's path. He took out his watch. There is no state of trance that can resist the agony of fire. Though the flame but quivered between the fragile fingers, yet it touched them again and again and was bound to destroy at least part of the cellular tissue of the epidermis and to cause observable burns. Anyone's finger brought within measurable distance of a flame recoils almost by reflex action. But Dozous saw ten whole minutes pass on the dial of his watch while the flame played upon Bernadette's painless and unharmed hand. Only then did the kneeling girl arise and approach the niche as though nothing had happened. The lady seemed to have called her. So soon as the vision had come to an end the physician immediately examined Bernadette's hand. Except for a tinge of soot it was entirely normal. Thereupon the physician had taken a burning candle from one of the women near by and had approached it gently to the girl's hand. Bernadette had cried out at once: "Why do you want to burn me?"

Dozous had couched his narrative in the soberest words. He closed it thus: "I saw it with my own eyes. But I swear to you, my dear Dean, that if anyone had tried to make me believe such a story I would have laughed him to scorn."

Marie Dominique Peyramale had jumped from his chair and was pacing up and down. "And your explanation?" he asked at last.

"I've read of Hindu saints and fakirs," Dozous replied, "who let themselves be buried alive and walk through flames unharmed and lie on beds of spikes. This may be true or it may not be. If it be true, medical science would be forced to assume that the human body, actuated by unknown mental and spiritual energies, is capable of conditions which contradict the laws of matter."

"Bernadette is neither a Hindu fakir nor a subtle practitioner of asceticism, but a plain, common, simple little thing!" Peyramale exclaimed angrily. "These explanations don't explain!"

Dozous, too, had arisen. He, too, showed impatience. "Ever since I've been here, Your Reverence, you've asked *me* for an explanation. But I came here in order to hear *your* explanation. I am still waiting for it."

Peyramale continued walking to and fro and said nothing. He was stirred to his very depths and at the same time tortured by his doubts of Bernadette, which he had not yet wholly overcome.

CHAPTER TWENTY-EIGHT

The Mayor Risks a *Coup d'État*

THE MAYOR fairly beamed; adventurously his square iron-grey beard protruded from below the purple pouches of his cheeks. For on the desk before him in the City Hall there lay the expert report of his excellent friend, the apothecary Latour. The report was not only a delightful act of friendship but a highly scientific and altogether favourable analysis of the spring-water of Massabielle. Adolphe Lacadé was totally ignorant of chemistry, but well versed in the propagandistic value of resounding and orotund foreign verbiage. In the neat chart presented by Latour—equal to some medical luminary's gigantic prescription—there appeared at the very head various compounds of chlorine and calcium and magnesium definitely present in great quantities. Good stuff, chlorine and calcium and magnesium, all prescribed by the best physicians. How pleasant of these three leading substances of the pharmacopœia to appear in curative combinations in one and the same bit of water. But that was only number one, Lacadé reflected, as he lost himself more deeply in the contemplation of this chart behind which he saw, as in vision, the glimmer of far more agreeable charts and accountings. In serried ranks behind the chlorates marched the carbonates. These carbonates, by God, were just as good as the chlorates, especially when, as in this case, they appeared in combination with sodium. The old gourmand Lacadé knew this much of medical chemistry, that after a twelve-course dinner a spoonful of bicarbonate of soda brings the desired relief. And this relief of gluttons was to be found gratis and free in the spring-water of Massabielle. Well, well, well, well! The mayor was not so sure of the value of the silicates, which occupied third place. But why should he distrust silicates, especially when appearing in aluminum compounds? That must be a reliable metal. But that he should come upon the notation of iron oxide, a specific given to anæmic children, and also of revivifying phosphorus—well, that was beyond his fondest hopes. There remained the notation of "organic substances" which concluded the analysis as part seven. Their presence, which somehow lent an air of mystery to everything, seemed most satisfactory to Lacadé. It sounded markedly philosophical and could be assumed to represent that scientifically unexplained residue which might conceal that nerve-renewing substance of which Dr. Lacrampe had recently spoken in the Café Français. The apothecary Latour had added at the end of his chart the following negative and not altogether unemphatic little sentence: "In the composition of this water the entire absence of sulphur is worthy of observation." Lacadé rubbed his hands. He was perfectly willing to get along without sulphur, a medicament, too, but of infernal origin. Latour summed up: "The peculiarity of this water is very worthy of remark. We must adduce not only its characteristic lightness so favourable to the digestive process but beyond that a refreshing energy calculated to fortify the entire life-process. In view of the presence of the chemical compounds which determine the value of the spring, we are very well justified in assuming that medical science will very soon place the spring of Massabielle, in respect of its healing qualities, at the very head of all our native curative waters."

The involved scientific style expressed more here than was to be desired. The appeal to medical science already implied the exertion of pressure on its representatives. The great Filhol would not hesitate to confirm the analysis of the humble

Latour, for even under the wide skies of science one crow is not likely to pick out another's eyes. One step at a time, Lacadé. He did not need Filhol yet. Filhol would be used in the final attack to assure victory. Perhaps in a year's time his analysis would grace the labels of the bottles sent out into the wide world by the "Lourdes Curative Water Company."

First, however, there was another battle to be won, a battle whose strategic preparation had been, alas, wretchedly impeded by the too proper Massy, the supersubtle Dutour, and the bumpkin Jacomet. To oppose these hesitant scribblers, squirming at their bureaucratic leash, there needed to arise a man of practical vision and energy who would cut the Gordian knot. Who else in Lourdes was fit to be that commercial Alexander save Adolphe Lacadé himself? For the sake of a great future it was necessary to make the grotto and the spring secure. Dutour and Jacomet had most immorally persecuted Bernadette and her family in order to defend the State against the impact of a miracle. But poverty, simple faith, and innocence had been their undoing. It was Lacadé who had attacked and brought home the miracle itself. So much was certain. He passed his hand over Latour's report.

Next came the crucial question: how was the grotto to be snatched from the lady, that is, from superstition, from ecstatic love of the inexplicable, from the yearning of simple humanity for a fairy-tale? The State had failed. The Church had failed. Both had collapsed before the twenty thousand people, before that popular uprising which had suddenly and unexpectedly come upon them. State and Church lived in fear of every manifestation of the rebellious masses' will. The deepest motive of those two endangered institutions is always their fear of mankind's own volition. Lacadé's motive, on the other hand, was the most sincere and strongest of the whole age, namely, good business.

The mayor had passed Easter, which came early this year, inactively and yet not idly. On his desk lay the yellowed documents recording all the laws, decrees, ordinances, and regulations of the French government in respect of the community of Lourdes that had been issued since the great year 1789. Lacadé's researches had been thorough and conscientious. He had not himself known to what an extent the constitution provided for the autonomy and freedom of decision of local communities. A mayor is something like an absolute monarch in his realm. He is not appointed but elected by the population. Nor can anyone demote him from his mayoral office except that population. He is in all matters of state the delegate but not the subordinate of the prefect. He has sole power to decide on all matters bearing directly and solely on his community. Vital Dutour many weeks before had called his attention to a certain very practical ordinance. But Dutour, like a true jurist, always hesitated between pro and con. Now the moment had come in which to make real use of the prosecutor's suggestion, in a very different sense, to be sure. The mayor summoned his two secretaries, Capdeville and Courrèges.

"Sit down and take dictation."

He walked up and down, carrying his belly with the stride of a victorious general.

"On the ground of and according to the laws of December 22, 1789, of August 24, 1790, and of July 22, 1791, and finally of July 18, 1837, all dealing with the administration of municipalities it is herewith made known . . ."

The far dates of the years fairly melted on Lacadé's tongue. Historic dates such as those add distinction to him who utters them with the intention of their living use. Pushing his pocketcomb through his hair, he continued his dictation in baroque official style: "In view of the fact that in the interest of religion itself the regrettable scenes at the grotto of Massabielle must be brought to an end . . . Paragraph."

The secretaries repeated after him. The paragraphs of Lacadé's dictation were like sword-thrusts.

"And in view of the further fact that it is the duty of the mayor to watch over the health of the population, and since that population, not only of this but also of other communities, is beginning to drink of the waters in the aforementioned grotto in great numbers, and since it has been discovered that the water in question contains powerful mineral elements and can therefore not be freely opened to public consumption until after thoroughgoing chemical analysis and only on the prescription of licensed physicians, and in view of the concluding fact that because of all the hereinbefore adduced reasons the consumption of the aforesaid water requires official authorization, now therefore, I decree as follows . . ."

". . . decree as follows . . ." the secretaries proudly echoed.

Lacadé swung his belly and stood still. He dictated so rapidly that the secretaries could barely keep up.

"Article I: It is herewith forbidden to take water from the aforementioned spring. Article II: It is forbidden at the same time to trespass on that side of Massabielle which is municipal property. Article III: A barrier of boards is to be erected in front of the grotto of Massabielle to prevent all access thereto. Article IV: Every breach of these regulations will be punished according to the letter of the law. Article V: The commissioner of police, the chief of the gendarmerie, and all watchmen in the service of the community are ordered to see to the strict enforcement of the above regulations. Given at Lourdes, in the City Hall. Date. The Mayor."

He drew a long breath after he had trumpeted forth these battle orders. Capdeville was instructed to copy the proclamation at once in elaborate calligraphy. Courrèges was sent to the prefect at Tarbes by a special coach which Cazenave had in readiness. It was now noon. By two at latest the messenger would have arrived. For Lacadé reasoned the matter out as follows: The government has risked no decisive action on account of irresoluteness or weakness or some higher political motive obscure to me. This political motive may be allied to the equivocal position of the Church, which flees from a miracle and yet hesitates to abandon it. But I, as mayor, happen to be an autonomous authority. My order to close the grotto is a *coup d'état*, but one which does not exceed the powers vested in my office. I'm not so insignificant and, by God, I've got them all on the run. No one can demote me. The prefectural office and the Ministry of Worship will, on the contrary, both be grateful to me for this step. It's the greatest service I can render the prefect. All the baron has to do is to see my proclamation and initial it: "Seen. M." A very small M. does it. He merely receives as information news of the measures independently taken by the mayor of Lourdes and helps to secure their execution. Nothing else. Yet so soon as the "Seen" of the prefect stands under my name he is responsible and not I. In the face of my city council and of the population, I can point to his approval and regretfully shrug my shoulders. They ought to make me president of the council of ministers of France. . . .

"Listen, Courrèges," said Lacadé, "if you don't get a strict counter-order you may stay in Tarbes and have a good time tonight. I'll wait till five. If you're not back by then I'll go ahead."

Courrèges had not returned by five and was doubtless having a good time in Tarbes, which to the gayer people of Lourdes represented metropolitan indulgence. The town even boasted a vaudeville theatre. Evidently, then, the signature of the baron had been secured. Lacadé went ahead. The prosecutor and the commissioner of police received copies of the proclamation, which was sent to the presses of *Le Lavedan* to be printed. Since the stroke was to be delivered with stunning swiftness, the mayor begged Jacomet to proceed to immediate execution. Hence on that very night a squad of workmen, headed by Jacomet, drew up in front of the grotto. It was not very late. The light of the torches attracted a considerable number of spectators who watched the goings-on in grim silence. A few days earlier a collection-box had been placed under the niche of the lady in order to gather moneys for the building of the chapel which she desired. Jacomet confiscated the box, the candles, the votive offerings, the pictures, the very flowers that had been placed before the pictures of the Madonna. As he was about to fling both the fresh and the wilted flowers with his own hands into the Gave a dangerous start quivered through the ever-increasing crowd. Jacomet stopped. He had the feeling that if he carried out his intention he would be grabbed and himself flung into the river. Quickly he changed his direction. He went to the cart which was to carry off the table and the devotional objects and thoughtfully heaped the flowers on the other things. The workmen erected in front of the grotto a wooden fence somewhat above average eye level. Warning placards were put up all around. Bernadette would no more be able to see the niche or the lady from the other bank of the brook.

It happened that during these days Bernadette stayed home and did not go to the grotto, whither the lady had not summoned her since Easter Monday. For the lady had taken to going on frequent and extended journeys. Bernadette bore this privation without complaint, for she knew that the most beautiful one would return.

Courrèges turned up early next morning. The baron's small "M." adorned the fair copy of the proclamation. The *coup d'état* had succeeded, at least in one respect: the lady had at last found a worthy adversary. Now it remained to be seen whether she could recover from this blow. An hour later the proclamation was being pasted on the walls of Lourdes. Callet's drum beat its rat-tat-tat-tat through the streets and people gathered about him. The little man loved to act as town-crier. It made him feel that he was a speaker and political leader. He was fond of his own crowing voice declaiming in bad French with wrong intonation and in the sing-song of the mountaineer: "In view of the further fact . . . I herewith decree . . ."

On the evening of this great day the company in the Café Français gave a farewell party in honour of the poet Hyacinthe de Lafite. Easter had seen the return of his relatives to Lourdes and the manor house on the Chalet Isle was full to overflowing. Lafite was going home to Paris, where small bare lodgings on the Rue des Martyrs were awaiting him. And he longed to go back, although he knew he would have to scribble silly things for the newspapers and although he already felt in his bones all the disappointments and humiliations that are the lot of the unsuccessful artist. Victor Hugo, who had once mentioned him agreeably, was in the ninth year of the most magnificent of exiles; Théophile Gautier, a native of Tarbes like Lafite himself, would nod to him now and then at the play or in a café. But if anyone were to ask Théophile Gautier: "Did you ever read anything by this Lafite?" the answer would doubtless be: "Didn't know the fellow had ever written anything." Thus in Lourdes Lafite yearned for the city of light, well aware of the fact that once there he would yearn for the dim little town of Lourdes. The few months spent here had been, aside from a few happy verses, not unfruitful for his thinking. He would never have admitted that the emotions which had shaken this place since the eleventh of February had by no means left him untouched. And in truth he was among the few who had never visited the grotto and had never seen Bernadette Soubirous's ecstasy with their own eyes. Now, there is no fierier pride in the world than that of the intellectual. Though hungry and shelterless, he is sure that God did not place him on life's stage, but invited him to sit in the royal box. The consciousness that he does not belong to the mimes who play the play but among the objective observers fills him with an intoxication of superiority which makes even a life of utter want endurable. The intellectual regards himself not as God's creature but as His guest. No emperor or pope can, it is clear, vie with a station so lofty. And that this station is often concealed from men serves but to heighten its secret luxuriousness. Hence Hyacinthe, the poor relation of the rich Lafites, regarded the affair which was taking place between Bernadette, the lady, and the powers of this world from the vantage-point of the icy and immeasurable eminence of the absolute spirit which touches human life with the ray of its playful irony alone. In brief, Lafite put himself in the place of that God in whom he feigned not to believe.

Tonight all the friends had assembled, even those who, like Estrade and Dozous, had been of late but infrequently seen in the Café Progrès. "I'll certainly miss you," said the elderly Clarens, Lafite's daily companion. "We've managed to get through some pretty good controversies together during these months. How am I going to get along without your contradictions, you incomparable non-conformist?"

"You have the lady to thank for this, my friend," Lafite jested. "She has put me to flight."

Estrade took the confession seriously. "Why the lady?" he asked. "I can't see what harm she has done you, either."

"Harm?" the poet laughed. "It seems to me that the lady

is of a most tyrannical disposition. She demands that one take a decisive stand for or against her."

With this view Estrade agreed emphatically: "You are right, Lafite. The lady demands of us exactly that."

"And you see, my friend," the poet continued, "it is just this demand which I consider a serious attack upon and interference with my personal liberty. I'm a poor enough fellow and not, I trust, particularly arrogant. But there is one luxury I hope not ever to have to renounce—the luxury of nonpartisanship. It pleases me to float about freely and airily, as it were, among the so-called fixed opinions of others. All these fixed opinions give me, if you'll pardon the expression, a deep pain. I don't consider man a mere creature of his belly-needs who has to be healed of his delusions concerning the supernatural, but neither can I stomach the religious beggar's brew which is being cooked up today. . . . Haven't you ever observed, gentlemen, that pious races or masses always give off a stale and unaired smell?"

"I've once before taken the liberty of observing," the pedagogue interrupted him, "that the writer of today has lost all relationship to the people itself."

"This so-called people," Lafite retorted, "is but another of those superstitious abstractions which you idealists have on your conscience." He added in closing: "Since the lady broke in upon Lourdes I am no longer at my ease here. I feel a real nostalgia for the sins of Babylon."

Lacadé and Vital Dutour took their places at the table. Already twice today the mayor had made the round of the Place Marcadale, a victor showing himself to his people. The Café Français welcomed him with applause. Duran and his minions were triumphant. Benevolently the victor turned to the departing poet. "You're leaving us, dear poet. You'll probably give our town a bad name in Paris."

"It is a privilege which I will not renounce," Lafite replied with extreme courtesy.

"I don't believe that would be very sensible on your part," Lacadé returned with a prophetic smile. "Paris and the world will soon witness a surprising turn of events. They will see a benefit to mankind proceeding from our little city, though in a very different sense from that now expected by most. And I had rather thought of you, Monsieur de Lafite, as the poet fitted to clothe this unexpected change in the splendour of words."

All eyes turned to the door, where a sudden tumult seemed to have arisen. Wild-eyed and sweating, the chief of the gendarmerie, d'Angla, rushed to the table of the notables. "Messieurs, we're facing an uprising!" he panted. "Crowds have stormed the grotto and torn down the scaffolding and overthrown the placards. . . ."

After a dignified interval of silence Lacadé said: "If you have an official report to make, d'Angla, you should try to do it in a more seemly fashion. . . . What exactly happened and when?"

"Half an hour ago, at nightfall, the grotto was taken by storm. I was the only one there."

"Do you understand now, Mr. Mayor, why I didn't congratulate you on your admirable courage?" Vital Dutour laughed with satisfaction.

"Well, what of it?" Lacadé asked, pale but calm. "We'll rebuild the fence tonight and station two armed guards there day and night."

"Courage may be a costly jest," the imperial prosecutor jeered. A minute or two later he said farewell to Lafite in these words: "Why do you walk out of this interesting play before the end of the fifth act?"

CHAPTER TWENTY-NINE

A Bishop Counts Consequences

MONSEIGNEUR LAURENCE gave the signal to rise. Outside of Dean Peyramale there had been but two other guests at table, a canon of the episcopal chancellery and the private secretary, a young cleric. Both the latter gentlemen soon made their excuses. Monseigneur desired to chat alone for an hour after dinner with the dean of Lourdes. A great distinction! For the bishop of Tarbes was not fond of distinguishing anyone above his fellows. He knew them all too well. Like many who have risen from the lower depths he retained upon his bright pinnacle the bitterness of former misery like a sediment of the soul. Within him the command to love one's neighbour was in steady conflict with an ill-restrained contempt for mankind. The result of this conflict was manifest in a rare type of icy mildness behind which a mind of adamant lay shyly in wait. Yet Bishop Bertrand Sévère entertained an unspoken weakness for the dean of Lourdes. The liking of males for each other is based upon the right blending of similar and dissimilar qualities. This Peyramale, a man in his late forties, had not yet learned to control himself. When something ruffled him his eyes burned with an unseemly fire. He did not guard his words and knew not the fear of man. He was rude and ready of retort and that amused His Lordship. Peyramale was a man of gentle birth and that impressed the son of the road-mender, surrounded by clerics of humble origin and therefore reeking with that unctuous servility which often, especially in southern countries, characterizes the lower ranks of the clergy. Monseigneur was proud of having a gentleman like Peyramale attached to his diocese.

The footman opened the doors of successive drawing-rooms through which the bishop, leaning on his ivory-headed cane, passed with his guest. All these rooms with their faded splendour were cold and uninhabited. For twelve years now Bertrand Sévère Laurence had been dwelling here without leaving the slightest trace of his personality on the rooms. As he had once taken them over from his predecessor Bishop Double, so they remained. Double, survivor of a different age, had been a lover of beautiful things and within modest limits a collector. Laurence did not care for beautiful things or for collecting them. He had, on the contrary, had a number of paintings and art objects in the episcopal palace sold and the proceeds devoted to charity. Men of the lower classes are commonly men of the practical reason.

At last they had reached their goal. A second distinction conferred on Peyramale was the bishop's ordering the coffee served in his own room. In this single room Monseigneur dwelt, worked, slept. Prior to being raised to the episcopate he had never had more than a single chamber of his own. As bishop now he wanted no more. The master of ceremonies protested quite in vain. His Lordship would have refused a roomier dwelling without hesitation. Nor could it be said that this single room was either comfortable or homelike. It was a room of medium size, containing an iron bedstead, a *prie-dieu*, a crucifix, a bad picture of the Virgin, an awkward couch, a desk, and sundry plain and upholstered chairs. But the room could not be called monastic or ascetic, either, for Monseigneur disdained no comfort that he had ever known. He quite simply and unaffectedly refused to change his way of living because he was a bishop. He had always been poor; a poor man and the son of a worker he would remain. Want, too, can be habit-forming. To stick to the exact truth, however, it must be added that the bishop's cuisine was good, nay, excellent, as Peyramale could confirm each time he was invited.

A third distinction: the footman handed Peyramale a long pipe, while Monseigneur himself stuck to the good old habit of snuff, of which his robe bore plentiful evidence. They moved their chairs close to the fire. What a cold spring! The one cosy element in this room was the fire. And Monseigneur was chilly even in summer. Perhaps it was his own mildness that chilled him.

"The events at the grotto," the bishop began, "of which you told us at table, served to confirm my conviction that we have acted correctly. But neither the prefect nor the mayor, I am sure, imagined that their fence would be pulled down over and over every day. Think of the harm that would have inured to the Church if any part of this fence could have been debited to our account. I must really tell you how much I value your attitude."

"Your Lordship," Peyramale replied with sincere reverence toward the old gentleman, "I ventured to request today's interview because I am not at all satisfied in my mind, because I do not think that things are going as they should, because I fear that a change in our attitude will prove to be necessary."

The bishop shook his pinch of snuff back from his fingers into the snuff-box without putting it near his nose. His eyes in their deep hollows were fixed with astonishment on the dean's face. Clearing his throat, he parried Peyramale's attack. "I want first to address a question to you as dean of Lourdes: Who is Bernadette Soubirous?"

"Yes, who is Bernadette Soubirous?" the dean murmured and looked at the floor. It was a full minute before he turned his furrowed face back to his superior. "Monseigneur, let me

confess frankly that I began by taking Bernadette for an
impostor, for another Rose Tamisier, and to this day there
are fleeting moments when I still do. I know too well this race
of tellers of fairy-tales, fantastics, and clowns and its ability
to take in not only others but itself. Oh, it's such a desperately
poverty-stricken people. I must also confess, Monseigneur,
that there were times when I considered Bernadette a lunatic
and that I do still at moments, though they are rarer and
rarer. And lastly I must confess to you, Monseigneur, that I
see in Bernadette a true vessel of grace and a worker of
miracles."

"Your account, my dear Dean, is neither very illuminating
nor very clear," the bishop grumbled. His juridically acute
mind had little understanding of the subtle contradictions of
the imaginative. With a vague gesture he pointed to his desk.
"I've got a letter there from a retired general named Vauzous.
He begs me to take steps against dangers that threaten the
reputation of the Church. About the same tune is played week
in and week out by the government—Massy, Roulland, and,
according to private information, the Emperor himself. But
there's one difference: the excellent general means what he
says. He's got a daughter among the teaching sisters of Nevers.
You probably know the nun, since she teaches in Lourdes."

"I know her and on two occasions discussed the case of
Bernadette Soubirous with her. Naturally I wanted the opinion
of the teacher who sees the child daily."

"Well, the opinion of this teacher, who ought to know
Bernadette Soubirous better than anybody else, is immensely
less equivocal than your own, Dean."

Marie Dominique Peyramale's eyes began to burn. "I have
gained the impression that this teacher's attitude toward her
pupil is by no means a kindly one."

After an observant silence the bishop went on: "I am informed that this Sister Vauzous is a credit to her order, distinguished in every respect. Enthusiasts have been known to ascribe to her the odour of sanctity. She comes of a most excellent family. Doubtless she will in due time be made mistress of the novices and later Mother Superior. Why should a religious of such virtue and merit distrust a creature like Bernadette without good reason?"

"Sister Vauzous," Peyramale made reply, "may lay claim to the highest offices and to a place of honour in heaven itself. But if you talk to her, Monseigneur, you are far from any feeling of confronting a very special or, above all, a chosen soul. Sister Vauzous leaves you cold. Bernadette Soubirous has just the contrary effect. I don't know what it is about the girl. She's a common little thing. She has a face like all these other Doutreloux and Ourous and Gozos and Cabizos. Sometimes you're enraged to think that all France holds its breath at the antics of this empty little boob. And then suddenly in all her simpleness of mind she gives you an answer, an answer, Monseigneur, which keeps you awake half the night. No use just trying to rid yourself of these answers. Not so easy, either, to get rid of the child's eyes. Monseigneur knows well that I am anything but an enthusiast or a hotheaded, mystical fellow. I am, by God's help, a practical man. Whenever I haven't seen Bernadette for some time, my doubts grow again. But when I summon her to me, as I did the other day again, it is not I who put her to confusion but she me. For, by the Blessed Virgin, Your Lordship, the child is of so wondrous a veracity, she is so profoundly in the right in her own way when she speaks, that I am utterly, utterly routed."

The bishop's features underwent no change. He nodded. "You have certainly sung the praises of Bernadette Soubirous," he said.

Peyramale steadied himself. "My point is, Monseigneur, that I do not deserve your expression of appreciation. I have done nothing except prevent my clergy from setting foot in the grotto. This has not been altogether easy, especially in respect of the gentlemen in the small country parishes. But I have not been able to contribute to the clarification or tranquillization of souls because I am, in my own person, a very centre of confusion. In spite of my years I stand in need of your paternal help, Monseigneur. Think of the spring! Think of the healing of the Bouhouhorts child! And since yesterday there is a persistent rumour that the spring of grace has given back sight to a blind peasant child. If we leave Bernadette Soubirous entirely out of the picture, we are still facing indubitable miracles. . . ."

"Stop, my dear Dean," the bishop broke in. "You know very well that neither you nor I am competent to employ that most hazardous concept. It is the Congregation of Rites at Rome which alone and exclusively has the right to determine whether a given phenomenon is a genuine miracle or a deception."

"Entirely correct, Your Lordship," Peyramale agreed cordially. "But in order that the Roman Curia may pronounce judgment it must be in possession of the requisite material. And therefore I, the humble and unworthy vicar of Lourdes, come to you, my Bishop, and I declare: I can't go on this way any more. My whole district lives in deepest spiritual uncertainty. Lourdes has become a battlefield, not only figuratively, alas, for the gendarmes drew their swords against men and women yesterday. Irresponsible enthusiasts like the Millet woman defy all discipline. The freethinkers draw advantage after advantage out of these events. Clear and sober heads no longer know what they would be at. Neither do I. For all these reasons, Monseigneur, I venture to beg you with the utmost warmth to disentangle this dreadful coil by convoking an episcopal commission for the investigation of the facts. That alone can steady my people."

Heavily the bishop lifted himself up with the help of his cane and dragged himself to the desk. Rummaging in a drawer he brought forth a bundle of documents and threw it on the flat part of the desk. "Here are the plans for the episcopal commission of investigation worked out to the last detail."

"And when will you give the signal for the work to begin?" Peyramale asked excitedly.

"Never, please God!" Bertrand Sévère replied harshly. Impatiently he motioned to the dean to keep his seat. He walked to the window and looked down at the blossoming lilac-bushes in his garden.

"A miracle is a very dreadful thing," the old man murmured, "whether it be acknowledged as such or not. Man is filled with voracious desire. Hence he yearns for miracles. Many of the faithful do not really want to believe; they want assurance. A miracle is to procure them this assurance. The Almighty rightly sends a miracle only most rarely. For what would be the value of our entire faith if every fool found it confirmed daily? Even the daily miracle of the Mass is hidden within such simple, natural things as bread and wine. No, no, my dear fellow, the extraordinary is poisonous to any institution, be it State or Church. Take what mankind is apt to call genius. Take a man like Napoléon Bonaparte. What was this so-called genius to his world and time? A cause of blood-drenched embarrassment. And many of the saints we invoke were in their time an embarrassment to the Church, though not of blood. To desire to tower above one's fellows or to tower above them in fact is an encroachment which we, official guardians of the Christian community, are bound to repel until we are overwhelmed by the unchallengeable proof of God's grace. The Church as the mystical body of Christ is the communion of saints; that is to say, each of its parts may partake of holiness as such. . . . But the moment in which I, as bishop, convoke this commission, I officially affirm not the vague possibility but the high probability of supernatural events. I dare do that only when every path to a natural explanation has been closed. If I do it before that I drag not only my diocese but the whole Church into the abyss of ridicule. What evidence are two or three healings whose actual character has not been sedulously examined nor irrefutably pronounced upon by a consensus of expert medical opinion? Not very much. You yourself, Dean of Lourdes, though you sing a song of praise in honour of Bernadette, are not ready to exclude entirely the two suspicions of fraud and madness. Have you considered what our very critical and very scientific age would say of a bishop who, impelled thereto by a little clown or fool, credited excited old wives' tales concerning a spring of grace and convoked a commission of investigation only to come in the end upon some prestidigitator's trick? The harm done would be immeasurable."

Marie Dominique Peyramale had grown restless and wanted to put in a word. The bishop silenced him with a gesture. "If the lady of Massabielle," he ended, "were in all truth to be the Most Blessed Virgin, a fact on which the ultimate decision must come from Rome, then I will do penance to obtain her forgiveness. Until then, however, it is my duty as bishop of Tarbes to make things as tough for her as ever I can."

CHAPTER THIRTY

Farewell of All Farewells

THE WEEKS passed by and the conflict around the miracle surged on without decision. The sub-prefect Duboë cursed and Vital Dutour cursed and Jacomet cursed most of all. The monotonous bureaucratic offices of Lourdes had been converted into general staff headquarters where new plans were daily forged against the enemy in the grotto of Massabielle, who, though herself gone journeying, sent her excited partisans into the lists by morning and by evening. Three additional brigades of gendarmes had been housed in the barracks of Nemours, since d'Angla and his men had long been insufficient for the needed service. Every two hours guards relieved each other at the grotto, which was now shut off from the world not by a few planks but by a firm wall of wood. Had the lady appeared in the niche at this period she would have been a prisoner. And this was, in fact, just the notion entertained by the embittered people of the Pyrenees, that she, the heavenly one who brought grace and healing, had been blasphemously imprisoned by the gendarmes. Hence it became a matter of honour to set her free again by fraud or force. These vigils night after night for weeks in a matter that seemed so damnably senseless to them was no small thing for the armed guards. The strictest disciplinarian could not fail to understand that these misused guards, driven from their beds every other night, were apt to fall asleep on duty now and then. They were not, after all, taking the field against Austrians or Prussians, but against the villagers of the Gave valley who stubbornly laid siege to the lady's grotto. In this undertaking the peasant lads of the vale of Batsuguère showed a real talent for tactics. They proved of great inventiveness in setting snares for the authorities. Toward three in the morning, for instance, the broad valley lay in total darkness. The moon had set. Only the Gave rumbled the rage of its monologue through the stillness. Now nothing more can happen, thought the black-bearded Belhache, who was in command that night. Two days ago he had acquired a new sweetheart, who was waiting for him in the Saillet woods. It was summer and she had promised to meet him at this unusual hour. Belhache always bragged that he knew women down to the ground. Yet his knowledge of the other sex was not nearly subtle enough to make him suspect that the little wench was calmly ready to risk the dark tryst with him if thus she could do the Blessed Virgin a favour and gain for herself the protection of Heaven.

"I'm leaving for just a minute or two," Belhache said to his assistant Léon Latarpe, who was on guard just then. Latarpe, a comrade of Bouriette, was disgusted with the whole business to the point of nausea. A man had to go without sleep for a paltry thirty sous. What could still happen? He made up his mind to give notice to the municipality and thought: All right, Belhache, you go and I'll hit the hay a little bit.

Meanwhile the lads of Batsuguère were lying in ambush in one of the caverns of the mountain. Their spies had been on the alert. When the field was clear they carefully sneaked up on the grotto, covered the fencing with oakum and other inflammable material quite noiselessly, and set it thoroughly on fire. Next morning a thousand pilgrims found only the charred remains of the barrier that separated them from the lady. They gathered the remnants of this sacrificial fire and took them home as trophies. Yet the Parisian press was very wide of the

mark in assuming that the fanaticism of either faith or superstition was alone responsible for the rebellious mischief per-
petrated against the government. The gendarmes knew well
that among the very ring-leaders whom they arrested now and
then were the most arrant freethinkers and even atheists. They
should have been glad to have the State fight their battles. But
man is not a logical creature and those unbelievers were preju-
diced not only against the Blessed Virgin but against the State
as well. Merrily and against their own convictions they took
advantage of an opportunity to create difficulties for the government. They perceived quite accurately that Bernadette's
lady was a fomenter of unrest, that she had driven the priests
into a corner, and that the bishop no less than the prefect saw
a miserable thing in any popular uprising, however motivated.
After the fourth demolition of the barrier an unexpected circumstance arose. Every workman in Lourdes refused flatly to
re-erect it. Carpenters and cabinet-makers were sent for from
the surrounding villages. They came, they heard, they marched
back home. Increased wages did not lure them. To the government's shame the grotto was open for many days. Gnashing
their teeth, the gendarmes themselves were finally obliged to
take tools in hand and board up the grotto.

Little Callet was assigned the hardest job of all: he had to
see to it that no one drank of the lively spring, which had long
dug itself a channel to the Savy. Callet scarcely ever turned his
back but someone crouched along this channel and dipped
water. The policeman leaped upon everyone he caught and
subjected him to an official examination. Five francs was the
fine imposed for contravention of the order not to drink of the
spring. Whoever had the money on his person had to pay on
the spot, else the fine was deducted from the individual's next
wage. On some days Callet conducted more than thirty of
these examinations. Rives and his colleague Duprat, justice of

the peace, tried to think up crazier chicaneries. If several persons simultaneously were guilty of the contravention a group fine was exacted in addition to the individual fines. Callet was indignant. The town gets a damned good additional income, he thought, and what the hell do I get? . . .

The only person in authority who showed himself wherever possible in undiminished dignity and abounding nervous health was the originator of the stroke pregnant with all these consequences, His Honour the Mayor. Lacadé grinned at the disquietude of the government representatives. They had no proper aim, that was their trouble. He had one. Soon the bomb would be made to burst. A specimen of water had already reached the hands of the great Filhol. And once science had spoken its lofty truth, and not only confirmed but extended the little apothecary's report, then would the most unexpected of victories have been won. Nor did Lacadé for a moment doubt this victory. Like a liberating flash of lightning would Filhol's expert opinion blaze upon all France and illuminate and solve once and for ever the whole question of Massabielle. Then it would but remain for a convocation of illustrious men of medicine to hurl at the suffering and ignorant public swollen sesquipedalian verbiage—chlorate, carbonate, calcium, magnesium, and, above all, phosphorus.

During a secret conference Lacadé had already communicated a bold conception to the postmaster Cazenave and the café-owner Duran. Not only was a great hotel to be built, but also a magnificent casino with classic columns, if possible, in the midst of a well-kept park on the banks of the Gave. But in the grotto of Massabielle the prettiest girls of Lourdes would offer healing draughts in daintily painted beakers to distinguished invalids, to the accompaniment of waltz and can-can strains played by the orchestra of the establishment. In his mind's eye Lacadé already beheld these rich visitors rolling toward Lourdes, rolling thither in the new railroad whose long whistles would awaken the sleepiest valleys of the Pyrenees.

Bernadette was busy at home. Bernadette went to school. Bernadette was waiting. Bernadette was waiting patiently. On Easter Monday she had experienced the closest communion with the lady that had been granted her since the beginning. Shaken by the alien nature of the world of her awakening, she had barely been able to readjust herself to life. She now knew that the lady had meant that there be yet no ending and that her last salutation had held the presage of their being reunited. This fulfilled Bernadette's whole dream. Like every deeply loving soul she gave no room to thoughts of a remote future. Nothing seemed to contradict her hope that her communion with the lady would last the span of her life. She considered it wholly natural that the intervals between meetings tended to be prolonged, for how many problems in all the wide world did the lady not have to solve and how little could Bernadette offer her. Where future meetings would take place, whether in the grotto or not, was a matter which did not trouble Bernadette. She knew the lady's character too well by now to fear that a few guards or a few boards could present a serious obstacle to her will. The lady would call her and would find her—no matter when. Thus April, May, and June passed by. . . .

The public conflict which she herself had instigated was regarded by Bernadette with complete apathy. It would be an exaggeration to say that she was indifferent to it; for her it simply had no existence. She did not grasp it and looked on like a sleepy child. What was important was that the prosecutor, the judge, the commissioner gave her no more trouble. Her ear was totally deaf to the daily exclamations of her adherents: "O thou full of grace . . . thou chosen from on high . . . thou seeress . . . thou worker of wonders! . . ." Incredible though it may seem, she did not understand these words, either. People seemed quite crazy to her. She was conscious of nothing miraculous. The lady had bidden her to drink of the water of the spring and to wash herself in it. She had obeyed. Where was the miracle? The lady had just known that there was a spring under the earth. Concerning all these things Bernadette spoke no word to any. If a remark was made, though it were by Mamma or Marie, she slipped silently away.

Life was not made easy for her. From all over the world people came to the Cachot with their silly and annoying questions. Bernadette hid herself as best she could. But the vain neighbours, these Sajous, Ourous, Bouhouhorts, Ravals, not least Aunt Piguno, managed to drag her forth to show off with her. She had to talk to the strangers and answer them. Her way of doing so was deeply disappointing. She had adopted an absent-minded monotone in which she reeled off her story as though it were not her story at all but as though she were forced at some country fair to tell a bloody tale of long ago. Behind this sing-song recital she hid her shame. The visitors continued stealthily to offer the family money. Bernadette was hard put to it to keep strict watch lest any of them, especially the little brothers, weaken. It was the one matter on which, for all her equability, she brooked no jest. Thus the abyss between herself and her family grew deeper day by day. Father and mother, sister and brothers, all stood in eerie fear of her. Weird to them seemed a member of their household who sustained a forbidden relationship to Heaven. François Soubirous never renewed his vow and slunk to Babou's whenever he knew that there were not too many people in the bar. In dull silence he brooded in a corner. The days of need were over. Cazenave had made his job secure and raised his wages. Louise Soubirous was jangled of mood and quarrelsome. She had had time to get used to the fame of her wonder-child. The high and radi-

ant February days were at an end. Now she had a seeress
daughter. But poor people must get along as best they can.
From time to time Bernadette approached her mother with shy
tenderness. As on that first sleepless night of the eleventh of
February she felt the need of hiding her head in her mother's
lap. But at such moments Louise's heart seemed, much against
her will, to grow curiously hard. She feigned not to have observed. Then later, fetching water, scrubbing linen, she felt
utterly miserable and could not restrain her tears.

Matters were worst at school. Jeanne Abadie and the other
girls went through the oddest contortions and approached Bernadette in a manner in which reverence and mockery were unnaturally blended. Her neighbours moved away from her in
embarrassment. Hardly a word was addressed to her. During
recess she walked about alone, carrying her white bag. The
teacher simply pretended not to notice her. She was not even
summoned to the place of trial any more. For the nun Vauzous
was a hundred times more embittered than any member of the
clergy at the heathenishness of the mob which kept running
after a beggar wench who pretended to have had visions of an
elegantly modish fairy without a single trait to remind one of
the Mother of God. Everything within General Vauzous's
daughter fought against attributing a shred of value or meaning to the ecstasies of this low-born brat or the heathenish
goings-on of these mountaineers. The whole affair seemed to
the nun a malicious and mocking revolution of forces, hitherto
beneficently held in check, against the appointed highway of
true religion and of true piety. Hence at the unavoidable moment she addressed Bernadette with the utmost curtness: "According to the dean's order you will approach the table of the
Lord, Soubirous Bernadette." Behind the dry words there was
an echo: As a matter of grace and charity and not of right!
Thus the very bread of the angels was made salty for her.

School closed, as everywhere in France, on July 15. The day after, as the evening shadows lengthened, Bernadette was sitting on a little meadow near the Lapaca brook. The spot was in a direction opposite to that of Massabielle. She preferred it since she had been going to the grotto no more. It was very quiet here under the immemorial evergreen oaks of Provence. From the far notch of the valley the Pic du Midi thrust its tall blue-white peak into the unmoving sky. Now Bernadette had endless hours in which to go over her thoughts and her emotions. And this rehearsal of all thought and all feeling turned about the single word: When? The clock of Saint Pierre's steeple in Lourdes was striking a quarter after seven. Before the lonely chimes fell silent Bernadette had the answer to her eternal: When? "Now!" This Now was embedded in a slowly moving solemnity of a strange kind. More powerfully than ever hitherto Bernadette felt herself divided into an almost inert corporeal being and a great uprush of self-determining instinct. The uprush lifted her with incomparable force. She raced back to the city in order to inform her aunt Lucille. But on the way she changed her mind. She wanted no one with her on this day. She wanted to be all alone with the lady. Unluckily she could not keep her intense haste from being observed, and already a few of the most zealous were at her heels, the while others hurriedly passed the news from house to house: Bernadette is on her way to the grotto.

She knew not why, but she did not choose the shorter forest path; she pursued the precise way which she had gone with Jeanne Abadie and Marie on the eleventh of February: along the Savy brook, across Nicolau's little bridge, over the Chalet Isle to the meadow of Ribères on the tongue of land. On the opposite bank in front of Massabielle, Callet and the gendarme Pays were lounging. As soon as they caught sight of Bernadette and those following her they assumed a hostile and officious attitude. But Bernadette made no attempt to wade through the brook. She knelt on the very spot on which she had knelt on that first day, now so unimaginably long ago. With an adjuring gesture she motioned to the people behind her to stay as far from her as they could. The crowd, increasing momently —mother, sister, aunts, the Nicolaus had all joined it—formed a wide and reverential semi-circle about her. A few women lit candles. But how could candle-flames be visible within the gigantic burning of the sunset which now flooded the valley of the Gave? The mountain and the forests seemed on fire, the river a burning stream of molten lava. The purple peaks at the world's edge seemed to melt like wax.

Even the interior of the grotto, half hidden by the wall of boards, flamed with the sunset. Or did it flame with a quite other fire? All that the kneeling girl could see was the upper part of the niche, the apex of the pointed curve. (The gendarmes had seen to it that new "apparitions" should be invisible even at a distance.) Yet immediately under that apex veritable clouds of golden glow seemed to issue forth. And yonder moving whiteness? Was it not the lady's bridal veil? Yes, there she stood in the rock, the lady, beyond all doubt, even if Bernadette could not see her. Oh, how little like a dream, how utterly real was the lady, since a few wooden planks could make her as invisible as any ordinary body! Seeking for help, Bernadette glanced about her. What could she do to find a place whence she might behold the lady?

As she looked about her in this manner, her glance rested for a second upon the bank of the Gave, a few paces from the point at which the river was joined by the brook. She looked away, then back again, then blinked her eyes. It was not possible. Then, as on that first day, she rubbed her eyes. Then suddenly came the pallor as of death, the tension of the skin of the face, the enlargement of the pupils. She cried out: "There she stands! . . . Yes, she is there. . . ."

And the constricted voices of the women far behind her took up her cry: "There she stands! . . . Yes, she is there . . ."

The lady stood in front of the grotto near the bank of the river. The guards did not see her, although Bernadette was seized by immediate terror lest Callet and Pays approach her too closely. Luckily the two men retired to the other side of the grotto the better to keep an eye on the dangerous women and to see to it that none drank of the spring. For the first time the lady stood with her inviolate waxen feet upon the flat earth. The roses on those feet were radiant. More than ever was the lady she of the eleventh of February, a creature all youth, all floating dainty maidenhood. In the great fortnight during which she had daily bidden Bernadette to the grotto she had been full of plans and secret intentions. She needed Bernadette to go to the priest and demand the chapel and processions and also to scratch the spring from the earth. Today it was otherwise. Today the lady harboured in her heart no aims beyond those whereby the isolation of these two in their love could be diminished. Today for the first time was the full and undivided love of her who brought such bliss turned wholly toward her who needed to absorb it. Never yet had the bridal veil fluttered so gaily in the wind; never had the brown ringlets escaped so freely from beneath the veil's border; never had the eyes been of a blue so crystalline nor ever had the half-open mouth been so ravishingly curved. Nor yet had the white fabric of the dress or the blue of the veil been so breath-takingly unheard of as on this day on which the fading sunset splendour lent them an added glow. And the smile of the lady yonder was more that of a playmate than of a great and gracious being.

Slowly Bernadette stretched out her arms and let them fall again. Then without removing her eyes she felt in her bag for the rosary. Scarce perceptibly the lady shook her head. She seemed to be saying: You will tell your beads a thousand times yet. But today even prayer would be wasteful. The time has come to gaze, only to gaze.

Bernadette's silent heart would stammer a message. But thoughtfully the lady laid a finger on her lips. That might mean: Be silent. What could you convey to me that I do not know? Nor have I any further annunciation to make to you.

But Bernadette had not the strength to restrain the dreadful question which despite all broke forth from her silent heart: "Is it the last time? Ah, Madame, is it indeed the last time?"

The lady, who understood this question well, gave no answer, not even a silent one. Only her smile grew brighter, gayer, more encouraging, more comradely. And in reality this smile had its own meaning, which was this: A last time—that does not exist for such as we. Assuredly we are saying a long farewell today, but you remain in the world and I remain in the world. . . .

And now the lady made still a third gesture. Very slowly she passed her pale fingers over her body from the breast to the girdle. That might have meant: I am still here, and therefore Bernadette renounced both dread and questioning, and sank wholly into contemplation, more deeply than she had ever done. Unconsciously she gazed, yet with an incomprehensible tension of all her nerves, as though she had to fill with what she saw all the chambers of her soul, as though she must, while it was still with her, store away the object of her vision into every cranny of her being against the lean days that would stretch from this hour even to the hour in which she came to die. For Bernadette knew this was farewell. But the lady, too, was giving her utmost. She offered and she gave herself in steady waves of drawing close and closer to the very boundary of the possible.

Twilight had long set in. Night fell, wave by wave. The July sky, studded with stars, had been gradually unveiled. The candle-light, brighter and brighter behind the kneeling girl's back, created before her eyes a world of darkness. Not yet had the lady withdrawn. With thoughtful tenderness of heart she had chosen this hour in which the fading of the light would make her fading indistinguishable. She did not desire to leave Bernadette as at other times, nor yet to deepen the girl's trance in order to steal away. She desired to dislimn airily and imponderably and leave behind as little pain as may be. So when at last Bernadette could hardly see any longer and the lady's figure was but an uncertain gleaming, then did she begin to withdraw. She did so very slowly and without taking her eyes from Bernadette. It all but seemed as though she raised her hand and waved it to her darling even as human beings are wont to wave to one another in farewell. Bernadette, too, lifted her hand, but her strength failed and she could not wave back. She stared into the night. Was that brightness yonder by the bank still the lady? Or was it she no more? The stars waxed more and more. They seemed to grow great with joy at receiving their queen. Was Bernadette to raise her eyes to the stars? She kept staring into the darkness at the spot where the last white glimmer had faded into night.

She remained for a few more minutes on her knees before she staggered to her feet and sought to approach the crowded candles and their holders. What a long way it was! She walked and walked and the others came toward her and yet there was no meeting. At last she stood in front of the people and saw the candle-light flicker in their faces: the face of her mother, who threw the little cape about her shoulders, since the night had grown chill; the stern face of Aunt Bernarde, who wanted at once to ask questions; the kindly face of Antoine with its searching look into her eyes. She still recognized all these faces. Also she recognized the voices that were insistent and famished for interesting news concerning the lady. But she repeated the lady's gesture and put her finger slowly on her lips. Then, quite unexpectedly, she suddenly sank to earth; she sank into a swoon and fell, not like one who himself fails and falls but like one whom a great hand has dropped.

Foreshadowings of Grace

CHAPTER THIRTY-ONE

The Departure of Sister Marie Thérèse

At first Bernadette's swoon was considered to be a particularly deep form of the trance into which all had seen the girl fall. Hence no one was anxious. Not until Bernadette opened her eyes after a long period in her mother's lap, and her face did not regain its colour as usual but was contorted by the struggle for breath, did Louise Soubirous cry out. The lack of breath developed into a severe attack of cardiac asthma. The girl's face was utterly without colour and the wide-open eyes gazed into emptiness for some relief. She was being throttled to death. The attack passed after a quarter-hour, but Bernadette remained prone and broken and could not stir.

Then, for the second and last time in life, Antoine Nicolau gathered her up in his arms, and carried her carefully the long way back to the Rue des Petites Fossées. Behind him thronged the whispering, horrified mass of women, some with their candles still lit. It looked like a funeral procession, and Uncle Sajou's prophecy that a coffin would soon be carried out of the Cachot seemed not far from coming true. Very odd was the behaviour of Louise Soubirous, who as a rule acted quite reservedly in public. She addressed loud and almost screaming abuses to the lady. How did it happen that her child and herself and her whole pitiable family were sent such bitter trials by uncanny powers whom neither priest nor bishop would acknowledge to be heavenly and holy! The lady was not the Blessed Virgin at all, but probably some spook risen from the abyss and an emissary of Satan, and the wise priests knew what they were doing when they avoided the grotto. How could the lady be a kindly being when she so muddled and upset poor Bernadette's head that the girl was really good for nothing any more? And now instead of curing the "athma" the beautiful phantom of the darkness was secretly throttling the child to death while she lay there unconscious. She shrieked thus like a very fishwife until her sister Bernarde Casterot angrily forbade it. "Hold your stupid tongue at last!"

Dr. Dozous was summoned to the Cachot immediately. He gave orders to have Bernadette removed at once to the Hospital of the Sisters of Nevers. After examining the patient, however, he reassured the parents. There was nothing new or dangerous; merely the same old asthma from which Bernadette had suffered since her childhood. This was doubtless intensified just now by a bad exhaustion of the nerves and the heart incurred by the child during the exciting weeks of the visions.

Exhaustion—that was quite the right word. Mortally exhausted by her dealings with the incomprehensible, Bernadette lay in a room of the hospital. During the first days phantasmal images beset her. But of the lady she did not dream. Of the lady she never dreamt. Of the lady she might not dream. She had still to undergo three or four attacks of asthma. But the intervals between attacks grew longer. Thereafter her breathing was easier and the phantom dances on the wall began to fade. The weight of exhaustion departed gradually from the delicate limbs. For though at first glance Bernadette seemed frail enough, there were tough powers of resistance in her young body. A new well-being seemed to pervade her muscles. One morning, somewhat more than a week after that farewell of all farewells, she felt well and resilient. She leaped from her bed and asked the sister on duty whether she might not go home. The sister bade her await the attending physician's call.

Meanwhile Dr. Dozous had paid the dean another visit on

behalf of Bernadette. His point was that for a frail developing girl with a bad case of asthma the Cachot was an extremely undesirable dwelling-place. The lack of light and air would sooner or later induce a tubercular condition in this case of initial predisposition. A remedial measure was indicated at once. The two men agreed quickly, whereupon Peyramale sought out the Mother Superior and proposed in his name and the physician's that Bernadette Soubirous be permitted the status of a patient for the present; not merely, he explained, for reasons of health but for additional and equally serious ones. The Mother Superior had not only taken a liking to Bernadette but was glad, too, to be able to render herself agreeable to the formidable dean.

Peyramale caused Bernadette, who was waiting to be discharged, to be summoned to his presence. She looked at him with eyes less intimidated than in the February days. She could not imagine what he wanted. But what a change had come over the black man in the priest's habit since the days when he threatened to drive her out with a broom! Peyramale seemed actually to contract his huge frame so as not to overwhelm the frail girl with his ardent massiveness. He even eliminated from his rough, veiled voice those thunderous echoes that were wont to accompany his friendliest words. Behind his kindliness today something hovered that was between shyness and timidity.

"Dear Bernadette," he said, "you're perfectly well now and could easily go home. But Dr. Dozous and I have decided that it would be better for you to stay here for a while. The Mother Superior has kindly consented. What do you think about that?"

She looked at him apathetically and did not answer, so that he thought life in the hospital might have irked her. "Of course you won't live with the sick," he went on. "I wouldn't like that either if I were well. The Mother Superior will give you a little room in which you can do what you please all day long. By night the supervising sister will share it with you. You'll be quite free. You can pass as much time with your family as you like. Of course, you must stick to the schedule here and come promptly to meals, because the doctor and I think it most important for the good sisters to feed you up as well as possible. Do you agree to that?"

Still silent, Bernadette nodded and her dark tranquil eyes rested on the dean.

"And that isn't all." The dean was persuasive. "I know how strangers pester you and how the curious question you without any regard for your feelings. I'd like to put a stop to that. You'll be protected here. The Mother Superior also asked me to say to you that you can use both the big and the little garden as much as you like. Does that please you?"

"Oh, yes, that pleases me very much, Monsieur le Curé," Bernadette said and smiled frankly at the dean, fearless for the first time in life. It did please her very much to have a place of refuge and to be free. Much as she was attached to her parents, the common life at home had grown very oppressive in recent weeks and for the little attic room of the Sajous she had had to pay by listening to endless idle chatter. Now she could go to the Cachot when she would and yet have an excuse for disappearing. Her need to be solitary was greater than ever. For to be alone was to be alone with her love, which had not been so much as touched by that farewell, but which that farewell had sweetened with continuous longing. What she felt in such hours and housed within herself of memory, and of re-experiencing—that was communicable to none and scarcely fathomed by herself.

She asked for work to do. They gave her work in the hospital kitchen. So she washed dishes after meals. She had never liked this work at home. But like all girls she did cheerfully out in the world things she had despised at home. Among the serving sisters there were several young and merry girls. They even sang in the kitchen. That pleased Bernadette. Everybody in the place treated her carefully, a little shyly, a little suspiciously. None knew quite how to take this miracle-worker. Thus it appeared.

The room they had given her was tiny, bare, whitewashed. But it looked out on the garden. She could sit for whole half-hours by the window, as she liked to do, and, lost in thought, stare at the tops of the trees. Now and then she was surprised in this mood of reverie and idleness, which seemed incomprehensible and irritating to the stupid, for empty heads cannot endure keeping still. Idleness means somnolence. One of the nursing sisters, angry at the idler, told the janitor, an old friend of François Soubirous: "There she sits, that funny creature, with her face all faded and doesn't move and stares out of the window like an idiot. I called her three times and she didn't answer."

The janitor of the Hospital of the Sisters of Nevers, a regular customer at Babou's bar, repeated this observation in the "medical corner." That was the name given to the table where the men-servants of physicians of Lourdes gathered. Dr. Lacrampe's valet, a tested diagnostician, whose acuteness penetrated to the character of the obscurest cases, gave his opinion, which none of his boon companions had a chance to contradict: "*Dementia paralytica progressiva sed non agitans!* I knew that months ago." The council of physicians' men nodded with that dumb matter-of-factness with which medical science faces disease and death. The obscure Latin death-sentence pronounced by the serving-man soon made the rounds of Lourdes as that of the man's master.

In Bernadette's little room there was a narrow iron bed and a day-bed. The day-bed was meant for the supervising sister. Since the convent and the hospital of the Sisters of Nevers were not under the same roof, some responsible person was needed in this building by night. The Mother Superior assigned this duty to nuns of ripe years and responsible character. It was the duty of the supervising sister to see to it that in serious cases the physician and priest were summoned, as well as to soothe and console restless patients. The supervisor also had the key to the pharmacy, with which ordinary nurses were not entrusted. The job was not very arduous at present; there were few patients seriously ill. Hence the supervising sister and Bernadette were very rarely aroused. The nuns slept very soundly, since, under these circumstances, they received dispensation from night devotions.

All changed when Marie Thérèse Vauzous was appointed supervisor. Bernadette had to pass the night with her too. And it was an almost sleepless night for the girl, although she never stirred and closed her eyes and feigned the regular breathing of sleep so as not to annoy her strict adversary. There was no call from the hospital. Since the bright light of a full moon of July shone through the window, Bernadette was able to observe her teacher from minute to minute from under her long, half-closed eyelashes. And she did so because she could not get the better of her curiosity.

While the other supervising sisters had undressed in the dark and slipped into bed, Marie Thérèse did not even take off her heavy habit. All that she took off was the conventual cap. She thus revealed her shorn head, which, with its dense blond hair, resembled a boy's. Would she take off her shoes? Bernadette wondered. Sister Marie Thérèse wore heavy flat laced shoes. Oh, how her feet must hurt at night! The nun kept her shoes on all through the night. She did not get under the covers but lay on top of them. First, however, she knelt and prayed for a whole hour. Not the comfortable rosary, like everybody else, but evidently a very exciting prayer, for she could be heard sighing as in great suffering. At times it sounded as though she were contending with someone. Bernadette could not take her hidden glance from the woman. She wondered whether the back and shoulders of the praying figure would not move just once. They seemed of stone and did not move.

Bernadette assumed a position in bed which enabled her from under almost closed lids to observe her roommate. In the sharp moonlight the nun lay on the day-bed, her hands crossed on her bosom, like a Gothic stone figure upon its catafalque. She did not sleep. Her eyes were open. Movelessly as the nun lay there, Bernadette nevertheless perceived the anguish of the sleepless woman's soul. Several times in the course of the night Marie Thérèse got up and knelt before the crucifix and indulged in long prayers. Bernadette could not help recalling that painful hour at school during which her teacher had told of holy men and women, of hermits and anchorites of the desert, who had lived on roots and wild honey and water or else had fasted for long periods and prayed all the prayers in the world when they were not thinking up new ones. The image of the iron girdles with rusty spikes under the cowls of the anchorites had become fixed, like all sharp images, in the dull pupil's mind. Doubtless Sister Marie Thérèse was as holy as the female hermits of the deserts and naked mountains. Perhaps she was even now fighting against evil thoughts and wishes, though it was hard to suppose that any such could be hidden in her breast.

On the small table by the side of the day-bed there was a plate with a fine fresh peach on it. Peaches were now in season and there are none better than grow in the province of Bigorre. Even by the moon's chalk-white light the round piece of fruit looked rosy and juicy. Bernadette was seized by a mighty hunger for that peach. Suddenly, however, the thought came to her that the nun had placed the peach there with the purpose of fighting her own terrible desire for it all night. Thus did the anchorites and hermits whom the implacable nun seemed so closely to resemble. The lady, Bernadette considered, who had always called people to do penance, had never forbidden them to eat peaches. Why shouldn't one eat them? They're delicious and you can get several for a single sou, so that even Mamma was able to buy a few now and then. Bernadette wished that the sister would at last bite into her peach. But the rigid figure of stone remained lying on the day-bed till the setting of the moon.

When Bernadette awoke she had the feeling of eyes having been fixed for a long time steadily upon her. Sunshine came in.

"You certainly are a good sleeper," said Sister Marie Thérèse Vauzous.

A swift glance showed Bernadette that the peach had not been touched. "I'll get up right away, Sister," Bernadette answered in an agreeable tone. While she slipped out of bed feet first, the straps of her little shift dropped from her thin shoulders.

"Aren't you ashamed even in front of yourself?" the nun whispered. "Cover yourself."

Since Bernadette started to leave the room as quickly as possible, the teacher held her back. "Wait a minute. Sit down on the bed. I'd like to talk to you."

The girl looked at the nun with her dark tranquil eyes. Sister Marie Thérèse could never puzzle out how much Bernadette suspected about her.

"When you return to school next year, which I strongly advise you to do," the nun began, "you'll not find me there any more. I am leaving Lourdes tomorrow. I am being recalled to the mother house of our order at Nevers."

"Oh, you are leaving Lourdes, Sister," Bernadette repeated neither regretfully nor yet the reverse.

"Yes, I am going away from here, Bernadette Soubirous, and I can't say that I am sorry. Look, what a little seducer you are! You've seduced the stupid mob and also the officials, since they don't lock you up. And now you're using your wiles successfully on a man of such strong character as the dean. You whistle and everybody dances. Except one person. Myself. For I simply don't believe you."

"I never wanted you to believe me, Sister," Bernadette said truthfully and without the slightest desire of wounding her teacher.

"Of course not! That's one of those answers of yours that are supposed to strike one silent." She nodded. "You've stirred up the whole country. Do you know, Bernadette, what was done in former times with creatures who, like you, boasted of equivocal visions of lovely ladies and produced springs by magic and stirred up the mob to violence and were guilty of infractions of the laws of the State and of Holy Church? One burned them at the stake, Bernadette!"

Bernadette wrinkled her forehead tensely but answered nothing. Marie Thérèse Vauzous drew herself up to her full height. "One more thing I must say to you, Soubirous. You may have thought at school sometimes that I was always finding fault with you and was unjust to you. You were utterly wrong. There was none among my pupils over whom I have been in such dread and sorrow as yourself. All this night I have been praying for you. And henceforth, too, I shall pray daily that God let not your soul be destroyed but save it from the frightful danger to which you are exposing it."

With this she took the plate with the peach from the table. For a moment she seemed tempted to offer it to Bernadette. But she could not bring herself to do so and gave the peach to the first patient she met in the corridor.

CHAPTER THIRTY-TWO

Psychiatry Takes a Hand

THERE WERE two men in France who truly and sincerely suffered under their defeat at the hands of the lady of Massabielle. One was Vital Dutour, the bald-headed prosecutor of Lourdes; the other was Baron Massy, the very conventional prefect of the department of the Hautes-Pyrénées.

The deepest motive of most people seems to be one of arrogance or, more accurately, the burning desire for a constant feeling of superiority. Social conventions demand that this passion be more shamefacedly concealed than even the passion of sex. Hence it ravages their souls all the more devastatingly. Now, every class has its specific kind and degree of arrogance. It may be fairly argued that the arrogance of bureaucrats, when provoked, surpasses that of all other classes of society. For in his own eyes the bureaucrat is not simply a chance functionary of the power of the State. At his desk he has the feeling that he himself is that power. Even though he is only stamping letters, he deems himself of another and higher order than the public, as, let us say, any angel is of another and higher order than mortal man. In his capacity of judge, chief of police, collector of imposts or taxes, he has a far more visible control over the fates of men than Providence itself. All surround him with the obsequiousness born of fear, for the law is as putty in his hands. From the crown of the Emperor, of which he is in his own conceit the co-bearer, he derives his magic power. He knows very well that in actual fact he is less and knows less than any scholar, physician, engineer, or even than any smith or locksmith who has learned his trade. Rob him of the magic which power radiates, and there is left a rickety and declassed scrivener. Human arrogance tends to defend itself with a bitterness in proportion to its vulnerability. If a bureaucrat is made ridiculous, so is the divine principle of power itself. That cannot be endured.

It is not to be endured that things should go on as they are doing, Baron Massy reflected. The case of the lady of Massabielle cannot end with a jeer at the divine principle of power. The great dailies had calmed down a little since the grotto had been boarded up. Perhaps grass would soon be growing over the grave of this business of phantoms and miracles which was a slap in the face to the spirit of the age. But the baron's arrogance prevented him from exercising a wise and far-sighted resignation. He had had to suffer ministers of state to find fault with him. Twice he had had to wait in the episcopal antechamber and then accept an ironic repulse. Every step he had taken for the suppression of this irritating nuisance had ended in bitter futility or open recoil upon himself.

Baron Massy was not the man to leave unfinished a sentence either spoken or written by himself. His predicates followed his subjects, and sand or blotter succeeded the final stop. It would have made him ill to yield, that is, to abstain from further persecution. His dislike of Bernadette Soubirous was acute, although he had never seen her. He was convinced that in her and in her alone was to be sought the origin of these endless and mischievous annoyances. Until Bernadette had been obliterated from the consciousness of all France, there would be no tranquillity in or around Lourdes. All attempts to convict the girl of fraud or at least of the selfish exploitation of the credulity of her fellow-men had been brought to naught either by her own astuteness or by the awkward silliness of Jacomet. But Massy still had a weapon in reserve.

It was one of the dog days. The summer sun flooded the huge office of His Excellency. The prefect had on his black morning coat, as always, the high stiff collar which scraped his very chin, and stiff cuffs, while all the other officials in the building worked in their shirt-sleeves. In spite of that they sweated. It was against the baron's principles to sweat. He was studying a document that had been sent him many weeks ago. It contained the findings of a committee of physicians who had examined Bernadette Soubirous toward the end of March. The committee had consisted of Drs. Balencie and Lacrampe, both in practice at Lourdes, and one humble country doctor of the vicinity. Vital Dutour had stubbornly insisted at the time that Dr. Dozous, though actually attached to the municipality, be not a member of that committee. He had had his fill of the reports which this unreliable customer had let loose in the Café Français. Frowning, the prefect read and reread the final report:

"Except for the asthmatic condition with which she was born Bernadette Soubirous is in entirely normal health. She never suffers from headaches or any other kind of nervous disturbances. Her appetite and sleep are excellent. There is no evidence of any pathological tendency whatsoever. Her nature is doubtless a very impressionable one. We are dealing with a hypersensitive temperament which can easily become the prey of its own imaginings, and these may become as intense as hallucinations. It is quite possible that a ray of light in the niche in the rock deludes her into seeing form and outline. These hypersensitive natures often tend to exaggerate such experiences and in severe cases this tendency may end in a pseudologia phantastica. But there is no ground for assuming any such condition in the case before us. The undersigned are of opinion that so-called ecstatic conditions may obtain here. These conditions constitute a psychical affliction, comparable to somnambulism, of which very little is known but which are of no danger to the patient."

" 'May,' 'could,' 'possibly,' 'perhaps,' " Baron Massy growled and pushed this cautious report from him in disgust. Then, just at the right moment, the visit of the psychiatrist was announced. This was a man who was at the head of a sanatorium near Pau and whom the baron had very specially invited. Now and then the State needs to employ a neurologist to get rid of some crude and stubborn fool. Especially in matters concerning the misuse of great fortunes, crazily eccentric wills, the infatuation of grey-beards and fathers for frivolous beauties, do State and entrenched families call upon psychiatrists for help. Why, then, should not the State invoke the psychiatrist's help against the supernatural in an age that can just manage to get along successfully with the natural?

The psychiatrist had both charm and a red beard. His pompadour was arranged to be flame-like. One might have called him handsome had not a muscular paralysis drawn the left corner of his mouth slightly upward. His mouse-grey eyes moved impishly to and fro, for the physician who treats the insane never wholly escapes the contamination of their maladies.

The prefect gave an accounting of the matter in hand and made clear the governmental point of view. To the baron's satisfaction the red-beard proved himself a delicately attentive listener. Himself completely indifferent to all philosophical speculations, he resented bitterly anything that seemed to produce a suprasensual rift in his fixed and wholly explicable universe. Thus Bernadette offered his mind no alternative but that of fraud or madness. And since madness was his specialty, he was a natural special pleader on its side. Nor could he see why in these hard times the heavenly powers, without having passed the requisite and severe medical examinations, should offer unfair competition like any quack. The prefect pointed out the law of June 30, 1838, according to which the prosecutor's office was empowered to put under restraint any citizen suspected of mental derangement whenever medical diagnosis justified such action and the patient might become a public menace. The psychiatrist smiled.

"We need to employ no hard and fast rule, Your Excellency. There is a proper and legal middle way between entire liberty and complete internment which I often use in difficult cases. I place the patient under observation. After all, a psychiatrist is no orthopædic surgeon who can set a broken foot on the spot."

"Excellent, my dear Professor," the baron happily agreed. "I fear that this patient will of necessity have to be placed under observation."

On the very next morning the psychiatrist made his appearance in the hospital of Lourdes. He was accompanied by an orderly as able-bodied as if Goliath himself were to be taken into custody. Bernadette was presented to him forthwith. Her eyes were cool, thoughtful, and very guarded, as always in times of conflict. The red-beard put on an avuncular act to gain her confidence. He laughed delightedly, pursed his crooked lips, patted and petted her. Angrily Bernadette avoided the man's touch. The psychiatrist involved her in a long discussion which in its own way aimed at the same end as that of Jacomet once upon a time. Bernadette was to be lured into all kinds of traps in order to display her feebleness of wit. She refused to afford the man that satisfaction. As always her replies were curt and telling. She knew how many hours there are in a day and days in a week and when the sun rises in July and who was the ruler of France. She could multiply seven by five. She could not multiply seventeen by eighteen, but quite seriously threw out the remark: "You had to do that sum first yourself, Monsieur."

Questioned concerning the events of the last few days, she was able to give a neat account in chronological order. Two of the younger nuns who were present at the examination began to giggle. Bernadette had not lost her old art of making a fool of anyone who tried to make a fool of her.

The psychiatrist asked permission to be alone with his patient in a dark chamber. The Mother Superior, though granting this request, had the wisdom to send messages to Bernadette's parents and to the dean. Bernadette sat attentively on a bed while the red-beard moved about like a shadow in the summery twilight. Like a tailor he drew out a tape-measure; like a tailor's, too, were the many pins stuck under the lapel of his coat. Skull and brain anatomy happened just then to be in triumphant vogue. The brain centres of thought, emotion, and motor impulse had been localized and neatly delimited. Man, so to speak, was suspended by these centres like a supple mechanical jumping-jack. They were the sum total of what old-fashioned people called "soul." The psychiatrist took Bernadette's skull-measurements and entered them in a little note-book, again just like a tailor. Then he pricked her with his pins in various parts of her body.

"Ouch!" Bernadette cried.

"You're very sensitive to that!" the psychiatrist rejoiced. Impossible to tell whether his meaning boded good or ill for the patient.

"So would anybody be," Bernadette answered in accordance with the facts.

The red-beard now examined her muscular reflexes and, above all, the reactions of the pupils of her eyes. He bade her walk backward and forward with eyes open and closed. "Why do you walk so unsteadily?" he asked.

"Because I'm worn out, Monsieur."

He told her next to sit down and chat with him. He was

very avuncular again. "So you see the Blessed Virgin in the grotto?"

"I've never said that, Monsieur."

"What, then, do you say?"

"I used to see the lady in the grotto," Bernadette replied with emphasis on the past character of the event.

"But the lady must be someone," the red-head insisted.

"The lady is the lady."

"Whoever sees ladies that do not exist is ill, my child, and not normal."

Bernadette let a little while pass. Then she explained with precision. "I used to see the lady. I will never see her again, for she has gone away. Consequently, Monsieur, you can no longer make me out to be sick."

For a moment the man was taken aback by this unanswerable logic. "Listen, my dear child," he said thereupon. "There are symptoms to prove that you're not quite as you should be. But I'll give you my word of honour that your cure will be very rapid. Wouldn't you like to be really well and be rid of these conditions that are so harmful to you? For a short time you'll live in a beautiful house with a large garden. You'll fare like a little princess. Are you fond of hot chocolate with whipped cream?"

"I've never had any."

"Well, you'll have it, if you like, with breakfast in the morning. You'll never be better off anywhere than with me. Your parents needn't pay a sou. You'll be taken care of, and your whole future will be better."

"I don't care particularly for chocolate and whipped cream," said Bernadette. "I'll soon be fifteen and it's better that I stay here."

With a smile the red-beard shook his head. "My dear girl," he said, "it would be better if you went with me of your own volition. Your parents, to whom we'll talk, won't be the losers, either. I have noticed that you're a clever girl. It won't take beyond three or four weeks. Then these morbid conditions will be over once and for all. You'll see no ladies in grottoes any more, but you will be a splendid human being well equipped for the struggle of life."

"I'm not a bit afraid of that struggle, Monsieur," Bernadette said, looking at those small hands of hers that had already done a great deal of work in their day. And with this, before the psychiatrist suspected anything, she leaped up and ran from the room and without hindrance from the house.

Two hours later the psychiatrist and the imperial prosecutor together entered the Cachot. The gentlemen were not a little startled when near the door there met them no lesser man than Marie Dominique Peyramale. Implacably that huge form barred the way so that the ensuing conversation was carried on in the low doorway while the Soubirous family sought refuge in the farthest corner around the fireplace.

The red-beard bowed in some embarrassment. "Have I the honour of addressing the dean of Lourdes?"

"You have that honour, Monsieur. How can I serve you?"

Vital Dutour cleared his throat. "Wouldn't it be better to go elsewhere?"

"It is you gentlemen who have chosen this place of action, not I," said the dean, not yielding a foot of ground. "The presence of the Soubirous family as witnesses is very welcome to me. I know Monsieur the Prosecutor. The other gentleman I do not know. He is probably the neurologist of Pau whom the prefect was pleased to send us."

"I am professor extraordinary of psychiatry and neurology," the red-beard admitted with crooked mouth and an aplomb that failed to come off.

"I'm afraid you won't find Lourdes a very fertile field for your studies," the dean observed regretfully.

"Mr. Dean, I am here on behalf of the medical department of the provincial administration. We have the findings of a medical committee under date of March 26 which establish the presence of definite anomalies in the youthful patient in question. It is the desire of the prefect to check these findings and to place the girl under my observation for a period. Such is my mission here. . . ."

Peyramale seemed to grow more and more massive. "I know that entirely empty document of March," said he. "Now you have subjected the girl to an examination, Monsieur le Professeur. Tell us what anomalies *you* were able to establish."

The red-beard was hesitant. "There are anomalies that are not exactly spectacular."

The veiled thunder of Peyramale's voice began to swell and fill the room. "Let me recall to your memory, my good Professor, that Hippocratic oath which you swore when you became a healer of men. I ask you: Is Bernadette Soubirous mentally deranged or inclined to mania or a menace to her fellowmen?"

"Good Lord, Monsieur le Curé, who ever mentioned such things as mania or public menace?" The fellow fairly writhed.

"Then what right has the prefect to desire to rob the girl of her liberty?"

"A right that is given him in the written law of France," Vital Dutour said with infuriating equanimity.

It took a few deep breaths for Peyramale to preserve a show of calm. "The law of France is too lofty to be used toward the perverting of justice."

The red-beard tried the role of pacifier. "But, my dear Dean, if we invoke the law of 1838 it is purely to serve our little patient, who at the direction of the prefect is to be placed under observation for a period and treated according to all the methods of modern science."

The end of Peyramale's self-control had come. The organ of his temperament rolled forth its music: "That is the most shameless piece of hypocrisy I have ever encountered! I give you my word, gentlemen, that I will unmask that hypocrisy and raise an alarm in all the land of France that will echo a thousandfold in the ears of the prefect of Tarbes. . . . Come here, Bernadette Soubirous!"

Quite instinctively Bernadette had already drawn close to the dean. The bogyman of her childhood took her and pressed her close to him in token of the protecting power of his arms of steel.

"I know this child!" he cried. "So does the imperial prosecutor. We have both had intimate conferences with her. Anyone who asserts that Bernadette Soubirous is deranged is himself either deranged or a scoundrel. The law of 1838 is directed against dangerous maniacs. Are you gentlemen still minded to apply it? Well and good! But be assured that I will not stir from this child's side. And now you may call the gendarmes!"

"And when the gendarmes come, what then, Dean?" Vital Dutour asked, his angry challenge sheathed in carelessness.

Peyramale laughed aloud. "When the gendarmes come, gentlemen, ah, yes, when they do come, I'll say to them: Load your guns well, my men, for your path lies over my dead body."

Checkmated, the prosecutor and the psychiatrist withdrew from the room, into which, thanks to the dean, they had penetrated but a few paces. Vital Dutour knew that Peyramale was capable of making good any threat. And he had not foreseen this sudden shift of attitude in the dean of Lourdes. Bernadette was a veritable witch as in the good old days. He would have to wire to Tarbes and Pau for new directions.

A little after one o'clock a closed special stage-coach stopped at the corner of the Rue des Petites Fossées and the Place Marcadale. At this hour the streets were always somnolent and empty. Louise and Bernadette Soubirous entered the coach. Dean Peyramale was already seated inside. The quiet journey took the direction of the high mountains, to the watering-place of Cauterets. Thither Peyramale was taking the persecuted girl and her mother to be sheltered in a little house which was parish property. Protection and care were assured by the parish priest of Cauterets. Thus Bernadette vanished and remained so. Not even the prefect's special police were able to discover her hiding-place.

CHAPTER THIRTY-THREE

Digitus Dei:
The Bishop Gives the Lady a Chance

A<small>T THIS</small> time Monseigneur Thibaut, bishop of Montpellier, was taking a brief cure at Cauterets. In the parish house he made the acquaintance of Bernadette Soubirous. Monseigneur Thibaut offered the sharpest possible contrast to Monseigneur Laurence. He wore his silky white hair rather long. His mouth was not at all sarcastic but gentle as a child's, and his eyes were of the deep blue of cornflowers. The bishop of Montpellier was a man open to pleasing appeals. His was a poetical nature. In his leisure hours, as was no secret, he composed tolerable verses, both French and Latin, in praise of God, of Nature, of Heaven, of the Blessed Virgin, and of Friendship. Like most people, Monseigneur knew of the apparitions of Lourdes only by what the papers had printed. Nor did he differ from the general opinion of the French clergy that in view of the prevailing temper of the times extreme caution was to be observed in respect of mystical appearances of any kind. Nothing could be more dangerous, he quite agreed, than any attempt to obliterate the sacred boundary between religion and ghost-mongering. Nevertheless, he asked Bernadette for an exact account of her experiences. And a remarkable thing took place. Though she never refused such requests, she had been acceding to them merely by a mechanical repetition of facts as by rote. But the glowing eyes of this listener inspired her. For the first time in her life she seemed to be meeting a soul like her own, one able to embrace with equal breadth and depth the mysteries of ecstasy, of love, of being shaken to the very core. Almost from the start she abandoned her mechanical repetition. She leaped from her seat. She knelt. She played her own part and she played the lady's. February 11. Behold, the brook was here, the grotto yonder. So powerful was the act of recollection that Bernadette herself felt how by a force unknown she was drawing and drawing the lady hither, more and more, almost into the niche at the right of the room. She grew pale and Louise Soubirous feared lest she fall into a trance. And when at last Bernadette, acting the lady's part, said as though to herself with half-outstretched arms and in that tone of lovely earnestness: "Will you render me the grace of coming here each day for fifteen days?" Monseigneur Thibaut suddenly arose and left the room. The old man's eyes were bathed in tears. He panted. In the garden he leaned against a tree and kept repeating: *"Quel poème . . . quel poème!* . . . What a poem!"

Two days later the bishop of Montpellier went on a visit to Lourdes. He took lodging in Cazenave's hotel. He at once requested Dean Peyramale to send him trustworthy witnesses of the visions and ecstasies of Bernadette. Peyramale selected Dr. Dozous and Jean Baptiste Estrade. The latter declared literally as follows: "Monseigneur, I have in my time seen and admired the greatest actresses of the French stage, among them an artist like Rachel. Compared to Bernadette they were all but grimacing statues who exaggerated false and affected passions. The little seeress of Massabielle mirrored for us states of bliss and blessedness for which language has no words."

"C'est cela, c'est cela! . . . Just so, just so!" Thibaut exclaimed.

Dean Peyramale seized the opportunity to advise as follows:

"Monseigneur should not miss the chance of having a chat with the bishop of Tarbes."

Monseigneur did not miss the chance. Although his physicians had insisted that his strenuous cure be followed by two weeks of rest, he proceeded to Tarbes instead of returning to his own diocese and had a three hours' conference with Bertrand Sévère Laurence.

Shortly thereafter the dean of Lourdes was summoned by telegram to the episcopal palace. This was no friendly visit with dinner and reception in the bishop's private quarters. He had to wait in the chancellery for two hours.

Angrily the bishop brought his cane down on his desk. "Are you proposing to have me hounded by the entire episcopate of France, Dean of Lourdes?" Before Peyramale had a chance to reply the bishop handed him one of those impressive scrolls, hung with seals, which are used for pastoral letters and proclamations. "*Lege*, read!" Monseigneur commanded him in Latin.

In view of the solemn parchment Peyramale observed with satisfaction that the unorganized mass of papers formerly in the bishop's drawer had made considerable progress toward final form and fair copying since his last visit. "Is this the order for the episcopal commission of investigation?" he asked softly.

"*Sedę et lege*," ordered the bishop, whose icy mildness had today given way to an almost passionate rudeness. Obediently the dean sat down on an office chair and read the Latin title inscribed in elaborate lettering of blue and red and gold: "Ordinance of the Bishop of Lourdes Looking toward the Appointment of a Commission for the Investigation of Those Events Which Stand in Any Relationship to the Alleged Appearances in a Grotto West of Lourdes."

And under the antique baroque style of this title he read: "Bertrand Sévère Laurence, by God's mercy and the grace of the Holy Apostolic See, Bishop of Tarbes, to the clergy and the faithful of our diocese, salutation and blessing in the name of Jesus Christ, Our Lord. . . ."

The dean looked at the bishop, whose glance sent him back promptly to his reading. Many, many lines of small calligraphy followed the Roman salutation and benediction. Peyramale, who was far-sighted, had trouble enough deciphering the script; but the tension was not only of the eye, it was of the mind too. For deeply implicit in the clear words of the pastoral letter the bishop's scrupulous distrust could be felt in all its anguish. In his introduction Bertrand Sévère argued the how and why of the case. Peyramale recognized that it had been Monseigneur's purpose in these arguments to make it clear that he had been forced to take action, not by an inner urgency, but by such outer circumstances as the hatred of the unbelievers and the fanaticism of the credulous. Again and again Peyramale came upon reservations well concealed under the smooth surface of the pastoral style. "There is nothing," he read, "that can be acknowledged *a priori* and without the most serious and sober research." Hence it were better to disregard as far as possible all subjective affirmations and to direct the acutest observation possible to the scientific clarification of the alleged phenomena of healing. "It is easier to confuse than to convince men," the bishop wrote. But Peyramale could read even more between the lines. A new confusion would be another blow at Christianity which even now was defending its eternal truths in one of the severest conflicts of all history. The modern spirit, even when it did not deny God, was so constituted as to refuse its intellectual or emotional recognition to breaches of the general order of nature. If the Church, even though eternally and in principle prepared to do so, were to admit such a breach, it would involuntarily strengthen the enemies of the divine and cause widespread bitterness. Hence before an ecclesiastical commission can grant the fact of super-natural interposition, all methods of natural explanation, pursued with every instrumentality of modern critical science, must be exhaustively employed. Hence this commission must be composed not only of professors of dogmatic theology, of moral and mystical theology, but of an equal number of professors of medicine, chemistry, physics, and geology. . . .

Peyramale read on and on. There seemed no end. The small script danced before his eyes. Monseigneur, becoming impatient, took the document from his hands. "He who denies miracles is no true Catholic," the bishop growled. "He who denies God the power to manage the universe as seems best to Him is not of the faithful. And yet—miracles of this kind cause offence. They offend me. I don't like them. A miserable brat in a shabby provincial hole, her father a drunkard, her mother a washerwoman! Heaven's mercy knows no bounds and I am only a humble human creature. And yet—God forgive me the sin—it nauseates me. And you're all hounding me into it."

"It is not we, Monseigneur," Peyramale said. "It is the thing itself that compels you even as it did me. I am, by the living God, no adherent of the easy and stupid mysticism of elderly females. But who, Your Lordship, will explain the mad course of events? She's the daughter of people who have come down in the world. Granted. But this truly guileless child, almost wholly ignorant of the simplest tenets of religion, nor ever given to waking dreams or reveries—this child sees a lady whom she takes for a real human being of flesh and blood. The child tells her sister and her schoolmate. The sister tells the mother and the friend the other schoolmates. Out of this trivial gossip among working women and children and humble folk there rolls forth within a few days a very avalanche of contradictions that buries all France. Your immediate colleague, Monseigneur, the bishop of Montpellier, calls it the most beautiful of modern poems."

Bertrand Sévère laughed not without contempt. "My colleague, the bishop of Montpellier, is a gentleman of facile emotions."

"But my emotions are far from facile, Monseigneur," Peyramale declared. "Yet this incomprehensible development of what seemed a childish triviality keeps me uninterruptedly stirred. Now, however, you are convoking a group of men who will instruct us and either say: '*Hic est digitus Dei*,' or else they will say: 'This is not the finger of God.'"

The bishop lowered the corners of his mouth and lifted his brows. "And among these men who are convoked," he said, "there will be the dean of Lourdes with all his uncertainties. . . ."

For once the dean looked frightened. He was strongly tempted to refuse to serve on the commission. But that was not to be thought of.

"When will you command the commission to assemble, Monseigneur?" he asked in a reserved voice.

"Not yet, not yet," the bishop answered grimly and closed his hands over the document as though determined to have no one snatch it from him.

"But the ordinance is ready for the printer," Peyramale argued.

The old man growled: "It can wait. It bears no date yet. Will you please explain to me, my dear man, how the scientists, the chemists and geologists, are going to conduct their researches if the grotto remains barred?"

"Your pastoral letter will force them to open the grotto for inspection, Monseigneur," Peyramale incautiously asserted.

The bishop's voice was high and mordant. "I don't want to

use force. I refuse to exert the slightest pressure on the secular power. The Emperor is going to command that the grotto be opened. Then the commission may assemble. Not the other way round."

"Did the Emperor reserve that decision to himself personally?"

"The Emperor will decide because the feeble underlings will leave him no other possibility." After a while, in a voice lowered almost to a whisper, the bishop added: "I'm giving the lady her last chance. Do you understand that, Dean of Lourdes?"

"No, I do not understand that, Your Lordship."

"Then I'll have to explain. I give the lady the chance of overcoming the Emperor or being overcome by him. If she overcomes, the commission can go to work. If she is overcome and the grotto remains barred, she is not the Blessed Virgin and she and the commission too can melt into thin air."

After these words the bishop read off the specific provisions of his plan. Peyramale's ears heard the names of the vested members of the cathedral clergy who were entrusted with the administration of the commission and the names of professors at the seminaries who were to take the scientific research in hand. Thereupon the dean was dismissed. But the bishop recalled him once more from the very door: "And what's to become of Bernadette, Dean of Lourdes, eh?"

"Exactly what do you mean by that, Monseigneur?" Peyramale asked, playing for time.

"I mean something quite simple. What's the girl's idea of her own future? You've constituted yourself her knight. You've probably asked her."

Peyramale answered with extreme circumspection: "Bernadette is very, very simple of heart. She has no ambition of any kind. Her sole desire is to return to the anonymous mass from which she arose and to live as do all the other women of her station."

"Easy to understand, that wish," the bishop laughed. "But you, as a theologian, do you believe that this idyllic future can come to pass after all that has happened?"

"I hope with all my heart it may and yet do not believe it possible," the dean said at last. In his answer was all the equivocalness of his mood in relation to Bernadette and her lady.

The bishop, leaning on his ivory-headed cane, came forth from behind his desk and approached the dean, face close to face. "The commission, my dear fellow, can render only one of three decisions. Number one: You're an impostor, little Soubirous. Hence off with you to an institution for juvenile delinquents. Number two: You're a madwoman, little Soubirous. Hence off with you to an asylum. Number three: You have been visited by the Most Blessed Virgin's special grace, little Soubirous. Miracles issue from your spring. The day will come when we will turn over the documents concerning you to the Congregation of Rites in Rome. And therefore . . . therefore what, eh?"

Marie Dominique Peyramale preferred not to reply.

"Consequently," Monseigneur went on, raising his voice, "you are one of those rarest of mortal beings who can demand to be honoured at our altars, and therefore you must disappear —make no mistake—because we can't let a saint loose in the world. A saint who flirts with boys and takes a husband and bears children, that would be a rather too amusing innovation, wouldn't it?"

The bishop's tone changed suddenly to one of gentleness and thoughtful softness. "Therefore, little Soubirous, the Church must take you under its guardianship. Therefore, little Soubirous, the Church must plant you, like a precious flower, in one of its best gardens, that of the Carmelites or that of the Carthusians, where the rule is very strict, whether you desire it or no."

"She will certainly not desire it, Monseigneur," Peyramale broke in, in a voice scarce audible. "Bernadette is a natural child of this world and has, so far as I know, no vocation for the life of a religious. And she's so frightfully young, under fifteen."

"She'll grow older," the bishop said curtly. "But the ordinance has not yet been published. The permanent commission has not yet met. When once it does meet, its sessions, my dear fellow—so much I can promise you—will continue for years and years. For I shall be contented with nothing less than a quite ultimate clarification. Until then your protégée, this little one, may live in the world, though under strict supervision. I do demand that. And if you wish the child well, Dean of Lourdes, persuade her to retract in time. Then she can go for a bit to a reform school. And that would be the wisest thing for Bernadette Soubirous and probably also for the Church, seeing the times are what they are. . . ."

CHAPTER THIRTY-FOUR

An Analysis and Two Cases of

Lèse-Majesté

Serious insurgency arose in a quarter which was generally not at all well affected toward the lady of Massabielle. Among the factory workers of the province the rumour circulated that Bernadette Soubirous had been kidnapped and locked up in either a prison or a madhouse. The red-bearded psychiatrist's visit to Lourdes had not passed unobserved. Jacomet had to get the man out of town in his own coach and under police protection, for Antoine Nicolau had sworn by all he considered holy to hold up the regular stage at Bartrès and not only give the professor a beating equal to that administered to the "English millionaire" but to make a clean end of him.

And after the red-beard's visit Bernadette could not be found. Therefore the miller Antoine went in for wild political propaganda. He addressed the hands of the Lafite saw-mill and of the Claverie mills, of the Duprat wagon-works, the Soutroux brick-works, and the Paguès distillery. He also made speeches before the slate-miners, stonemasons, woodcutters, and road-menders, most of whom he knew personally.

"Are we free men in France or slaves?" he sharply incited his hearers.

"Slaves!" the answer rolled back, and the answer was, in point of fact, not wholly wrong, for by virtue of the laws of *sûreté générale* or public safety the Emperor had made himself absolute and was unrestrained by constitutional checks. Thus

Antoine Nicolau found ears willing to listen to his demagogic appeals in favour of Bernadette. Though the scene was the Catholic South of France, these were the same working-class people who in 1789 and 1830 and 1848 had mounted the barricades to fight the privileged classes to which, in their view, *le bon Dieu* and *la très sainte Vierge* belonged. Bernadette Soubirous was a daughter of this working-class, one of the very poorest of them. For months and months the privileged classes had been tormenting this child through the police, the prosecutor, the examining magistrate, official psychiatric snooping, and the very Church. And why? one might ask. Because *la très sainte Vierge* had appeared and caused a well of healing to gush forth from the infamous grotto of Massabielle through a simple child of the common people and not through an aristocratic nun in an exclusive cloister. Was that any goddamned business of Jacomet or Dutour or Massy or even the Emperor? It was quite squarely none of the goddamned business of any of them. They might better have seen to the elimination of starvation wages and unemployment and the frightful misery of the common people. But, oh, no, from the Emperor down to Jacomet all they're intent on is that the possessing and ruling classes don't lose a sou. On the contrary, they barricade the harmless grotto and in very mockery forbid plain people to drink of the waters that had already cured many a sick person. Just why? So as to be able to sell it at good prices by and by and fill both their bottles and their pockets. And now the last and most monstrous performance! They kidnap this innocent child of the people in order to bury her for ever in some prison cell or madman's den. . . .

On the first Thursday of August the storm broke. More than a thousand workmen laid down their tools at four o'clock in the afternoon and marched in close formation toward Massabielle. Jacomet had barely time enough to send his available force of fifteen gendarmes in hot haste to the grotto. The armed men constituted themselves a wall in front of the scaffolding. After preliminaries of rage and abuse it came to open combat. The gendarmes had to draw their swords to repel three attacks. A rain of stones next rattled down upon them. Belhache was quite seriously wounded beneath the right eye. The mayor, the commissioner, half the members of the provincial courts appeared on the scene of action to save the situation. Jacomet tried to speak and was howled down. The same thing happened to Dutour. Lacadé, that former tribune of the people, had a happier touch. His first sentences were listened to. Then Nicolau interrupted him: "Where is Bernadette?"

"Bernadette is safe and sound!" Lacadé cried. "I stake my life on that. Wasn't I always on your side, men? Didn't you elect me of your own free will? Give me your confidence and I'll give you mine. If you'll put an end to this criminal mischief, Nicolau, you'll be told where Bernadette is."

That promise carried weight with Antoine Nicolau.

Jacomet's report was calculated to plunge Baron Massy into blackest melancholy. On the very heels of the foiled attempt to intern Bernadette through the red-beard came this blow, the severest yet. The press seized upon the "incidents" at Lourdes and spread them with a hypocritical air of misgiving. The French people was a people of independent reason, not of blind obedience. An absolute regime could daunt Cossacks or Prussians, not the great nation of Voltaire and the Encyclopædists. The Gallic race had enough of the gift of irony to use an episode of superstition for the raising of its voice. Even as the poor girl Bernadette saw a mystical lady in the cave of Massabielle, so might certain circles behold in that same grotto the letters of fire in which the sovereign people was admonishing all those who would curtail its rights. Such were the words which *La Petite République* dared to print. The censor confis-

cated a part of the edition, but most copies had already reached
their readers.

And consequently on the bureaucratic Jacob's ladder there
began once more the up and down of inquiries and answering
reports. No decision had yet been obtainable from the Emperor. He played at being husband, father, summer visitor at
Biarritz. He enjoyed sea-bathing, and when the Minister of
Finance, Fould, turned up with troublesome business he sent
word that he was out. Baron Massy was tired of all the fruitless ways of official business. He registered an oath of vengeance against the grotto of Massabielle which had so often
humiliated him beyond endurance. After his first amazement it
seemed to him suddenly that the way of revenge was clear.
Let the "subversive elements" gather by thousands, nay, by
tens of thousands; let it come to a regular revolution in Lourdes;
he would merely rejoice. On his own responsibility and at any
cost to himself he did not intend to hesitate. He would order
the hellish grotto demolished under the fire of the regiment of
artillery stationed at Tarbes.

He dispatched the sternest possible orders to the sub-prefect,
the mayor, and the police commissioner of Lourdes: "If these
tumults recur, and violence be renewed against the armed
power of the State, the gendarmerie as well as any troops summoned to its assistance is herewith ordered, after due warning
according to law, to make unrestricted use of its firearms."

Lacadé was badly frightened when he read these words.
"The battle of Massabielle" with many dead and wounded, that
would be a devil of a prologue to a successful world export
business in curative mineral waters! You can't use a bloody
field of battle for a casino with gardens, bandstands, croquet
lawns, Italian fiestas, and fireworks! Good Lord! Horrified, the
mayor ran to the dean's house.

There now ensued a week during which Peyramale had

little time either to eat or to sleep. First he got hold of Antoine. "What an ungodly ass you are!" he roared. "Brainless!
Why do you incite people to violence? Do you want human
blood mixed with Bernadette's spring? That would be the end
of her. Rightly one would get rid of her as a criminal. And the
spring, which may be a great blessing, would be accursed for
all time. Do you get the consequences through your head, you
abject ass?"

Antoine turned pale and hung his head.

"You're going with me this instant and you'll show me all
the ring-leaders!" the dean thundered.

That Marie Dominique Peyramale had been from the beginning of his ministry the shepherd of the weary and heavy-
laden now served him in good stead. He knew the workers, the
peasants, the poor, and they knew him. He spoke their language. With a very subdued Antoine he entered the shops of
Lafite, Claverie, Soutroux, and Paguès. His irresistible rough
voice recalled the men to reason.

"I know your plans for next Thursday. You want to come
in your tens of thousands from all directions, eh? Nothing will
come of it except that the military will fire and many of you
will die and many be crippled. To what end? The liberation of
the grotto? Don't try to pretend to me! You're mixing up your
own cause with something else. That will lead to no good. That
will end in more misery."

"We want to see Bernadette," the men replied.

Peyramale continued on his mission. He went into houses
and huts. He besought the women to make life so bitter for
their men that the latter would desist from their madness.
"Suppose the lady is really the Most Blessed Virgin!" he cried.
"What will she think of such ingratitude?"

The women yielded to the force of this argument but also
demanded to see Bernadette.

Two days before the planned insurrection the dean summoned Louise Soubirous and Bernadette back from Cauterets. Wednesday he hired a carriage and took them both for a ride back and forth through town and country. And the girl's fresh aspect, a visible result of her stay in the mountains, made a deep impression. Bernadette smiled inattentively to herself. Wherever she was seen she was greeted with jubilation. The victory was hers.

Mayor Adolphe Lacadé brooded dully over a weighty letter that he had opened but a few moments before. The hour has come, he had thought. The great Filhol had sent in his analysis. In the sight of all France and of the world the most effective of all curative springs could now be presented to suffering humanity by the incorruptible hand of science. Not for a moment had he entertained any doubt of this radiant result when with solemn hands he had broken the seal of the letter. But a cursory glance had sufficed to make him collapse.

Oh, they were all present, these fine carbonates, chlorates, silicates, calcium, iron, magnesium, and phosphorus listed by the good Latour. As was due his fame as a hydrologist and balneologist, the thorough Filhol had added several impressive items to the list, although of these substances only mere traces could be observed, namely, ammonia and potash. And what a fine sound that had—potash, a very cleansing substance for the sinful entrails of the gluttonous. But of what avail were all these noble technical terms of healing in view of the perfectly devastating final conclusion? For below his neat tabulation of the chemical analysis Professor Filhol had written in red ink the following crushing sentences: "From the above analysis it is evident that the specimen of water presented from the spring of Lourdes may be designated ORDINARY DRINKING WATER, the composition of which corresponds exactly to that of the

spring-waters of mountain ranges of a strongly calcareous character. It does not contain a trace of any active substance of
therapeutic value. It may therefore be freely partaken of without either advantage or harm."

"Without either advantage or harm," Lacadé murmured bitterly to himself. He then discovered in the envelope a brief note
addressed to him personally: "The extraordinary effects which
have been allegedly ascribed to the use of this water cannot be
explained, at least from any scientific point of view admissible
today, by any of the various salts soluble therein and tabulated
in the above analysis."

The monstrousness of that sentence as such enraged the
mayor. Well, if the salts can't account for the cures today,
they will tomorrow. What two-faced malice! The professor
excluded the miracles by the front door, but with a wink kept
the back door open for science's get-away. Two-faced. Exactly. The last thing to be expected of him. A stab in the back
of progress and good business. What was the man's purpose?

For even as the prosecutor always asked *Cui bono?*—To
whose advantage?—so Lacadé always asked *Ad quem finem?*—
To what end or purpose? He did not ask it in Latin, to be
sure. But he knew himself too well not to assume that every
human action was calculated with an eye to profit. He had
probably underestimated Filhol. These scientists were no fools
any longer. A man of Filhol's repute knew very well that his
analysis was worth so much cold cash. Yet he was in no position to send a bill. His dicta created watering-places out of
nothing and could cause them to wither again. Why should he
enable the city of Lourdes to establish a gigantic business for
sweet charity's sake? Lacadé struck his forehead with his fist.
Idiot that he was! Too stupid and too stingy to have gone to
Toulouse and let the professor cost him a few thousand. He
had trusted the empty chatter which had seemed so strongly

to suggest that a marvellous analysis would arrive from Toulouse. And he had yielded to the impulsive folly of having Latour's analysis printed in *Le Lavedan*. Day before yesterday, goddamn him for a fool, he had been vain and incautious enough to brag before the city council of his committee for founding a balnearic establishment, despite the dagger eyes of that rogue Labayle upon him. He was past sixty and still so rash merely because of this mad, unconquerable greed. What next? There was no retracing of steps. Filhol's analysis could not be hushed up. It could not be burned; it had to be published. In all likelihood the professor had himself already published it in the *Dépêche de Toulouse*. This particular brew had to be drunk to the dregs. And always these headaches, these goddamned headaches. . . .

Lacadé pressed his hands against his temples. But his old, old headache which came from his bad digestion, grew worse and worse. He kept groaning and puttering around in his office for a long time. Suddenly he stopped and gazed into a corner. Suppose this clever Filhol was even smarter than he had dreamed of giving him credit for being? Suppose he were a hundred times cleverer than himself and was actually on the only right track? At that reflection Lacadé's headache passed all common bounds. His imagination teemed with immature but fascinating notions. He rang for his secretary Courrèges and gave the secret order that a bottle of the water of Massabielle be fetched at once. In half an hour it was on his table. He poured the clear water into a crystal jug. It sparkled in the old gold of the afternoon sunshine, this strange liquid which under its aspect of common drinking water had no therapeutic properties and had yet brought about cure after cure. Bouriette did see with the eye that had been blind and the crippled Bouhouhorts child was running about. For many minutes Lacadé contemplated the lights that played in the crystal jug; they threw a quivering

tracery as of rainbows upon the wall. Nothing to be done, he
reflected, in the present state of science. That did not mean
that his purpose could not be achieved. There was no retreat,
to be sure. What was needed was an offensive action in another direction. Visitors were visitors and money money,
whether the visitors spent their money on carbonates and phos-
phates or on miraculous healing. Was that not the whistle of a
locomotive that he heard?

He went to the door and locked it very carefully so that his
secretaries might not hear the turning of the key. He also
pulled down the heavy hangings of the windows, as though he
were ashamed before God Himself of the experiment he was
about to try. The room now lay in purplish dusk and the pris-
matic gleaming in the jug was extinguished. Lacadé tested the
intensity of his headache. Wretched enough, he found. He
filled a glass with the miraculous water, retired to a corner of
the room, knelt with a groan, and began to say a few Aves.
Since his knees, having to sustain so heavy a burden, ached
mightily and soon, he emptied the glass at one draught after
the tenth Ave. After this exertion he lay down quite exhausted
on his sofa in order to await the effect. From time to time he
asked himself: Was the ache in his head diminishing or not?
Very confusing. He could not really tell. Perhaps another trial
was indicated. He knelt and prayed and drank once more. At
the third attempt he was almost sure that his headache was beginning to improve. And now Adolphe Lacadé, mayor of
Lourdes, began to laugh at the old Jacobin and freethinker
Lacadé and began to speculate on the lengths to which the
most enlightened of mortals was capable of going when he was
all by himself. And the headache was really gone.

That simply goes to prove, Lacadé reflected, that he who
suffers pain has faith. But since many people suffer from pain
worse than a mere headache, many are bound to have faith.

Therefore those who have faith and whom pain has robbed of all else but this faith—they will come.

Probably not a public of the first class, this kind of public, the mayor could not help thinking before he fell asleep.

This was certainly the worst year in the entire career of the imperial prosecutor Vital Dutour. It had begun with the stubborn cold in February. A wretched head cold and a red and swollen nose had certainly not been calculated to sustain the self-esteem of a very proud and imperious man. Next had come the curious examination of Bernadette Soubirous ending in the first defeat. A sound jurist must, of course, draw a sharp line between the professional and the personal. How could one live at all if the fate of the accused, if doubt in the equity of any given decision were to leave traces graven on the soul? Members of the judiciary must early acquire the art of throwing off the lamentable burdens which their profession imposes on them the moment they leave court. In this respect they are in quite the position of physicians who equally cannot burst into tears at every death-bed. Thus Vital Dutour had acquired the habit of automatically forgetting the conferences and examinations that had just taken place at the very door of his courtroom or his chambers. Yet he could not forget that examination of Bernadette Soubirous. It kept burrowing deep within him on this very day, six months later. It seemed to him as though he had been examined instead of examining another and as though the tranquil, inviolable, unreachable soul of the girl had demanded of him that he change his way of life. To the shame of the imperial prosecutor's office it had to be admitted that a deep moral dismay had afflicted Vital Dutour for many weeks. And it was this dismay and no philosophical considerations that served to explain the bitterness, the actual hatred of Bernadette Soubirous, the lady, the grotto, the spring, the whole miracle business by which his nerves were tortured in his very sleep. He had argued out the matter to the point of enmity with his table companions at the Café Français, with Estrade, Dozous, Clarens, and several others who were either wavering or had, like the revenue men, frankly joined the camp of the mystics. On the other hand, Vital Dutour could not take pride in the community of opinion which united him to the banal Duran and others of the same kidney. Now, a bachelor whom the inscrutable providence of the French administration of justice had condemned to live in an overgrown village was bound to seek in his eating-house and his café substitutes for home, family, the theatre, and all forms of civilized entertainments. And Dutour had abandoned the pleasant group composed of the few really keen minds of the town. He was now confined to the dreary Jacomet and several equally dreary lawyers and military men.

After that unpardonably crude incident of the *agent provocateur*, of which he was ashamed to the gnashing of his teeth and which, though in a modified form, had found its way into the press, his superiors in Pau had administered a stinging rebuke to him. After the tumult at the grotto during which Belhache had been wounded Dutour had been personally summoned to Pau. His immediate senior officer, Falconnet, an elderly gentleman, had received him, wringing his hands. "The Emperor complains bitterly of our department," Falconnet had almost whined. "I've received a dreadful letter from the ministry. There's got to be a change. I'm not near the spring. You are. Do something, man!"

"Do something . . . do something . . ." the horses' hoofs had said on the drive back to Lourdes.

But what was he to do? Easy enough for Falconnet to lay down the law. Well, he had once more called in all members of the gendarmerie and of the police force and had given them emphatic orders to listen carefully to the talk of the people who were always gathered about the grotto. They were to arrest without pity anyone guilty of remarks disrespectful of the government, not to mention such as indulged in treasonable words.

The very next day little Callet had triumphantly brought a prisoner to the office of the prosecutor. Jacomet had happened to be there. The prisoner was a certain Cyprine Gesta, a lady belonging to a prominent family of Lourdes and a friend of Madame Millet and that whole group. The good, plain policeman Callet had a grudge against people in good society in general and Madame Gesta in particular.

"She declared," he squeaked hoarsely, "that the scandal wouldn't end till the Emperor and the Empress had personally visited the grotto."

"Is that correct, Madame?" Dutour inquired.

"Entirely so, Monsieur." Cyprine Gesta, a plump lady in her thirties, had the most tranquil expression imaginable. This tranquillity on the part of one arrested by his orders irritated the prosecutor.

"Is it really your opinion that Their Majesties will visit a place barred by the orders of their own government?"

"It is my firm conviction, Monsieur, that Their Majesties hold this silly government in contempt and will undertake an early pilgrimage to the grotto of Massabielle."

The hardened prosecutor unluckily lost his head at this mockery. As though possessed by an evil genius he sprang from his seat and cried: "That is *lèse-majesté!* I formally charge you with criminal disrespect toward Their Majesties."

"You go ahead and do that," Madame Gesta said with finished irony. "But may I be permitted to ask wherein my insult to Their Majesties consists?"

"In that you identify the mental characteristics of Their Majesties with your own."

When a reasonable man loses his reason he is apt to lose

every shred. A once well-disciplined temperament takes revenge upon that discipline by amazing outbreaks. Vital Dutour, bitter as gall, really had this laughable charge brought against Cyprine Gesta. The case was tried almost immediately before Justice of the Peace Duprat. Amid the roars of laughter, half of gaiety, half of irony, of the packed courtroom, Duprat, a friend of the prosecutor, was obliged to acquit the accused Cyprine Gesta of the misdemeanour of *lèse-majesté* and had to turn and twist to manage to impose even the quite customary fine of five francs.

But by now Dutour's rage had turned into a kind of maniacal obsession. It knew no bounds. What had failed in Lourdes might not fail in Pau under the eye of Falconnet. Hence Dutour appealed from this sentence of acquittal and took the case to the next higher tribunal in Pau. On the day of the trial Cazenave had had to run an extra coach, since a great crowd of laughing and jesting ladies clad in light summery frocks insisted on accompanying the accused criminal. The whole tone was that of a celebration. Not only did the tribunal at Pau sustain the sentence of the lower court but even revoked the imposition of the five-franc fine. The chief prosecutor Falconnet was heard to remark in front of witnesses: "Poor Dutour needs psychiatric treatment ten times more than that Bernadette Soubirous."

A broken man, the imperial prosecutor slunk about in his offices. The wound which, God knows why, he had inflicted on himself seemed incurable. The press, and not only that of the clericals by any means, made him the object of its ridicule. His career, he had every reason to suppose, was at an end. He was sentenced for time and eternity to the filthiest of provincial back-waters. No doubt of that. He could not see his image in a mirror without a grimace of complete disgust.

Callet, however, the "sorcerer's apprentice," was not to

be restrained. In less than a week he turned up with another victim. This time it was a pompous lady in an enormous bell-shaped crinoline. Brown silk. Violet sunshade. Blond hair arranged in a tall coiffure on which swayed a flower-trimmed little hat. With an emphatic bang Callet placed the *corpus delicti*, a large bottle, on Dutour's desk. "The lady took water from the spring," the little policeman began his accusation. "She wouldn't give up the bottle. Then she began to pick flowers and grass on the rim and refused to move on."

"What is your name, Madame?" Dutour asked in a bored voice.

"I am Madame Bruat," said the lady with that tinge of deprecation used by those who would rather not make display of an eminent name or station.

"Madame Bruat?" the prosecutor looked up. "Bruat? Are you by any chance connected with Admiral Bruat, former Minister of Marine?"

"He is my husband," the lady answered.

Rather put out of countenance, Dutour rose and pushed a chair toward the lady. "Perhaps you will do me the favour to be seated, Madame?"

The lady refused. "This gentleman arrested me and led me through the town. I don't wish to be treated differently from other accused persons here, either. May I inquire after the nature of my crime?"

The bald-headed man did not have to feign exhaustion. He got rid of the terrible Callet with a glance and spoke softly.

"Madame, you are the bearer of a great name. Your husband, as I well know, is very close to the Emperor. We, however, the servants of the government in this town, have been for many months engaged in a struggle against one of the maddest oddities of the century. We are carrying on this struggle at the behest of the imperial government and with the full knowledge and consent of His Majesty. Certain elements, though politically not at one among themselves, have taken advantage of the hallucinations of a feeble-minded female and of rumours of alleged cures to forge a weapon against the imperial regime and the Emperor himself, calculated to strike at the weakest point of that regime. I am speaking of the laws of public emergency upon which the present government founds its powers. Once an authority thus constituted is flouted in any respect, it begins to totter. In order to protect the absolute authority of the regime from dangerous infractions we have barred the grotto of Massabielle to the public. And now come ladies like yourself, Madame, who belong to the highest circles of imperial France and you show the masses of the people that you yourselves despise this highest authority by putting yourself in opposition to it. What is there left for a civil servant to do, Madame?"

Madame Bruat smiled. "You could always accuse me of *lèse-majesté*, you know."

Dutour endured this poisonous thrust without lifting a lid. After an interval he said: "I am forced to require you to pay the prescribed fine of five francs. The competent police officer will receive it."

"Delighted, Monsieur. And I'll add a hundred francs for the poor of Lourdes. Now, please, let me have my bottle."

"The bottle is confiscated and remains confiscated," said the prosecutor.

The lady smiled a little. "I don't believe it will remain so, Monsieur, for I filled it at the desire of a very high personage."

Dutour was firmly determined not to yield on this point. Spasmodically he grasped the bottle. "May I ask who this personage is, Madame?"

"Her Majesty the Empress Eugénie," Madame Bruat replied.

"I have the honour to be the governess of the little crown prince."

Yellow of face, Dutour thrust the bottle toward her. "Take it, Madame!" And without offering an apology he added: "I begin to see the folly of being the only one to do one's duty in a feeble-minded world."

CHAPTER THIRTY-FIVE

The Lady Overcomes the Emperor

THE WINDOWS of the Emperor looked out on the Atlantic. The thunder of the surf could be heard in the rooms, for the summer villa at Biarritz had been built high on the cliffs. Despite the mild September night the windows were not open. Cigarette fumes were dense in the room and gathered in clouds about the chandeliers and the pretentious petroleum lamps on the two desks. The Emperor immensely valued this solitary hour right after midnight. Like so many devotees of tobacco he found it hard to fall asleep until late, and his mental clearness and productivity heightened after midnight. This was an hour of dreamy planning for the most powerful monarch of his contemporary world. He was fifty. The face, whose cheeks usually gleamed oddly as though polished, was yellowish now and relaxed and furrowed. The long moustachios waxed to stand out straight all day long now drooped as they would. The black-dyed hair, usually combed over the forehead from left to right, was in disorder. The monarch wore a pleasant silken dressing-gown and soft bedroom slippers. To plan prophetically the future of a continent in this state of contemplation and bodily ease evoked in him the conscious thrill of power.

Napoléon III walked up and down between the two desks as though invisible demonic secretaries sat at them to whom by night he was dictating the battle orders of the century. On the larger of the desks lay a map of Northern Italy dotted with mysterious marks in red and blue and green ink. This map had been appended to the sealed fivefold campaign plan of the General Staff which the Minister of War had brought to Biarritz in person yesterday. The world had no suspicion of the ripeness of the Italian plan. Even Count Cavour, the great man of Savoy, was still being hammered into pliancy on the anvil of uncertainty. The papers, however, wrote about the Emperor's modernity of outlook and his passion for nature which impelled him to take a long daily dip in the sea.

On the smaller desk, under mountains of official acts and petitions, there also lay maps of Algeria, Equatorial Africa, and Central America. The Emperor's dreams were polyphonic. His uncle Bonaparte had dealt with a smallish world. His vision had always been bounded by Europe and the Mediterranean; he had not even conquered the narrow Channel to punish Britain. In spite of the cult devoted to the founder of the dynasty, the third Napoléon felt superior to the first. His achievement consisted not in battles which were lost even while being won. It consisted in the network of railways that in seven brief years had been made to cover the whole of France. He did not aim at conquests to boast of. He desired the harmonious organization of a world, civilized by the French spirit, that should extend as far as the Congo, Eastern Asia, perhaps as far as Mexico itself.

The Emperor kept poring over the General Staff's map of Northern Italy. The war with Austria was unavoidable. Cavour, quick-minded as lightning though he was, was convinced that he was pulling the strings of all marionettes and did not dream that he himself was but a puppet in the hands of a greater than he. Cavour's plan was a united Italy under the house of Savoy. That was not at all to the Emperor's mind. He would not dream of placing a Vittorio Emmanuele at the head of another great power. Once upon a time in his adventurous youth he had, to be sure, solemnly sworn to the Carbonari and the Giovane Italia that he would lead to victory the movement of an arising and united Italy. But these had been the republican fancies of a youthful and indigent tourist who had then been the mere hopeless pretender to a throne. Louis Napoléon had certainly never vowed to raise the house of Savoy beyond its merits and thus set a bad example to the house of Hohenzollern. His plan was far more original as well as more expedient. Italy was to be united, not under a single monarch but under four, who could, if need were, be played off against one another. There would be formed a tight alliance of states and dynasties with very limited freedom of movement. The presidency of this federation he, Napoléon, intended to assign to none other than the Sovereign Pontiff and ruler of the Papal States. Thus could the circle of Italian politics be squared. It would be, moreover, an immense benefit conferred on the clerical parties of all nations and yet would tend to function as a control over all Catholic factions everywhere. The liberals would rage, of course; the Emperor was fully aware of that. They would cry murder and treason. The clericals and the liberals were the two poles of the balance on the scale of the imperial rule. His whole art consisted in holding this balance level. The gigantic gift intended for Rome proceeded from no religious feeling on the Emperor's part. He himself was intellectually and emotionally a liberal, like everybody else. But the pre-eminence of a French world empire demanded that neither Italians nor Germans be permitted to attain a unitary national state. That could not of course be mentioned without enraging all the sentimentalists and foolish shouters of all Europe, including France itself. Everything had, on the contrary, to be done to keep the liberals from the right scent lest they grieve in disillusion over that master-stroke. Was it mere accident that, despite a rigorous censorship, the radical sheets became more openly rebellious day by day?

Consequently this affair of Lourdes was not the mere bagatelle which all those incapable fellows, Fould, Roulland, De-langle, were trying to make it out to be. Clearly not, else why had they got nowhere at all in eight full months in this business of miracles? The Emperor felt as though a sixth sense of his were functioning. Unbelievable how during those eight months this depressing town of Lourdes had been the very showpiece of the international press. From all sides pressure was being brought to bear on the Emperor for a decision. His well-tested art of seeing nothing and hearing nothing, of feigning, so to speak, a tactical death, was daily being tried to the utmost. Only yesterday Monsieur de Ressegnier, a former deputy from the Hautes-Pyrénées, had called and today even Monseigneur Salinis, archbishop of Auch, had paid a visit in which he had passionately protested against the interference of the civil authorities in Lourdes. Strange enough was this visit of the prince of the Church in view of the cautious silence and watchful attitude of the French episcopate. The Emperor had given both the deputy and the prelate evasive answers. Ressegnier must have left a petition behind him. Where can it be? Where did I put it? If only these damned lackeys and secretaries weren't so intent on putting my desks in order. There's more order in my disorder than in a well-kept depository of archives. At last the Emperor found Ressegnier's petition. He read it but superficially.

"Your Majesty is requested graciously to leave out of consideration the question of the visions, although hundreds and even thousands of witnesses are of the opinion that a revelation of higher powers did in fact take place. What is a fact, however, and one now irrefutably demonstrated is this, that the water of the spring originating in so wondrous a fashion and now barred by the police could not possibly work harm to any. The analysis made by Professor Filhol of Toulouse leaves no possible doubt in respect of this fact. A further fact, and one proven to the very hilt, is this, that a not inconsiderable number of the afflicted have regained their health after drinking the water of the spring. In the name of freedom of conscience, therefore, grant access, Sire, to the spring of Massabielle. Grant healing to the sick in the name of humanity and grant opportunity for scientific investigation in the name of freedom of research."

The Emperor could not help laughing aloud as he flung the petition into the waste-basket. Aha, gentlemen of the reactionary parties suddenly take the side of freedom of conscience, humanity, and untrammelled research, exactly as gentlemen of the progressive parties are much concerned over Heaven when it happens to fit in with some little scheme of theirs! How hollow and unveracious are the things of this world. What each desires is to hunt down for himself and his party the bit of might which a full belly and a little superiority give him a chance to pursue. Science and Heaven are to each but the purposeful extension of this fragment of power into the realm of the abstract. The gentleman of the clerical party, Monsieur de Ressegnier, cares no more about the spring, the Virgin, or the health of his fellow-men than about some handful of dust by the roadside. He wants success, that is all. He wants to be revenged on his opponents, having been beaten by a liberal in the last elections. . . . A high thing to be Emperor and have no need to go lying or whoring after power, since one has it. In some ways the Emperor is better off than God Himself, for here on earth *le bon Dieu* leans on the clericals, but my prop consists of opposites, of clericals and liberals. Well, gentlemen of the clerical parties, a succulent mouthful is in store for you. Hence I will shower my undisguised favour on the liberals during the months to come.

The Emperor looked at the clock. Half-past twelve. He had been restless all this time. He had wanted to ask how Loulou was feeling before retiring. For Loulou, his only son, had not been too well the past two days. Nothing special—slight temperature. But with a two-year-old child dangerous surprises are always possible. Louis Napoléon had not spent his youth in palaces but in quite middle-class dwellings. His nerves were well tested. He was frightened but not so excessively as Eugénie. Yet upon Loulou's health depended the future of the imperial house of Corsica.

He rang and asked for his coat and shoes. He was not young enough or sure enough of himself to appear too familiarly before Eugénie Montijo. Since her origin was not high, she was insistent on formalities. Louis Napoléon was informed that the doctor had been awakened half an hour ago. Disquieted, he entered the nursery. He found his wife with streaming tears at the baby's bedside. Loulou seemed unconcerned, though his cheeks and eyes gleamed too brightly. Only when Madame Bruat or the nurse changed the compress on his forehead did he whine a little. The physician smiled reassuringly at the Emperor. "Nothing of consequence, Sire. A light fever, as we know. . . ."

"It's diphtheria; it's croup at least," Eugénie groaned.

"There's not the slightest reason to assume that, Madame," the physician contradicted her. "The prince's throat is very slightly inflamed, but that's all. We've gone through the same thing often before."

"Is there any danger of a children's disease, such as scarlet fever or measles?" the Emperor asked.

"That's always a possibility to be reckoned with, Sire. At present, however, there is no room for anxiety at all. May I suggest that Her Majesty go quietly to bed?"

"I just know it's croup," Eugénie said in a toneless voice.

Very pale, the Emperor approached her. "You should really go to bed, dearest," he said tenderly and placed his hand on the child's chest. "Loulou is going to be brave and let Mamma go to bed, aren't you, Loulou?"

Loulou did not agree with this at all. He sobbed now: "No, Mamma mustn't go to bed; Mamma must stay with me!"

Eugénie looked up at the Emperor with impassioned, tear-stained eyes.

"Oh, Louis, there's one wish you must grant me!" she cried. "Bruat has brought a bottleful of the spring-water of Lourdes. We'll give Loulou a glass of it."

"Is that necessary, my dear?" the Emperor asked, somewhat rasped.

"It is necessary, Louis. This water has cured many people. A two-year-old child just like Loulou was cured and on the instant."

"But that's an unverified rumour, my dear."

"Anyone who has even a trace of faith knows it to be true, Louis."

The Emperor found it hard to conceal his unhappy perplexity. "Other people can afford to make themselves ridiculous, my child. *We* shouldn't; *we* mustn't. . . ."

"I don't mind making myself ridiculous to save my child's life, Louis."

The old doctor gave the Emperor a meaningful glance. "The water is quite harmless. If Madame is so set upon it, there's nothing against letting the prince drink of it."

Before this proposal of a skilled physician the Emperor had to retreat. "All I ask," he said slowly, "is that the fact doesn't become public knowledge."

But Eugénie flared up at that. "How ignoble that would be! What vulgar ingratitude that would show, Louis! How is the spring to help if one denies it in advance? On the contrary, I swear here and now in the presence of God and man that if

my child be saved I shall publicly acknowledge my faith in the
spring and in the Blessed Virgin of Lourdes."

Madame Bruat arrived with the glass. Shrugging his shoulders, the Emperor left the room.

On the morning after the next, the Empress made her ap-
pearance in the Emperor's bedroom in order to announce that
Loulou's temperature had returned to normal. "The spring of
Massabielle did help him, Louis."

"That's a very frivolous observation, darling. Loulou has had
a number of attacks like this and has always got well quickly,
by God's help. You're doing a great injustice to the doctor's
prescriptions."

"You're an atheist, Louis."

The Emperor smiled. "That's about the most stupid thing a
sovereign could be."

"Then you're worse than an atheist, Louis. You haven't the
humility to thank God for the grace He has accorded us. And
yet all day yesterday you shook with terror that it might be
scarlet fever or croup. . . ."

The Emperor, who, in the five years of their marriage, had
not received five such early visits from his wife, was exceedingly embarrassed. He had been caught with his hair-net and his
moustache-tie on. "You do me wrong, my dear," he said wearily. "I know that we owe Loulou's life wholly to God's grace.
But that's no reason at all for abandoning all sense and reason
and believing that a glass of ordinary water brought from the
Pyrenees has saved Loulou from scarlet fever."

Eugénie Montijo's classic countenance grew hard and sharp.
"You deny the slightest possibility of its having been the water
of Massabielle which reduced Loulou's temperature to normal
within twenty-four hours!"

"That again is unjust." The Emperor half closed his eyes

with an expression of suffering. "In addition to the many natural explanations I don't regard a supernatural one as wholly impossible. But I have no ground for assuming miraculous interference so long as the explanations offered by nature and medical science are amply sufficient. Let's leave that sort of thing among old wives' tales, where it belongs. Our child is well. That God helped, I know. That science and nature helped, I also know. That Lourdes helped is conceivable, but I do *not* know it."

"But I know it, Louis." The Empress was militant. "No one shall prevent me from showing my gratitude, not even you!"

"Why should I prevent you, my dear?" the Emperor asked conciliatorily.

"Then I may take it, Louis," she broke in upon him, "that you are ready to grant my wish? I vowed for us both that if the water of Lourdes helps our child, you will command the grotto to be opened to the public. . . ."

Now Louis Napoléon found it hard to restrain his irritation. "One vows vows for oneself, not for others, my dear. Lourdes, moreover, has come to be a delicate political fact. Very weighty reasons demand that I do not offend the liberal parties at this moment. . . ."

"My motives as wife and mother are much weightier than any political tactics of a given day." Eugénie turned pale and the stubbornness, ambition, and rude power of her countenance displeased her husband intensely.

After an interval he spoke and his voice was hoarse. "From the beginning my government has taken a negative attitude to this business. And not only my government, but also the French episcopate. And not even you will accuse the bishops of open atheism. We are all dependent on public opinion, and the public opinion of our time is definitely hostile to the stuffy mysticism of an undeveloped peasantry. And this is so because we are engaged in fighting for a new spirit, a spirit which works in my favour. If I seek to halt the advance of that spirit, it will destroy me. Note well: if I open that grotto I make my own government ridiculous and also myself. Is that what you want me to do? You want me, in a word, in opposition to all political good sense, violently to affront the spirit of the times and, without any need, publicly to retract a well-considered policy."

Eugénie went close up to her husband and took both his hands. Her voice was deep and dark: "Louis, an emperor is dependent on far greater powers than that of public opinion. You are very sensible of that. Else why would you consult Madame Frossart, the fortune-teller and *clairvoyante*? In your position you can't draw an indifferent breath nor seek refuge in opportunism. Your very dreams make history. A sovereign, I have heard you say, can't outwit Heaven. And yet you would do so on this occasion? Now, at the outset of the greatest year of your reign. Consider! In France there flows a spring of grace that has accomplished cure after cure. Your own son being in danger, you gave him of the water of the spring. . . ."

"Let's stick to the truth, Madame," Napoléon said and his teeth grated, "it was not I, by God. . . ."

"No matter," Eugénie Montijo, the Spaniard, said: "Loulou is well. That power which by means of an innocent and highly graced maiden brought forth within an hour that potent spring, that power has shown you its grace. And you would venture to withhold its meed from this power? Do you really think it safer to affront God and the Blessed Virgin than this so-called spirit of the times? And you would do that after you had vowed a vow of gratitude? . . ."

"You vowed, not I," the Emperor insisted, though without hope.

"No matter! The vow is vowed. It must be kept. Less for me than for you. For your empire is at stake, Louis. . . ."

The Emperor conducted Eugénie back to her chambers without uttering another word.

The day was a most uncomfortable one for him. This beautiful woman had an irresistible power to upset him. She would grow cold and colder and finally so icy that flight to Paris would seem desirable. Moreover, on such occasions she had a chance to make implications of which his conscience was far from guiltless. Bathing was not enjoyable. Work was stagnant. The happy midnight hour of creative solitude was spoiled. Worst of all was the sting which the woman's words had left in the man's heart. She was right. She dared not break her vow. Nor dared he, though he had not vowed it. Whatever power it was that stood behind the visions and the cures of Lourdes, it might be the same power that stood behind the scenes of history and therefore, too, behind his Italian undertaking.

It was easy for insignificant nobodies to be freethinkers. What did they risk? Could the greatest of earth's monarchs, however, venture, merely in order to conciliate the freethinkers, to challenge that vastly more susceptible power which determines the victory or decline of nations? Even these cold considerations seemed dangerous to the Emperor. He walked up and down between his desks. Who knows whether that power which demands a boundless submission was unaware of these subtle calculations? A man who scribbles legal papers or sells merchandise has no trouble being witty at the expense of what he calls superstition. He who rules the world knows as a matter of daily experience that all things hold a transcendent element of the unknown, that the concatenation of events depends not on him, that he is the play-ball of mysterious forces and counter-forces which demand adoration and propitiation and must be ever either lured or conciliated. Whether or not the bullet of an assassin reaches its mark is determined not by the science of ballistics but by those same inscrutable powers, be they a triune God or the will of the constellations. None but a ruler knows how wholly outside of the common laws of nature he stands. His sphere is the miraculous. Hence from of old the faith of princes and men of might has partaken of the nature of superstition. . . .

On the third night of his silent battle with the woman the man admitted defeat. Nothing remained but to find a form in which to clothe his capitulation. After long inner arguments the Emperor decided on a very unconventional step. He would avoid regular bureaucratic channels. He was ashamed before his ministers and determined simply to avoid them. Fould, Roulland, Delangle were all left in ignorance. The Emperor scribbled a telegram to the prefect of Tarbes:

"Access to the grotto west of Lourdes is to be immediately granted to the public. Napoléon."

That was all. The telegram was sent. With a copy in his hand the Emperor sought out the Empress. She blushed with joy. "I always knew, Louis, that you have a great heart and one that can conquer even itself. . . ."

"The fact is, Madame," he replied icily to her declamatory outburst, "that the lady of Lourdes found a most effective ally in yourself."

CHAPTER THIRTY-SIX

Bernadette among the Sages

Baron Massy held in his hand the Emperor's telegram. During the first minutes of dismay an uprush of pride had almost persuaded him to send in his resignation without delay. Quickly enough cold self-control returned and he proceeded to analyse the situation with his accustomed acuteness.

Take first the telegram itself. Its form was as curt and dry as that of a military order. This was contrary to Louis Napoléon's way. He was wont to clothe his directions to the civil servants in courteous phrases and even to give his reasons. This brevity spoke of moral discomfort. If the telegram was genuine, it had doubtless been wrung from the Emperor against his will. A conspiracy, in all likelihood, between Eugénie, some bigoted ladies of the court, and so and so many cassocks who seemed from day to day more aware of the propagandistic value of the "apparitions of Lourdes." The only one not to be moved was the bishop whose business it was. The rest of the clergy had recently become as fluid as a river in thaw. A miracle supported by proven but inexplicable cures meant so enormous a breach in the official deism and non-official nihilism of the age as to shake to their foundations both the certainty of unbelief and the uncertainty of faith. No more living proof of that than the Emperor's telegram. The only remaining question was: was the telegram authentic? The baron decided that, lacking confirmation, the telegram was neither authentic nor the reverse. A telegram emanating from the court but without certified signature could have been dispatched by any lackey. To guard the Emperor himself from the results of a possible mystification it was necessary to await the confirmation of an autograph signature. His Majesty's action, moreover, was so contrary to all official use and wont that delay would be wholly justified.

The prefect, to whom the prevailing of his opinion in the affair of Lourdes had become an obsession, had the courage to leave the telegraphic order unanswered for a week and to do nothing about it. At the end of a week he sent it off to Roulland with a request for precise directions. The Minister of Worship and his colleagues flew into rages over Napoléon's cowardice and treachery. Napoléon the Little, by God! First through his vacillation and his attempt to curry favour with the Freemasons he had egged them on into this affair which, lacking their opposition, might have died a natural death; now that he had himself given it exaggerated prominence he stabbed them all in the back. A curse upon this ill-starred Spanish woman who ruled him! If the excellent Massy had not acted so bravely and so cautiously at once the entire ministry would have been made to look so foolish and absurd as to have been forced to resign. Censorship of the press was at once made even more stringent and a letter of appreciation from the council of ministers sent to the prefect of the Hautes-Pyrénées.

Not bad, Massy reflected. To gain time is always something. So that he could not be reached at his Tarbes office he went on a tour of inspection, during which he spent some days in Lourdes. He conferred with Lacadé and told him that he intended taking his vacation in October. Since the mayor had originally taken action looking toward the closing of the grotto, the baron would be very much pleased should certain things eventuate during the following weeks, if in the prefect's absence Lacadé, in his capacity of mayor, would himself take whatever steps were necessary to reopen the grotto. Lacadé refused in fright. In view of all developments, such measures went far beyond his authority. The matter of Lourdes had come to be one of high and national import. He himself was only the humble chief of a community. Moreover, since he had received the luminous analysis by Professor Filhol his own opinion concerning the water and the grotto had undergone a complete change. The government whose approval had closed the grotto would have to give its approval to the reopening as well. Baron Massy was suddenly interested in his pointed patent-leather shoes, tugged at his cuffs, and left the mayor's office without a word. He's finished, thought Lacadé, who had a sharp scent for political corpses.

The prefect summoned Dutour and Jacomet separately to his room in Cazenave's hotel. He had a most unpleasant way of finding fault and insultingly made them responsible for the present lamentable state of affairs. He knew all the time, of course, that the two men, far from being guilty, had fought the nuisance far more energetically and persistently than himself, who had wanted to stay in the background to the very last minute. In this damnable business every step had retrospectively been proven a false one. And so Massy, daily more scared of his own rashness and desiring nothing now but to avoid a resounding personal defeat, adopted new tactics—those of retreat. The prosecutor and the commissioner were instructed to deal lightly with those contravening the order not to drink of the spring and to impose no more fines. The scaffolding and placards were to remain. The State never retracts. But the gendarmerie was to be withdrawn and supervision left to the local police. Thus, the baron thought, the government would give the impression of having attained its ends. He hoped that the pilgrims and the curious would gradually occupy the forbidden left bank and unobtrusively repossess the grotto. Formally the regulations would remain in force; practically they would fade into forgetfulness like a lost sentry. Thus his chief purpose would be achieved—not to have to append his name to his own disgrace.

A good idea and worthy of the Massy type. Unluckily the enemy refused to co-operate in the idea's execution. The enemy was the crowd in front of Massabielle. When it no longer saw the visages of the gendarmes and observed that Callet no longer brandished his notebook when he caught people drinking, the impression prevailed that a trap was being laid. Antoine Nicolau, the grotto's loyal neighbour, issued the watchword: "Stay on the right bank!"

He was obeyed. Never since the closing of the grotto had the regulations been so strictly observed as now, when tacit infraction would have been a perfect solution for the prefect. The scaffolding, the rope, the placards stood forth in the translucent air of early autumn like instruments of torture of an unknown passion. And many a one who cared no whit for the lady or the spring yet muttered angrily: "Disgusting to bar this grotto like the scene of a murder and to treat free men like criminals!"

Once as the prefect and the commissioner were crossing the Place Marcadale, Jacomet beckoned to a young girl in a white *capulet*. "This is Bernadette Soubirous, Your Excellency."

"Aha, yes, yes." The baron was inarticulate but his heart began to palpitate. He was ashamed of the excitement he could not understand. He lost all adroitness and found no words. Bernadette looked at him as she looked at all those in power, with big, attentive, guarded eyes. Finally in his embarrassment he gave the girl his hand, lifted his hat, and turned to go. A little farther on he said to Jacomet: "You didn't describe the girl correctly. She's not at all coarse or common."

Jacomet defended himself. "Your Excellency should have known her when I first did. She's changed so you wouldn't know her since the visions."

"Magnificent eyes the girl has," replied the baron, deeply lost in thought.

During the prefect's last day in Lourdes the ministers Fould and Roulland had proceeded to Biarritz. There ensued a very painful scene between the Emperor and his chosen advisers. The Emperor had been caught in the act of yielding to one of his weaknesses. And the strongest man is not strong enough to forgive those who tear the mask from his feebleness or faults. Louis Napoléon had reckoned with the prefect's immediate execution of his order, so that the government, faced by an accomplished fact, would have no chance to indulge in argument. Now this insolent creature had dared not only to disregard his order, but to turn it over to the government like the unsatisfactory homework of a stupid schoolboy. The Emperor's face was quince-yellow and the long ends of his moustache vibrated. To crown it all these idiots now repeated his own rigmarole about the liberals and Masons who ought just now to have been conciliated. Was he to cry out to them: A monarch has every right to be superstitious. A monarch knows day and night that he is in the grip of dark forces which determine the causes of things. Your pedestrian minds are unaware of the universe.

What he actually said was: "I am holding you responsible, gentlemen, for the contempt with which one has been pleased to treat my decisions as non-existent."

Luckily the ministers were cowards and the Emperor, especially in this matter, not quite a hero. Hence at the end of the scene all agreed on who should be the common scapegoat. Baron Massy, of course. The next day Massy was in receipt of a rebuke from the government which was as unexpected as it was terrifying. His Majesty's command was to be obeyed on the instant. The baron's mouth went dry. He knew he was ruined. He wired to Lacadé and Jacomet. That was October 7. On the eighth almost at dawn Callet went drumming through the streets of Lourdes and in his self-conscious sing-song cried out to all and sundry the revocation of orders: "The ordinance regarding the grotto of Massabielle is revoked and nullified as of this date. Given at the City Hall of Lourdes. Signed: A. Lacadé, Mayor. Seen and approved: The Prefect, Baron Massy."

Once again, as when the barrier was to be erected, the workingmen of Lourdes refused to tear it down. Jacomet was forced to set out with Callet and two deputy constables and supervise his own disgrace. Thousands witnessed this capitulation after so long a siege. The crowd remained on the farther shore and observed an ominous silence. The commissioner mounted the same boulder he had occupied on the Thursday of the great vexation when he told the people how the miracle had come to naught just before out of the naught of the earth the miracle had gushed forth. Today too he raised his most official voice in speech in order to save what shred might still be saved.

"Good people, you see we are removing the barriers that were erected by the government. I'm only a servant of the State. And that's just like being a soldier. You don't ask questions; you just obey. We never fought against you, as you may have thought, but for you. Till we were sure if the water was good to drink or not we had to keep you from drinking it. Now, however, after we've got the word of the University of Toulouse about the water, further precautions are unnecessary. Therefore the purpose of the government is now accomplished. And so we decided, the prefect and I, to open the grotto and put no more obstacles in your way."

A dignified speech, it must be admitted, which demonstrated admirably the benevolent behaviour of the authorities. The speech dropped into the mass like a stone into a swamp and barely called forth a few notes of ironical laughter. At home Jacomet spoke as follows to his wife and daughter, who were serving the meal: "It's a good thing that we're leaving this rotten hole. The commissariat of police in Alais means a definite step ahead for me. Next to Nîmes, Alais is the biggest town in the department of Gard and the seat of the sub-prefect. We'll have a real gentleman's house to live in and after Madame la Sous-Préfet, Madame la Commissaire de Police will be the first lady of the town."

In these words did Jacomet communicate to his family the news of his transfer, which on the way home he had found on the desk in his office. His pleasure in the removal from Lourdes was, despite the circumstances, quite sincere. For the past weeks the papers had been telling of the heroic exploits of a group of criminals the scene of whose devastations was between Nîmes and Alais. Train-robberies were the specialty of these rogues. That was more up to date than healing springs and mystic visions. Doubtless, too, a criminologist could do more against train-robbers than against the lady.

The government sheet *Moniteur* contained an item on November 1 to the effect that Baron Massy had been transferred to the prefecture of Grenoble. It was true. In an access of shame the Emperor had disdained to sacrifice the man entirely and thrust him into outer darkness. But according to the secret traditions of the French administration the department of Isère with its capital city of Grenoble was the transition to chaos. Grenoble was a kind of last stop from which no road led to the radiant government house in Paris. That dream was finished. Nevertheless, he remained a prefect. The lady's very vengeance was mild.

The imperial prosecutor Vital Dutour fared worst of all. He was left where he was. He was not transferred but condemned to stay. Day after day the bald-head carried his pale, nauseated face across the Place Marcadale to the courthouse and back again. Twice daily he stopped at the Café Français. He was condemned to listen to the fruits of Duran's reading and join the trivial provincialism of lawyers, army officers, and small businessmen. It was a great day for him when now and then he could hurl one of his shafts of arrogant malice at the renegades Estrade and Clarens.

At eleven o'clock on November 17 the chimes of Saint Pierre's in Lourdes began unexpectedly to ring. The meaning was this, that His Lordship Monseigneur Laurence could no longer, with the best will in the world, continue to make life bitter for the lady. All the conditions he had made had been fulfilled to the very letter. Beyond all expectation the Emperor had given in. The government was in full flight. The prefect had been transferred to the other end of France. The barriers before the grotto had fallen. No official obstacle any longer gave the bishop any right to put off the investigation of the sacred and delicate matter. Once the most significant foe, Monseigneur could not but admit defeat. Well, not entirely yet. He was merely withdrawing to his last line of defence. As late as yesterday, when he had assembled about him the members of the commission of investigation, he had in a brief allocution strongly emphasized the fact that an authentic miraculous cure must be characterized not only by utter unaccountability on medical grounds. To render it wholly irrefutable it had to exhibit a very special trait, namely, the overwhelming immediacy of the "arise and walk" of the Gospels. In view of this circumstance the bishop reserved to himself ultimate decision in respect of all cases of cure acknowledged by the commission.

The rites prescribed for the solemn inauguration of similar commissions had been carefully studied. Such bodies are under the special protection of the Holy Ghost, whose inspiration is indispensable to the fruitfulness of their activity. This activity, then, was inaugurated, as was fitting, by a sacred service at Saint Pierre's in Lourdes, perhaps to find its final echo, if the investigation should confirm the presence of supernatural powers, in a far distant future, in a far mightier ceremonial and in a far mightier church of the same name. Today the theologians of the bishop's commission assembled in front of the modest high altar of the parish church of Lourdes. The seats of honour at the foot of the altar steps had been reserved for the learned laity, the physicians, chemists, geologists. Behind them in the first rows of pews sat the most respected witnesses of the visions: Madame Millet and her friends were radiant in their role of paladins of the fame of Heaven. Mademoiselle Peyret had furnished them with dark dignified robes befitting the occasion. She too sat in the front row and by her side sat the aged Philippe. All Bernadette's schoolmates were present, at their head Jeanne Abadie, who had cast the first stone but who today claimed the honour of the earliest disciple. The Sisters of Nevers were here, all but Marie Thérèse Vauzous, who had returned months ago to the mother house of the order. Densely thronged were the neighbours of the Cachot, Uncle and Aunt Sajou, Bouriette, Madame Bouhouhorts, radiant with her restored child in her arms, Piguno, the Ourous, Raval, and Gozos women, and, grandly throning in their midst, the clever Bernarde Casterot and her serviceable sister Lucille. Mother Nicolau and son, however, sat in a row far in the rear.

Nogaro, canon of the Cathedral of Tarbes, intoned the "*Veni, Creator Spiritus.*" At that moment a whisper of amazement rustled through the rows. Where was Bernadette? Where were the Soubirous? The chief figure of all was found at last among the nameless crowd, wedged in between her parents and Marie. She resisted but was pushed forward. Yearningly Madame Millet stretched out her arms. People moved nearer to each other and Bernadette was finally placed next to her first patroness, who dissolved in tears of joy. Bernadette's emotion was far from joyous. She was scared. Formerly Jacomet, Rives, and Dutour had tormented her with questions. Now the priests and doctors would follow suit. That is what she feared. And what was it all for? Nor was her fear groundless.

After the service the commission held its first plenary session in the presbytery. Twenty gentlemen, clerical and lay, sat in a semi-circle at a huge table. Benches against the wall had been provided for the witnesses. Bernadette was summoned as the first witness. Yet she seemed less witness than one accused. Over and over she had to tell her story. She did not use the apathetic mechanical tone of mere repetition she had so often used nor yet the ravishing reproductive pantomime that had so moved Bishop Thibaut. She spoke in a terse and dry but very living manner. She spoke like one fighting for life before a tribunal. Again and again she was interrupted in order that other witnesses might confirm or correct her delineation—Marie, Jeanne Abadie, Antoinette Peyret, and her mother and Aunt Bernarde and Madame Nicolau and Antoine. And now it appeared that the memories of the adult witnesses often failed them but that in Bernadette no smallest detail of those for ever perished days had been extinguished. One was tempted to say that she lived beyond time and wholly within the great happenings of the story of her love. Every glance, nod, turning of the head of the lady was graven unfathomably deep upon her memory. Nor was this all. She summoned all these gestures, in shape ever new and vivid, and not only these gestures, but all other details and all that had come to pass before and after her ecstasies. And the irresistible superiority of this memory of hers was the first powerful impression received by the investigating commission.

Again and again she made her astonishing replies. Thus, for instance, Canon Nogaro inquired after the secret that the lady had entrusted to her.

"But that was for me only," Bernadette declared with some impatience. "If I told you, Monsieur, it would no longer be a secret."

Another member voiced the common objection to her having eaten the grass and herbs: "I can't understand the lady's demanding anything so repulsive of you. It doesn't fit into the picture you have drawn of her that she bade you act like an animal."

"Do you act like an animal when you eat salad?" Bernadette calmly retorted. The gentlemen looked at one another, not knowing whether they should take this answer as an impertinence. The girl's tranquil eyes contradicted this suspicion. But Antoinette Peyret on her seat among the witnesses gave forth a squeaking sound.

Among the secular powers of Lourdes who had led the battle against the lady, Lacadé was the only one who had not been broken by it. This elastic gourmand certainly had a gift for sucking sweetness from the most critical circumstances. In what respect, anyhow, had the situation been critical for him? Let the miracle of Massabielle give the lie to all regnant philosophies, it is hardly the business of a practical man to shed his blood for the universal validity of the laws of nature. The times were incomprehensible, the world a mere mad soap-bubble, and A. Lacadé no fool. On that summer evening on which he had secretly thought of testing the power of the spring by his headache the scales had begun to fall from his eyes. Within every human being exists innately the degree and kind of his possible conversion to life in the spirit. Lacadé, too, had been converted in his very own way.

The sudden conviction that had come to the mayor was that a spring of grace was no worse than a spring of medicinal properties and was in some respects unique and more profitable. Lacadé's personal taste would a hundred times have preferred a brilliant watering-place to any place of pilgrimage, however sanctified. But what could he do? The learned Clarens had been right when, long ago, he had explained in the café that Lourdes had been a sacral locality even in remotest heathen times and that such sites never lose their mystical character. So Lacadé resigned himself. True, he had to renounce his favourite dream of a casino in a park, of a band in a pavilion, of a café on a terrace, and of croquet lawns. The merry life of rich and happy vacationers would hardly be suitable to the miraculous grotto area. No concerts or fireworks or flower-festival, no handsome women in charming frocks or children in lace-edged pantalets playing ball. Lacadé loved life. What a pity that gaiety and all its play of colours would have to be sacrificed to sombre processions of pilgrims! So, too, the water of health had turned into holy water and the whole idea of a company with stocks and shares and a flourishing export business had to be given up. Bottles with labels showing the Virgin restoring a blind child's sight, well, that would be in very bad taste, nor would the Church stand for it. Much had to be renounced. But even more might be gained if the thing were properly taken in hand and firmly administered by the right man. Luckily it was not too late. There was still a chance of getting ahead of the Church, which had not yet pronounced its great affirmation. Thus one might still be reckoned among the pioneers.

The aged Philippe was mightily astonished when he had to announce to his mistress that the mayor was calling. Lacadé

proposed a pious project to the pious woman of wealth. Before
the commission had a chance to pay its first visit to the grotto
tomorrow, one should turn the grotto into a floral bower in
order to demonstrate to the bishop's sceptical delegates the
genuineness of the population's faith in the miracle. Since it was
after All Souls' Day, little would be left in Cazenave's gardens
except asters. But these graveyard flowers of many hues could
be used to fill all available space. The commission was due at
the grotto at eleven. An hour earlier, under municipal leadership, a procession of the best people of Lourdes should proceed
to the grotto in order to demonstrate by participation or
absence who were the friends of the lady and who were not.
None was so clearly indicated by Providence to arrange this
manifestation as Madame Millet. The widow, charmed by the
sudden conversion of a former sceptic, at once took the matter
into her capable hands.

And thus in fact at nine o'clock next morning a goodly part
of the better people of Lourdes assembled in front of the
mayor's office on the Rue du Bourg. The gentlemen appeared
in formal dress, the ladies hid their hair under chaste veils. The
weather was very favourable. Lacadé issued from the portal,
his secretaries at his side, the gentlemen of the city council in
his wake. His purple cheeks were clean-shaven; his square grey
beard stuck out like a block. Across his belly shone the tricoloured sash. In his left hand he carried his tall silk hat and
in his right a burning candle.

"Let us intone a song," he said to Cazenave before giving the
signal to start. "Perhaps '*Nous voulons Dieu . . .*' "

The singing procession passed the Café Français. Embodied
in Duran, the spirit of the times beheld it thunderstruck.

CHAPTER THIRTY-SEVEN

A Last Temptation

Sadly the dean had said to the bishop: "Bernadette is still so young." The bishop had replied: "She will grow older," and he carefully saw to Bernadette's growing older before the final judgment concerning the lady and herself could possibly be pronounced. Between the miraculous and its acknowledgment as such the bishop sought to place the densest isolating substance known to man—time. He followed very precisely the wise rules of Benedict XIV, as these are laid down in the fifty-second chapter of the third book of his great work, *On the Elevation and Canonization of Saints.* Time is the sharpest of all acids, a supreme test it is. Only the purest and heaviest gold can withstand its action. Any lighter metal, though with a value of its own, is finally corroded and dissolved. Most things that stir men for a day are not more than a dream on that day's morrow. The memory of the most glorious as well as of the most grievous days in the history of peoples pales at the cock-crow of a new sensation. The matter of Lourdes had been discussed in the press beyond all proper measure. The bishop had a right to hope that now, toward the end of the first year, the excitement would be allayed. Perhaps at the end of another year no one would any longer speak of Massabielle, and the story of the visions and healings would remain a lovely memory without important consequences. Therefore Monseigneur Bertrand Sévère Laurence had granted his commission four whole years for the execution of its task. Within that period the material was to be examined, tested, and tabulated, but no final conclusion was to be drawn. For a great space of time is more potent in the cognition of truth than the operation of any human intelligence, however acute. It remained, for instance, to be seen whether the miraculous cures would continue or cease. It would likewise be seen whether the popular movement which had spread from Lourdes all over the country were to be lasting or if it had been but a fleeting mood evoked from masses wearied by the nihilism of the upper classes. By the long interval of waiting the bishop sought finally to subject the supernatural principle itself to the severest testing of its authenticity.

As far as the cures were concerned, they seemed indeed not only not to end, but from month to month their number increased. The medical members of the commission, quite disinclined professionally to favour the competition of Heaven "like that of any quack," examined each case meticulously. Their findings were gathered by the commission and submitted to the bishop. The latter sifted them and divided them into three classes. First there were the cures that appeared to be far beyond the order and custom of things. Medical science professed itself unable to understand or define the organic processes involved. The bishop's judgment was that what science could not define need not therefore be miraculous by any means. Next followed cases so completely inexplicable that the commission was unanimously ready to ascribe a miraculous character to them. Among these cases were tumours the size of a human head which had diminished and finally disappeared wholly after steady use of the spring-water. And there were paralyses which were greatly improved in a few days. The bishop did not deny the high value of these phenomena, but did not wish to base a conclusion on these alone. The curative properties of the spring were in themselves no decisive proof, for on some later day science might well reduce them to the

order of nature by discovering a hitherto unknown ingredient
in the water. Not even the marvellous many-sidedness of the
spring's curative power, which seemed applicable to any and
every human ill, satisfied the bishop. The future might reveal
an immanent causative principle for this too. Only and alone the
phenomenon of lightning-like immediacy was the one which,
according to Monseigneur's conception, would remain for ever
inexplicable. If a blind eye becomes a seeing eye in an eye's twinkling; if the dead nerve in an atrophied muscle shows living
tension on the instant, then and only then has man's justified
doubt reached its own limitation and must be ready to give in.

Contrary to his expectation the bishop found several cases
of this irrefutable character which he had to record in his own
first category. In the end there were fifteen of these instantaneous healings beyond the cavil of any criticism, however
sharp. Two of these cures were very early ones.

There was the case of Marie, oldest daughter of the Moreau
family of Tartas. This sixteen-year-old girl, who was attending
school in Bordeaux, was quite suddenly afflicted by one of the
most dreaded diseases of the eye. Dr. Bermond, the famous
ophthalmologist of the University of Bordeaux, diagnosed
retinal detachment of both eyes leading to inevitable total
blindness. The prognosis was soon confirmed. In a few weeks
the blood-suffused veil had wholly darkened the comely girl's
eyes and the shadow grew deeper after each awakening. As is
common in these desperate cases the family struggled and
struggled and would not submit to the cruelty of fate. The
blind girl was tormented by a hundred attempts at cure. Since
none helped, it was decided at last to repair to Paris and consult
scientific luminaries there. A last attempt. On the day before
departure Moreau, the girl's father, happened to pick up a
newspaper that contained an account of the sudden healing of
a certain Madame Rizot through the spring at Lourdes. Moreau

suddenly remembered the hour of his poor daughter's birth.
That birth had been an extremely difficult one. The doctor and
the midwife had given the baby up. In that hour Moreau had
vowed that if the baby girl survived he would call it Marie,
even though Marie Moreau was a stumbling and uneuphonious
name. He changed the journey's goal and took his family to
Lourdes. The grotto had but recently been reopened. A kerchief drenched in the spring-water was applied to Marie's
blind eyes. When it was removed, the girl uttered a cry so
piercing that none who heard it ever forgot it. The purple
veil that hid the light had been rent. Marie could see. They
held a page of printed matter before her eyes. She could read.
A delegation of the episcopal commission went to Bordeaux to
interview Dr. Bermond. He was asked to submit the notes he
had made concerning his patient's hopeless condition during the
last examinations. The whole business was so repulsive to the
professor's temperament that he resisted for some time before
surrendering his notes.

The second case was no less immediate. It concerned another
young person of Bordeaux. It was Jules, the twelve-year-old
son of an official in the revenue department, Roger Lacassagne.
This gentleman affected a martial air and, quite unlike Moreau,
could not be accused of any stirrings of a religious instinct.
Now, Jules was afflicted by the rare and curious disease popularly known as Saint Vitus's dance. This affliction is less dangerous on account of the morbid contortions of the limbs than
on account of the swelling and progressive closing of the
œsophagus which gradually makes almost impossible the in-
take of solid food. The family physician Noguès and the con-
sultant physician Professor Roquer applied all remedies prescribed in the medical textbooks as well as some that were not.
They displayed the opportunistic pragmatism common to all
physicians who are unwilling to admit their powerlessness.

The boy's œsophagus closed up more and more. At last the channel left was no thicker than a knitting-needle and admitted even a few drops of milk or soup only with extreme difficulty. Jules Lacassagne had become a mere shadow and seemed doomed to die of starvation. His mother took him to a seaside resort: perhaps the ocean's energy would help. It did not. On the beach whither they carried the boy he found a torn piece of newspaper. Holding it in his feeble hands he read an account of the healing of young Marie Moreau. He pocketed the piece of paper but dared not at first utter his wish. He knew his father's character and convictions well and was afraid of being laughed at. Not until many days later, when, obviously doomed, he was taken back to Bordeaux, did he hesitantly tell his mother the story of Lourdes and Marie Moreau. Madame Lacassagne besought her husband to set out for Lourdes on that very day. The husband consented without debate. In the face of death, unfaith is far unsurer of itself than faith. In his own arms Roger Lacassagne carried his son to the grotto. A former army man, he was disinclined to stand for any nonsense. If miracles can happen, let them! Hence he had brought with him a bag of soft biscuits. After Jules, endlessly agonizing, had succeeded in getting down a glassful of the water drop by drop, the absurd father handed him one of the biscuits and gave an order in his military fashion: "Now, then, eat!" And now an absurder thing happened: the boy ate. He bit off a piece, chewed it, and swallowed it like any ordinary mortal. The tall Lacassagne with his grey pompadour turned aside, reeling like a drunken man, and beat his breast and panted: "Jules is eating . . . Jules is eating. . . ." And the people around the grotto burst into tears. But Jules kept on eating in silent thoughtfulness and it seemed to many as though the first flush of recovery were even then tingeing his cheeks.

Marie Moreau and Jules Lacassagne were but two out of

fifteen cases which Bishop Laurence considered as inexplicable by natural processes and as fulfilling his specific demands. He was always guided by the medical evidence recorded immediately prior to the cure and also Monseigneur welcomed most the testimony of physicians either not of the Catholic faith or confessed enemies of all faith.

Fifteen human beings were cured between one breath and the next during this early period. Hundreds recovered as incomprehensibly but more slowly. Thousands and tens of thousands came to Lourdes seeking new health and life. Arbitrary as the lady, who in the days of her appearance never did what was expected of her, even so was the spring. Its way of choosing was unfathomable.

In the midst of this stream of men and events Bernadette lived as though it did not concern her. And it did not indeed. The discovery of the spring had not been hers. She herself had been the lady's business in the world. That men should praise her, Bernadette Soubirous, for the spring of grace and healing remained incomprehensible to her. The lady's reality grew sharper to her as time went on. But she was impatient of things being taken for what they were not. When people thanked her, she considered it as absurd as if one were to thank the postman for bringing money and not him who had sent it. She was constantly troubled by gratitude and praise and fame. People blocked her path and knelt down and touched her garments, especially on days when some great cure had taken place. When she was tormented and beset thus, the anger of her resolute soul was aroused. One of the many women who pursued her kept following her in the streets crying: "O Bernadette, thou who wast chosen, thou saint!" The girl turned on her with flashing eyes and exclaimed: "Good Lord, but you are stupid!"

Bernadette lived a life outside of and parallel to time. Nay, it were better to say that she lived in a time of her own. And this time of hers was a very monotony of waiting, though she was unaware of what the bishop and the dean had said to each other. It was like that provisional state of consciousness, blended of strangeness and distaste, that had succeeded each of her ecstasies. But now this provisional state had become a permanent one. For Bernadette knew with an infinite certainty of knowledge that on this earth the lady would never come to her again. Time passed slowly and yet ended swiftly. All others moved with and in time. Bernadette had the feeling that time flowed by her and she herself stood still. She was growing older, though she knew it not. The contact with the all-beautiful had not failed to affect her outer being. At sixteen the ailing girl was very beautiful. Nothing in her face recalled the common features of François and Louise Soubirous. A wholly alien subtilization, never intended by nature originally, shone from her face. The roundness of her childish face had developed into a pale oval; under a well-modelled forehead the still strangely apathetic eyes grew ever larger. The peasant raiment to which Bernadette was accustomed did not harmonize with this increasing distinction of aspect. Yet it was her desire to look not otherwise than her mother and sister.

Sometimes she lived at home, sometimes in the hospital, where a small room was held in readiness for her. This was done at the bishop's bidding because he had insisted that constant watch be kept over her and also because at certain times the importunities of the curious were no more to be borne. Many of these, especially such as could boast of rank or name, were hard to repel even in the hospital.

"Oh, how lovely it is to be sick in bed!" she was once heard to sigh. A pedantic cleric had arrived from Toulouse with a couple of ladies whom he wanted to impress with his own importance. Bernadette had no shrinking reverence for the professionally religious as such. They kept pestering her with questions. She had had trouble with the commission but recently. There was nothing either fey or feigning in her. When she spoke, each word was her very own. She was frank to the point of rudeness.

"Let us see whether one can believe you, Bernadette," said the cleric from Toulouse.

"It isn't important whether Your Reverence believes me," she retorted with withering directness.

The priest raised his voice. "If you lie, you're the cause of our having gone on this long journey in vain."

Bernadette regarded him with sincere astonishment. "But, Your Reverence, I didn't at all want to be the cause of your going on a journey."

A schoolmaster of the region named Loyson once mocked: "The lady might have taught you better French."

"That's the difference between her and you," Bernadette had answered after reflecting briefly. "She tried her best to speak dialect, which was hard for her. But she wanted me to be sure to understand."

The Soubirous went on living in the Cachot. But Uncle Sajou had given them an additional room. In the fourth year of the commission's sessions Marie got married. Her husband was a farmer near Saint-Pé de Bigorre. It was odd, for Marie had always regarded Bernadette's love of country life with contempt. At the marriage feast the older sister was gay with the others, but rather with the air of a kinswoman who had come from afar and must return to that distant dwelling of hers. The sisters were alone for a few minutes on this day and Marie wept suddenly, pressing Bernadette passionately to her. She sobbed: "Why, why is it that one can never have you? I was present there too and yet I lose you now, Sister."

Jeanne Abadie left Lourdes, too, to become a chambermaid

in Bordeaux. Cathérine Mengot, on the other hand, the premature nymph of Monsieur de Lafite, had now become a far maturer nymph in Tarbes. And many of the other schoolmates and early witnesses were scattered about the world. When the aged Philippe died, Bernadette asked whether she might not be a servant in Madame Millet's house. But Dean Peyramale, whom she consulted privately, was horrified. "Good Lord, that's not the proper station for you, Bernadette!"

"But look how old I am, and I don't help my parents a bit and I could do the work very well."

He shook his head. "Do you believe the lady meant you to be a servant?"

Bernadette gave the dean a long, veiled glance that held the shadow of an indescribable smile. "I'd be well content if she'd let me be her servant girl some day."

"Maybe you have an agreement of that kind with her, child?" the dean asked.

Bernadette was sad. "She'd never take me. I'm far too awkward."

Toward the end of the last year of the four years of waiting Marie Dominique Peyramale was once more summoned to Tarbes. A very long conference between himself and Monseigneur took place, again in the bishop's unhome-like study and bedroom. It was shortly before Advent. On his return the dean immediately sent for Bernadette to come to the vicarage. Heavy snow lay on the acacia and plane trees of the garden. Icy gusts made the cold penetrate to the very bones. It was the old fierce breath of the Pyrenees, the piercing message of those crystalline peaks, the Pic du Midi and, far behind, the demonic Vignemale. The cold was raw in the Cachot, but the dean's study was deliciously warm. The fire of larch logs crackled busily. Bernadette came in half frozen. Even in winter she would wear only a *capulet*, though not the same old one. "How you've grown, child!" the dean said as she entered. "I can scarcely call you my little one any more. But you'll have to let your bad old parson go on calling you the same as always."

He placed an armchair near the fire for her and poured brandy into two tiny glasses. "Listen, my dear, you probably know that the work of the bishop's commission of investigation is practically concluded. After New Year's everything will be in Monseigneur's hands. How clear an idea have you of the work this commission has been doing, Bernadette?"

"Well, Monsieur le Curé," she answered in her schoolgirlish tone, "the gentlemen examine and test all the people who have been cured."

"Quite correct. But do you think this was the entire purpose of the commission?"

Bernadette was evasive. "It's hard for the commission. There are always more and more people being cured."

The dean seemed intent on cleaning his pipe. "But how about yourself, child? Do you imagine that you and your case are not part of the commission's task?"

"I answered all the gentlemen's questions," the girl answered in a quick and frightened voice. "I hope I won't need to have anything more to do with all that."

"Oh, Bernadette," the dean sighed, "don't pretend you don't know. You've got quite a logical little head, more so than most women. The lady chose you from among all children. The lady bade you bring the spring out of the earth. And the spring is a spring of grace, a miraculous spring which heals the sick day after day. The lady said many things to you and entrusted a secret to you and even named her name to you. Under the most binding of oaths you repeated her words to the commission. You are the centre of a story such as our age has not hitherto witnessed. Do you really believe that all this is part of the common trend of life and that you can now say: 'I've done my share; now let me live my own life'? Do you?"

"But I did do my share," said Bernadette, pale now to the very lips.

The dean thrust his index-finger out into the void. "You are like a bullet that has been shot, Bernadette. No one can change your course. Listen to me carefully. The commission has written a very extensive and very important report about you. This report admits the possibility that you are one chosen by the powers above and that to your hand and to your hand alone which brought forth the spring itself are to be traced a great number of proved miracles. Do you understand just what that means? This is the report which, signed by our bishop, is being sent to Rome to the Holy Father himself and to his cardinals, and the greatest and the wisest men of the Church will be watching you for years, nay, for decades, and then . . ."

The dean, now a man in his fifties, stopped because his furrowed face was blushing to the roots of his grey hair. "It's hard for me even to utter such words, little one," he went on hoarsely. "Never would I have believed that the Lord would choose me to speak them some day. But it's not at all out of the question that this Bernadette Soubirous who sits facing me, this daughter of François Soubirous, this girl that I was once going to drive out of my house with a broomstick—Jesus and Mary, a man's tongue freezes—it isn't out of the question that this ignorant little thing who was at the foot of her catechism class, that she—that you—how shall I say it?—that you will not be forgotten long, long after all the rest of us are dead and thought of no more, but will be . . ."

She had understood. Deathly pale, she jumped up. "But that is frightful!" she cried. "It can't be; I don't want it!"

"I understand you very well, my child," the dean said, nodding to himself. "It's no small matter, that!"

Bernadette recoiled and fought for breath and sobbed and kept stammering: "I don't want it. . . . No, no, I don't. . . ."

"Yes, yes, I understand," said the dean. "But what's to be done about it?"

His hands behind him, he paced to and fro. Nothing broke in on the stillness save the fire's crackling and the girl's sobs. At last Peyramale stopped and faced her. "Aren't the good sisters in the hospital and in the school very sweet?"

"Indeed they are—very sweet," she stammered.

"Well, then, couldn't you imagine yourself as one of them some day?"

"Dear God, no, that's far above me!" She was startled into fright and new tears. "Why didn't you let me take the maid's job at Madame Millet's?"

He put his hand gently on her head. "I understand it all. Life in the world is life in the world. . . . And no one must be forced to take the three sacred vows. One takes them only if the soul desires passionately and earnestly to sacrifice itself to God. The demand is stringent. The third vow, that of obedience, would probably be the hardest for you, little soul. You were obedient to the lady. True. But otherwise you love your own way and your freedom. Yet the bishop is right. Can we let little Soubirous, to whom the Most Blessed Virgin condescended, run about like a little savage? This was his question. Next the Holy Father and the cardinals will be sitting in council concerning her visions and miracles, and she desires to live as other women do! No, no, the bishop said, Bernadette is a precious flower which we must take under our care. . . . Don't you see that, child?"

Bernadette sat deeply bowed and made no answer.

"Long, long ago," Peyramale reminded her, "I said to you: 'You are playing with fire, O Bernadette.' But it is not your fault that you did so. Your lady was the heavenly fire, O Bernadette. She raised you high above all men. It is actually possible, little one, that your name will survive your death. Do you think that that imposes no obligation on you? You can't suddenly play truant from your destiny, as though it were school, and be an old widow's servant. Heaven chose you, by my faith. Nothing is left you now but to choose Heaven with all your soul. Isn't that true? Tell me yourself."

"Oh, yes, that is true," Bernadette breathed after a long silence.

Peyramale changed to a lighter tone. "One of these days Bishop Forcade of Nevers will turn up here. He's a very amiable gentleman; not such a rough customer as our bishop. He'll ask you one or two things and you'll answer him and tell him exactly how you feel. The mother house of the order of the Sisters of Nevers, whom you've always known so well, is in his diocese. The rule of the order is beautiful and lofty, and the women are certainly no grey cellar-growths but very much involved in practical life. And you don't really believe it would be better for you to be the servant of strangers and wash their linen. . . ."

Bernadette, now wholly calm, did not take her eyes from Peyramale, who was pacing up and down again. "One more thing," he said suddenly. "Of course, you'd rather bite your tongue off than ask a favour of me. But I know very well how the condition of your family weighs on your heart. Your parents work themselves to the bone. But they haven't a happy touch and don't know how to manage cleverly. Well, Bernadette, here's my hand: I promise you that even before you leave Lourdes your people will be established in the mill on the upper Lapaca and I'll see to it myself that things don't go wrong again."

He held out his huge hand, into which her small one disappeared. Suddenly she bent over the dean's hand and kissed it.

"Well, I guess that's all," Peyramale growled. But when she wanted to take her leave he frowned and held her back. "No, Bernadette, not even yet quite all."

His voice was soft and deep. A while ago when he had blushed, speech had been difficult for him. It was more difficult now. Elaborately he went about lighting the kerosene lamp.

"Don't misunderstand me, Bernadette," he said, clearing his throat, "I believe you; I have full faith in you. You've convinced me. But in respect of one detail I've never quite overcome my doubts. It's the words '*l'immaculada councepciou.*' Everything your lady said was as inimitable as life itself and couldn't be made up by wanting to. But those two words sound so consciously emphatic and so fit for propaganda and laid on so thick that they seem the utterance of a dryasdust theologian rather than of the ever-loveliest whom you beheld. Now strain your soul to the utmost, I beg of you, and search your memory and conscience. Didn't those words somehow come to you from somewhere in the world and in your trance you thought they were the lady's? It is a terrifyingly serious question I am putting, Bernadette. As dean of Lourdes and member of the commission I ought not to utter it. But if you could remember one who first spoke those words in your hearing; if you could admit the possibility that you were weary, dreamy, inattentive, and that it seemed to you only later as though the lady had spoken these words, why, in that case a good deal might be different. You would then have to retract this single incident before the commission. The lady's character would not be so rigidly defined as it is now and the entire report of the commission would need to be rewritten. Do you understand me? But of course you do! It's certainly not my business to talk to you like this. But if you were to make retraction on this single point it might not be wholly impossible that somewhere in all the wide world there would be a little corner where you could hide and lead a normal human life. . . . Would you like time to think this over?"

The fire sputtered and the lamp whistled and the two human beings' breathing could be heard. A cold draught blew through a crack in the door. Bernadette stared at the lamp as though nothing interested her except the too tall flame which began to cover the chimney with soot.

"I don't need time to think anything over," she said at long last, "for I never lied to you, Monsieur le Curé."

Peyramale turned down the wick of the lamp. "Who spoke of lying?"

Bernadette smiled up at him. "And I don't want a little corner to hide in. . . ."

CHAPTER THIRTY-EIGHT

The White Rose

THE BISHOP OF TARBES, the most sceptical of all opponents, had been vanquished. He yielded to the five contradictions inherent in the healings of the spring of Massabielle, that is, those which, according to the admission of the scientific branch of the commission, could not be explained by human reason.

The first contradiction was that between the insignificant means and the greatness of the results. The second contradiction was that between the sameness of the means and the variety of human ills cured thereby. The third contradiction was that between the briefness of the application of the means of cure and the previous long employment of medicaments prescribed by medical science. The fourth contradiction was that between the instantaneous effectiveness of the means and the previous ineffectiveness, often extending over years, of all others. And, finally, the fifth contradiction was that between the chronic character of the ailments investigated and their sudden disappearance through the means of cure. None could deny these contradictions save minds consciously and voluntarily closed to documentary proof and determined to consider both patients and physicians as the dishonest propagandists of a belief in miracles. These five contradictions seemed to Bertrand Sévère Laurence the sure foundations on which to base the pastoral letter in which he at last acknowledged the supernatural character of the visions and healings of Lourdes. Nevertheless, as was expressly said in this acutely and brilliantly reasoned pastoral letter, the bishop submitted his own judgment to the judgment of that Vicar of Christ on earth, to whom had been mandated the governance of the Church of God.

In spite of these decisive events Peyramale succeeded in obtaining one more respite for Bernadette. He had the nineteen-year-old girl undergo a medical examination which not only confirmed the chronic asthma but revealed a general state of low physical resistance. Moreover, there supervened a new sensation which diverted public attention from Bernadette. Monseigneur had added to his pastoral letter an appeal to the members of his diocese. The people were admonished to fulfil the lady's emphatic wish for a chapel. Especially in view of the difficulty of the terrain on the Montagne des Espélugues and the high consequent cost, the bishop would be unable to carry out this undertaking without the help of the faithful.

What took place now was like another miracle, since it seemed to contradict the natural law of the reluctant human purse. Within a few weeks the sum of two million francs had arrived in Tarbes from all over the world. And because this sum was largely composed of the sous or pennies of the poor, it should be expressed in the more eloquent and glowing terms of forty million sous. It was twenty-five sous that François Soubirous had received from Cazenave on that eleventh of February for burning the hospital refuse before the cave of Massabielle, and he had felt that the money had saved him. Monseigneur, not ignorant of his own limitations, appointed the dean of Lourdes head of the architectural enterprise. Therewith set in the great period of Peyramale's life. He agreed with Lacadé on the price to be paid the municipality for the mountain of caverns and the surrounding lots. The mayor proved far too pious a man to be unreasonable. His busy mind was relieved of the necessity of utopian dreaming. Six modern inns and hotels had already sprung from the blessed soil of Lourdes and he had a share in each establishment and its profits. And his highest achievement, the railroad line from Tarbes to Lourdes, was under construction. He who knows his goal and knows the laws of navigation governing the sea of this world will never know shipwreck. To Lacadé success was no miracle, not even the success of a miracle.

Architects crowded the vicarage. Peyramale was far from gentle with these artists. One brought the model of a little church sitting on the top of the mountain like a baker's ornament on a wedding-cake. The dean simply smashed it. Artistic taste is integrated with physical constitution. He who breathes from a mighty breast loves long-curved songs. A powerful and gigantic man such as Peyramale loved a muscular style of building. Out of the very flank of the rock the new cathedral should emerge, massive and slender at once, as though the mountain were the trunk of its own body. For this cathedral had been wrung from both State and Church as the symbol of a victory over the all-powerful doctrine that twice two is always four. Peyramale's plans matured. The Gave had been diverted, the brook filled in in part. A broad esplanade fronted the grotto. Workmen and gardeners converted the mountain of Massabielle into a floral slope that sent streets down the valley like embracing arms.

At this time Bernadette, too, knew the visitations of art. Two aristocratic maiden ladies of Tarbes, the de Lacour sisters, had made a donation for a special purpose. A committee of ladies under the chairmanship of Madame Millet had been appointed by them to entrust a worthy artist with the task of modelling a statue of the Madonna which was to be placed in the lady's niche. The worthy artist chosen was Monsieur Fabich of Lyon. In velvet beret and armed with his sketch book, he turned up in Bernadette's little room. Squinting his eyes, his left thumb out, he begged the "charming seeress" to indicate to him the exact gestures of the visionary lady. Also would she please describe to him, to the very last detail, countenance, hands, feet, robe, veil, girdle. Bernadette did her utmost, a hundred times over, alas. The charcoal quivered across the rough paper. Sheets covered the floor.

"Did she look like this?" the zealous artist asked.

"No, she didn't look like that, Monsieur."

"But I have been strictly guided by all your indications, Mademoiselle. What is wrong?"

"I don't know what is wrong, Monsieur."

A few days later the sculptor had executed a statuette that was to serve as model for the future work. He was very proud of the fact that, in imitation of sundry antique works, he had painted the lady's girdle a watery blue and tinged with bronze the roses on her feet. Mesdames Millet, Cénac, Baup, Gesta were filled with enthusiasm. What luck to have found so mild a master, one of such ideal sensibilities yet so skilful a craftsman. The ladies praised above all the industry of this able man who even in this first sketch had omitted no fold of the garment and no fingernail. How filled with happiness would be the little visionary, poor ignorant girl that she was, to find the lady again. Bernadette, called in by the jury, was not only not happy but quite visibly dismayed.

"Isn't it like your lady?" asked Madame Millet, equally devoted to the artist and his work.

"No, Madame, it is not like." Bernadette could not answer otherwise without lying.

Master Fabich's eyes grew wild. For what on earth is like the fright and bewilderment of an artist the value of whose work is denied to his very face? He threw out a life-belt, as it were, both for himself and for his critic. "It could not be my aim to create a resemblance to the incomparable," he said. "My aim was to create an approach to supernal beauty." His beseeching glance swept over Bernadette. "Is my lady not very beautiful, too, Mademoiselle?"

"Oh, yes, Monsieur, she is very beautiful," Bernadette said with great good will, knowing well that she was a nobody and a child of the Cachot and really had no right to an opinion.

The master wiped his brow, breathed more easily, and grew bolder. "And now I would appreciate it deeply, Mademoiselle, if you would point out to me wherein lies the difference between my lady here and yours. . . ."

With a lost smile Bernadette gazed beyond the statue. "Oh," she said softly, "my lady was much more natural and not a bit tired-looking, and she wasn't praying all the time. . . ."

These awkward but telling words meant: Here is another Mother of God like a hundred others in a hundred churches. But my lady was unique, the one and only, and none dreams how she looked, and she is mine alone. This much, however, was true: Fabich and Madame Millet and the rest imagined nothing that had not already been imagined a thousand times. That served to satisfy them. Their faith and their doubt, their very seeing and hearing were like a rubber-stamp. But what of a soul who had been face to face with an arch-image?

Long before the completion of the basilica of the rock the common people of Bigorre who had conquered the grotto for themselves four years ago demanded that it be consecrated. The bishop, who had so long driven the lady hard, determined to do fitting penance as a prince of the Church by means of the highest and most radiant festivity his diocese had ever known. He would himself lead the procession of a hundred thousand pilgrims. It was to be also the day of the highest honouring of Bernadette. Spring was chosen, the fourth of April, the beginning of the time of the overwhelming blooming of all trees in the Pyrenean countryside. Lacadé had the whole town hung with flags. On the eve of the day thousands of candles burned in the windows of all houses. Bishop Bertrand Sévère arrived in Lourdes on that evening. All the canons and prelates of his cathedral chapter accompanied him. Five hundred priests were to assist him on the morrow at the mightiest Te Deum of his career. The garrison would turn out in full dress led by its colonel. Members of many orders were to surround the bishop, Carmelites of both sexes, Christian Teaching Brothers, Sisters of Mercy, the Sisters of Nevers, the nuns of Saint Joseph. The bishop would wear his richest vestments, rochet and stole, the mitre on his head, the golden crosier in his hand.

On the morning of the great day, Bernadette meant to get up early. She could not. Her legs were as though dead. After a number of attempts she sank back in exhaustion. Then her breath failed her and she was overcome by the severest attack of asthma in years. Her temperature climbed. Dr. Dozous was obliged to inform the committees that the girl's joining the procession was out of the question. The bells began to ring. More than a hundred thousand souls filled the town and the valley. The people ached to pay its child an incomparable tribute. Bernadette heard the gigantic hum without. She paid no attention. It took all her strength to get a little air to breathe. Promptly at noon the celebration came to an end. Promptly at noon Bernadette was well again. The attack had lasted exactly long enough to confirm the lady's prophecy and prevent her from experiencing a happy earthly day.

Monseigneur Forcade, bishop of Nevers, had put to her one question or another, Bernadette Soubirous had answered one thing or another and, at last, said that it was not only necessary but most welcome to her to renounce the world and take the veil as one of the Sisters of Nevers, whom she had known all her life. Benevolently Monseigneur welcomed this decision and

gladly undertook to make all necessary arrangements. He did
so even sooner than had been expected. The call came to
Bernadette, and two sisters of the house in Lourdes were
commissioned to conduct her to the mother house at Nevers.

The Soubirous couple had now been managing the mill on
the upper Lapaca brook for a year. Business was not bad. To
ruin a mill that could really grind would have been something
of a trick in Lourdes, now that the town was overrun by
strangers. A new hotel opened its doors every six months.
Restaurants flourished. The fat baker Maisongrosse had many
new competitors. When François Soubirous dropped in on
him now his reception was quite different from what it had
been in 1858. Now the fat man urged him to come into the
parlour and partake of some fine old brandy. The postmaster
and hotel proprietor Cazenave was no longer Soubirous's employer but his very best customer. It was rare for him to hear
the appellation "*mon capitaine*" from Soubirous. At Babou's,
where the miller still dropped in now and then, even the
police would not have dared to make a dirty allusion. D'Angla,
Belhache, and Callet got up respectfully in the presence of
Bernadette's father and gave a military salute. Soubirous had
risen high above all the neighbours in the Rue des Petites
Fossées. The Cachot was empty. Uncle Sajou would rent it
no more. But on a certain rainy summer's day all the old
neighbours surrounded the ruined old prison. Bernadette was
leaving to enter upon her novitiate. All the old friends and
foes, adherents and deniers of other days, the whole tale of
the conquered, would say farewell to her now. The clever
notion to celebrate this farewell at the Cachot had originated
in the brain of the seamstress of the crooked shoulder, Antoinette Peyret. It was an ordinary workday and a new company of the sick had just arrived. All hands were busy and
the Lapaca mill was fairly distant. Bernadette had passed re-

cent weeks there with her family. But they, too, had persuaded her to confer this favour on the Sajous and the other neighbours of the great days and go to the Cachot.

The room with its thick damp walls and its two barred windows of unequal size was empty. In its desolation the Cachot was like a house of mourning from which a corpse has just been carried. The Soubirous family stood in a solemn row. Beside François and Louise Soubirous were the two young sons, Jean Marie and Justin, who were pretty big boys by now. The thirteen-year-old Jean Marie and the twelve-year-old Justin displayed on their coats the honourable dusty stains of their father's trade, for they were both his helpers. It was a strange court ceremony of farewell which Bernadette was forced to conduct. The people passed in front of her and gave her their hands and many sought to kiss her own and many embraced her and many had tears in their eyes. The Bouhouhorts woman had come with her child, who was all of eight years old now and sound to the marrow, despite his little bow-legs.

"Look on this angel once again, my child," Madame Bouhouhorts sobbed. "All your life you will think of this hour even though you live to be a hundred."

The Bouhouhorts child gave Bernadette a glance, half frightened and half curious, made a quick little bow, and took to his heels. Very long was the train of those saying farewell which passed by under the unmoved friendly eyes of Bernadette. "Au revoir, Monsieur Bouriette, au revoir, Tante Piguno, au revoir, Madame Raval, au revoir, Monsieur Barringue . . ."

Antoinette Peyret shook with woe. "Don't forget that I was the first to believe in you."

Madame Millet pressed her to her mighty bosom. "Pray for me who am being left desolate."

And Aunt Bernarde, still the family oracle, hastily added a few rules for her behaviour in the convent. Aunt Lucille, the ever gentle, pressed a tiny gold cross into her hand and whispered: "Oh, how I envy you, oh, how much!"

And finally Mayor Lacadé turned up, too, with a little box of crystallized fruits. "A little snack for the journey of the blessed child of Lourdes."

Bernadette was surprised that Antoine Nicolau was not among those who had come to bid her farewell.

At last it was over and the family was alone. They accompanied Bernadette to the hospital, where the carriage was waiting to take her and the two nuns to Nevers. The final farewell was brief. François Soubirous, within whom paternal dignity and a vague sense of grief were in conflict, displayed a stiff and sombre grandeur, as he always did in great moments. Though the corners of his mouth twitched he thought it due himself to give his daughter a final admonition: "Be good, dear child, and be a credit to your parents in the cloister, too."

Mamma, who in recent years had lost her front teeth, looked old and very worn. She took refuge in the empty little activities of all mothers who see a child depart. She hastily repacked Bernadette's few possessions in the shabby little valise. She produced from it, too, her farewell present, a silken headkerchief. Bernadette wore a new black frock of modish cut. "Wear this kerchief, darling," Louise begged. "Let them see how pretty my daughter is."

Obediently Bernadette fulfilled her mother's wish. Suddenly Louise's face turned quite grey. "We'll never see each other again, Bernadette."

The girl tried to laugh. "But why shouldn't we, Mamma?"

"*Praoubo de jou*, you'll be so very, very far from me." She burst into tears.

Bernadette clung to a light tone. "But visits are allowed, Mamma. And it's not far to Nevers by train. And Papa is earning enough money now so that you can all have a pleasant trip."

Not till the carriage was rattling over the stones, and Bernadette saw her family no more, did she feel a piercing sorrow. It was less the pain of parting that suddenly flooded her than an obscure pity for her parents and her sister and brothers, a pity that would never know consolation. Her companions observed that Bernadette was huddling in a corner of the carriage with closed eyes and tense limbs. They had agreed beforehand to afford the girl a last joy. She should take leave of her beloved grotto and say a prayer to the invisible one in the niche. The coachman, who had received his orders, stopped at the new esplanade, three minutes from Massabielle. But the good sisters were mightily astonished. Not as in her great days did Bernadette cast herself passionately on her knees. She made an ordinary sign of the cross. She stood at the grotto as any sincere human being stands at a grave. The place of miraculous blessing to tens and tens of thousands was to Bernadette a grave of love. Others received what she had lost. She no longer saw the real lady. What she saw in the niche was Master Fabich's imitation of innumerable other empty imitations and less, infinitely less, like her ever-beautiful one than is some mortuary image like him above whose grave it stands. Bitter enough had it been to stare into the empty niche after that farewell of all farewells. Yet that desolateness and dark void had been a frame of what had once been and possibly might be again. Now a stranger stood there carved of Carrara marble, which under Fabich's treatment resembled plaster, stood there with her girdle painted blue, accessible to all at every moment and banishing from the eyes of her who had beheld the veritable and supernal what once those eyes had seen. Anguished, Bernadette turned and left. The dismayed sisters were inclined to regard this strange behaviour as a sign of impious coldness.

At the city limits the carriage had to stop once more. For the miller Antoine Nicolau suddenly appeared running by its side, in his hands a bunch of white roses which he very shyly offered to Bernadette. "To the future bride of Christ and the favourite child of the queen of all roses," he declaimed, glad not to have forgotten the words learned by rote.

"Oh, Monsieur Antoine, they're much too beautiful and they'll wilt on the long drive," said Bernadette, frightened, while one of the nuns took the flowers for her.

"I didn't want to come along with the others this morning," he said falteringly. "There was something I wanted to tell you."

"What did you want to tell me, Monsieur Antoine?"

"Yes, what was it exactly? Oh, Mademoiselle Bernadette, it is very hard to say. . . ."

There was a long silence. The two nuns sat very stiff and erect. Bernadette's eyes were fixed intently on Antoine Nicolau. Desperately he twisted his black moustache; beads of sweat stood on his forehead.

"I wanted to say," he finally brought out, "that my mother is getting old. She and I are used to each other and get along real well. And I'm thirty-four now. And so I've decided never to take a wife, Mademoiselle Bernadette, because, you know, a mother-in-law and a daughter-in-law—that doesn't work so well. I'm going to stay unmarried, too, that's what I wanted to say. . . . And now I wish you luck on your journey, Bernadette."

She pulled one of the white roses out from among the others and gave it to him.

"Farewell, Monsieur Antoine. . . ."

CHAPTER THIRTY-NINE

The Mistress of the Novices

JOSÉPHINE IMBERT, mother superior of the Convent of Saint Gildarde, descended the stairs to the reception room where Bernadette Soubirous had been waiting for a full hour. No one could have detected in her demeanour that the venerable nun had been praying with devout passion in her cell and that this troubled supplication's subject had been none other than the famous miracle-worker of Lourdes who was to enter the convent as a novice on this day. As though she did not know who it was that had been waiting, Mother Imbert glanced at the girl who had risen at her entrance.

"So you are the postulant brought from Lourdes today?" she asked rather sternly, and Bernadette was frightened by her suspicion that another examination was about to begin. Her answering voice was feeble. "*Oui*, Madame la Supérieure."

"And what is your name?"

Heavens above, as if she didn't know it! The same old thing over and over. But better not to make a fuss. "Bernadette Soubirous, Madame la Supérieure."

"How old are you?"

"Just past twenty, Madame la Supérieure."

"And what can you do?"

"*Oh, pas grand'chose*, nothing that amounts to much, Madame la Supérieure." It was one of those answers of hers that were so veracious that they could easily be considered pert. The mother superior looked up a little and tried to probe those dark, calm eyes she saw. "*Mais alors, mon enfant,*" she said, "what are we going to do with you here?"

Bernadette did not feel it her duty to reply to this question. She remained silent, wherefore the venerable nun was obliged after a space to reopen the conversation.

"But out in the world, what would you like to have been?"

"Oh, Madame la Supérieure, I thought I might be good enough to be a servant girl. . . ."

But a mysterious overtone vibrated in this sentence which the mother superior knew not how to interpret. How was one to take this girl? The furrows on the sides of the nun's mouth grew sharp. Her next question was almost offensive in tone. "Who recommended you to our congregation?"

"I believe it was His Lordship the bishop of Nevers."

"Aha, Monseigneur Forcade!" The mother superior turned with the shadow of a laugh to a tall slender nun who had just entered. "Did you hear that? Monseigneur Forcade, *ce saint et cher homme!* His child-like heart always makes recommendations of the same kind. This is the postulant from Lourdes. What did you say your name was, my daughter?"

"Bernadette Soubirous, Madame la Supérieure."

"And this is the reverend mother, the mistress of the novices, to whose guidance you will have to look from now on."

"We know each other," said Mère Marie Thérèse Vauzous, betraying no surprise. The handsome face of the former teacher of Lourdes, that Amazon of Christ, as Father Pomian had called her, had grown long and horsy during the past year. The narrow lips now showed far too much gum. In her small deep-set eyes glowed not the peace of self-conquest but an unknown grief. Bernadette looked at Vauzous as she had often done when she had faced her in the place of trial and disgrace. Mère Imbert now asked the mistress of the novices: "Didn't the novice Angéline recently return to the world at her own request? Who is doing her work?"

"The novice Angéline didn't leave till yesterday," Mère Vauzous answered. "Her place as kitchen maid is still open, Madame la Supérieure."

"All the better. Then the postulant may start in tomorrow. . . ." Then, mildly and indulgently she turned to Bernadette. "All this on the supposition, *mon enfant*, that you won't be too tired tomorrow and that your health is equal to the work. You'll be asked to wash dishes, prepare vegetables, pare potatoes, scrub floors, sweep corridors and stairs, in brief, perform all the lowly tasks that need to be done. But please observe: I do not command you; I am merely proposing this. If you don't feel equal to what I propose, or if work of this kind is repellent to you either physically or spiritually, I wish you would tell me now. . . ."

"Oh, no, Madame la Supérieure," Bernadette broke in. "It's not a bit repellent to me, and I'm very happy to be able to take the place of the kitchen maid."

She did not know how well she had stood the deliberate testing of her humility. Yet this very testing represented a crookedness of approach and a misunderstanding on the part of the mother superior, like a good deal else that took place between people and Bernadette. She was not a general's daughter like the mistress of the novices nor that of a landowner like Mother Imbert. Washing and scrubbing and sweeping, her mother's daily tasks, meant no humiliation or lowering of herself to her. These things were routine in her childhood and were what she had always meant by work. The sisters had expected a vain girl drunk with her celebrity. After the triumphs of Massabielle, that was almost taken for granted. But Bernadette was sincerely happy to have been chosen for the lowliest tasks. Her smile was one of relief and the mother superior nodded with satisfaction.

"Good. Now let Mother Vauzous take you to the refectory, where you can have supper at the table of the sisters from Lourdes."

"With your permission, Madame la Supérieure, but there is one other matter to be considered," Marie Thérèse Vauzous declared. "The postulant bears a name that has made a great noise in the world and has been printed in the papers over and over again and has even been mentioned with distinction in the pastoral letters of a bishop. But among us great names have no meaning even when they have been acquired by far greater effort. We disassociate ourselves from all we have meant to the world or it has meant to us. Moreover, the name Bernadette is a childish and trivial diminutive."

"Quite right," Mother Joséphine agreed. "Before actually entering upon her novitiate the postulant will want to choose another name. It were best to do so at once. Have you given the matter any thought, *ma fille?*"

Bernadette had not.

"What is the name of your godmother?"

"My aunt Bernarde Casterot was my godmother, Madame la Supérieure."

"Then surely you will be happy to bear the name of Marie Bernarde, my child," the mother superior said with finality.

Thus happily and easily Bernardette made her first sacrifice —her name in the world, by which all whom she had loved had ever called her.

Next day at the noon meal there were about forty women present in the refectory, among them nine novices, already in their robes, at whose table Bernadette had the lowest place. The reader at the lectern was just about to open the devotional work that had been chosen to be read from that day when at a sign from Mother Imbert the mistress of the novices raised her voice.

"You know, my dear Sisters, that a new postulant entered this house yesterday. Her name is Bernadette Soubirous and she is a native of Lourdes. Within a few days she will be received as a novice and will assume the name of Marie Bernarde. Some of you, at least, will have heard of the visions and mystic experiences of Mademoiselle Soubirous and of their beneficent effects which have made such a stir. A pastoral letter of the bishop of Tarbes treats of these matters. . . . Would you please step forward, my Daughter, and give us a brief and simple account of those experiences?"

In profound dismay Bernadette stood at the lectern and regarded these older and younger female faces, singularly without eagerness, equally peaceful and yet visibly tired after the forenoon's toil. Some looked at the postulant with child-like curiosity, others with eyes long lifeless, three or four with friendly warmth. Bernadette, who had told her story so often, felt very helpless in the face of this strangely gentle stoniness. She added faltering sentence to faltering sentence like a child of seven.

"My parents once sent us for faggots, my sister Marie and me and another girl named Jeanne Abadie. Marie and Jeanne left me behind on the Chalet Isle near the brook opposite the grotto. And suddenly in a niche in the rock there stood a very beautiful lady wonderfully dressed. And later I told Marie and Jeanne about it and my mother, too. And my mother forbade me to go back there. But I did go back. And the lady was there whenever I went. And the third time she spoke to me and asked me to come back every day for fifteen days. And I went for fifteen days and the lady stayed away only twice, on a Monday and a Friday. On the third Thursday she bade me wash in the spring and drink of its water. But there was no spring to be seen and the spring began to flow only on the second day after the day on which I had scratched a little hole in the right corner. After the fifteen days the lady appeared to me three times more. The last time she went away from the grotto and I never saw her again."

That was Bernadette's dry and dusty and awkward account. It fell on stony ground. There was no stirring in any face.

"We thank you, my child," said the mistress of the novices. "And now I believe that our dear sisters, as well as the novices and you, too, Marie Bernarde, will understand me correctly if I express the conviction that from this moment on that matter will not again be referred to in this house. We shall not annoy you with it, Marie Bernarde, nor will you want to refer to it yourself. . . . And now let us not linger over our meal."

When Bernadette returned to the table her neighbour asked: "Was that all, Mademoiselle? No more than that?"

Bernadette nodded to the disappointed girl. "Yes, that was all, Mademoiselle. No more than that."

On the eve of her being robed and received as a novice— it was the twenty-eighth of July—immediately after the Adoration in the convent chapel, Bernadette was sent for by Mère Marie Thérèse. The mistress of the novices received her in her own cell, which was barer and bleaker than that of the other nuns. Nothing but an iron crucifix hung over the bed of bare planks, for permission to use which she had had to apply to the mother general of the order.

"Listen, *ma fille*," she began, "you are starting out upon a difficult way tomorrow. It is the way that leads through disassociation from the temporal to eternal life. To be sure, the novitiate is but a side-path which leads to the road itself.

Yet to some it is the hardest part of the way. When once we had made our final profession we find that it supports us against many temptations. I have summoned you because I would like to clarify a few things between us. First of all, I don't know whether you have a right conception of my office, that of mistress of the novices."

Calmly and without answering, Bernadette looked at the nun.

"The task imposed on me by our superiors," Mère Marie Thérèse explained, "is to be the goldsmith of your soul, Marie Bernarde, in no other sense, to be sure, than that in which every mother is such, in that she brings up her immature child and seeks to fortify it in soul and body against the perils of life. What, then, will be demanded of you in the immediate future has but the single holy purpose of so forging your soul that the gold be utterly purged of the dross. Is that clear to you?"

"Oh, yes, *ma mère*, I believe that is quite clear."

"I am called to be your spiritual leader henceforth. That is the reason why I mention your visions once again, though I know that you are not fond of having them spoken of. I confess to you frankly that for a long period I did not believe in you and considered your visions hypocritical pretences. Meanwhile, wondrous circumstances have prevailed upon high princes of the Church to decide the case in your favour. I bow to the judgment of these superiors. Nothing else would befit me. For who am I? I therefore believe that at the time of the apparitions you were one of the chosen of Heaven and that an utterly incomprehensible grace did descend upon you, Marie Bernarde. You don't seem to pay attention. Aren't you able to follow me?"

"Oh, yes, I am quite able to follow you, *ma mère*."

"Try to understand, dear Daughter, how your entering

your novitiate among us renders my office more difficult. In general the novices are young things whom we try to train to be genuine and able religious. To what extent these young souls prepare their eternal future ultimately depends upon their spiritual reach. But your case, Marie Bernarde, is no ordinary one. If you are one chosen of grace, my responsibility is increased not only toward you but toward the source of all grace. At fourteen you accepted that ineffable grace as a child does the shining of the sun. But then that is the secret of grace, that it is granted for the merits of our Saviour and for no worthiness of our own. Do you understand that, my Daughter? If you're tired, do sit down on my bed."

"Oh, no, I'm not at all tired, *ma mère*."

"So a new chapter begins for you," said the mistress of the novices with a deep sigh. "You have now, as it were, to catch up with that free grace through your own worthiness of it, in so far as that is humanly possible. That is probably the reason why you yearned to take the veil. The immortal soul continues its life in the beyond, and what it has earned here it possesses there, and what it has not earned here is what it lacks there. You will be favoured in that beyond as we others, the unfavoured of Heaven, will not be. Now wouldn't it be a shame if suddenly in Heaven there appeared that old Bernadette whom I, being her teacher, was able to observe so long: a lazy, dreamy, indifferent creature without the slightest interest in the truths of religion, barely able to read and write and fluttering through life like a moth? A frivolous creature, moreover, who despite an outer modesty was full of stealthy trickery and proud stubbornness, a girl who never wanted for self-conscious and even impertinent reply. The old Bernadette, in other words, who liked best to see the whole world at her feet. That is my opinion of you, Marie Bernarde, as I had occasion to form it years ago. Yet it is your good right after so long a time to say: Mother Vauzous, you are mistaken in me. I am not as you describe me. I haven't any of these faults."

"I have very many faults," Bernadette hastened to say.

The nun suddenly changed the subject. "Did our house physician, Dr. Saint-Cyr, examine you?"

"Yes, when he was here yesterday."

"And what did he say, my child?"

"He said that I was quite well."

"Were those the words he used?"

"Yes, except, of course, for my asthma. But I've always had that."

The mistress of the novices smiled faintly, displaying her gums. "I catch you in your first unveracity. Dr. Saint-Cyr told you frankly that there was something wrong with your lungs."

"It doesn't matter," Bernadette laughed. "I feel quite well."

"Your pious little lie pleases me, *ma fille*. It proves that you suspect that our sufferings and infirmities may become the instrumentalities of help from above. Of these sufferings and infirmities rooted in original sin we must strive to make such instrumentalities. Do you comprehend?"

"I believe I do, *ma mère*."

"Doubtless you will some day, Marie Bernarde. For the moment it remains to be said that it is your right, indeed your duty, to abstain from any work that exceeds your strength."

"Oh, kitchen work doesn't ever bother me, *ma mère*. I'm used to it. . . ."

Marie Thérèse Vauzous rose to her full height. "The chief thing is, Marie Bernarde," she said in a restrained voice, "that you grasp the meaning of our third vow, namely, the vow of obedience. It has nothing to do with obedience as the world conceives it, not even with military obedience, which, as a soldier's daughter, I know thoroughly. Our obedience is not blind or enforced or mechanical; it is freely given; it is seeing and alive. We never lose sight of the truth that in fulfilling our third vow we are working toward our ultimate goal, the preparation and sanctification of the human self for eternity. You and I, my dear Daughter, are from now on united in the pursuit of this goal. I beg you from my heart not to believe that I will bedevil you like an arbitrary teacher. Voluntary giving is the secret. Without it every sacrifice is fruitless, offensive, superfluous. A convent is no prison. No force is exercised here. Until you have made your final profession you may leave this house when you will. No difficulties were made for your predecessor, the novice Angéline. The door was open. This is no place of suffering but one of joys so keen that they rise far, far above all the pleasures of the world. But whatever you do or fail to do, remember the great grace which you must still earn by your sacrifice. And that is all, Marie Bernarde. Good night."

"Good night, *ma mère*."

Bernadette's hand was on the doorknob when Mère Vauzous gave her a last piece of advice:

"Learn at once to fall asleep quickly. The right way of sleeping is the great art of monastics." Speaking thus, the mistress of the novices looked upon her hard couch with its rough blanket. Bernadette, not knowing why, remembered the beautiful round peach which had lain untouched on Vauzous's plate in the chalky whiteness of the moon.

CHAPTER FORTY

This Is Not Yet My Hour

BERNADETTE FAILED to acquire that great art of monastics. Night after night she lay wakeful on her straw sack. It was not the hard couch that prevented sleep. The bed she had once shared with Marie in the Cachot had been much worse than this. Nor was it the hard day's work constantly interrupted by choral prayers, contemplation, searchings of conscience, which kept the brain tense and the nerves from relaxing. It was the flame of life in Bernadette which flickeringly struggled against extinction. Mother Marie Thérèse plied a mighty hammer in order to make her subjects smooth and alike. It was, to be sure, her high aim to forge the souls in her care and to induct them purified into eternal life. In spite of the excellent programme of the general's daughter these young souls always ended up very much like a well-drilled company of recruits. If ever this company were to enter that dwelling where truth and joy are seen face to face, it would probably first have to get rid of the habit of standing in rank and file and feeling in rank and file. Human education always imposes the same hard cross. Unhampered freedom creates a senseless jungle. The uniform creates a sterile wasteland. Hyacinthe de Lafite had probably been quite near the truth when, to the horror of Estrade, he had once said at the Café Français that the world had been made for those few souls of genius who, through what they are, escape the jungle and avoid the wasteland.

Excellent as Bernadette's intentions were, the mistress of the novices failed to hammer her quickly into the smoothness and the evenness of the others. "Marie Bernarde, you loiter as though you were taking a walk in the fields. This is no recreation period." . . . "Marie Bernarde, will you never learn to discipline your eyes? We don't stare but cast our eyes down." . . . "Please don't look at me as full of curiosity as though I were a freak." . . . "Marie Bernarde, you are dreaming again. Don't you understand yet that this wandering of thought and attention is a great fault? We are here for the purpose of concentration, not of reverie and wool-gathering." . . . "Please, Marie Bernarde, what a coarse and common way of speaking! The dialect can still be heard behind your French. And why so loud? What would you do in the house of a contemplative order, of the Carthusians, let us say, who take the vow of silence? We lower our voices in answering. You are definitely falling behind your fellows, Marie Bernarde. . . ."

It was true. Bernadette did not keep up with her fellows. They were already dragging their feet through the halls with short conventual steps; they did not gaze out upon the world with Bernadette's large, wondering eyes, but cast down their lids before Mère Vauzous. Their thoughts did not wander and they answered in subdued voices. Within a few weeks they learned that shadowy, unreal, falsely shy behaviour which Mère Marie Thérèse Vauzous demanded of them even as a hollow rigidity is demanded in a barracks. They submitted easily and hardly knew that they did so. Only the favourite of Heaven found it hard to be engulfed by this convention of appropriateness to sanctity.

Night after night Bernadette lay awake. For the first time she was inclined to quarrel with the lady. She was not presumptuous enough to desire a renewal of vision. But why did the lady never come to her in her dreams when Bernadette dreamed of so many, many things, of long-forgotten people and objects? Only of the most real figure in her life, of her unique and eternal love, she might not dream. If only the lady had come to her in dreams and had said: "Leave this place. Go back to Bartrès and work as Madame Laguès's shepherdess," she would have obeyed instantly, despite her age. But the lady deliberately withdrew from Bernadette's dreams and Bernadette was like a rusty tool that has been cast aside. Another pain increased by night in the novice's breast, the pain she suffered on her mother's account. It was the same piercing pity she had felt on that day of parting. Just because Mamma could not easily give herself and had so rarely been inclined to tenderness, the daughter suffered all the more. There was so much unspoken, so much of life uncommuni-cated between them. A hundred times Bernadette recalled all the misery of the Cachot when her mother went to wash clothes for strangers and there was nothing but corn-mush in the pot and Papa snored in bed under the bright light of day. Her mother was far better off now. Yet Bernadette harboured a dark feeling of guilt because she was permitted to strive for the perfection of her soul here instead of helping her mother. Often the hour of awakening at half-past four found her in tears.

One had to arise quickly and proceed in closed ranks to join the sisters in chapel for early prayer. Thereafter Mère Imbert or one of the older nuns would utter brief reflections concerning some incident in the life of Jesus or concerning the rule of the order, the specific vows, or the striving after perfection. Next, the priest who was to celebrate Mass ap-proached the altar. There was daily communion followed by choral prayer in honour of the Most Blessed Virgin. In this Bernadette took a deep and heart-felt pleasure. Breakfast fol-lowed and then the day's work began. And Bernadette re-joiced in her tasks because they were like her mother's. She fetched water, pared potatoes and turnips, and washed lettuce. Potatoes and turnips and lettuce were so real; the moist odour of earth clung to them. Thus had the earth in Bartrès smelled when she had pressed her face into it. After the noon meal there were more choral prayers. Later the mistress of the novices assembled her charges for earnest admonitory interviews, sometimes as a group, oftener individually. These interviews treated all questions of moral behaviour that did not fall within the secrets of the confessional.

"My dear Marie Bernarde, the sanctification of the self, to which we are obligated, concerns, as you know, our virtues and our faults. Which of your faults did we discuss last time? Help me remember."

"We spoke of my fault, *ma mère*, of still thinking myself extraordinary."

"And what right have you today to harbour such a feeling, *ma fille?*"

As once in school, Bernadette answered with head hung low. "I'm still proud, *ma mère*, because the lady appeared to me."

"After the decision of Monseigneur the bishop of Tarbes, you may openly speak of the Most Blessed Virgin, my dear child. But what do you do to combat your pride? Have you realized all the worthlessness of the howls of applause that once surrounded you?"

Swiftly Bernadette raised her flashing eyes. "I never paid any attention to that, *ma mère*."

"That is not the right answer, Marie Bernarde," said the mistress of the novices, illustrating her inexhaustible patience by the gentleness of her tone. "We've often spoken of this undisciplined way of answering. It would make me very happy to be able to hear an answer of a different kind."

"I have realized the worthlessness of applause, *ma mère*."

"And what penance are you doing in order to break your pride?"

"I have avoided the novice Nathalie for some days," Bernadette said very softly after some reflection.

"Uhum, that is well, *ma chère fille*." Mother Marie Thérèse nodded. "You should more and more limit your contacts with the novice Nathalie, whom I esteem very highly. I'm afraid you are attracted to her for unspiritual reasons. She is pretty and gay. But that is pardonable, my dear child, and I make no reproach of it. Also, the novice Nathalie is of an adaptable nature and that flatters your sense of superiority and dogmatic assertiveness. Were you always so intent on being right in your relations with people?"

"Yes, *ma mère*, I am afraid I always was."

"Then wouldn't it be better to choose for your associate among the novices some hard and unyielding character? Tell me yourself, wouldn't that be better?"

"Oh, yes, *ma mère*, that would certainly be better."

"And now we come to your virtues," the mistress of the novices proceeded. "Which one among them do you hope to cultivate?"

Bernadette was embarrassed and blinked and blushed a little. "I beg your pardon, *ma mère*, but I really believe I have a slight aptitude for drawing. I did a sketch of Nathalie the other day and everyone was pleased."

Marie Thérèse Vauzous struck her hands together. "Stop, my dear child. We don't understand each other at all. You're very far afield. Your aptitude for drawing, which I do not deny, is a talent and not a virtue. A talent is an inclination of nature which it is easy for us to exercise. A virtue is not as wholly natural and its development is a hard, hard matter.

A virtue, for instance, is the ability to bear pain without uttering a sound. Another virtue is that of abstinence. But let us talk no more of drawing. Or must we?"

"Oh, no, *ma mère*, we'll talk about it no more."

"Our order is no school of art," the mistress of the novices said with a chill smile. "We have been assigned the duty of nursing the sick and of teaching children. But it is always the same thing with you, my dear Marie Bernarde. Your whole tendency is in the direction of the extraordinary and showy. . . . It would really delight me if by next Friday you could mention a genuine virtue which you are minded to culti-vate."

But even these pedagogical interviews were not Bernadette's heaviest burden. That was laid on her by the recreational hours granted the novices. There was one each day, from one to two in the afternoon. The Convent of Saint Gildarde had a large and beautiful garden. In its middle was a circular plot of well-trodden lawn which served as a playground for the young novices.

Marie Thérèse, the soldier's daughter, placed a high value on open-air exercise. In that respect she was in her time an exception and an innovator. She considered physical exercise as of great value in balancing prayer, study, work, contem-plation, and the constant searchings of conscience. Yet play, too, was to be subjected to the reason and the will and not be a mere yielding to the perception of bodily delight. All day long the novices were obligated to a thoughtful gait, folded hands, downcast eyes, lowered voices. Between one and two, according to their mistress's system, they were to indulge in gaiety. Hence when they reached the playground Mother Vauzous would say encouragingly: "Now be merry, girls, be cheerful and light-hearted."

That was the signal for a game resembling badminton, or else they tossed a huge ball or threw about little painted hoops or jumped rope or indulged in other childish sports. During this hour the mistress wanted the novices to be the real right innocent chicks of the order who may even indulge in a bit of wanton mischief. Her own astonishing feeling of tact was to draw the boundary beyond which the heavenly Bride-groom might be irritated by a too temperamental behaviour on the part of His future little brides.

Though Bernadette had never been a tomboy, yet in earlier days she had taken a real delight in joining Marie, Jeanne Abadie, Madeleine Hillot, and other girls in such games as the children of the poor can afford. Now she was past twenty. The recession to a childish level which Mère Vauzous de-manded affronted her. Why did those who were in command in the world always desire one to lie? Did that do their hearts some good? The sight of the novices in their long habits hopping about on the plot of grass in a merriment partly natural and partly enforced afflicted Bernadette.

"Dear Marie Bernarde," said the mistress, beckoning to her, "why so depressed? You usually carry your head high. This is the time for recreation. Don't you want to show a little delight too?"

Bernadette did her utmost to show delight. She could not manage it.

It was a grey blustery day of late autumn. Adoration being over, recess threatened to approach. This was the hour at which mail arrived for the inmates of the convent. Marie Thérèse Vauzous called Bernadette. She looked solemn and seemed much moved. She went so far as to take the head of the novice Marie Bernarde between her long bony hands.

"My dear, good child, a heavy sacrifice is required of you

today. I myself know its meaning full well. Our most honest attempts at disassociation from the world cannot break certain ties of nature. I, for instance, cling to my father with anxious love."

Bernadette's eyes were even larger than usual. "My father . . . has anything happened to my father?"

"No, nothing has happened to your father. . . . Dearest Marie Bernarde, summon all the strength you have. It is your mother who has passed away, painlessly and provided with all the comforts of religion. It happened on the day of the commemoration of the Immaculate Conception. That should be a wonderful consolation to you as well as a mysterious confirmation!"

"My mother," Bernadette faltered. "Mamma. . . ."

So sudden a weakness overcame her that even the strict Vauzous pressed the girl to her bosom. "Lie down awhile on my bed here, my child."

Bernadette sat down and leaned against the wall. There was a silence of many minutes. When a tinge of colour returned to Bernadette's face Mère Vauzous said: "It goes without saying that for some days you are excused from all duties that you cannot or care not to perform. If you prefer solitude in your grief, the chapel, the garden, or any other place is open to you. But solitude is not what I would recommend, *ma très chère fille*."

On the nun's grey cheeks appeared the hectically defined red spots of a rising enthusiasm. "Marie Bernarde, in this hour you can aspire beyond yourself! Your mother has died. But there is no death. You will see your mother again. Our Saviour by His death has conquered death. Demonstrate your faith in this truth. Make of your loss a conscious sacrifice. Set an example. Join in the recreation. Let your unshakable faith convert your tears into a sublime gaiety. Don't misunderstand me! It is only a suggestion that I offer. Won't you come?"

After a while Bernadette replied: "Yes, *ma mère*, I'll come."

When the novices appeared two by two on the plot of grass Mère Marie Thérèse beckoned to them. "Our dear Marie Bernarde has just received a grievous blow through the death of her mother. It is the saddest thing that a loving child's heart is called upon to suffer on this earth. But Marie Bernarde is ready to make a sacrifice of her grief. Help your sister by your active play."

She forced into Bernadette's hand one of the badminton rackets. "Let us all play for a few minutes, my dear!" she cried and herself joined in the game, a thing she had never done before and was never to do again.

Bernadette hit the ball, tossed the hoops, ran a race, skipped rope. The latter she did with such speed and hard mechanical persistence that the nun stopped her. "No more, Marie Bernarde! Enough! You're overheated. . . ."

They gathered to go back into the house. An icy wind tore the last yellow leaves from the trees. No more outdoor recreation, the novices reflected. Bernadette and her friend Nathalie walked last. As they were passing through the door into the dark hall Bernadette suddenly crumpled up and had to sit on the flagstones. A throttling cough shook her. Nathalie knelt down beside her. Next she screamed: "Help, please help! . . . Marie Bernarde. . . she's coughing up blood. . . ."

It was one o'clock at night. Through the empty ill-lit streets of Nevers a solitary man was fighting his way against the wind. His own cloak flapped against his stocky figure. He had to hold his broad flat hat with both hands. The prelate was recognizable only by the violet band of this same hat. Monseigneur Forcade needed a long time to reach the convent, however much he hastened. He was driven by the fear that he would arrive too late. Rightly had they roused him from sleep. The approaching death of the miracle-maker of Lourdes required a bishop's presence and testimony. For history teaches that at the passing of the chosen of God miracles are wont to occur. It was furthermore necessary that a high authority of the Church receive the last confession and messages of such a one. Since, moreover, life is immeasurably complicated and the human heart a veritable abyss, there was the ultimate possibility that the girl on the very threshold of death and eternal reckoning might conceivably negate certain testimonies and retract a portion of that upon which the decision of the episcopal commission had been based.

At the door of the convent Mother Joséphine Imbert was waiting for him. The elderly, somewhat corpulent gentleman was quite out of breath and dried his forehead. "Tell me, how is your patient?"

The mother superior, usually the image of calm, was deeply disturbed. The lantern in her hand flickered across her withered face, from which the cheek-bones protruded sharply. "Dr. Saint-Cyr has given up all hope, Your Lordship," she replied. "What a trial, Holy Mother of God!"

"What has been done?" the bishop asked, frowning.

"An hour ago Marie Bernarde was to receive the holy Viaticum. But the steady vomiting made it impossible. She was then provided with all the holy sacraments, Monseigneur."

"Is she conscious, Mère Imbert?"

"Very weak, Monseigneur, but fully conscious."

The bishop, who was familiar with the building, entered the reception room, followed by the mother superior. He took off his cloak and sat down to recover from his exertions. "How could such a thing have happened?" he asked. "Weren't you careful enough of her?"

The mother superior crossed her hands over her bosom. "It was with Your Lordship's consent that we employed the novice in the kitchen. At the advice of Dr. Saint-Cyr we excused her from all hard tasks even during the first week. But we do know that it gave her satisfaction to work in the kitchen."

The bishop threw her a sceptical glance. "Was she too hard driven spiritually and religiously?" Monseigneur asked very frankly.

The mother superior stiffened. "Mère Vauzous was instructed to care for the novice Marie Bernarde with the utmost conscientiousness and attentiveness."

"I have heard from more than one quarter, *ma mère*," said the bishop, "that the recreational activities of the novices here take a somewhat unusual form."

The mother superior's lips seemed to disappear. She bent her head. "It is the opinion of our mistress of novices that playing out of doors is an excellent occasional antidote against the temporary discouragement of these young creatures. Dr. Saint-Cyr gave special orders that Marie Bernarde was not to be excluded from these harmless diversions."

The bishop's sigh came from his very depths. "I'm beside myself, my dear woman, I really am. They place Bernadette Soubirous under our care in the summer and the year is not yet at an end. And the eyes of the whole world are upon her. Imagine the consequences of this sudden death. Think of the talk and think of the scribbling. Good Lord! And the obscure suspicions! Monseigneur Laurence, my colleague of Tarbes, is an upright and admirable old gentleman . . ."

Monseigneur Forcade preferred to leave this sentence unfinished. He asked rather to be conducted at once to the girl's death chamber. It was the infirmary of the house, a rather large room. Bernadette was bedded on high pillows. She lay supine and without stirring. Her little face was shrunken after the severe hæmorrhage and the many hours of vomiting. Her eyes shone and kept their characteristic lofty apathy. Her breath, however, was so short and rattling that one would have thought her at the point of death. Dr. Saint-Cyr was watching the pulse. Fèbvre, the house chaplain, whispered the prayers for the dying, which two kneeling sisters murmured after him. The mistress of the novices stood upright, petrified, with folded hands. Her face had an odd greenish tinge and her deep-set eyes were fixed on Bernadette with a famished tension. Monseigneur Forcade approached the bed. He placed his chubby hand tenderly on the sick girl's. "Can you hear me, my daughter?" he asked.

Bernadette nodded affirmatively.

"Have you any wish to communicate to me as your bishop?" Gently she shook her head.

"Are you strong enough to speak?"

Again she shook her head.

Forcade knelt down and prayed. Deeply moved, he arose and requested the mother superior to provide him with a cell for the night. Following Mother Imbert down the corridor, he heard behind him the clatter of heavy shoes. It was the mistress of the novices.

"Your Lordship," Marie Thérèse said in a trembling voice, "will not the Blessed Virgin be angry at us to have to receive her favourite above without the final vows?"

"You think so?" the bishop asked rather harshly. A vague feeling of discomfort reached him from this nun. "Would you desire the dying girl to take the final vows?"

"I would indeed wish it very much, Monseigneur." The woman was excited and her breath came hard.

Bishop Forcade, a very clever man, was intensely disturbed at the thought of the upright and admirable old gentleman in Tarbes. A novice is neither fish nor flesh. Perhaps the catastrophe would be somewhat mitigated if Bernadette were properly admitted to the ranks of the religious who by virtue of their vows have attained special merit. Hence he said: "The bishop is empowered to receive the final profession of the dying. It wouldn't be the first time that I've done so."

They re-entered the room. Marie Bernarde's condition was unchanged. Monseigneur Forcade bent over her face and said in a tender voice: "Summon all your strength, dear one. She who so graciously appeared to you would wish you in time to take the three vows of poverty, chastity, and obedience, in your bishop's presence. You need merely answer my questions by an affirmative gesture. Did you understand me and are you willing?"

Bernadette nodded in a rather lively way. Whereupon the bishop, speaking very softly and with the utmost delicacy, performed this most unusual ceremony of the acceptance of final profession. The room was full of nuns who had thrown themselves to the floor, especially Marie Thérèse Vauzous. After the ceremony the physician gave the exhausted patient a few drops of water, the first thing she had been able to retain in many hours. The bishop smiled at her. "I congratulate you upon your new rank, my Sister."

An armchair was placed beside the bed for him. He looked up at Dr. Saint-Cyr. The look meant to ask: How much longer? The physician shrugged his shoulders. A fifteen minutes' utter silence. The eyes of Monseigneur did not leave the girl's face. Attentively he watched the desperate struggle for each breath, and thought: The end cannot be far. He made a last attempt: "It may be that there is some burden on your heart, my Sister. I am here to take it from you. All the others will leave. . . ."

No sooner had the bishop whispered these words than something most unexpected came to pass. Bernadette took several very deep breaths. Everyone thought they were her last and Father Fèbvre raised his voice in the prayers for the dying. They were not the last breaths, however, but the first normal ones that commonly succeed an asthmatic attack. And suddenly Bernadette said in a low but normal voice: "My mother is dead . . . but I'm not going to die yet."

She had spoken the truth, as she always did. Six days later she was able to arise from her bed and Dr. Saint-Cyr could actually hear fewer suspicious noises in her lungs than before.

The Wages of Affliction

CHAPTER FORTY-ONE

Faery Hands

ADJOINING THE chapel of the Convent of Saint Gildarde
there was a spacious room. It was part vestry, part depository
of art objects. The walls were hung with darkened old paintings which had been acquired in the course of the years
and for which no better place could be found. For the Congregation of the Ladies of Nevers was quite an old one. It
had been founded by Jean Baptiste de Laveyne almost two
hundred years before, and although the convent building had
had to be re-erected after the storms of the Revolution, many
previous possessions had been saved. The largest of the paintings that hung in the vestry was an eighteenth-century Holy
Family, a rather insensitive and awkward piece of work. The
Mother and Child were amid the straw. There were the ox
and the ass and the adoring shepherds, even as Bernadette knew
and loved the scene. The only unusual thing about the painting was that Saint Joseph, contrary to all tradition, wore no
beard but a sort of beret on his head. In chests along the vestry
wall vestments, paraments, and altar-cloths were stored. A few
religious utensils of gold and silver were in a vitrine. In a special chest a group of garishly coloured figures was kept for
the annual showing of the Christmas manger.

This sacristy or vestry became Bernadette's domain. A year
after the hæmorrhage she renewed her profession to the bishop
of Nevers. Thus she served her full novitiate after all. Thereafter the bishop insisted that she be relieved of nursing the
sick, as she had chosen to do. At his behest Mother Imbert had

to entrust to Sister Marie Bernarde the most delicate and the lightest office within the gift of the house. This was the office of the sacristan who every morning filled the ciborium with the prepared wafers. It happened that the very aged Sister Sophie could no longer fulfil even these light duties. A cerebral hæmorrhage had paralysed her left side and robbed her of speech. Sophie was one of those radiant child-like souls such as one does not meet out in the world. Though her lips could mumble only unintelligible sounds now, her eyes sent forth rays of such tranquillity and serene joy that Bernadette was happy whenever, hours at a time, the old woman watched her at her work.

Her new office involved a notable circumstance. Since the mistress of the novices had, on that certain day, repudiated with sincere misgiving Bernadette's passionate desire to be permitted "to cultivate the virtue of her aptitude for drawing," the young nun now become a sacristan devoted herself to a kindred occupation. Not even Marie Thérèse Vauzous regarded the embroidering of altar-cloths, vestments, and similar ecclesiastical articles as conducive to the pride or vanities of art. It was in fact a tranquil and pleasing occupation well befitting a nun of limited physical strength. Bernadette, who during her novitiate had felt within her the urge to create images and pictures, had now found the best possible field for her activity. Her soul and character were ever the same. To the observer she often appeared indifferent, wandering, and feeble. But whenever, impelled by a hidden power, she fixed her will upon a definite goal, nothing could deter her—neither Jacomet, nor Dutour, nor Massy, nor Peyramale, nor the bishop, nor the Emperor, nor, finally, the granite-like resistance of the nun Vauzous.

Thus Bernadette was enabled with faery hands to reproduce on the consecrated fabrics the forms and colours which arose

within her. In addition to the necessary materials she had been
provided with drawing-paper and crayons for making preliminary sketches of the work to be executed. Her designs were so
out of the ordinary, so highly individual in fact, that it took
the delighted appreciation of sundry connoisseurs of art among
the clergy to soothe the anxious fright of Mother Imbert and
the frosty astonishment of Mother Vauzous. After that people
asked now and then to see the new works of Sister Marie
Bernarde. Mother Imbert permitted them to be shown only
in the artist's absence. For the administrators of the convent
continued to mistake their young sister's authenticity of impulse for a vain hunt after distinction. Thus Bernadette had
not the slightest notion of the effectiveness of her embroidered
dreams.

She devoted herself insatiably to this occupation. She had
complete command of her time, since at the special order of
the bishop she had been relieved of all other tasks and even of
the severer regulations of the order. She who had never had a
drawing-lesson could be seen kneeling on the floor surrounded
by sheets of paper. At first she had followed models and pat-
terns. Next her small untaught hands began to invent flowers
her eye had never seen as well as ornaments that were like the
symbols of an unknown faith. There was a lamb like a unicorn,
a cross upon its forehead. The seeress who had had the supernatural power to see the lady's apotheosized body carried
within her soul innumerable forms and visions. The process
was wholly unconscious. She knew not what would come from
her fingers nor how it came. Whenever a few sketches were
completed she laid them in old Sister Sophie's lap. The speechless woman would then try to decide between the good and
the less good. A brief comparison, a nod or two, and the right
design was selected. Next the fabric was set in the embroidery
frame and the labour began, difficult and endless as Penelope's.

But Bernadette knew no impatience. It was as though with many-coloured silk she wove away the seconds of her own life, putting them behind her, one after another, with calm serenity.

Her work was interrupted only by common prayers, meals, the adoration, the rosary, the stations of the cross, and night itself. She joined the sisters' recreation only when she felt the impulse. In some free hour Sister Nathalie would slip into the sacristy. She, too, was fond of watching and judging the work. Once she asked: "You saw the Most Blessed Virgin with your own eyes, *ma sœur*. Why do you never delineate your vision on an altar-cloth?"

"Oh, no, *ma sœur*, what are you thinking of? The lady cannot be drawn or painted or embroidered."

Nathalie was surprised. "Perhaps your memory of the lady is no longer so clear?"

"Oh, it is so clear, so very clear." Bernadette smiled with gaze fixed upon the world beyond the window and spoke no more.

Nevers was a sombre medieval little town. As late as March it was dark in the sacristy shortly after four o'clock. Therefore by three Bernadette would take her work to the window so as to lose none of the last light of day. This was a quiet hour during which the nuns were wont to conduct their daily examination of conscience. In recent years the recess of the novices had been put an hour later. At times Bernadette could hear the many pairs of feet of the returning girls or an admonition of the mistress of the novices. Next to her in the chapel the sister organist began to practise.

There was a knocking at the door. The gate-keeper came to announce that a caller for Sister Marie Bernarde had arrived.

Madame la Supérieure was having the man directed to the sacristy. He would be here in a moment. Bernadette lifted her head in astonishment. A caller? There was almost none. What man could it be? Bernadette could not but gratefully remember that Mother Imbert permitted no curiosity-seekers to annoy her. Quite by accident she would now and then learn from the sisters that some outstanding personality or association had desired to make a show of the famous Soubirous. She had made the request once and for all to be permitted to remain in her cell whenever strangers were shown through the cloister. What caller could this be?

Bernadette rose. Her eyes, tired out by her work, were able to distinguish in the dim doorway only the tall slender figure of a man too shy to enter.

"Praised be Jesus Christ," the man greeted her softly and formally.

"In all eternity, amen," Sister Marie Bernarde replied. "What can I do for you?"

"I came just to find out how you are, *ma sœur*."

He took a long step forward and bowed. Bernadette's heart stood still. The embarrassed man was her father, whom she had not seen in many, many years. With outstretched arms she went slowly toward him and whispered: "Papa, it is you. . . . Is it possible?"

"Yes, yes, I came here by train, Marie Bernarde."

She bit her lips and tried to laugh. "Why do you call me '*ma sœur*' and 'Marie Bernarde'? Am I not Bernadette to you?"

She embraced him and laid her hooded head against his face. But the miller François Soubirous could not yet bring himself to relax. Since his daughter, the wonder-worker of Lourdes, had in addition become a nun of a strict order, his paternal embarrassment had assumed terrifying proportions. It still frightened him sometimes to think of the day when he had told this daughter to join the tumblers and gipsies. He returned her embrace with a reverent pressure.

Bernadette was mistress of herself again. "How good of you to come, Papa!"

"I inquired years ago, Bernadette. At that time they said it was not desirable. And after your mother died, you know, I was like a lost soul, I couldn't budge. . . ."

Bernadette closed her eyes. Her voice was soft and thoughtful. "Mamma . . . how did Mamma die?"

The miller Soubirous's hair had turned grey. He was now in his early fifties. His character, not without its solemn dignity even amid indigence and the fumes of drink, had acquired through the years and their circumstances a touch of the religious. He crossed himself.

"Your mother died an easy death, little Bernadette. She was sick only a few days and did not know how grave it was. Saint Joseph—may he help us all to an easy death—gave her his help. And you were her great joy, my child, you only. She kept your picture in her bosom. For there are many pictures of you to be had nowadays. And your name was on her lips to the last. . . ."

"Mamma knew that day that we would not meet again. I didn't know it." Bernadette nodded and whispered to her dead: "*Praoubo de jou.*"

"And we had little pictures of her made," said Soubirous proudly. "They are called miniatures and the painter gets good pay for them. I've brought you one."

François gave his daughter a gilt medallion on a little chain. The plain features of poor Louise had been vulgarly idealized. "May you accept it?" he asked, thinking of the monastic vow of poverty.

"I believe the mother superior won't object," said Bernadette, who took a child-like delight in the picture. She drew a chair forward for Soubirous. "Do tell me, Papa, how is everybody at home?"

Soubirous cleared his throat in a manner to show his satisfaction that the difficult ice had now been broken. "Well, my dear child, I can't complain. Business isn't bad. I was always an able miller, as you know, and it was only the lean years which got me down and truly not me alone. Nowadays we millers can't catch up with the work. Since last autumn we have fifteen hotels in Lourdes. Imagine that—fifteen. And Lacadé has built a huge municipal hospital with hundreds and hundreds of beds. It's called the Hospital of the Seven Sorrows. And the upper Lapaca mill has a contract for the partial supply of this hospital. And your brothers Jean Marie and Justin are pretty able millers and I don't let them have much time for follies. They both send you kind greetings. And your sister Marie has a boy and two girls. She'll come to see you tomorrow with other old friends from Lourdes. And I thank God that I've been able to put by a bit of money for my children and grandchildren against the day when I am no more."

Bernadette had been listening as tensely as though she had difficulty in hearing. "Ah, Papa," she said, "it makes my heart light to hear how well you are all faring."

François Soubirous could not keep his eyes from becoming moist. "And I often have a heavy heart, Bernadette, when I think by night of how little I could give you in those years in the Cachot and how much better I could do by you now."

Bernadette smiled. "In those days, Papa, I didn't feel it in the least. And now, now I lack nothing."

"Is that really so, my dear child?" Soubirous asked in a sombre tone. "It seems to me you look very pale."

"It's only the coif. It makes us all look pale. I'm very well. I never was better. I haven't even asthma any more. . . ." And as though to change this particular subject she asked intently: "When did your train arrive, Papa?"

"Just an hour ago. . . . And the others, they'll come tomorrow."

"Dear God, you must be hungry and thirsty." The thought startled her and she ran out and down the halls and dared to knock at the mother superior's door. Breathlessly she panted: "Madame la Supérieure, my father has just come from the train. He's had nothing to eat or drink all day. May I . . ."

"But of course, my dear. Ask the assistant sister for coffee and cake and a liqueur."

Bernadette brought in the tray herself and set the little table in her workroom for her father. Her cheeks were on fire with happiness that she could perform this womanly service, her mother's endless service, this one time. With delighted eyes she watched her father, who was hungry and also shy at the thought of eating among saints' pictures and vestments. At last she filled the little glass with liqueur. Soubirous half feigned to decline, but not quite sincerely. "For some time now," he said in his grandiose way, "I've been taking no more than an occasional drop of wine and no brandy at all. It doesn't go with hard work."

Bernadette smiled. "But, Papa, you have no hard work to do today." And her soul remembered the dangerous distillation which her mother used to keep under lock and key.

"Do you really think so?" The miller wavered. "Well, it was a long trip."

"Look, I'm going to drink to your health," she said encouragingly. "I'm not a bit afraid." She tilted the little glass without a grimace. That made a difference, Soubirous considered, and after the third glass he felt thoroughly comfortable in this consecrated environment of which his daughter was the mistress. There was not much more conversation; the well of communication between them had long gone dry. Bernadette lighted a few candles. The dark painting assumed colours it did not really possess. The young nun sat beneath it. Saint Joseph, patron saint of an easy death, seemed solemnly detached from the background. The Mother of God smiled at her Child. Father Soubirous could not quite repel the reflection that in some way this was the family of his little daughter, too.

He had long forgotten his drunken hour at Babou's and the blasphemous question of the brigadier d'Angla.

CHAPTER FORTY-TWO

Many Visitors

THE GROUP of visitors that arrived at the Convent of Saint Gildarde on the next day, though apparently assembled at haphazard, yet constituted a veritable delegation of the city of Lourdes to its most famous child. Mayor Lacadé had sent his secretary Courrèges and Dean Peyramale had sent Father Pomian to bring back authentic news concerning the wellbeing of Sister Marie Bernarde. For out in the world nothing was any longer heard of Bernadette. The newspapers wrote of her no more. Even the news of her mortal illness and recovery therefrom seeped through only gradually and vaguely.

Father Pomian was the leader of the group which had had a long and complicated journey to take. The emissary of the mayor had been joined by Bernadette's father, her sister, now the wife of a small farmer near Saint-Pé de Bigorre, Aunt Bernarde (the acute family oracle undulled by the years), Aunt Lucille, and also two strangers of sharply opposed character, the cured invalid Louis Bouriette and the proprietress of the most important dressmaking establishment in Lourdes, Antoinette Peyret. These two had also been delegated by others to bring back an account of the well-being of Marie Bernarde —the dressmaker by the widow Millet and Bouriette by the miller Antoine Nicolau. Madame Millet was now a very old sick woman and superstitiously afraid of the railroad. Therefore she had not, despite her yearning for Bernadette, been able to bring herself to undertake this exhausting trip but had sent her true and tried messenger. Antoine had not been able to bring himself to take the trip, either, for very different reasons, and had been obliged to send a far less expert messenger. The company had used the many changes of train required by the journey to view famous cities on the route. Only Father Soubirous had impatiently hastened ahead from the last stop.

Bernadette lay awake all night. Seeing her father again had told on her nerves. Her imagination, tamed at such cost to herself or forcibly directed into other channels, had been troublingly aroused. Images out of the past oppressed her. The announcement of tomorrow's visitors filled her with more fear than joy.

Mother Joséphine Imbert and Mother Marie Thérèse Vauzous insisted on personally receiving the delegation from Lourdes. At the behest of the mother superior, refreshments were provided for the guests. Bernadette was dismayed by these gatherers of news concerning her and the character assumed by the event. The people sat stiffly in the larger of the two reception rooms, a dreary chamber with red plush chairs, a clumsy sofa, an iron stove which usually smoked, a grey crucifix, and a blue picture of the Virgin on the wall. The greetings were as formal as though nobody had ever met anybody before. Father Pomian, abandoned apparently by his sense of humour, began the proceedings with formal words: "It is my pleasant duty, *ma sœur*, to convey to you cordial greetings from Dean Peyramale. He is very well in spite of being overwhelmed by work. You can imagine, *ma sœur*, how his responsibilities have increased since you left us. There are days when not only thousands of pilgrims arrive but whole trainloads of the grievously sick from all parts of the world. At times even our dean hardly knows where to begin. He will be overjoyed at a message from you, Sœur Marie Bernarde. What may I convey to him from you?"

"Oh, Father," Bernadette answered softly after an interval, "I am so very grateful to the dean for remembering me."

Madame la Supérieure nodded with delight at this formally faultless answer. Its deep, simple sincerity was lost on her.

Next Courrèges conveyed the mayor's greetings: "You have no idea how proud we are of you, *ma sœur*. The municipality has acquired the Cachot from André Sajou. It will be preserved just as it was."

"It ought to be torn down!" Bernadette was frightened and almost violent. "The yard was so dirty. . . ."

"That could never be done." The secretary smiled indulgently. "The house is of historical import. A memorial tablet will be affixed to it some day."

Bernadette glanced shyly at Mother Imbert. Heavens, what would she think! And it was no fault of her own. To change the subject quickly, she asked: "And how is your daughter, dear Annette, Monsieur?"

"Oh, she got married like most of the girls of her vintage, *ma sœur*, all except Cathérine Mengot, of whom there's not much good to tell."

Since the conversation leaped feebly across such areas the humblest of the callers, Louis Bouriette, took courage and delivered the greeting of him by whom he had been sent. The miller Antoine was well. He was living with his mother, who was still hale; and as one of the most impressive local figures Antoine could be seen carrying the great flag that headed the processions to Massabielle. This was no more than he deserved as the first man who had witnessed the visions. Bernadette smiled faintly at Bouriette's awkward words without returning the greetings of Antoine. But the clumsy messenger, desirous of interpreting some of the feelings of his patron, began, half in dialect and half in French, to boast of what had been accomplished by a little girl from the Rue des Petites Fossées in the world.

"A pity that you don't know the new Lourdes, *ma sœur*. You'd be amazed. Nothing but very big shops in which you can buy big images of the Blessed Virgin and candles galore and glasses and beakers for the spring and rosaries of all sizes and at all prices, and your picture, of course, *ma sœur*. There are pictures of you to be had, *ma sœur*, from two sous up."

"That's all I'm worth," Bernadette said curtly.

That frightened Bouriette. He was afraid he had disgraced Antoine by a stupid blunder.

"Oh, there are much more expensive pictures of you, *ma sœur*. The big ones in colours fetch two francs fifty apiece."

Bernadette looked down. Would the unhappy blunderer never stop? But Bouriette, the stonemason, was not Antoine Nicolau. Deeper and deeper he slid into the mire.

"And whole big books about you can be bought by those who can read them, *ma sœur*. In those books everything is recorded exactly as it was."

Bernadette folded her hands convulsively, as she was wont to do at moments of anguish. But nothing could stop Bouriette, who, in the name of his patron, was determined to make Bernadette's heart rejoice. "And they're planning to build a panorama in which the whole story will be told in paintings on a circular wall. And it's going to be called 'The Bernadette Soubirous Panorama.' "

After these words Mother Imbert arose. "I believe, dear Sister Marie Bernarde, that your guests will now want to view our beautiful chapel. If anyone desires to see your embroidery work, feel quite free to show some examples. Sister Marie Bernarde has very skilful hands, ladies and gentlemen. . . . Later you will want to be alone for a little with your family, *ma fille.* You are at liberty, of course, to receive your sister and your aunts in your own cell."

Bernadette, speaking in a monotone, constituted herself a guide and showed what was worth seeing in the cloister, as was done on Sunday afternoons. The news of her embroideries had reached Lourdes. Especially Antoinette Peyret, herself an artist of the needle, insisted on seeing something of them. Only after long pleading did Bernadette, visibly uncomfortable, spread out a few specimens on the sacristy table.

Peyret was confused. "Holy Virgin, think of all the things you can do, *ma sœur!* What originals did you copy?"

Indifferently Bernadette answered: "There are no models for such things."

"You mean to say you make up all these remarkable birds, flowers, beasts, decorative designs, out of your own head?"

"Yes, Mademoiselle, I make them up out of my own head."

"I always knew you had a lot in that head of yours," said she of the crooked shoulder who was accustomed to try to convince everybody that she had been the original discoverer of the thaumaturgist of Lourdes.

"And you see, Mademoiselle, I don't even yet know what is in that little head," Mother Vauzous said jestingly. She had just appeared in the door of the sacristy.

"And what work!" Peyret vicariously boasted. "Just the work alone. But nothing ever is difficult for you, *ma sœur.* Everything you touch succeeds."

"Oh, I found this work very difficult, Mademoiselle Peyret," Bernadette defended herself.

But the secretary Courrèges, true disciple of his chief, wagged his head significantly. "If one could offer some of these things for sale in one of our great religious bazaars, one could get hundreds and hundreds for them."

"Oh, no!" Bernadette hastened to say. "These things are only for our convent." Hastily she folded up her work and put it away.

Later she took her sister and her two aunts to her cell. Four people, including the robust Bernarde Casterot, so filled the cell that there was scarcely room to stand. "And you live here, my child?" Aunt Bernarde asked.

"Yes, I live here, Aunt, when I pray or reflect or sleep."

"I can easily see, my good child, that you pray and reflect more than you eat," said the oracle, not so willing as the others to resign an erstwhile superiority.

"We have very good food here," Bernadette assured her, "and I enjoy it very much."

Bernarde Casterot was far from being convinced. She shook her head. "I'd like to see you better nourished. I'll have a word with Madame la Supérieure. As your godmother and the representative of your blessed mother, I have the right to do so. You must take care of yourself. The Casterots have always been robust, in spite of the misfortune we had with your mother. I wish I could say as much for your father's family."

Bernadette drew Marie close to her. Her sister had grown plump and had been shyly standing aside. "You haven't told me a thing yet, dear Sister."

"There's not much to tell about me, Bernadette. I'm just a peasant woman."

"Papa tells me you're happy and have children."

"Happy!" Marie gave a sudden laugh. "If there's bread in the house and the harvest isn't a failure and nobody is sick or unhappy, then one is called happy. Yes, I have children, too, three of 'em, and a fourth is on the way."

"And yet you came to see me, dear Sister."

"Peasant women, my dear Sister, work up into the ninth

month. I'm not so feeble. And it was a grand trip and I did see you again. I want you to know, too, that I don't always look as big as a barrel."

"You look very pretty, dear Sister," said Bernadette, surveying the coarse-looking woman with her red, knotted hands. Her own hands were no longer those of a worker, but pallid and slim. But that woman was Marie, with whom she had shared the bed and who had inspired her with such loathing after the visions. Suddenly, with the unconscious immodesty of pregnant women, Marie grasped her sister's hand and pressed it to her belly. "Just feel how it stirs!" she laughed.

Bernadette felt the warm flesh under the garment and felt a light twitching which thrilled her strangely. Quickly she withdrew her hand.

The departure of the visitors was set for the next forenoon. The mother superior bade Bernadette, in company of another nun, to conduct her relatives and friends to the train. There was a long period of lingering on the train platform. The usual empty and anguished farewell phrases were spoken. All acted as though the parting were one for time alone.

"We'll come again, Bernadette. . . . We're coming soon again, dear child. . . . Can't you manage to be sent to the convent at Lourdes some time? . . . So many of you sisters live there. . . ."

"Oh, I might be sent to Lourdes some day. . . . At all events, Papa, Marie, we'll soon meet again whether here or there. . . ."

In spite of the chatter Bernadette knew that the farewell was not for time but for eternity. The whole thing made her dizzy. It was years since she had been among men on an open thoroughfare. She felt so wretched that she could hardly keep herself erect. But before the train left, Father Pomian took her aside.

"I have still one quite private message to you from the dean, *ma sœur.* He asked me to give you this little picture of the Mother of God. It's the same one he gives to the schoolchildren. But he bade me tell you that if ever you stand in need of him, just send him the little picture."

She thanked him absent-mindedly and put the picture away.

It is not very pleasant for nuns to walk through populated streets. Some people salute them, others give them hostile looks, a few of the superstitious cross their fingers. On the swift way home Bernadette reflected: The disassociation is complete, though I didn't know it. I have nothing more in common with all those people on the train. I am grateful from the heart to Mother Vauzous. Oh, what a trying day this has been! . . .

In the refectory at home the sisters were taking their seats at table. Again as on Bernadette's second day in the cloister Mère Marie Thérèse lifted her voice. "Our dear sister Marie Bernarde has had visitors from the outside world. After many years she saw her closest relatives again and a few friends. It would benefit us all greatly if we could hear something of the effect of such a meeting upon a soul striving for disassociation from the world. We'd be so grateful to you, *ma sœur,* for some edifying words on the subject."

But Bernadette did not stir from her seat. Calmly she said: "Oh, *ma mère,* you can't strike words of edification from a stone."

CHAPTER FORTY-THREE

The Sign

SISTER SOPHIE died. It was a quiet, smiling death, very creditable to Saint Joseph. They did not carry her to the infirmary. She kept indicating that she wanted to stay in the house. During her last days she could hardly bear anyone but Bernadette about her. Since Sœur Sophie had been the most beloved and venerated of the nuns, her preference for Marie Bernarde was the cause of many little pangs of jealousy. Again and again the character itself of the girl of Lourdes brought to naught the far-sighted planning of her life and conduct by Mother Imbert and Mother Vauzous. This plan's purpose was to make the given personality conform to a type which was to be that of all the ladies of the order, namely, a blending of Benedictine piety with sturdy activity of a charitable nature. In the recipient of the grace of Massabielle it had been hoped that a very paradigm would be found—a quite simple and passive child's soul without marked characteristics. Yet that kind of Bernadette would never have fought the valiant combat for her lady. An original and specially selected soul was to subordinate itself within the ranks of those who were most lacking in well-defined individuality. Bernadette would have been profoundly prepared to make this sacrifice, too, had she but been able to do so. But here, as everywhere, she was a secret divider of souls. Without opening her lips she aroused faith and unfaith, admiration and resistance. She created passionate partisans of herself, like that Sister Nathalie, for instance, who had meanwhile become so able a woman that Mother Imbert

502

planned soon to appoint her as one of her two assistants. And the dying Sœur Sophie had so emphatically preferred her that she had beckoned to the others to leave when the girl of Lourdes was at her side.

Now, death in a cloister is fundamentally different from death in the world. Death in the world may be likened to an accident during the building of a skyscraper. One of the sweating riveters plunges from the scaffolding; for a few seconds his comrades take their pipes out of their mouths; stealthily they blink into the abyss, knowing that today or tomorrow the same fate may be theirs. In the cloister death is the festivity that marks the completion of a soul, such as the guilds of masons and carpenters celebrate when a house has been finished. Tirelessly one has been working toward this unique day. Now one can take a deep breath and hope that one's sure dwelling-place is for evermore established. A day of someone's death in a cloister may well give rise to a sensation of festive curiosity. The nuns are fond of surrounding her who is dying and of praying fervently. They believe that they can help their sister in her final throes. They have the sense of being, as it were, midwives of the supernatural birth of a soul into another world. And this is so, above all, in a case such as Sophie's, who had been by far the oldest and most experienced among them and had celebrated the fiftieth anniversary of her taking the veil. From the death of such a one there was wont to emanate a great grace to encourage and sustain the survivors.

This grace was now received by Bernadette. It was the first death that she had witnessed with her own eyes, and though it was so easy a one, it ploughed up her very foundations. Youth ceases at the moment when death becomes a reality to us. Bernadette clung to the eyes of the dying nun, who consciously fought again and again to smile. This smile was to stream into the soul of the witness. Bernadette knew of a cer-

tainty that the speechless woman was speaking of her lady.
The smile was saying: Let nothing make you weaken. The
lady knows exactly what she is doing. She knows why she
came to you and to none other. She knows why she is giving
you this life to lead, too. It couldn't be different; it had to be
thus. But when one has come to the place where I am, one is
glad and light of soul and happier than any. But you will be
much more glad than I, for your lady beholds you in life and
in death.

After Sœur Sophie's funeral Bernadette tried to take up her
embroidering again. She could not do so. It was as though her
hands were frozen. Her eyes could not distinguish the colours
of the silken threads. It was as though the lady were saying in
her own person: Enough of this game! She understood and
abandoned the game. Now came a year during which Mother
Imbert and the chaplain Father Fèbvre observed a change
come over Marie Bernarde. She revealed herself to no one.
What happened was that she no longer took the life of a
religious as a task which she, a pupil, had to learn to master, but
as a path which must be consciously trodden to its end. Though
she still enjoyed all kinds of dispensations at the behest of the
careful bishop, she was now observed to share all exercises with
a new attentiveness and intensity. The nuns of Saint Gildarde
were not of a contemplative order; they were women active in
hospitals and schools. Nocturnal prayers were neither rule nor
custom. Only a few very old nuns who had been relieved of
toil arose at three o'clock in the morning and said their matins
in the chapel. More and more often Marie Bernarde was now
seen to join these, until the mother superior forbade this early
rising in view of her delicate health. It was as though Bernadette had now to exert herself to the utmost in combat against
something that pressed in upon her from all sides.

The convent paid for but a single subscription to a single

paper. It was *L'Univers,* whose famous editor, Louis Veuillot, had once upon a time broken a lance for Bernadette and the miracle of Lourdes. In reality even this paper was read only by the mother superior and the mistress of the novices. The other nuns did not take much interest in the news of the day and were too tired in their leisure moments to read a paper. Yet days now came on which the copy of the paper was passed from hand to hand. Bold headlines announced: War Is Declared . . . The Crime of Prussia . . . On to Berlin! Next, great victories were announced. Then lesser victories were announced. Then one read with terror the names of the French cities that had fallen into the enemy's hands and last of all one read that the Emperor Napoléon had been captured by the enemy who was laying siege to Paris.

During the very first weeks of the catastrophe the mother house of Saint Gildarde was quickly emptied. The first group of able-bodied nursing-sisters left for the war hospitals that had been established in Paris and elsewhere. But since the war proved a very bloody one and since epidemics broke out here and there, the authorities called for more and more nurses. Even the nuns trained to be teachers had now to answer the call. The few who remained behind in the mother house and the two hundred branch houses of the Ladies of Nevers had to pick oakum and roll bandages. Bernadette did the same. But her restlessness increased from day to day and she kept imploring Mother Imbert to assign her to a hospital, since she had learned nursing in the days of her novitiate. The mother superior put her off with the consolation that she would bring the matter to Monseigneur's attention at the first opportunity. But Bishop Forcade was not inclined to subject to any danger the precious being confided to his care by Laurence of Tarbes. Confusing circumstances now set in. An archbishopric fell vacant. Bishop Forcade was elected to occupy it. The bishopric of Nevers remained unoccupied for several days. During this brief interval the vicar general of the diocese granted Sœur Marie Bernarde's request. The hospital of Nevers was overcrowded, since wounded men had been brought from Paris even to this distant point. A great part of the former nursing-staff had been sent west and north. Every hand, above all every skilled hand, was desperately needed. Hence Bernadette Soubirous was assigned to nursing-duty at the hospital of Nevers. Mère Marie Thérèse Vauzous could not bear to remain inactive, either. Saint Gildarde's was empty and desolate. The mistress of the novices, though her training had been exclusively pedagogical, asked for hospital duty. She was attached to the local hospital, too, as a supervising sister.

Now a new Bernadette was again revealed. Aunt Bernarde used to say that all the Casterots were born half-doctors. Louise Soubirous had often proved the truth of this saying not only in her handling of the case of the Bouhouhorts child but of many other children in the Rue des Petites Fossées. Bernadette now proved that she was indeed a Casterot and the idea seemed not extravagant that the lady who had appeared to do something to stem the sickness of the world had made a prudent choice in this respect, too.

No one knew in the halls of the hospital that Sœur Marie Bernarde was the girl of Lourdes. She seemed a nursing-sister like any other, distinguished solely by her unusually large eyes and pleasant features. Yet it came to pass that ever more of the wounded and the sick asked for her, even in the rooms where she had never been on duty. Day and night there was a crying for Sœur Marie Bernarde. Alleviation seemed to flow from her touch; her glance brought refreshment. Victoriously there re-arose that resolute aspect of her character, the Casterot heritage, which the conventual life had repressed. In the hospital there were very many wounded of those regiments of the line and of cavalry which drew their supplementary recruits from Pau and Tarbes and all the Pyrenean districts. With these Bernadette spoke in the provincial dialect, which she still used more easily and naturally than standard French. Her use of the tongue was so unspoiled, her replies so telling, her jests so full of native country drollness, that wherever her occupation took her she left behind a trail of laughter and of ease. When a stubborn case made trouble, Marie Bernarde was called. The work was beyond the strength of any. Bernadette's energy grew to meet the demand. Colour returned to her cheeks. The doctors and the clerics in charge sang her praises, which reached the ears of Monseigneur Lelonge, the new bishop.

Marie Thérèse Vauzous no less did her utmost and beyond, and exceeded the limits of her strength. She sacrificed her nights and refused her hours of recuperation. She kept strictest watch to see that the directions of the physicians were exactly carried out and that the patients were punctually given generous portions of well-prepared food. For hours she would stand in the kitchen and in the linen-rooms counting and reckoning and recounting with her own insatiable scrupulousness. Then again she moved slowly from room to room and from bed to bed, her deep-set clear eyes alert to observe whether all was as it should be. Yet no voice asked for the nun Vauzous, although she was a hundred times more practically useful than Bernadette. She, too, said the kindest things to the sick and wounded, wrote letters for them, and to the poorest she promised help for the future. And yet at her appearance a slight sensation of fright passed from bed to bed, as though a high officer had arrived to inspect men subject to punishment. On a certain evening Marie Bernarde and Marie Thérèse happened to be alone in the nurses' sitting-room.

"I've known you for a very long time, *ma sœur*," said the

former mistress of the novices, "and I assure you that my respect for you grows from day to day. You do know how to enchant people and how to win over the ugly and stubborn in an instant. Long ago I was your teacher in Lourdes. Now I should really be your pupil in the arduous art of rightly handling the poor human soul. How do you do it, Marie Bernarde?"

"But, *ma mère*," Bernadette replied in amazement, "what is it I do? I don't do anything."

"That's just it, *ma sœur*." Vauzous kept nodding. "Exactly that. You do nothing at all."

The papers came with the news that the Emperor and the Empress had gone into exile to England. A new name was printed in huge letters, that of Gambetta. New conflicts arose and new wounded came. Then that too came to an end and with it all tumult came to an end. But the march of events is swifter than the healing of shattered bones or of infected entrails and other injuries of war. The year was far gone before the Convent of Saint Gildarde received the returning sisters and Marie Bernarde and Marie Thérèse were relieved of their duties at the hospital. Both were walking home from the hospital for the last time one evening, each with her little valise in her hand. Mère Vauzous observed that Bernadette dragged her left foot a little. She said nothing. Her heart was tormented by its old distrust. Aha, she wants to show me how the long service wearied and broke her.

During the nights that followed, Marie Thérèse Vauzous was repeatedly haunted by the same dream. She saw before her the grotto of Massabielle. Yet it was not the grotto that she knew but a maw-like abyss which led, despite the many lighted tapers, into the immeasurable depths of hell. Deep in the unfathomable lay in wait the monster, the evil one fallen from heaven through pride. Nor was it the Gave that thundered by, but a grey river, mightier than the Loire. Fogs rose. In the shallows of the bank stood hundreds of figures with filthy bandages, leaning on canes and crutches, the mutilated, too, with wooden legs. All stared yearningly toward the grotto. There they beheld Bernadette. She was a half-grown girl who was playing tag with other children and leading a circular dance and clapping her hands. And now and then Bernadette would laugh so loud, so piercingly, that in her dream the mistress of the novices blushed with shame. It seemed to the dreamer as though the playing girl were laughing the whole world to scorn.

This repeated dream filled Marie Thérèse with violent distress. It was fourteen years since the visions of Massabielle. Was this oppressive nightmare meant as a prophetic hint justifying her old doubts? Night after night she prayed for light from Heaven. She prayed that Marie Bernarde be not as her suspicion pictured her. She prayed that Marie Bernarde might not be dragging her left leg as an affected fishing for attention. For that circumstance continued to fill her pedagogic soul with hidden irritation.

One evening Marie Thérèse Vauzous appeared in the cell of Marie Bernarde. Her face was as grey as though after an illness. "Help me, Sœur Marie Bernarde," she said beseechingly and her whole being gave evidence of a distress and a moral confusion deeper than Bernadette had thought possible.

"So gladly, *ma mère*. But how can I help you?"

"You alone can help me, *ma sœur*, since it concerns you."

"Me?" Bernadette asked, taken aback. "Did I commit some fault, *ma mère*?"

"If only I knew, *ma sœur*," the other groaned. "I have no right to speak to you in this fashion. I'm neither your father confessor nor your mother superior, and even they would not have the right. But I am begging for your help in my agony of uncertainty."

"What uncertainty do you mean, *ma mère?*"

Marie Thérèse leaned against the wall as though she could not remain erect without support. "Bernadette Soubirous, help me! For I cannot believe you."

"But have I recently uttered an untruth, *ma mère?*" Bernadette asked searchingly in her dismay.

"You never utter an untruth, *ma sœur* . . . and yet it is the question concerning the veracity or unveracity of your whole life that has riven my soul in two."

"I don't understand that, *ma mère,*" Bernadette said with lowered lids.

"I have held to my purpose, Sister Marie Bernarde, and have not mentioned your visions since the day you came. I know how undisciplined it is in me to be untrue to that purpose now. And I also know that it is an unpardonable failing in me to continue in a state of doubt in the teeth of the decision of a theological commission of inquiry, against the judgment of a bishop, yes, against the opinion of the Holy Father himself. But God sees the great depravity of my heart and that I cannot help myself. Therefore I have come to you, *ma sœur,* beseeching your help."

Slowly and earnestly Bernadette lifted her eyes. "Just what is it that you don't believe, *ma mère?*"

"Oh, that is a good question, Marie Bernarde. I believe that you saw visions and saw them on several occasions. But I am unable to believe that these visions addressed you in dialect and made themselves explicitly known to you. For years and years my thoughts and prayers have been concerned with you. Concerning that I can give a true accounting before God. But I now know your dear and child-like and playful nature, your—shall I call it?—artist's nature. I know your unbridled imagination from the sketches you made for your embroidery work. Perhaps that imagination it was which in those days added its magic to the real visions which you saw, so that you yourself could no longer distinguish between the true and the untrue. Or it may be that in those February days the talk of the women and the girls so heated your imagination that you thought you saw what had first been suggested to you. That, too, would be a gift of God, but a dangerous one. You know how to cast a spell over men's souls as no one else. Thus each element may have lent aid to the others. You were a child. Nay, you are one still. You could yourself not tell where was the boundary line between true vision and your own imagining. The tale you told grew more real through the telling of it. Your feet once on this road, there was no retracing of your steps. Through your power over the hearts of men you won over the gentlemen of the commission, even as your words reduced to tears the venerable bishop of Montpellier. Could it not have been thus, my dear child?"

"No, it was not thus, *ma mère*," Bernadette said very quietly.

"Oh, you would set me free from horrible suffering if you could convince me. This way I am, except for the atheists themselves, that single unworthy one who still doubts. It is inexpressibly dreadful that I must speak in this way to you. But give me some sign that could help me."

"Are the cures of the spring no sign?" Bernadette asked after a long silence.

"A very great one, *ma sœur*, the very greatest. But my desire is for another, for a sign that concerns you in your own person. . . . Listen to me, I'll tell you something from the days of my novitiate. In those days there still lived among us the aged Sœur Raymonde. She was very like our dear and blessed Sœur Sophie. But in the days of her strength she had worked much harder and, of all places, in the prebendary infirmary at Nîmes where aged men are cared for, which is, as you know, the most repulsive kind of nursing. Yet was Sister Raymonde also the first at prayer and at hours of contemplation. And all the while she was as quiet and cheerful as a child. The world knew nothing of her. She didn't assert that she had seen visions. Neither the papers nor a venerable bishop wrote concerning her. Except for her father confessor none knew what grace had been granted her. None of us knew until her death that she had been the subject of the fairest of all signs of grace in that she bore on the palms of her hands the stigmata of Christ. . . ."

Bernadette shook her head violently, even indignantly. "I don't believe I can help you, *ma mère*," she said curtly. Then she sat down on her bed and did not stir. Vauzous, too, stared at her without moving. But after a while Bernadette lifted her head and smiled faintly as though a sudden thought had occurred to her.

"It may be that there is a sign for you too, *ma mère*," she whispered and slowly raised her habit until her left leg was exposed. The knee was frightfully deformed by a tumour almost the size of a child's head. The older nun tottered at the sight. She walked to the door, then returned and opened her mouth to speak. No word would come. She broke down at Bernadette's feet, felled to earth by a cognition of mystical coherences.

CHAPTER FORTY-FOUR

Not for Me Flows the Spring

AND THESE were the great coherences which Marie Thérèse Vauzous had seen in swiftest illumination when she had sunk to earth at sight of the terrifying sign revealed by Bernadette: The Virgin of Massabielle had chosen as her instrumentality an innocent creature and placed in that creature's mouth as a first communication a pertinaciously repeated summons to penitence, even though this very creature had in her child-like simplicity not even grasped this cry directed to the whole world's sinners. Penitence, penitence, penitence! Again and again. The world is foul. The world is sick. Pray for sinners. Pray for the sick world. As penitence is brightly related to sin, even so sin is darkly related to disease. The call to penitence was only a preparation for the lady's real plan. Amid fantastic circumstances—gorging earth and vomiting it—the simple presageless child scratched from the earth that spring which gradually revealed its power and by its incomprehensible cures set by the ears the very ends of the earth. The finding of the spring seemed to end the child's practical task and she was dismissed from the service of the lady. Now came the rulers of the Church and submitted these phenomena to a scrupulous, an almost hostile testing which took four whole years. Not until then did they declare their conviction and acknowledge the supernatural character of the phenomena. But what happened to Bernadette, mediatrix between the lady and the world? The bishop of Tarbes had long recognized it as his duty to take this wondrous child of God under the care and protection of the Church. He transplanted her in one of the noblest monastic establishments of all France, that hidden there she might blossom and strive for that perfection accessible to the religious which alone could correspond to the special grace with which she had been favoured. Among the gardeners of that spiritual garden Providence had placed none other than Marie Thérèse Vauzous, the general's daughter. Her mission it was to cultivate a desirable type according to the millennial wisdom of the Church, which knows man and his possibilities so well. In ninety-five out of every hundred cases no difficulty is experienced in adapting the varying personalities to this approved type. Strange circumstance, however, that the nun Vauzous, outwardly a faultless representative of the type in question, had at the core of her insatiably aspiring personality a powerful, self-directing ego which, despite the severity of her self-disciplining ascetic practices, permitted her to conform to the average type only outwardly and in mere seeming. Her descent, blood, culture, intelligence, energy became the unconquerable temptations of a deeply concealed pride. The unbending strength of her personality was the ultimate reason which prevented her from attaining peace either with herself or in her relations with Bernadette. For Bernadette was adamant in her own way. Yet there was no question here of an arithmetic of the soul. The process that took place in the dark was one of attraction and repulsion. No one knew the innermost truth, not her father confessor nor the mistress of the novices herself. Ever and again Bernadette had to be a stumbling-block to her. It had been so in Lourdes. But in those days Bernadette had been a stumbling-block to all, the secular authorities, the clergy, the dean, the bishop. Up to the commission's final verdict all had been as distrustful as the child's teacher. It was Marie Thérèse's misfortune that, despite the sun-clear testimony of events, she was condemned to continue in doubt. She fought this doubt in endless hours of prayer. Yet her prayers seemed not to be heard. Ever again some trait of Bernadette or even some chance and innocent word plunged her back into her agony. No matter what the proof might be, her innermost soul refused to accept the fact that this common, superficial, and stealthily rebellious creature should have been chosen from among all the living as the object of divine grace. In the obscurest corner of her being bled, as it were, the frightful question: Why she and why not I? And yet another question even more terrifying: Is my way of a lasting convulsive tension of the will the right way, seeing that one may unconsciously dance one's path through all difficulties to heaven itself? For many years Marie Thérèse succeeded in concealing this anguished inner division of soul from Marie Bernarde, from everyone else, above all, from her own conscience. The repeated dream concerning that hell's mouth at Massabielle first tore asunder the fog which had veiled that division. Thus she, the embodiment of self-discipline, broke down and demanded of the poor child a sign in proof of the grace accorded. And behold, she was given to see the sign and understood its meaning in a sudden overwhelming flash of illumination. Bernadette bore a stigma. It was the stigma of her fatal illness. This illness made her who, under the guidance of the Most Blessed Virgin, scratched forth from nothingness the spring of thousandfold healing, the protagonist of all the ailing in the world. Thus after all the miracles of which she had been the instrument, God granted her yet a second grace, the grace of a passion, the grace of the imitation of Christ Himself. The nun Vauzous felt lightheaded. Her bony hands holding her dry face, she lay prone on the floor. Ungraspable by mere thought was the horrible and yet glorious fate of Bernadette. Boundless contrition and utter reverence in the face of the mystery kept Marie Thérèse lying there. Yet she of the terrifying grace had covered her knee and was smiling a little, as though this were all as it should be and a mere matter of course.

The nun Vauzous had been illuminated to the point of a correct diagnosis. The tumour on Bernadette's knee was not due to a passing infection. It was and remained the symptom of a mortal illness. Tuberculosis of the bone is one of the slowest as well as one of the most painful of mortal ills. Long intervals accentuate the final hopelessness. In acute periods inflammations of the nerves are among the cruel complications. The passion of the girl of Lourdes was to take not seven days but more than seven years. Seven years are two thousand five hundred and fifty-five days.

Bernadette yielded herself to her illness even as she had always been obedient to all that life had brought her, unquestioningly and from her very heart. Thus had she fulfilled the lady's bidding and eaten the bitter herbs and devoured the slime of earth and ventured twice on the same day into the den of Peyramale, the lion. Thus had she faced unfalteringly the official questionings and the psychiatric examination and the silly insistence of the curious and the insults and the shallow adoration and the pestering of fools. So, too, she now accepted her illness as something wholly natural, without for a moment formulating the mystery which the nun Vauzous had recognized and which was not hidden from her own heart. Once she said to Nathalie: "This illness was sent me because there really was nothing else to be done with me."

She had smiled faintly but without a trace of conscious conformity to some pattern of humility. The words had been like the words in which, on her first day in the convent, she had answered Mother Imbert's inquiry as to what she could do. "*Oh, pas grand'chose*, nothing that amounts to much, Madame la Supérieure." And this answer, too, had not had humility as its source but an even rarer virtue—an acute and soberly accurate estimate of the self which neither the grace of Heaven nor the plaudits of the world had ever shaken. Nor did Bernadette throughout her long illness ever for a moment affect the part of a heroic and strong though much enduring soul. When the pains became too excruciating, she cried out and wept and asked for mitigating narcotics. The nun Vauzous, had she ever been ill—only she never was—would have uttered no lament amid bitterest suffering but, rigid and pallid as a medieval queen, would have made a silent sacrifice of her torments. Not so Bernadette. She never thought of making a sacrifice of the inevitable. She had no stealthy eye on some reward. She had kept the tumour on her knee a secret only because she did not want to be relieved of her duties as a nurse. Now she needed no longer to keep her secret. If she still restrained her plaints as best she could, it was simply in fear of being taken to the infirmary. She wanted to stay at home, like her sainted friend, Sœur Sophie.

Her sickness faced Bernadette like a mighty mountain through which she had to dig with her frail hands in order some day to see the light again. For hundreds of days she dug and dug without losing courage, with the tireless intrepidity of a good worker. She was fully employed. No breathing-space was granted. Lying down became a special art, and sitting up and every movement in bed and breathing and going to sleep and waking up. She devoted herself to being ill as ardently as she had devoted herself to her embroidering. She showed no impatience nor ever wished that the end might come sooner. To their extreme amazement the nuns observed that Marie Bernarde clung to life, though it was mere martyrdom. The destruction of bone tissue in her legs and shoulders made necessary repeated operations. At such times she had to be taken to the infirmary. When she was permitted to return to the mother house she would jest and, despite her great weakness, celebrate the day in joy.

Bernadette's old power to change the souls of men was more confirmed than ever during the course of her illness. The sisters of Nevers were now able to recognize the preciousness of the treasure given into their keeping. Nothing tangible happened, yet Marie Bernarde's cell became, as it were, the heart of the house. As ever before, so now too the girl of Lourdes spoke no word that aspired beyond a common sober reality. Her mouth uttered no matter of devotion nor any mystic hints. Yet now and then there gleamed behind the plainest words a significance which much later drew tears to the eyes of Sister Nathalie and even Mother Imbert.

Chief of the changed souls was Marie Thérèse Vauzous. Even this change of hers, however, was a matter of self-discipline. After she had been vanquished by Bernadette and had condemned her stark voluntaristic way of attaining salvation, she strove after a simple humility which was foreign to her nature. Above all she, the general's daughter, took it upon herself to minister to the eternally superior child of the common people by day and by night. With iron will she insisted on that entire service. Hence the mother superior was frequently obliged to intervene between the former mistress of the novices and the second assistant, Sister Nathalie, who did not wish to be wholly separated from her beloved Marie Bernarde. And it was bitterly ironical that when her former mistress and monitor performed certain services for Bernadette with all her old stringency, the girl was far from happy but rather much dismayed over the unseemly reversal of roles and circumstances. Thus it came to pass that, despite conversion and sacrifice, her old scourge became, under another aspect, a scourge once more.

The course the disease ran was such that in the second year

Bernadette could walk no more. But since she desired to share prayers and meals she had to be carried both to the chapel and to the refectory. This led to another conflict between Nathalie and Marie Thérèse. But this time it was easy for Mother Imbert to compose differences. Nathalie was far from robust. Mère Vauzous, bony and sinewy, could have carried three creatures as elfin as Bernadette. Hence several times a day she took the sick girl in her arms and carried her upstairs and down, which made Bernadette feel not a little shy.

There was a subject which the sisters had often discussed among themselves but which for rather vague reasons none had hitherto seriously and frankly mentioned to Bernadette. Now it came about that Bernadette seemed better during several weeks and even gained some weight. So toward the end of a meal Mother Imbert turned to her and said "I'd wager, dearest child, that you've often had the thought we all have had. But while you were suffering so acutely, the long trip seemed out of the question."

"I really don't know what you mean, Madame la Supérieure," Bernadette said cautiously.

Mother Imbert forced herself to smile. "Should not you, of all people, take advantage of the benefit that has come to the whole world through you?"

"What do you intend to suggest, Madame la Supérieure? You know how stupid I am."

"In your present condition, *ma sœur*, when you're so much easier than you have been, a trip to Lourdes could be well undertaken. . . ."

"Oh, no, *ma mère*, that can't be done!" was Bernadette's quick and startled reply.

"Why can't it be done, my dear daughter?"

"Because the spring is not for me, Madame la Supérieure."

There was a long silence. At last Nathalie said: "I don't

understand that. Why should the spring not work in your case, of all cases, *ma sœur?*"

"No, no, the spring isn't for me," Bernadette reiterated stubbornly.

"How do you know that, *mon enfant?*" asked Vauzous with a long glance at the sick girl.

Bernadette nodded. "I know it, that's all."

"Did the lady tell you?" asked Vauzous.

"The lady speaks to me no more."

"Did the lady communicate the feeling to you?"

"Oh, no, the lady concerns herself with that no more."

And once more before she turned the conversation to other subjects she said curtly: "I simply know. . . ."

CHAPTER FORTY-FIVE

The Devil Afflicts Bernadette

In the last two years of her life Bernadette's body became a mere shadow. Nevertheless, the illness seemed to have become arrested or, rather, to have reached a stage of self-exhaustion. The pain-filled nights came more rarely. On the other hand, she was assailed by psychical weaknesses. In her well days she had never been prey to morbid scruples or exaggerated feelings of guilt. On the contrary. It had been the supremely enchanting thing about her soul that that soul had dwelt in inviolable security. Now it was suddenly turned into a boundlessly sensitive, trembling scale in matters of conscience. The infinite outer void of an invalid's existence tended to bring into sharp relief the past, Lourdes, and the world of other days. This process rendered ever more acute the remorseful promptings of her heart. Gradually that which was and that which had been blended into a supersensitive oneness. It would happen, for instance, that Nathalie approaching her bed found Bernadette bathed in tears.

"For the love of Christ, *ma sœur*, what happened?"

"I behaved so abominably, *ma sœur*."

"What do you mean? Toward whom could you have done so?"

"I did, I did, Nathalie. Abominably, and toward my mother. Just now . . ."

"Your mother has been dead for over ten years."

". . . and she had cooked an onion soup and served me a plateful. And I was irritated, goodness knows why, and scolded: 'Please spare me your nasty onion soup. I can't bear the smell of it any more.' I really said that, really."

Nathalie shook her puzzled head. "But that's so very long ago. It must be a matter of sixteen years."

"Nothing, nothing at all is long ago. Everything is always present." Bernadette sobbed. "Oh, my poor mother; she had such a hard time of it in life. And I treated her so badly."

Another time she blinked at Marie Thérèse Vauzous. "You don't know, *ma mère*, that I tore two pages out of my catechism."

"What catechism do you mean, *ma sœur?*"

"The one I had at school, of course. . . ."

"You still remember that, *ma sœur?*"

"Remember, *ma mère?* But I still have it among my things. And I tore out the two pages in sheer rage. I was so angry at Jeanne Abadie because she kept boasting and boasting about how much she knew."

Next to her mother it was the pure memory of Sœur Sophie which became the subject of her shadowy feeling of guilt. More than once Bernadette told Nathalie about it. "Look, there she sat next to me hour after hour. And I kept on drawing or embroidering like one possessed and she couldn't speak, the poor darling, nor express herself and she'd keep moving her lips because there was something she wanted to say. And I paid no attention, thinking I wouldn't be able to understand her anyhow, and didn't even try to help her, Nathalie—didn't even try. How can one be so wicked?"

Many such small sins oozed forth like drops of blood. Anyone but she could have been thought of as unveracious and affected by indulgence in self-tormenting plaints over such trifles. In Bernadette's case these things were forced from her by a veracity so deep and keen that they brought tears to the eyes of Nathalie and other witnesses. In proportion as the past grew more vivid to her, the present paled. When a telegram from her brothers informed her of the death of the miller François Soubirous, she crossed herself and spoke no word.

There was another and most uncommon trial which she was called upon to endure. It caused not a little terror in the cloister. But the human soul, athirst as it is for the light, has roots deep buried in horror and in night. Bernadette's soul was no exception. Even in her childhood and long before her sight of the heavenly one, her visionary eyes had had the gift of filling the frame of things with faces and forms. The splotches of moisture on the walls of the Cachot, the clouds at Bartrès, leaves moving in a breeze, the white stones in the Gave and in the brooks, the tongues of flame in the fireplace— all these had been as frames to frame the crowding images that had poured from her child's soul. Most of these images did not belong to the realm of the lovely, the pleasing, or even the indifferent, but rather to the counter-realm of darkness, strange as this was in view of the girl's love of beauty. A splotch on the wall was Orphide, the goat. Quivering spaces amid foliage became gnome-like monsters. Stones in the water were the bleached skulls of the drowned. And all these things blended to produce an indescribable cosmic fear in the heart of this child of the Pyrenees. And very early had Bernadette learned to identify this ultimate terror with the character and name of the evil one.

Now that the stream of her life was forcing its way through the last narrows, the whirlpools of this terror issued in dreadful cascades. It seemed as though a soul so powerfully grasped by grace must at a higher bidding be painfully purged, before its farewell to earth, of all the images of horror that had ever lain in ambush in its depths. The whitewashed walls of her cell or of the infirmary, branches of trees outside her window, forms and shadows of all things in the twilight sprang into strange life as never before.

Had not the grotto of Massabielle been a place of offal and abhorrence before it had been redeemed and glorified? Had not the Gave's howls of woe and rage protested against the breaking of demonic powers? Had not the lady herself been obliged to curb these powers with a stern glance what time they roared above the raging river in her very presence? Always had this power been present and allied to the soul through fear.

In other words, Bernadette was being plagued by the devil. It was a sufficiently poverty-stricken devil, who had nothing to offer. He could not offer the Soubirous child the kingdoms of this world, for that was a lure she would not even have understood. He could not even tempt her with a succulent peach, a trick that might still work with the nun Vauzous. For the fading body of Marie Bernarde had no desire left now save absence of pain. So evil had a hard time with her. Nothing was left it than to send a very local and primordial sort of devil, one who was at home in the chasms of the Pyrenees and under the glaciers of the Pic du Midi or the Vignemale and who had at his disposal no subtle lures but only throttling fear and naked terror. Bernadette, child of the people, who had attained the highest level of exquisite spirituality, was exposed to a devil with horns and tail, even as the simple people of Bigorre had imaged for centuries. He plunged muttering past her bed embodied as the Gave and growled his: "Away from here!" And: "Flee while you may!" In the shape of black sows he wallowed, grunting, on her oppressed bosom. He appeared in the most repulsive human forms and combinations. Sometimes he was but a painted jumping-jack who tried to singe her with a torch. Again he resembled Vital Dutour, the imperial prosecutor with two goat's horns growing out of his bald skull. Odd that of all her persecutors the devil picked the embodiment of Dutour, who had caused her far less immediate misery than Jacomet or Rives, the examining magistrate, or the *agent provocateur* or the red-bearded professor.

"Consider well what you bear witness to, little girl," the devil Dutour admonished her with hellish nose of red protruding from his face. Bernadette groaned. The devil Dutour was quite friendly. "I hope you won't repel the hand stretched out to save you. . . ."

"*Apage Satanas!*" cried Bernadette, as she had been taught to do, while her painful hand covered her face and breast with the sign of the cross. Now and then one of her piercing cries shrilled through that quiet house. Then would the nuns, one by one, come into her sickroom in order with long-tested prayers to help their sister in her fight against the great afflicter of souls.

"Oh, my dears," she would whisper with chattering teeth, "he besets me sorely today."

Mother Vauzous proved herself a valiant warrior and Bernadette hid her shivering soul under the military resonance of Vauzous's prayers.

After Epiphany of that year Dr. Saint-Cyr notified Mother Imbert that the end of Marie Bernarde's martyrdom would soon have to be reckoned with. The mother superior at once betook herself to the bishop, Monseigneur Lelonge. The bishop of Nevers at once wrote to inform the bishop of Tarbes, who was now called Pichenot and no longer Bertrand Sévère Laurence. When Monseigneur Laurence had been summoned by Pius IX from among the bishops of the whole earth to attend a Vatican council, he had been eighty and seriously ill. Attempts were made to keep him from the hard journey. But Monseigneur, who had made it hard for the lady in his time, answered his advisers: Is a grave in Rome so small a goal that a man will not risk for it thirty hours on the train? The old man attained his goal. His successor Pichenot now sent two learned theologians from the great seminary at Tarbes to Nevers who were joined by two equally learned theologians of the seminary of the latter town. Thus another commission was set up, whose task it was to make a definitive audit of the mystery while the chief witness retained consciousness. Distorted rumours concerning Bernadette's pangs of conscience and afflictions by the demonic had leaked, no one knew by whose indiscretion, from the cloister walls into the world. A certain journal, however, dared to write that the troubles of conscience afflicting the dying thaumaturgist of Lourdes were clear enough indications of her fear of a heavenly reckoning for her hard-boiled career of mystic swindle.

On an icy winter day Mother Imbert approached the bed of Bernadette and spoke as follows: "My dearest child, Their Lordships the bishops of Tarbes and Nevers desire to hear from your lips a final confirmation of all that the Most Blessed Virgin did for you and through you. They have sent four learned gentlemen who desire this afternoon to receive your solemn confession concerning the visions by which you were graced. In your honour the general mother superior and the council of our congregation will be present too."

Bernadette could grow no paler than she was. But she closed her eyes and fought for breath. The mother superior sought to calm and encourage her: "Resign yourself to it, Marie Bernarde, as to a duty imposed by obedience. But I give you my word that I will guard against their tiring you out."

The solemn ceremony took place in a large cold chamber in which two dozen armchairs had been placed in a semi-circle. The general mother superior, bowed by her great weight of years, the twelve venerable nuns of her council, the vicar general of Nevers, the four emissaries of the bishops, and sundry other clerics all arose and remained standing while, preceded by Mother Imbert and Mother Vauzous, Sœur Marie Bernarde was carried on a stretcher into the bleak room. The sisters of the house remained modestly in the background.

The oldest of the appointed theologians bowed with tender considerateness over Bernadette. "We will avoid whatever might exhaust you, *ma sœur*. We shall proceed to read to you the final protocol of the commission of investigation assembled in 1858. It contains a record of all the testimony which you offered exactly twenty years ago. We ask nothing of you except to confirm that testimony of yours. Do you feel equal to that?"

With great and fearful eyes Bernadette looked about her and nodded almost imperceptibly. Was this another examination? A monotonous reader's voice reached her ear. As out of an immeasurable distance she heard the tale of a child of fourteen who went out for faggots and met a beautiful lady. It was a very, very long story and her limbs grew stiff with icy frost. Her feeble breath was visible above her lips. Yet Bernadette tensed every nerve, seeking to be equal to the inquiry. At the end of the long tale the senior theologian asked tenderly: "Sister Marie Bernarde, can you once more confirm the truth of all you have just heard?"

Bernadette's beseeching eyes were fixed on empty space. Then in the lilting voice of her childhood she breathed: "Oh, yes, oh, yes, I saw her. . . ."

The reader continued. Time seemed to stand still. Again and again she heard the soothing voice of the old priest: "Sister Marie Bernarde, can you once more confirm the truth of all you have just heard?"

Her beseeching glance upon some distant point, Bernadette answered in almost the same words: "Oh, yes, I saw her. Yes, I saw her."

When an hour later she was carried back to her cell and was alone with Nathalie, the stiffness melted and a fit of convulsive weeping shook her and seemed to shatter what was left of her body. "Dear God," she sobbed when she could speak once more, "they will come again and again, tomorrow and on the next day, and ask and ask till the very last day of all."

Nathalie knelt beside her and laid a hand on her forehead. "You've given a final solemn confirmation now, dear friend. They won't torment you any more."

"Oh, I know more about that than you, dear," Bernadette moaned. "They'll torture me as long as I live, and keep asking, asking, asking. So soon as they've left, they've forgotten and want to hear it all over again, all over. . . ." And finally when she had sobbed all she could, she said: "They don't believe me, they just don't. . . . I understand that, too . . . it was too much grace for one like me. . . ."

She seemed to have fallen into slumber. Nathalie remained silently beside her. But suddenly she raised her head. "Would you be so kind as to give me my white bag, *ma sœur?*"

Sister Nathalie took from the drawer the little, faded old bag which Bernadette had carried when she was a schoolgirl. Her primer had once been in it, her catechism, a piece of knitting, a crust of bread, a morsel of rock-candy, and a little donkey with a broken leg. When Nathalie emptied the bag on the coverlet the primer and the little donkey with the broken leg were still there. Bernadette nodded with satisfaction. The treasures of the rich are fleeting; the treasures of the poor are abiding. Bernadette pointed to the little picture of the Mother of God which Peyramale had once sent her. "Take that little picture, *ma sœur,*" Bernadette begged, "and put it in an envelope and address the envelope to the Reverend Dean Marie Dominique Peyramale at Lourdes."

"Nothing but the picture?" Nathalie asked, surprised.

"It will suffice."

But as Nathalie was about to go she called her back.

"Write, too, *ma sœur*. Write: '*Cher Monsieur le Curé*, Bernadette is thinking of you!'"

That very evening Sister Marie Bernarde had a serious attack of weakness. She was taken to the infirmary, never to leave it again.

CHAPTER FORTY-SIX

The Hell of the Flesh

ON THE very day on which the aged Dean Peyramale was finally able to set out for Nevers, a stranger arrived in Lourdes. It was the man of letters Hyacinthe de Lafite, who since that spring twenty-one years ago had not set foot in Lourdes again. Two obvious reasons and one secret one persuaded Monsieur de Lafite to take this trip. One of his nephews, who had called on him in Paris, had issued a most pressing invitation to him to spend a few weeks prior to Easter in the Lafite villa near Lourdes. The Lafites had long sold the old manor house on the Chalet Isle. Like the isle itself it had been acquired by the diocese of Tarbes and had been sacrificed to the regulation of the Gave and the new parks. Several members of the family had built themselves agreeable summer residences in the environs, far from the goings-on of the sick and the pilgrims of this strange town.

Hyacinthe de Lafite was the same poor and obscure fellow that he had been thrice seven years ago. His youthful ambition to awaken the classical alexandrine verse to renewed life and to give the romantic soul a marble body had been sadly cast aside or left behind. None gave thought to alexandrine verses these days or to classic or romantic movements. It had become the aim of literature to catch up with man's development. Realism was in breathless haste. Writers delineated the lives of locomotive engineers, stokers on ships, factory workers, coal-miners. The least and least striking formed the subject matter of fiction. Analyses were offered of the sexual conflicts of small-town women and the emotional confusions of commercial travellers. To Lafite's deep discomfort the noble tongue of France was spending its time in suburban markets, shops, and bars, intent in servile fashion on catching the precise accent of the most vulgar slang. And all these trivial attempts were still made in the name of the worn and dated metaphysics of progress and science. No wonder that in such an age a truly unusual work, such as his own *The Founding of Tarbes*, could not even be completed, not to speak of receiving adequate acknowledgment.

Well, a man who lived on a forgotten word of praise from Victor Hugo and occasional articles for the papers could hardly afford to refuse invitations that would house and feed him for weeks to come. Lafite's second reason was that some weeks before he had met one of the old friends from Lourdes. It was Jean Baptiste Estrade, who had long been advanced to be chief of the revenue office at Bordeaux. Estrade had the habit of passing his annual vacation, which he took around Easter, in Lourdes. And he had so insistently and cordially expressed the desire to see his former friend of the Café Français and show him the utterly changed miracle city that Lafite had promised to come.

The third and secret reason was hidden even from him who entertained it. Hyacinthe felt ill; nay, he knew he was ill. The trouble was in his larynx. Growths had appeared there; they had disappeared again. A physician, sharply questioned as to whether the trouble might be cancer, had admitted the possibility. In accordance with his innate melancholy the man of letters was sure that he had cancer. He had quite given himself up, convinced that neither science nor Lourdes could help him. His proud consciousness rejected both. Yet the cure of Lourdes had been declared efficacious in many, many cases and not by the clerical papers alone. A sober man like Estrade asserted that he had been eye-witness of several instantaneous cures. Since his last conversation with Estrade, Lafite had been subject to an obscure and incomprehensible restlessness. On the journey south he reflected: Not bad to spend a few weeks in the old Pyrenean hole and revive memories. That was all.

Hyacinthe de Lafite was now fifty-nine. The acquaintances who met him privately thought that he looked older than his years. They also thought that the beautiful white-haired head with the sharply defined temples and the pale sunken cheeks was more impressive than his former aspect and pointed to the possession of real genius. Of the acquaintances of earlier days some had died, among them the pedagogue Clarens, his adversary in so many brilliant debates, as well as Lacadé, old and full of honours, who had always treated the writer with such condescending joviality. In the hour of his death Lacadé had known that all his dreams of the watering-place of Lourdes had been surpassed.

Between Estrade and Dr. Dozous, Lafite strolled down the new Boulevard de la Grotte which led by way of the recently built Pont Michel to the miracle area. It was a day of radiant sunshine. Fairly aghast, Lafite squinted at the change which the old mountain town had undergone. Hotels stood in rows. But these buildings did not display the monastic simplicity, tranquillity, and dignity that might have harmonized with the character of the place. No, there was exhibited a witches' sabbath of stucco façades, the miscarriages of a poisonous architectural manner which ill-concealed its grimaces behind sacred inscriptions. Looking about here one would think oneself in a cheap watering-place or in the festive quarter of a maritime town rather than in Lourdes of the miracles. The regnant taste was that of the third-rate casino, the provincial vaudeville theatre and hippodrome. Lafite was horror-stricken by the endless rows of shops that sold religious articles. The sacred trash offered for sale fairly took his breath away. A good many years ago Master Fabich of Lyon had succeeded in making the Carrara marble of which he had formed the Virgin look like oleomargarine. A thousand copies in screaming plaster of this piece, from which Bernadette had averted her face in misery, were now for sale, further vulgarized by the acidulous blue of the girdle. It was a Babylon of religious trade-goods. Bernadette was the chief figure. In her white *capulet* she knelt, adoring a syrupy Madonna, not only on chromos, lithographs, and picture-books, but also embroidered on covers and shawls and plastically wrought on paper-weights and table centre-pieces. Hyacinthe de Lafite could not contain his indignation.

"It was a lovely legend that happened here twenty years ago. An innocent child saw the Madonna and conveyed her experience in a quite new and vivid fashion. Now comes this infamous age and its inhabitants and drags that legend down to the filthy level of its own conventions. And the Church patronizes these horrors. . . ."

"As far as all that abominable trash is concerned, you are right," Estrade said. "But perhaps the Church in tolerating it is wiser than we think. Strong minds have turned aside from her. What she has left is a sterile aristocracy and the simple countryfolk. So the Church lets these people turn the town into a fair according to their taste. Nothing else would appeal to them. Or do you expect the Church to order its sacred pictures of some modern artist who wants to shock the Philistines?"

"I disagree most emphatically, dear Estrade!" the writer cried out. "In ages when the Church was a great Church the highest art was her handmaiden. For nothing human is holier than that high beauty which is found incarnate in high art. I cannot consider a Church as partaking of holiness when it is faithless to beauty either because it shares the taste of these cave-dwellers or is unwilling to offend it."

Estrade smiled. "Suppose we reverse your saying, dear friend. When art was high art, the Church stood at its side. . . ."

Dr. Dozous, who had walked along in silence, pointed to a large building beyond the bridge. "We shall now see the most deeply serious thing in the whole world," he said. The old physician led them through the outer courts of the Hospital of the Seven Sorrows. Here waited row on row of rickshaw-like carts in which the orderlies, called *brancardiers*, conveyed the patients to the grotto, the baths, and the basilica. From the outer halls the three men entered an apparently endless dining-room in which hundreds of people were just sitting down to a meal at long tables. The order was excellent. Each patient seemed willing, for the sake of the hope he harboured, to co-operate toward a smooth functioning of the daily routine. In long single file the serving sisters passed between the crowded tables and filled plates with soup and glasses with dark red wine. The diners seemed not at all downcast but visibly excited. They chatted and laughed. Perhaps they were swapping anecdotes concerning the battlefield of miracles. For in Lourdes miracles were an everyday occurrence.

"These are the ones who are suffering no pain," Dr. Dozous said softly to Lafite. "We are, as it were, in an upper circle of this most Dantesque house. These are the cripples and the blind."

As Hyacinthe de Lafite's near-sighted eyes took in the crowd more clearly he saw that these were indeed nearly all crippled or blind. On crutches and sticks they hobbled to the tables; crippled limbs hung slackly. The opalescent twinkling smiles of the sightless grinned at the emptiness before them. Lafite fought down the oppression of his breast. "How many of these poor wretches can expect healing?" he asked the physician.

"In the course of several decades many have been cured. Nevertheless, indisputably supernatural healings are rare. They have to be specially investigated and confirmed by the medical research division here. And I can assure you that the scepticism of my profession has not been diminished by one jot. Alleviation and improvement of severe organic diseases are quite frequent. Look at these people. If but one among hundreds or even thousands experiences a miracle and regains sight or motion, the souls of all are immeasurably uplifted. Hope reaches indescribable heights. If not this year, why, then perchance next. . . . Do you understand?" Dozous opened a door. "These are still without pain. But they cannot move."

Three more long halls. Endless rows of beds. The sick lay still under white coverlets. Here and there a piece of orthopædic apparatus might be seen. Next to many a bed sat a husband, a wife, a mother, or some kinsman. Under the bedsteads one could glimpse the luggage of the poor, the handbags at six sous each. Stiff silence, unlike the dining-hall. These moveless creatures seemed infinitely weary, still exhausted by long train-trips to the station of the last of all hopes. From some of these pallid faces eyes stared dreamily into the void; others had lapsed into a strangely torpid slumber.

Now Hyacinthe de Lafite had to take himself firmly in hand, for they were entering the lower circles of this house. All his life he had sensitively avoided sights of disease or ugliness. Although as a romantic writer he was on principle devoted to the darker aspects of life, he had in practice sedulously shunned them. Never had he known that such things existed as he now saw. He often closed his eyes; he could not close his ears to the waves of feeble lament, the sudden outcries, the phantasmal groans heard in the halls of the afflicted. Here lay those who were diseased within: people with lungs decayed who had to have the blood-stained foam wiped from their lips; those with cancerous entrails who could not contain their excrement. Lafite wanted to flee from these circles. But the pitiless Dozous forced him into a small side-chamber. There in a complicated invalid's chair sat a boy of about eleven with a look in his eyes that Lafite was never to forget. The boy's deformed legs exhibited from hip to sole all shades of red, from bright salmon to a deep reddish brown like that of lacquer. Blood and pus oozed from open gangrenous fissures. The soaked bandages lay on the floor beside him. Next to him sat a wrinkled old lady, the only one who had stayed with him on the train, for from him came an unbearable stench of putridity.

"Well, how are you, Monsieur?" Dozous asked with imperturbable cheerfulness.

"The Holy Virgin is helping me," the boy answered, panting. "Several places are drying up already. Just look, Monsieur."

"That's splendid, my dear boy. And tomorrow she will help you again, and so every day for a week, until all the places are dry. . . ."

"Oh, yes, Monsieur, I have firm faith," said the boy with an utterly weary but sweet look in his eyes. Lafite ran from the room, but into the chamber of the dying. Here lay those who had collapsed on the threshold of the last of hopes. Most of them had already been provided with the final sacraments. Priests stood beside the beds. Horrified, Lafite became aware of his own death which lay in ambush in his throat. He tried to swallow. An hour ago he could. Now he felt a knot-like object on his larynx. His own death was being fed by all this dying roundabout him. He knew that he himself was one of these condemned, though he might still play the part of a distinguished gentleman visiting this inferno and unthreatened by it. He gasped for breath. He was afraid of being overcome and making a fool of himself before his companions.

The way led on. They entered the chamber of lupous women. These sat on their beds silent and without moving, their heads hidden in black veils, for even they could not endure each other's aspect. The physician asked one of the women to lift her veil. Lafite and Estrade turned aside for a moment. A death's-head of the colour of raw ham with unnaturally sparkling eyes in bloody hollows. No nose. No lips. The nose-holes in the bone closed with cotton stoppers. For this woman had just drunk a cup of coffee and had to see to it that the liquid did not get into the wrong apertures. Dr. Dozous addressed this vermilion death's-head with normal, natural objectivity: "We had a case last year that was much worse than yours, Madame. And the woman got relief, complete relief. Do you understand me? I want you to give me your word that you'll be patient and not do any more foolish things."

The death's-head nodded in eager affirmation.

On leaving, Dozous whispered to his friends: "She tried to kill herself yesterday."

"And is it true that a case like this ever has been cured or can be cured?" Lafite asked not without difficulty.

"It is true," the physician replied, "and you can see the photographs in our office yourself. The last patient of this sort who was healed didn't at first notice that suddenly she had a nose and a mouth again."

In a small adjoining chamber a little woman stood immovable, her face turned to the wall, like a sad and naughty child that has been sent to a corner in punishment and that now stubbornly turns to the wall.

"I am your attending physician," said Dozous. Slowly the woman turned. Her face was not as human as that corroded ham-coloured death's-head had been. It was a tobacco-brown mass of swellings, dominated by two lips that were not lips but huge violet dewlaps proliferating in every direction like a tree-blight. This unimaginable Medusa head began to speak insistently. The sound was like that of a dull mumble behind padded walls. Dozous understood and nodded courteously. "Your wish will be fulfilled. You will be taken to the baths at midnight, when you will be quite alone and seen by no one."

Slowly Hyacinthe de Lafite descended the stairs, his fist pressed against his diaphragm. Clear thought was impossible here. Horrified questions rose rebelliously in his breast: Was it mere empty Nature, careless of quality or value, a goddess unallied to mind and feeling, who through a constant process of proliferation not only destroyed her creatures but condemned them to the living putrefaction of such plagues? Were the brilliant hues of a Brazilian butterfly's wings and the equally brilliant colour of decay in a lupous face one and the same thing to her, then? Did she not distinguish between beauty and horror, by which is guided that most ill-starred of her creatures, man? Or did there exist a barbaric earth-deity like the Huitzilopochtli of the Aztecs who drew a perverse sacrificial ecstasy from such faces of horror and such forms of torment? Or was it really the theological God of the Hebrew Bible and the Christian Church who permitted these absurd diseases as incomprehensible syllogisms linking the primal guilt of matter, which had been drenched with soul till it became man, to its final redemption?

When at last they were out in the fresh air Dr. Dozous said to Lafite: "You have seen, my friend, how deeply hell reaches into human life."

"Yes, Messieurs," Estrade agreed. "And Lourdes is that geometrical point of our planet at which this hell transects heaven."

They walked on. The physician took Lafite by the arm. "You have seen but a small section of the suffering that fills the world; there's far more than most imagine. And the pilgrimage

of suffering streams here, of course. Tomorrow we expect
five more trainloads. And not only the simple faithful come
to be cured here, my dear fellow, not only Catholics even, but
also Protestants and Jews. They are the despairing who come,
those who have no way left but this. . . ."

"And oftener even than of their sickness are they healed of
their despair," said Estrade softly.

Dr. Dozous stopped and looked about him. He smiled.
"Would we have dreamed when, two decades ago, we sat at
Duran's café and argued about matters literary or scientific
that this city of Lourdes would arise as at the stroke of an
enchanter's wand? And all this only because one of the children
of poverty from the verminous Rue des Petites Fossées saw the
most beautiful lady in the cavern of Massabielle and fought for
her? If there be miracles here, Bernadette Soubirous remains
the greatest. What is your comment on that as a writer, Lafite?"

But Lafite, to whom the gift of speech had been granted,
was speechless.

The Lightning Strikes

As early as three o'clock the *brancardiers* take the rickshaws with the sick to the magnificent platform facing the basilica which rides the mount of Massabielle as a high-masted ship rides a great wave of ocean. Many hundreds of these carts, usually supplied with a canopy-like top, form the wide semi-circle of the chorus which accompanies this spectacle. It is an unbelievably mad spectacle when one considers that some member of the chorus may suddenly become the protagonist of a miracle and that from his corroded lupous face the old, old scabs may drop like dry mortar and give place to a new and healthy skin. And this possibility is no stage-play or rumour or gossip, but visible reality of which anyone who is present may convince himself. And it is in very truth a matter so mad and delivers such a stunning blow to the nature of the human intelligence that even those who are eye-witnesses later distrust their own memories.

Immediately behind the rows of carts bearing those who cannot move and are in pain were assembled the crippled and the halt and the blind who were able to drag themselves here. Behind these, however, surged the great mass of pilgrims and spectators, who looked forward to a tremendous and stirring experience such as no other spot of mortal habitation on earth could provide. A fire of yearning filled the hearts of some, a keen fret of curiosity those of others. In the midst of the crowd stood Dozous, Lafite, Estrade. It was the physician's purpose to let the poet experience the hour of the throbbing of this assemblage's heart. Their station was so well chosen that they had an unimpeded view of the platform.

"You're in luck, Lafite," said Estrade. "Today is a great day. Monseigneur Pichenot, the bishop of Tarbes, has arrived to conduct the sacramental procession in person."

"Does Dean Peyramale usually conduct it?" Lafite asked.

Dozous regarded him with surprise. "Didn't you know that Peyramale has been almost entirely pushed aside? The poor man is still irascible, despite his years. He can't endure the monastic clergy nor they him. Even Monseigneur Laurence, his friend and patron, had to drop him years ago. The Fathers of the Grotto now rule the roost, above all Father Sempet, the former chaplain, to whom Peyramale gave his entire confidence."

Lafite showed no great interest in these personal items of clerical life. He inquired as to the nature of this sacramental procession of Lourdes.

"The bishop bestows the eucharistic blessing upon every sick person," Estrade explained. "Most cures take place after the reception of this blessing."

"After the blessing and not after drinking of the spring?" Lafite asked again.

"At both times," Dozous replied. "To me, however, those cures are the most marvellous that have no theatrical element. A few days ago, for instance, a young woman recovered from a hopelessly stiff knee-joint while she was thoughtlessly sitting on a park bench and gazing into the river. She had neither used the spring nor prayed. It was a wholly unforeseen surprise of grace. . . ."

The shadows of the afternoon were growing longer while the crowd still kept increasing. The strangest of tensions became more and more acute. Dozous and Estrade, experienced witnesses, asserted that each time it was precisely the same excitement which had shaken the crowd at Massabielle on that great Thursday of vexation when the miracle of roses had been expected. Restlessly people changed their places. A hum as of the tides of ocean flooded from the Celtic cross at the far end of the park to the basilica platform. It seemed to dash itself against the silence of the mortally afflicted who were crouching in their carts. No silence of earth could be likened to that of these heads which, weary with the weight of fate and waiting, inclined toward breast or shoulder.

Lafite observed the people among whom he was wedged in. They were far from being only the familiar simple Frenchmen of the South: worn-out old women dressed in cheap black stuffs, knitted mittens on their scarred hands, crudely shaved men in their Sunday best with bright dreamy eyes fixed on nothingness. Figures like this made up a considerable proportion of the crowd; not a majority. A striking number of well-dressed persons were to be seen. Very near Lafite there was, for instance, a gentleman of middle age, presumably a scholar. Bushy eyebrows and moustache and gold-rimmed pince-nez with a black cord. This intellectual face had doubtless until recently answered the question of all questions with a sincere "*ignorabimus*"—"we shall not know," not otherwise than Hyacinthe de Lafite, who confessed that materialistic atheism was a religion too, though the worst in the world. Now the gentleman with the bushy moustache nervously shifted his weight from one foot to the other. Ten times he took off his pince-nez, polished the lenses, put them back on. He sighed with anxiety. He dried his perspiration. He seemed to await something and knew not whether to desire or fear it. And the same vague feeling had invaded the writer's breast.

The bells struck in sign that the bishop's procession, obedient to the lady's behest, was setting out for the grotto where the Body of the Lord was to be placed in the monstrance. A mo-

tion passed through the crowd which thronged against the
barrier of the sick. A few minutes later muffled calls were
heard: "They are coming!" And these tens of thousands grew
as still as though each held his breath. On the platform a little
man carrying a banner of the Madonna was seen leading the
other banner-bearers.

"Do you see that chap with the bow-legs?" Dr. Dozous
asked softly. "He takes precedence over even the miller
Nicolau, for he is, so to speak, the first-born of the miracle. We
still call him the Bouhouhorts child hereabouts, though he's
over twenty-three now. You probably remember the excitement when a working-woman immersed her dying child on
one of the first days that the spring flowed?"

Hyacinthe de Lafite did not remember.

The bishop appeared under his brocaded canopy. The reddish violet of the bishop's robe gleamed in the great sun among
his numerous attendants in white vestments. He came forth
from under the canopy. The radiant eucharist in both hands,
he approached the semi-circle of the carts. The bells were
silent. Only the thin tinkle of a Mass bell was heard as the
bishop reached one end of the semi-circle and with the sacramental Christ made the sign of the cross over the first of the
sick. All fell to their knees, including Dozous and Estrade.
Lafite looked at the strange gentleman next to him. He, too,
hesitated before kneeling. The writer had not knelt since his
earliest youth. He did not like to form part of a mass-movement
in any event. God had invited him to the royal box. He was
ashamed before himself and the others, too, ashamed to kneel
as well as not to kneel. Therefore he bowed as deeply as he
could and remained in this attitude.

The bishop went from sick person to sick person, bestowing
the blessing. His way was long. Suddenly from the midst of
the many thousands a shrill cry rose:

"Lord, grant us to see!
Lord, grant us to walk!"

This prayerful ejaculation and magic formula was taken up in choral fashion everywhere. From all sides the voices stormed Heaven to force it down to earth. It was as though one were no longer in Europe, home of the mathematical and inventive mind, but in some primordial dwelling-place of man where human masses had not yet lost the energy to release great streams of magic feeling wherewith to force down to them the powers above. Lafite felt this stream suck him into its spiral whorl. He was not surprised when suddenly the strange gentleman beat his breast and uttered a variant of that wild and grandiose prayer:

"Lord, grant us to see!
Lord, grant us to walk!"

Slowly the bishop had made the complete round of the semi-circle. Now he strode solemnly up the incline of the platform. With a gesture of inexpressible eloquence he raised the eucharist high above his head in blessing of all the people. The little bell tinkled thinly through infinite space. Then the great chimes began to ring once more. The blessings were over. Nothing extraordinary appeared to have taken place.

The bishop and his clergy vanished inside the basilica. The mass, released from the spell that had forged it into oneness, began to stream hither and yon and to be divided into groups. The *brancardiers* took their places behind the little carts. They waited for the clearing of the platform in order to take back to the various hospitals the sick entrusted to their care.

"Let's go now," said Dr. Dozous.

Lafite lingered. Had anything happened! Something must

have happened. At first the feeling was vague. Then there arose at the very other end of the row of carts a sharp tumult of voices. Many outstretched hands pointed to the spot. Human whirls rushed forward. Lafite and his two companions were swept along. Dozous made his way energetically forward and pulled the other two along. They came to the row of carts where the *brancardiers,* used to such scenes, had formed a barrier by joining hands. Yonder, however, in the wide space between the carts and the platform, a space that seemed momently to expand, there was to be seen a solitary woman.

This woman was an awkward mass of fat. She had lifted her skirt a little, as though to avoid puddles. Her legs had quite disappeared in the rolls of fat, so that her feet were like mere stumps. And on these poor stumps the formless female colossus trod slowly, step by step, very slowly, exactly like a marionette, wholly absorbed by this act of walking, with a uniform and stiff and unelastic rhythm. The woman had thrown back her head, so that her wretched flower-trimmed little hat had slid back toward her neck. She had let her skirt fall again. She held her arms stretched out to balance herself as though she were walking not on the ground but on a rope. A *brancardier* followed her with practised attention, ready to catch her if it were necessary. Another followed with her cart. She walked and walked as though she were within an invisible sphere that had rolled out of time and space and were moving with her. Breathlessly the crowd stared. Lafite heard someone whisper: "I know her well. She hasn't been able to take a step these ten years."

When will she collapse? Lafite wondered. The woman did not collapse, but on her swollen legs continued this strange staccato dance-like walking until, growing smaller and smaller, she disappeared at the door of the basilica. Now only did the death-like stillness break. A little man, tears coursing down his cheeks, intoned the *Magnificat* in a high tremulous voice: "*Magnificat anima mea Dominum.*"

A group of priests who were mingled with the spectators joined in: "*Et exultavit spiritus meus.*" And over the whole wide place resounded the Psalm in which it is said of God "that He dethrones the mighty and uplifts the powerless and shows mercy to Israel, His son, mindful of the mercy promised our father Abraham and his seed for evermore. . . ."

Lafite had the feeling that all his entrails had dropped lower in his belly. Merely to hear the sound of his own voice he asked the physician: "Is that a genuine cure?"

Dozous made a vague gesture. "Days pass and sometimes weeks," he replied, "before it is possible to pass a certain judgment. First, all medical evidence concerning the particular case must be gathered. . . ."

Dozous invited Estrade and Lafite to accompany him to the bureau of confirmation. Lafite glanced into the room, which reminded him less of a doctor's office than of the chart-room of a sailing-vessel. But at the very door he turned. He felt wretched. He needed to be alone.

CHAPTER FORTY-EIGHT

I Never Loved

THE GROTTO at twilight. The Pyrenean sky was still pregnant with light and radiant colours. But earth was turning grey. The great iron stand in front of the niche in the grotto, a strange palm of candles, quivered with its hundred flames and drove the last vestiges of daylight from the interior of the grotto. The statue of the lady in the oval was clothed in dancing shadows. The bush of thorns and the wild rose-vine already green had both remained unchanged these twenty years. The dark rock beneath the niche gleamed with moisture. Drop after drop rolled down. The projecting rock on the other side of the grotto which had the form of a gigantic skull-bone showed a yellow sheen. If one slowly approached the grotto now from the shore of the Gave, as Hyacinthe de Lafite was doing, one might have the impression that an openwork curtain or carpet or Gothic grillework were covering this skull of rock. But it was only an intricate tracery formed by the crutches, sticks, iron braces, and orthopædic casings hung up here by the cured. The grotto itself seemed to have nothing left in common with the wild cavern of Lafite's walks of former days. Yet no one had touched the grotto itself. A beautiful tall fence of metal grillework had been erected in front of it with two small entrances to the grotto at either side. The whole length of this fence there extended a threshold on which those might kneel who desired to take holy communion here at Massabielle or desired to offer their prayers at the very portal of the vision. About twenty rows of benches divided by a middle aisle afforded seats for several hundreds of the devout. At the left of the grotto on a high pulpit stood a young priest who repeated in a gentle voice the Lorettan litany. More and more clearly as he approached, Lafite heard the French words of the invocations: "Mother of divine grace . . . thou purest Mother . . ." After each pause made by the priest arose the murmur of the responses: "Thou most chaste Mother—thou strong Mother—thou lovely Mother—thou wonderful Mother—thou Mother of good counsel—pray for us. . . ."

What beautiful verses, Lafite thought, and what a tranquillizing rhythm! And in truth the restrained voice of the young priest and the antiphonal murmur of the responses blended to form a somnolent cradle-song which lulled the senses in the deepening dusk. Many of the kneeling prayed with arms stretched out, thus symbolizing in their own bodies the form and the agony of the cross. By forcing their muscles to endure the strain and pain of this posture for whole quarter-hours at a time they obeyed the call to penitence which the lady had issued through Bernadette.

Hyacinthe remained standing at a suitable distance from the last benches. But it was sheer shyness that kept him from approaching. He felt like a stranger whom accident had brought quite uninvited into the midst of a circle of intimates. Many decades had passed since he had entered a sanctuary for any purpose but the appraisal of artistic values. I am not as these people are, he reflected, I haven't their uncomplicated faith. All the corrosive thoughts that have ever been thought have penetrated my brain. My reason stumbles at the head of the human caravan over a darkling land. I know that we are a wretched animal species, distinguished from the insects and amphibians by but a few nerve centres and fallacious syllogisms. Truth is a million times more inaccessible to us than the differential calculus is to a louse. Our contemporary form

of thought, critical and objective, deems itself to be far
exalted above former religious forms. Yet it, too, forgets its
limitations in that it also is but a form of thought. And I have
the intuition at this moment that the past forms of thought
will some day be the future forms and may look down with
a smile upon our entire critical period. I have often had the
wish that we might be satisfied with small results, but my
voracious heart was not made to be thus satisfied. True, I
know that all gods are but the mirrored images of our own
corporeal nature and that if the pelicans were to believe in
a god, it would have to be a pelican. Yet is that no disproof
of the being of divinity, but only a proof of the narrowness
of the mortal mind limited to its own words and imaginings.
Never could I have endured the thought of being eternally
excluded from the cognition of God, to whom I feel myself
akin in spite of all. I do not belong to you yonder who believe
in a Heaven in the heavens. But neither am I to be reckoned
among those dullards who believe in a heaven on earth to be
provided by better laws and machines. To them I would prefer
you yonder who believe in a Heaven in the heavens.

Lafite walked a few paces nearer to the grotto of Massabielle.

"Thou wisest Virgin—thou venerable Virgin—thou praiseworthy Virgin—thou mighty Virgin—thou kindly Virgin—thou
faithful Virgin—thou mirror of righteousness . . ."

If dear old Clarens were here beside me I'd be impelled to
tease him. Listen to that extremely beautiful litany, my friend.
Not otherwise did the pious Ephesians once celebrate the
praise of their Diana. Isn't that so?—I'm no historian, my dear
Hyacinthe, and hence I don't overestimate history. It is nothing
other than the refraction of eternal happenings in the water
of the river of time. Each epoch sees objects assume different
shapes in the mirroring stream. Whether Apollo or Christ,
whether Diana or Mary—names and their specific representa-

tional contents are but the changing names for a presence eternally felt by man. At this moment you feel that presence more keenly than any of the others, my friend.—Do you really think so, dear Clarens? In spite of my critical intelligence I am, I grant you, an old-fashioned fellow. Poets are always old-fashioned. But perhaps men will come after us who will not know the visitation of such feelings.—You need not worry, my dear Hyacinthe. There will always be a Bernadette who will render her invisible lady visible to the world. *Per sæcula sæculorum.* . . .

Lafite moved still nearer to the grotto of Massabielle. He had now reached the last row of benches.

"Thou cause of our joy—thou vessel of the spirit—thou venerable vessel—thou excellent vessel of devotion . . ."

Listen, Clarens. I won't fool you any longer. A cancer is feeding on my body. A heartless doctor told me so bluntly. But I need no doctor. The disease first attacked the larynx. Later it will attack the stomach, the liver, the colon. These phenomena are called metastatic. I read up on it all. My days are numbered and their number is few. Don't reply, Clarens, that I still look truly human. In a year or even a few months I'll be like one of those lumps of fleshly misery that I had to see in the Hospital of the Seven Sorrows. And I'm far from being a hero, my friend, rather a quivering coward. Yes, my days are numbered and my nights heavy upon me. Yet is the fear of death not the worst. One can manage with it. You stretch yourself out and you wait. But in my heavy nights, Clarens, I've come upon a far more ghastly thing. You won't laugh at me, for you've come to believe. Since age has not made me duller but wiser, I've come upon the cognition that I'm the greatest sinner in the whole world, I, Hyacinthe de Lafite, the nameless scribbler, the zero who means nothing to anyone. And don't believe, Clarens, that I'm indulging in

Byronic coquetry in this hour. I'm not talking about the thousand sins of slackness and weakness with which my soul is stained day by day. I'm talking about the crucial sin according to Genesis with which I'm rotten, of that insane, laughable, and most absurd pride which stood at the very cradle of my mind. At ten it had hold of me. I was too proud to be beholden to anyone for anything, even to my dear mother. Out of pride I wanted to be something which is self-productive and hence self-sustaining. The notion of being a human creature, a sort of grown-up fœtus, conditioned by descent, land, speech, blood, metabolism—this notion seemed intolerable to me. Independent to an insane degree, I swore to be the only human being that belonged to no community. According to my conviction nothing had served to educate, influence, or guide me. I was to be the fruit of my self. The self-consciousness of a vain spirit exalted itself above all human thought. If I did not acknowledge the being of God, it was because I could not endure not being He. Therefore the analytical processes became a throne from which I ruled the world. And now it seems to me today as though I were standing behind my own back and saw myself in the round at last like any stranger. My sin, Clarens, was the sin of Lucifer, even though I'm a dirty nobody and sick unto death. In the heavy nights of the past year I have also come to see that our sin harms us far more than it does God. It is evident that my pride has destroyed me.

A few of the people at prayer looked with astonishment at Lafite, who was standing in the aisle between the benches.

"Thou rose of the spirit—thou tower of ivory—thou golden house—thou ark of the Covenant—thou gate of Heaven—thou morning star . . ."

Where was I? Yes, thou tower of ivory. I, too, am a tower. But the tower is ruined and full of rats and woodlice. Oh, yes, thou golden house. My self is a house, too. It was lent me and I made a pig-sty of it. But now the period of the loan runs out and I shall be driven forth and there is no time left in which to put things to rights. O thou morning star, what have I made of my life? For it was a good life, despite all need. Never was I punished with rotten limbs, like that poor lad in the hospital. Lupus never corroded my face, though I deserved it far more than those poor harmless women. I never had to cower in a corner for shame of my face. Yet I should cower more miserably than that woman, for the visage of what I truly am is more that of a Gorgon than hers. I've wasted all my hours in a low titillation of the senses and in utter confusion. That was, next to pride, my second sin, which now wallows toward me like a very hippopotamus. What have I left to show for the million seconds of this goodly life? The women I have embraced are mouldy ghosts within me. What of the ecstasies of beauty and thought that were granted me? I was not sufficiently possessed by them nor industrious enough to give them wings. What is left is a bitter, bitter taste, thou morning star. . . .

"Thou healer of the sick—thou refuge of sinners—thou comforter of the troubled—thou helper of Christians . . ."

Am I even a Christian? I don't know. All that I know is that all dazzling formulations of my mind are no more than the croaking of frogs and the chirping of crickets. Nothing is left me but solitariness. For my pride has lost me mankind. When the disease attacks me again I will neither tell my kinsmen nor seek a cure; I'll go back to Paris and hide in a hole to die in. No one will be with me in that hole of death, thou refuge of sinners, thou comforter of the troubled. And I do not complain. For it was not the world that abandoned me but I who abandoned the world. . . .

The *Agnus Dei* completed the litany. The priest and the

murmuring chorus intoned their Aves one by one. The iron
palm of candles was ever more radiant in the increasing dusk.
The white statue of the lady was but a white shimmer in the
interior of the grotto. The devout, with arms outstretched,
were shadowy crosses.

"It's perfectly logical," Lafite sighed, half aloud. This sigh
had been preceded by a long, vague chain of reasoning which
ended with the following conclusion: My desolate aloneness
is a logical result. For I have loved no one. No one and
nothing and not even myself. . . .

In the meantime he had, without knowing it, come face to
face with the grotto. He could have pressed his forehead
against the grille work. His empty eyes stared into the disappearing hollow. Yet the longer and the emptier his gazing,
the more evidently did the bodily discomfort that had tortured
him for hours disappear, the desolate sensation of his entrails
being loosened and having sunk down. He breathed calmly
and yielded to a weariness which made his self seem less important.

Even and mechanical was the voice of the young priest!
Even and mechanical were the murmured responses of the
devout! Scarcely distinguishable were the words of this endless cradle-song: "Pray for us . . . now and in the hour of our
death. . . ."

The rhythmic murmur became a beneficent rustling. It
was like a soft support against which one could lean one's
back. And with it came the feeling as though one were surrounded by a helpfulness, encircled, taken into its core. The
prayers of men took Hyacinthe de Lafite into their midst.
Something like smiling irony came over him. Proud and without love? Yes! But am I really so deserted, so much more
than others? Would it not suffice, seeing the vast incertitude
of all knowledge, to be no vainer than these here? What's

the difference between myself and them? Bits of sophisticated power over speech which enable me to dress up my total ignorance, more frivolous in itself and less honest than theirs. Did I not sink so low merely because I did not believe that there were arms which could lift me up? O maternal power of the universe, O Morning Star! The support came nearer him. The prayer behind him seemed to lay many gentle hands upon him. He who had always despised numbers as a conglomerate of low instincts and low interests now felt the devout behind him become a single loving incorporeal body that helped him more and more. Without any other sensation than that of the fading of his shame, the writer Lafite now also sank upon his knees and murmured into the grotto of the lady the familiar words of the angel's greeting and of his mother's lips and his own childhood. There was no new element in his consciousness. But he knew that the emptiness, the critical emptying of the soul's content, of which he had once been so proud, had always been fulfilled by a certainty which was merely being unveiled and brightened as by a breaking fog. There is no such thing as a conversion to faith, only a reversion, only a return. For faith is not a function of the soul. It is the soul itself in its last nakedness. In a peace unknown to him Lafite remained thus until night had fallen and most of the worshippers had risen and gone and only the flames of the candles were left alive. But ere he arose there came to his lips, he knew not how, the invocation: "Bernadette Soubirous, pray for me!"

And Bernadette Soubirous was still living at this hour. For days pain had once more most terribly beset her. The infirmary lamps had been lighted. Bernadette's eyes were tensely directed at a shadowed crucifix upon the wall. She did not dream that at this moment her lady's proudest foe was lying on his knees before her.

CHAPTER FORTY-NINE

I Love

MARIE DOMINIQUE PEYRAMALE at sixty-eight was still a giant. Only his eyes were less fiery than of old. They now looked out from a broad, somewhat puffy ecclesiastical face with glances held in check. Of all his enemies it was his own temperament that had led to most of his troubles. When seventeen years ago the pastoral letter of his patron Bertrand Sévère Laurence had been published and had made of Lourdes a new centre of Catholic Christianity, Peyramale had believed himself to be the chosen ruler of the transformed town. He quarrelled with the architects, he rejected their plans; he drew his own plans for the basilica, for the crypts, for a future Church of the Rosary below the basilica. His masterfulness caused much bitterness. People stormed the old bishop's door with their grievances. That upright and admirable old man, in Monseigneur Forcade's description, was not the one to forgive the originator of these annoyances. He thought that Peyramale had let the development of things make a megalomaniac of him. A rebuke was in order. It was delivered with a good deal of severity. Peyramale's monumental plans, the pride of his heart, were partly abandoned, partly reduced to fit the taste of little people. The gossips and intriguers had the last word. The artistic taste of sextons and narrow bigots of both sexes prevailed. Marie Dominique, descendant of three generations of scholars and physicians, a man of knowledge and some creative imagination, had dreamed of a complex of sacral edifices which by sheer grandeur was to overshadow all in that kind that this century had built. Reality destroyed his lofty dream. The confectioners of sugary ecclesiastical art and architecture were victorious all along the line.

The ambitious dean had desired to make Lourdes into a second Rome. And if one considered the streams of men and women who made the pilgrimage thither year after year it did, after a fashion, become a second Rome. But in this Rome the masterful dean was anything but pope. The millions of pilgrims and sick who arrived in the course of each single year required an army of clerics for their spiritual needs. Only the monastic orders were able to provide such numbers. Hence these orders took in hand the administration of both the hospitals and the sacred places. Peyramale lived to see himself limited to his local parish duties and deprived of all influence upon this new and important Lourdes. Once upon a time, before the days of the grotto, he had been a very monarch in his district. When people bowed down before him it was in the nature of a tribute. Now he felt like a king dethroned. A greeting was a narrowly personal matter. The bitterest circumstance was that, according to his own not wholly just conviction, he owed his downfall to a shrewd intriguer, a very snake that he had nourished in his bosom. Father Sempet, member of an order, had long served as his third chaplain, whom he had always preferred to his other two co-workers, the sharp-tongued Father Pomian and the harmless Father Penès. Actually Sempet seemed more inoffensive than Penès himself. But while the third chaplain bowed down to him obsequiously, the monkish pussyfooter had used astonishing shrewdness and energy to get complete control of power. Now he was curator of the grotto and the biggest man in Lourdes and also, of course, the enemy of enemies and very scourge of the aged dean.

While Marie Dominique Peyramale was leaving the station

at Nevers with his shabby hand-bag he could not but remember the whispered comment of Sempet, who had made fun of Bernadette longer and more sharply than either Pomian or Penès or anyone else: "Do you know, Monsieur le Curé, what this capital saint does the moment she comes out of her trance? She begins to scratch the lice out of her mat of hair." Peyramale was inclined to regard the inglorious end of his career as a deserved punishment. Had he not been a doubting Thomas even in that last great interview with Bernadette which had taken place around Advent of '63? Inscrutable Providence, he could not but reflect, you have raised up this confounded Sempet, who was far more sceptical than I.

The big man stamping with his bag through the streets of Nevers was deeply stirred. The approaching meeting with her whom he had once threatened to sweep out of the temple weighed on his heart. Bernadette had been his whole life's deepest experience of grace. Blind, stupid ass that he had been, found worthy without merit of having stood at the cradle of the greatest of modern miracles. Of him the lady had made her demand to build a chapel and establish processions. In thanks he had teased her with stupid counter-demands for money and blooming hedge-roses. Quite properly had she crossed all his plans and placed the processions in others' hands. But how about Sempet? How could she endure him? Clever rogue! He had never come out in the open. Peyramale had been on the point of visiting Bernadette more than once. But the thought that she might not be glad to see him had always held him back again and had finally, years ago, given him the idea of sending the little picture of the Madonna. Her illness had been a matter of rumour for long. But definite details were not available, not even in Nevers. So it had taken her own strange words, *"Cher Monsieur le Curé*, Bernadette is thinking of you," to shake him deeply enough to set out on the long trip without delay. Even after he had bought his ticket troublesome affairs had forced him to delay his departure. While he was arranging these matters he was filled every hour of the day and night by a profound discomfort, a restlessness at his very core which often rose to a dull feeling of guilt. He could not rid himself of the notion that Bernadette was calling him as her old protector. When he had performed all troublesome duties, Holy Week had set in. Truly unheard of that a pastor should leave his flock in the lurch at that, of all seasons. Peyramale did it. "What if I were no more here?" he asked the substitute who took over his duties. "I am old and sick and live on by some mistake, because the Lord indulgently closes an eye."

Mother Imbert received the dean of Lourdes with friendly veneration. His violet collar proved that, though dethroned, all kinds of honours had fallen to his share, including the appellation of Monseigneur. The mother superior at once offered him the hospitality of the house. In regard to Sister Marie Bernarde all she could say was that she was alive as by a miracle, since all physicians agreed that the sickness had wasted her wholly away. It was only the unbelievably strong and persistent soul of the poor darling child that prolonged her life. Perhaps Providence desired the object of the grace of the Mother of God to see one more Passion week. Yet three days ago Dr. Saint-Cyr had expressed the conviction that the death of the seeress of Lourdes could not but be a mere matter of hours now. The pains, however, were gone since yesterday. Monseigneur Lelonge, the bishop, had given orders that no callers be admitted to see the dying girl without his express permission. Mother Imbert was afraid that an exception could not be made even in the case of the venerable dean of Lourdes. She would, however, send a messenger at once to the episcopal chancellery. Meanwhile Monseigneur was begged to rest a little from the journey and to partake of some refreshments.

Peyramale was about to fly up at the bishop's orders, but restrained himself and said in his still powerful, veiled voice: "Bernadette Soubirous is a child of my parish. For many years Providence entrusted her to my poor care."

The mother superior smiled and bowed. "We know it well, Monseigneur. Although we of this house were ordered by our superiors not to pay too much attention to those great events, yet they are well known to us in all their details."

Early in the afternoon Mère Vauzous and Sœur Nathalie came to conduct the dean of Lourdes to the infirmary. The old man's heart beat hard. "Will she recognize me?" he asked.

"She is clearer of mind and calmer than ever," Nathalie replied, not seeking to hide her tears.

It was a quite spacious sickroom with two tall windows and three beds, each with a pointed canopy of veiling. Two of the beds were empty. Bernadette lay in the third in the room's right corner. On the opposite wall was a narrow chest of drawers and upon it a statue of the Madonna, though not the one by Fabich. A crucifix hung above. That was all except a single armchair and a couple of very small ones of wood. With heavy tread that creaked disturbingly in his own ears Marie Dominique Peyramale approached the bed in the right-hand corner. What he saw was not a nun of thirty-five, but a very young girl with a delicate face of alabaster. The exquisitely delicate nostrils quivered. The child-like mouth had a breath of colour. The rather high forehead was half concealed by a compress. The large dark eyes were at once watchful and apathetic. They were still the eyes of Bernadette Soubirous. The dean, all but seventy years old, blushed shyly. He cleared his throat and said after a while: "Well, I've come. . . ."

One of the small chairs was pushed toward him. Cautiously he lowered his great bulk into it. He had reason to fear that it might go to pieces under him. On the coverlet lay two small hands of old ivory which were trying to stretch out toward the guest. They could not. Most carefully the dean of Lourdes took one of these frail miniature hands into his own huge one and breathed a reverential kiss upon it. Two full minutes passed before Bernadette raised a very soft voice which nevertheless sounded strangely distinct and clear through the room: "Monsieur le Curé, I didn't lie to you."

Peyramale fought down a sob. "God knows that you did not, *ma sœur*," he whispered. "It was I, I, who was not worthy of you."

A shadow of fear flitted over the girlish face. "They question me again and ever again. . . ." And then, after an interval of waiting, Bernadette declared with trembling breath: "I saw her. Yes, I saw her."

The dean did not know why he was suddenly impelled to speak to her in the old familiar way, as though no two decades had passed and as though she who lay before him were not the nun Marie Bernarde, the sublime seal of perfection upon her face, but the old Bernadette Soubirous, a little creature clear as well-water and yet somehow inscrutable. Peyramale brought his heavy, weary head near to the dying girl.

"Yes, my little one, you saw her and you will see her again."

A shadow of reflection appeared in those large eyes. Memories came to light. There sat the dean by his study fire. And she was there too and had kept her white *capulet* on because it was very cold. And she had wanted to be maid at Madame Millet's and he asked if the lady had no better position for her. . . . And so with a sigh the words came from Bernadette's lips: "Oh, no, Monsieur le Curé, it's not at all sure that the lady would let me be her maid."

At last the dean managed to strike the free, light tone that he had sought to use from the start. "If anything is certain, little girl, it's that. It's the very least that the lady will do for you."

The tiniest gleam of roguish irony came into her eyes. Everybody was so sweet and gentle with her now. Did they really mean it or were they pretending out of pity?

"I'm not at all sure, not at all, no," said that small clear voice, incorruptible as of old. "All I could achieve was being sick. And maybe I didn't even suffer enough."

This time the sob escaped Peyramale. "You've suffered enough, little child, for the Heaven of heavens. You may believe me."

Now a vestigial smile seemed to flicker across her still face. And suddenly the clear small voice no longer spoke French as heretofore, but the coarse dialect of home and childhood. "Not a bit, Monsieur le Curé." It was the girl from the Rue des Petites Fossées who spoke. "I know about sick people. We all exaggerate a little. Our pains aren't so terrible. . . ." And falteringly, after a violent struggle for breath: "I believe I had far fewer pains than joys . . . in those days . . . in those . . ."

It had been too much for her. The face of alabaster became contorted. The eyes protruded. Dr. Saint-Cyr in the background gave a sign. Peyramale got up with difficulty from the little chair. His country parson's shoes creaked.

It was the sixteenth of April. A Wednesday, bright and cheerful. Next day was Maundy Thursday with its mighty liturgy. The sisters of Saint Gildarde were kept very busy at this time. Toward noon Nathalie came back from an errand. At the gate of the cloister something seemed to hold her fast. A strange compulsion kept her from entering. Marie Bernarde, it flashed through her mind, and she hastened over to the infirmary which was one of the conventual buildings. The nurses had lifted Bernadette into the armchair. She had no longer been able to breathe in bed. Now she sat awkwardly in the chair and with eyes wide with horror cried out to Nathalie: "*Ma sœur . . . j'ai peur . . . j'ai peur . . . ma sœur! . . .*"

Nathalie knelt down beside her and took her hands. "Why are you afraid, and of what, dear?"

The sick girl's chest heaved with difficulty. She stammered brokenly: "So much grace was shown me . . . I must make up for it . . . and I can't. . . ."

"Think of our sweet Saviour, *ma sœur*," Nathalie said and tried hard not to weep. But Bernadette's thoughts remained at the same point, that she had not been equal to the grace granted her.

"I'm afraid," she moaned again and again. "*J'ai peur . . . j'ai peur, ma sœur.*"

Nathalie looked for some narcotic. She found none. At last she laid her hands on Bernadette's head to help her. "Are the pains very bad?" she whispered from between clenched teeth.

"Not bad enough . . . not enough . . ." Bernadette panted.

Nathalie bent low over her. "We'll all help you, dearest Marie Bernarde. We'll keep praying and praying for you all the time, both now and later."

"Oh, please, *ma sœur*, be sure to do that," Bernadette pleaded like a child.

Sister Nathalie sent word to Mother Imbert that the patient was very low and that Dr. Saint-Cyr and Father Fèbvre should be sent for at once. The pains continued for some minutes to toss Bernadette to and fro. Suddenly she could take a deep breath again and asked in the matter-of-fact way of one asking the time: "What day is today?"

"It's Wednesday of Easter week, *ma sœur*," Nathalie told her.

"Then tomorrow is Thursday!" Bernadette seemed astonished.

"Yes, tomorrow is Thursday—a very great Thursday!"

"A very great Thursday, indeed," Bernadette repeated. And the glory of the goal suffused her eyes. Nathalie did not understand her friend's happiness. She could not remember that Thursday, the eleventh of February, when the Soubirous girls had gone to look for faggots and Bernadette had sat by the Savy brook, one stocking in her hand, one on her foot, and had rubbed her eyes, wondering whether she were dreaming or awake. And again it had been a Thursday when the lady had spoken: "Go to the spring yonder and drink and wash yourself." And a Thursday it had been, too, when the lady had named her name. Thursday had been the day of the lady and of her great gifts. And tomorrow was another Thursday. . . .

"I'm not afraid any more, *ma sœur;* I'll be quiet now," Bernadette said with the air of a guilty child promising an impatient nurse to behave.

Shortly thereafter she slumped on her left side in the chair. They carried her to bed, thinking all was over. Yet breath returned, brief and heavy. The room was filled with people. The physician and the priest were beside her. Mère Imbert, Mère Vauzous, and the other nuns were on their knees. Marie Thérèse herself looked like a dying creature. Near the door stood Marie Dominique Peyramale, far too big and weighty for this room and this delicate death. His hands were folded in an impassioned gesture.

Bernadette had opened her eyes again. She understood all that was going on. With astonishing force, such as she had not shown for days, she made one of those great and glowing signs of the cross which her vision had taught her. The prayers for the dying were begun. Father Fèbvre intoned the

Song of Songs, the words in which the human soul greets its bridegroom: " 'I was asleep, but my heart waked. It is the voice of my beloved that knocketh, saying: Open to me, my sister, my love, my dove, my undefiled; for my head is filled with dew, and my locks with the drops of the night.' "

Bernadette's eyes flashed̄ strangely into the void. They thought she was seeking the crucifix on the wall. They placed it on her bosom and passionately she pressed it to her. Yet her eyes sought a farther distance and suddenly a great thrill made her body quiver and a new strength lifted her up. Therewith came, long echoing from her breast in a round vibrant mature woman's voice, the cry of her confession: "*J'aime* . . . I love. . . ."

Deeply as a stricken bell the word vibrated in the room. It was so great a cry that the prayers ceased and all were silenced. Only Marie Thérèse Vauzous, her arms stretched out and crossed, slid toward the bed to be nearer the blessed one. Her face was riven by grief. Few had ever seen her weep. But she believed now that the lady was in the room. The most blessed, the ever lovely had come in her own person to receive her child and take her with her. Alone with her in the ineffable solitude of death the needy child had cried to her returning lady: "I love . . . I love you. . . ." And now she, too, the nun Vauzous, sceptic so long against her will, was granted, she thought, the grace of presence at a vision. Look down upon the outcast, the hard of heart, who was full of envy in her gracelessness! Sobs wrung themselves from Marie Thérèse. In a broken voice she began to pray her Ave. But Bernadette regarded her old teacher with a look whose attentiveness strove after obedience. She knew that they desired her to repeat the prayer after them. But what remained to her of breath she had used for the mighty cry of love. She kept her lips busily moving and in the second part of the Ave she succeeded in murmuring: "Now and in the hour . . ." Then her voice failed.

Commonly death extinguishes a human face in the twinkling of an eye. But death illuminated the face of Bernadette Soubirous. At the very moment of her last breath's ceasing her countenance assumed the aspect of the ecstasies, as though through all the sights and things of the world she had remained bound to the lady of her vision. And in the presence of this countenance all felt what Antoine Nicolau had felt once upon a time and expressed thus: "One ought not even to touch a being like that."

"*J'aime.*" That confession of love did not fade from the consciousness of Marie Dominique Peyramale. He was still kneeling by the door without motion. The window had been thrown open. The nuns knelt shadowy around the bed. Others moved shadowily about and clad the dead girl in habit and coif and fetched long thick candles and stuck them in the holders and lighted them. Not much of this quick hushed activity reached Peyramale, who was left reverently undisturbed in his devotion. Yet now and then he glanced at the window in which the radiance of spring faded to a silvery thinness. He could see sundry fruit trees of the cloister garden in blossom; he could see voyaging clouds. All life seemed marvellously light to Peyramale and the lightness communicated itself even to his own massive body. He utterly forgot that he was still kneeling on his elderly rheumatic knees. Only gradually did he begin to suspect how deeply this death had refreshed his vital powers. All things had changed. Could any sting or any bitterness ever again assail him? Silvery was the light of the day, golden was the light of the tapers. And daylight and candlelight played over the eternally remote face of Bernadette. Peyramale could not bear to leave this sight. To his own surprise he heard himself whispering: "Your life begins, O Bernadette."

The meaning of these soft words was not only: You are in heaven now, O Bernadette. It was also: You are now in heaven and on earth, O Bernadette. Your eyes beheld more than ours. In your heart was more love than our hard hearts could ever even understand. Therefore are you effectually present in every hour of every day not only in the spring of Massabielle, but in each one of those blossoming trees out there. Your life begins, O Bernadette.

With youthful lightness the huge man arose. With a last look and a last sign of the cross he said farewell to Bernadette and turned and went.

CHAPTER FIFTY

The Fiftieth Ave

ON THE greatest of all the days in her honour there were
many Soubirous, the children, grandchildren, nephews, and
nieces of the sister and the brothers of Bernadette. The day
centred, however, not in her blood relations but in the first-
born of the miracle, the Bouhouhorts child. The latter, more
precisely Justin Marie Adolar Duconte Bouhouhorts, was now
seventy-seven years old, a little old man with merry eyes and a
shrewd mouth under a moustache that was still dark. Despite
his years he was still very active as a florist in Pau. He had been
given a second-class ticket to Rome and assured of free board
and lodging there, too. For the first-born of the miracle of
Lourdes was to share the joy of that great day of celebration
on which Pius XI was to enrol little Bernadette Soubirous in
the calendar of saints. Christendom does not afford a more
magnificent ceremony than the canonization of a saint by the
Vicar of God on earth. Of the Bouhouhorts child the tale was
told that seventy-five years ago the new saint had often carried
him in her arms when the neighbouring families went calling
on each other. This the florist of Pau could in no wise remember. In the course of time, however, frequent questionings and
others' tales had heated his imagination and helped out his memory. The old man was fond of depicting in elaborate detail the
appearance, voice, character, demeanour of her to whom he
owed his miraculous recovery and all the modest blessings
of his long life.

"When I was a child I was paralysed and had convulsions,

as you have certainly read," he would say. "Bernadette and her mother used to carry me up and down and shake me till I came to myself. And I kept on seeing her until she said good-bye and went to the convent in Nevers. I was about eight or nine years old then. The Soubirous were our best friends; I know that from my parents. And so here, seventy years later, I am the only human being alive who was really personally close to our sweet intercessor of Lourdes when she was herself little more than a child. And I see her dear face before me now, as though she had left but a few hours ago. The good members of the Soubirous family can't equal that experience. All they know they know from books and pictures and hearsay. . . ."

Fifty thousand strangers had come to Rome to witness the canonization of Bernadette. They represented forty different nations. The most numerous group, both clerical and lay, was that of fifteen thousand Frenchmen, the core being representatives from the countryside of Bigorre. No wonder that immense attention was paid to the only human being who had seen Bernadette with his own eyes during those great February days and the first through whom the spring of grace had revealed its instantaneous and unanswerable power. The old gardener of Pau was surrounded by crowds and confused by the many hundreds who wanted to shake him by the hand. He was presented to all sorts of illustrious laymen and clerics. Monsieur Charles Roux, the ambassador of France, conversed with him repeatedly and saw to it that a good seat on the rostrum of honour was reserved for him. And so the Bouhouhorts child came to sit in the midst of dignitaries in Saint Peter's in Rome and blinked shyly about in the vast circular space.

It was a Holy Year, the thirty-third of this century. It was December 8, date of the immaculate conception. It was nine o'clock in the morning. Next to the Bouhouhorts child was seated a friendly and well-informed gentleman, a fellow-Frenchman, who lived in Rome and was more than generous in his explanations.

"Only on the occasion of canonizations are the gigantic windows here hung with red damask, as well as the small windows of the cupola, in order that no daylight enter. It is an impression never otherwise experienced. Though I'm half a Roman I've witnessed but a single previous canonization. Remark that, aside from the searchlights, there are six hundred chandeliers with twelve thousand bulbs, each at least a hundred-candlepower bulb. Accordingly the illumination is that of one million two hundred thousand candles."

Triumphantly the statistician regarded Bouhouhorts, who nodded his agreement. But the friendly gentleman had not by any means finished his calculations. "The surging masses fairly scare you. San Pietro holds eighty thousand. I'm convinced there are ten thousand more than that today. And still the middle aisle has to be kept clear for the entrance of His Holiness. He'll be followed by the entire College of Cardinals. I need recall to you only such famous names as Gasparri, Granito di Belmonte, Pacelli, Marchetti. No one can remember the names of the bishops and archbishops, because there will be a hundred and eighteen of them. A magnificent spectacle, eh, Monsieur?"

"Magnificent," Bouhouhorts echoed.

"And what must be your own feelings, my dear sir! When you were a child you were closely allied to the Soubirous. You yourself witnessed their poverty and misery. Oh, you probably remember it all, for the impressions of childhood are not easily lost. . . ."

"It was a pretty rotten life," the old man sighed with frankness.

"And now this magnificence, this radiance!" The friendly neighbour waxed enthusiastic. "Earth can offer nothing comparable. And that fifty-four years after her death. What is any ruler or head of state or dictator in comparison? They're washed up on time's shore and disappear in a hole in the earth. What remains? A name in dust-covered books. Think of our own Napoléon III, Monsieur. Nothing on earth is dustier or, in fact, funnier than a man of might when his might is gone and he can harm no one any more. The death of a man of might is his final defeat. Great minds are in far better case. But, to speak profanely, nothing surpasses the thorny career whose goal is heaven. Don't you agree, Monsieur Bouhouhorts?"

The Bouhouhorts child both nodded and shook his head, thus offering no decisive judgment in this matter.

By this time the silver trumpets had sounded their peals. Already the sedia of the Pope had been carried up the aisle in the midst of the Swiss Guards, the Guards of the Nobility, the Maestri di Camera, the scarlet-robed sediari, the consistorial advocates in black velvet, the prelates of the Signatura, the penitentiaries with their long wreathed staffs. The friendly French neighbour had pointed out and explained everything to the gardener of Pau, who sought with blinking eyes to distinguish and appreciate the sights.

The throne of the Pope was erected in the apse under the *Gloria* of Bernini. Sixteen cardinals sat on either side of him and at his feet the prelates of his court. The Bouhouhorts child not only heard all the names but was told the meaning of the sublime ceremonies which now began. A figure in black approached the throne of His Holiness, knelt down, and recited some Latin words. This was the consistorial advocate who had last conducted the case for the canonization of his client, Bernadette Soubirous. This case had been pending at court for decades, involving thoroughgoing discussions of *pro* and *contra* and subjected, above all, to the implacable intervention of time, that acid which separates the authentic from its contrary. Among the assembled advocates of the consistory he too was present who in the conduct of the case had represented, as it were, the opposing litigant, the faction of doubters, wherefore he was called by his vulgar title *advocatus diaboli.* He had had no easier time with Bernadette than once long ago the imperial prosecutor, Vital Dutour. Even in death she invalidated, with all her old tranquil pertinacity, every objection. For her corpse was from the beginning a very strange phenomenon. When, four days after her death, they carried her to eternal rest in the chapel of Saint Joseph, her body despite the long destructiveness of disease showed not the slightest trace of corruption or the odour of corruption. At the roots of her fingernails the astonished witnesses saw the dainty pink of child-like life. Thirty-nine years later the court of canonization appointed a commission in Nevers which opened the sarcophagus and exhumed and examined the body. Several physicians, including the municipal physician, were present. Bernadette's girlish body showed no sign of corruption. It was almost unchanged. Face, hands, and arms were white and their flesh soft. The mouth was a little open, as though breathing, so that the shimmer of the teeth was visible. The lids over the slightly sunken eyes were closed. The expression of dreamy remoteness still dwelt upon the features of the seeress. The body itself was rigid and so firm that the ladies of Nevers, who witnessed the official exhumation, were able to lift it and deposit it unharmed in a new coffin, like that of one just dead. The protocol concerning these facts made a great noise in the world. Voices arose in the press which declared this story of the uncorrupted body to be a fraud of the grossest sort. Of course the body had been skilfully embalmed soon after death and now an ordinary mummy was being shown off as a body miraculously preserved by special grace. The *advocatus diaboli*, whose duty it was to oppose canonization, adopted this argument and succeeded, seven years later, in having another commission appointed which once more opened the grave and subjected the unchanged body to a new examination. No evidence was found to support the suspicion. This was in 1925. Bernadette's opponent dropped all objections. Sanctification followed.

And now, after the passage of eight more years, down there at the end of the apse, under the *Gloria* of Bernini, the advocate of Bernadette who had conducted her case victoriously through all its phases humbly besought the Pontifex Maximus to enrol the name of the girl of Lourdes in the calendar of saints. The Pope did not answer in person, but by the mouth of his interlocutor, Monsignore Bacci, who was seated on a stool at the foot of the throne, his profile turned to Pius. The Holy Father, Bacci declared, had no more ardent wish than that this canonization be accomplished. Before the solemn enrolment could take place, however, it was necessary once more to invoke the divine light. Upon their knees the whole assembly sang the litany of the saints. Then the Pope gave the signal for the singing of the *"Veni, Creator Spiritus,"* which, taken up by the voices of the priests and the boys of the choir of the Sistine chapel, flooded the mighty edifice. Thereupon Bernadette's advocate repeated his prayer to the Pope. Monsignore Bacci arose, knelt before His Holiness, stretched out his arms, and said: "Arise, Peter in person, living in thy successor, and speak!" Then, turning to the immense assemblage, he cried resonantly: "And do ye listen in reverence to Peter's infallible oracle!"

A microphone had been placed in front of the Pope. Amplified by loud-speakers, the sonorous voice of the eleventh Pius penetrated to every corner of the church of Saint Peter.

"We declare and render decision that the blessed Marie Bernarde Soubirous is a saint. We enrol her name in the calendar of saints. We decree that her memory be annually celebrated in the name of the Virgin on the sixteenth of April, the day of her heavenly birth."

This was the formula. Scarcely had it been spoken when the thousands of voices were raised in the Te Deum to the accompaniment of pealing silver trumpets and the deep thunder of Saint Peter's chimes. The bells of three hundred Roman churches and of innumerable other churches all over the world chimed in to proclaim the eternal glory of little Bernadette Soubirous of the Rue des Petites Fossées. It was now eleven o'clock. The Pope began the celebration of High Mass. He celebrated the Mass in both Latin and Greek in order to mark the all-embracing universality of the Church and of this day. After the reading of the Gospel he delivered the sermon. And again his strong, warm, manly voice resounded through the loud-speakers. The saints, said Pius, were to be compared to the telescopes of astronomers. Instruments permit us to see stars which the naked eye could never discover. Through saints we learn to see those eternal truths which the world's common day veils from our feeble eyes. He lauded Bernadette's purity, simplicity, and the fearless fight she had fought for the genuineness of her visions against a whole world of doubters, mockers, haters. Not only in the beneficent miracles of Lourdes but in the whole life of the new saint there was contained a message of inexhaustible wealth. Pius now spoke of the confusion of demonic voices which had accompanied the visions of Bernadette. This tumult had increased immeasurably since her time. It was filling the world and a considerable portion of mankind was under demonic sway. The fever of maniacal false doctrines was threatening to plunge the human spirit into bloody madness. In the battle against this, which man must win, not only did Lourdes stand like a very rock, but the life of Bernadette Soubirous retained its prophetic activity within time.

The head of the aged Bouhouhorts child began to wobble suspiciously amid this intoxicating wealth of words and music and colour. The friendly commentator had translated the Pope's sermon for his benefit. And still the celebration went on. Cardinal Verde chanted for the first time the prayer addressed to Saint Bernadette. That must have been at twelve. It was after one before the Bouhouhorts child, wedged in amid the swaying mass, could leave Saint Peter's.

The square was flooded with people. Bouhouhorts had lost touch with those he knew. He let himself be carried along by the crowd to a side street. Despite December the sun shone in a cloudless sky. The old man was not only exhausted but hungry and thirsty. Suddenly he sat down in one of the little inns which still kept their tables on the sidewalk in this fair weather. He ate a great dish of noodles and drank the violet wine of the Campagna. He felt very comfortable after this meal. Gaily he watched the traffic flooding past him in the street.

Look, he said to himself. The gentleman next to me was quite right. What a career it is, to be sure! And Bernadette Soubirous carried me in her arms. And I was part of it all in those days. And don't I remember how it looked in that wretched Cachot? And now Bernadette is a great person in heaven itself and the Pope and cardinals invoke her. And come to think of it, since I sort of belonged to it all in the Cachot, why, I might soon belong to it all in heaven too, provided I don't manage to slide into a couple of juicy sins at the last moment. . . .

The old man blinked up at the great clear sky of Rome. He was convinced that localized in that patch of sky above him all the saints of the Church dwelt close together on their thrones. And maybe Bernadette was now looking down on him sitting in the pleasant sunshine, all alone in this gay street, and hale and hearty at seventy-seven. And so he felt a real need to place himself in contact with Bernadette Soubirous. He did what he had always done. His fingers felt for the rosary in his pocket. The street was no proper place for prayers which ought to be said in church. But wasn't this city of Rome like one great church? The gardener of Pau turned his soul not to the rosary of sorrows nor to that of joy but to that of glory which is to lift the thoughts of man to victory, glory, and the ascension into heaven. His lips whispered one Ave after another while he sought to master his great weariness. His smiling small eyes still watched the lively traffic in the street. Motor-cars flitted by. The ice-cream man rang his bell to attract street-boys and servant-girls to buy his wares. From near-by alleys sounded the tragically tinged cries of the venders of oranges, fennel, and onions. Under the heaven of Rome, where the saints were gathered to welcome their new comrade, flew a military plane.

After the fortieth Ave the smiling old eyes began to grow heavier and heavier and precisely during the fiftieth the Bouhouhorts child fell asleep. But great gladness was in his heart the while he slept.

Other Works by Franz Werfel

EMBEZZLED HEAVEN

HEARKEN UNTO THE VOICE

THE ETERNAL ROAD

THE FORTY DAYS OF MUSA DAGH

THE PASCARELLA FAMILY

THE PURE IN HEART

TWILIGHT OF A WORLD

VERDI: A NOVEL OF THE OPERA